The Return of the Wizards

Volume I
The Twelve Companions
The Making of Wizards

Vic Broquard

"From far above in misty heights
Mighty Mizziniti issue forth
To conquer all our fears and foes
Isel freed once more."

The Return of the Wizards
Volume I
The Twelve Companions
The Making of Wizards
ISBN: 978-1-941415-63-4
2nd Edition

Artwork by Crooked Willow Studios.

Broquard eBooks
103 Timberlane
East Peoria, IL 61611
author@Broquard-eBooks.com

To Morgan and George
To L. Ron Hubbard

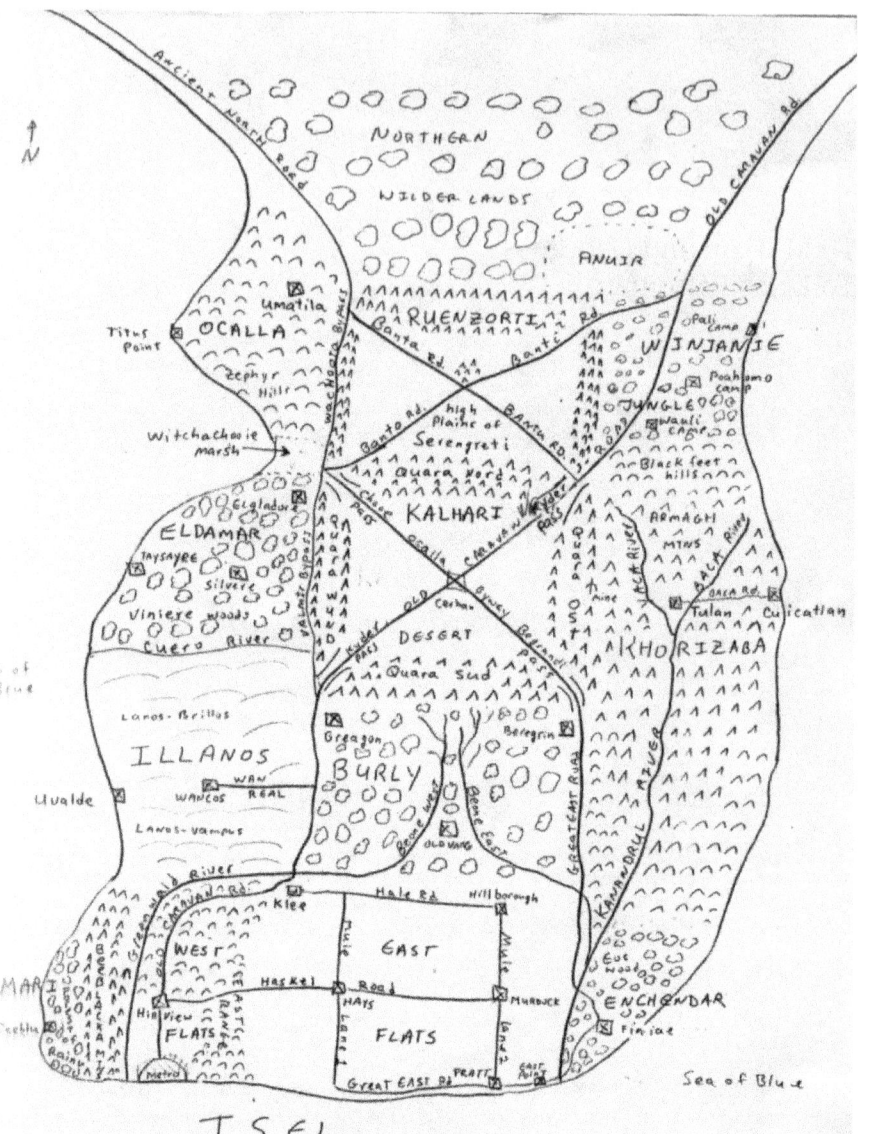

Table of Contents

Chapter I—The Encounter

It was a lazy Sunday afternoon. White billowing clouds slowly meandered across the deep blue sky. Marcos gazed thoughtfully into space. Marc's Bellview villa stood at the edge of Whitegate, a suburb of Metro. Beyond his second story balcony stretched the gently rolling hills of green that formed the East Range. Not quite mountains, these hills marked the eastern edge of West Flats, a large, fairly flat land that sloped uniformly to the sea. West Flats was bounded on the north and west by the great river, Grenwald, which was nearly a mile wide at Greenside, where it fed the sea. Nestled between Grenwald and the East Range was the huge ancient city of Metro, with its magnificent harbor. In all of Isle, Metro was the biggest city and, in its younger days, the most splendid.

In the olden days when Metro was built, a giant, semi-circular wall or fortification was built around it, the Round. These days, of course, the Round was crumbling—at best, in disrepair. Metro had expanded, being noted as the City of Merchants. It had prospered. Today, the wealthy lived on the east side, beyond the Round, in the suburbs of Whitegate and Southview. The poor had generally taken over the areas known as Dunky and Harlos, bordering the sea on either side of Metro. The northern parts of Metro's suburbs were filled with sprawling industries. Black Bone Tools were renowned throughout Isel.

Metro proper was a vast maze of shops, stacked endlessly, end on end. It has always been said there was nothing you could not get in Metro.

Marcos, who was turning twenty, came from the Blancas family, one of the more prosperous merchants of Metro. Marc became heir to his father's business at the early age of fifteen. Being exceptionally bright and alert, in only five years, he had taken the business and expanded it fivefold. He had made excellent transactions with the Mariners, cornering the markets on fish, tobacco, and tea. Marc, now of age, was known in Metro as a Master Merchant.

He had studied extensively in the Academy and had virtually perfect marks, but now he had grown tired of the constant hassling of the markets and had retired to Bellview, his father's old retreat at the east edge of Whitegate. From here he conducted his ever-multiplying marketing. Marc leaned his long arms on the balcony rail and stared off at the vast green hills and blue sky. He was bored. "Yes, that's exactly it," he thought, "I'm utterly, completely, positively bored!"

The markets, he found, offered no new challenges because he knew, or so he reflected, all there was to be known there—or at least "necessarily worthy of knowing," as he'd put it. He had already invented a system by which his enterprises could almost run themselves by a process of slow expansion. "There is no more game here." He continued to gaze.

Since his parents died five years ago, he'd become very independent—perhaps too much so, as it was frequently discussed by those in the pubs. Indeed, he had no permanent servants, only Sheeba, who came to fix dinners three times a week and handle the laundry. Aunt Gertrude, he recalled, put up such a fuss. "You must have at least five servants. You are noble now and very successful. Now, the Freedors's have six servants. I'm sure you make more money than they do. It's quite unbecoming of you to cook your own meals; and it's too horrible to think of you, Marcos—well I just can't say it—cleaning, you know." He remembered how he'd just smiled, saying "Ok," and kissed her lovingly on the cheek and asked her to bring some more tea.

So partly to avoid isolating himself from the rest of Metro, he'd consented to hiring Sheeba. Later, he had contracted for Bill Jacks to take care of the buildings and grounds at Bellview. This way the rest of Whitegate didn't think he was too weird, just an eccentric young man who had not settled yet.

The clouds billowed now and rolled by him. "They feel so close, it's like I could almost touch them," he mused. The hours drifted by with only a shifting of feet to mark their passage.

He was well built, tall, and slender, with long straight black hair, and piercing black eyes—handsome and quite bored. It was nearly four, when a soft voice behind him called to him, so gently, that for a second, he felt as though the white forms were speaking. Turning around, his eyes fell on Mindi standing in the doorway. For an instant, her long black hair and light robe gently swaying seemed to match the clouds. As if coming out of a dream, he said, "Huh?"

"Come in and have some tea," she repeated in her gentle voice.

"Hi, Mindi. Sure. Actually I guess I'm glad you dropped by. You know," he said sitting down across from her and accepting the cup, "you know—well, I've decided I'm bored! I've been here thinking for hours, and I've really decided that. I've mastered all that's here—in Metro, I mean. Merchants now bore me. It's the same old conversations day after day. You know that I can buy anything I want, but I cannot think of anything to buy! What would I do with five houses? I'm quite comfortable here at Bellview. I can run a good mile and I'm mean at the swords," he concluded.

Mindi watched him with her pale blue eyes, and occasionally sipped her tea as he talked. She replied softly, "Yes, I know." A thoughtful silence followed, broken only by occasional sipping noises. Mindi Francos was the closest thing to a best friend Marc had, ever since they were kids playing in the streets.

He had pretty well spotted what had been going on by the age of ten. He was something of an eccentric then, or more exactly, he seemed a bit different from others in West Flats. He had had difficulties as a child. Everyone that he played with soon found that Marc easily surpassed them. So it was each time he made a new friend—within a few weeks the friendship terminated—Marc was just plainly not in their league.

Then one day he had been playing hide and seek with some new friends in Southview, where he first met Mindi. Time after time, when no one else could find him, there would come Mindi. It was as if she could always find him. Right then, they struck up a friendship that had endured, and they were now very close.

Mindi was twenty as well and quite a fair young woman. At times she could be the most beautiful, quiet, soft spoken young woman you'd ever want to meet; and at others—well, let's say she could give Marc a battle at swords. She was widely known in long distance running events and had won a number of trophies in gymnastics. It was quite an enigma to Metroites, when at the annual fair, one day, Mindi would take top prize for a roast leg of lamb, and the next day, one for the mile run.

She and Marc had grown so close that, at times, he felt she could read his mind. But they were not lovers, as each felt they were not yet ready to settle into family life. Except for Marc, she was the only person in Metro, or West Flats for that matter, who was of comparable magnitude. She felt similarly of him. Hence, for over ten years, they had been very close.

These last few days, a new feeling had been spreading over Marc. As if guessing it, Mindi asked, "What's it feel like, Marc? Can you describe it?" There was a pause and then he said, "Well, it's like I want to just get up and go somewhere— nowhere—wandering. Oh, I don't know." Marc's mind was troubled. Merchants were never inclined to wandering or even to farming as their distant relatives in East Flats. Merchandising, marketing, and more recently manufacturing were their prime interests.

Had he been talking to his aunt, he could have predicted a sudden gasp. But Mindi only raised an eyebrow. "I thought it was something like that, but I was not totally certain, Marc."

"Yes, I know—well don't give me any of those lectures on you know these are dangerous times; the world is cruel, full of unknowns and evil things—yuc! I've heard that since I was a kid. You too, I suppose?" he said.

"Yes," came the brief and frank reply.

"Well, I know only too well how bad the times are. Only yesterday, we lost three prize lambs to them—the Scavengers. They broke open the shop over in Black Bone around one p.m., Henry guessed. Hardly a day passes when some new report comes into Metro concerning their wickedness. So far the Patrol has been useless."

Metro, once the splendor of the south of Isel, had fallen into hard times. Actually, Isel was isolated from the rest of the world except by sea. The Old Caravan Road going northwards

4

had long been abandoned. In olden days it was the main artery, filled with many caravans and travelers of all types. But that was in the days of the wizards, who were now long gone.

In these times, people spoke only in hushed whispers about the Desert King who had taken over Kalhari Quad, the desert up north. None can pass through his realm—at least alive and free, it is said. Many servants and armies were rumored to be wielded by the Evil One. Scavengers was the name used for all of the servants, whether tormented men, goblins, wolves, or other ghastly beasts. By night, these would pillage where they might—taking slaves as well as goods. It was heinous but none so far had defied them. Travel, these days, was very risky and wholly unthinkable at night. People kept big bolts and locks on their doors. There even was talk of rebuilding the Round, though none possessed the skill to do so.

"Yes, I know it's a stupid thought. I bet you just want me to up and marry you, have three children, and stay home and play. Well darn it, I don't feel like that!" he angrily burst out.

"Whoa Marc, you know I don't want that any more than you," she said taking his hand in hers and confronting him squarely. "That's enough of that! You know, as well as I, that if you're angry, you miss the target. So sit down, relax, have some tea, and tell me more about this feeling you've felt."

Grumbling, Marc sat down and fingered his tea. As usual, Mindi was right; they'd discovered that bit about anger long ago. It served them both very well in life. "I mostly feel very restless, almost like a great uneasiness has come over me. I cannot say if it's connected to the evil tidings or not. Perhaps not, dear, since I'm sure I'd have it anyway. Things—life—all; it's just boring to me here. I feel just like walking and seeing Isel. But it's unheard of for a merchant of Metro to do that, or even consider it," he continued.

"I understand," she acknowledged. "You feel yours is bad, consider mine. Here I am twenty years old and no thoughts of marrying. By now, all young girls should be married; so says mom nearly every day. You know how muck opposition I get every time I compete? You yourself have handled mom by telling her not to worry—girls should be well rounded, and they've a right to their own life and viewpoint." She paused and continued, "I feel, Marc, as if I too have a great gap in me, a void so to speak. Something's missing. And it's not a bunch of kids, I assure you," she said laughingly.

Marc broke up and began to laugh too. He knew very well her plight was even worse than his. Grinning, he said, "Come on, let's go for a walk. You're right as usual, love. At least I have an idea what I need; you don't. Come on." So arm in arm, they strolled out onto the grounds of Bellview around sunset, as the rose-colored clouds met the deepening green hills.

It was about seven o'clock when they parted with a loving kiss. Mindi left him standing in the doorway, and his eyes followed her as she gracefully, yet swiftly, walked off south towards Southview. He went inside and picked up the cups off the balcony. It was nearly dark now. As if remembering the afternoon, Marc gazed off to the east, across the rolling hills towards the old city and tower. That's when his eye caught the pale blue light coming from Obelos Sud, the two hundred foot tall ancient tower.

He nearly dropped the cups; he was startled. In olden days, Metro had another part, called Obsel, now called the Ancient City. It was built right against the base of the rolling hills, about one mile from where he stood. It had been abandoned for centuries; most of the buildings were in very ruined condition. In olden years, it was the City of the Watchers, the Protectors, the Wizards.

The wizards used to be the guardians of all of Isel and had built the strange obelos, twelve in all. Each was a tall tower—all nearly two hundred feet high, according to the legends. There was only one door and no windows, except at the top. The tower ended in a platform-like room from which the wizards operated. Tales tell of how the wizards would stand vigilantly watching and protecting the lands. That was before the Great Battle.

Many stories had been told of the Great Battle. Briefly, the wizards were destroyed, some say by their own hands. And the world and Isel fell into a great darkness. Out of that darkness, the Merchants with the help of the Mariners had continued and now were thriving. No one ever went into the ruins. Some say it's full of evil things. Most were just plain scared, although they did not admit it. That's why the teacups nearly crashed when Marc saw the pale light.

Almost without thinking, Marc grabbed his blue cloak, his torch light and his sword and immediately left the house. Quickly he began to cross the grounds of Bellview. He was not sure of what he was going to do. Curiosity was the biggest thing. Who was up there? Why seemed an even bigger question. Stealthily and quickly, he moved across the grounds, barely perceptible as a shadow. Were the Patrols there? Should he alert the Patrols and just go home? Let them do their jobs? He knew he should.

After covering a half mile, the going got rougher; small hills kept rising up in front of him. He was breathing deeply now. He resolved to be a spy. If it were Scavengers, it's best not to be discovered. If it's the Patrol, he shouldn't be found there anyway. His nerves were tingling with excitement. He hadn't felt this alive in years!

He kept on going, being as quiet and as quick as he could. Fifteen minutes later, he was scrambling over the ruins of Obsel, the ancient town. The old city roads were mainly blocked by fallen rocks from the houses. Going was bad in the daylight. He found it very difficult to be both quick and quiet now. The situation, he figured, would require stealth; so he slowed down and carefully picked his way.

Using the torch as little as possible, he continued scrambling. Even then, he covered it as best he could with his hands so that only a little light came out. His excitement grew. He found himself heaving heavily for breath. At last, he was within fifty feet of the Obelos. There it stood, a pale grey, ominous tower rising to a great height. There was an old wooden door at the base. It was ajar! Nothing else was insight.

He paused a minute, caught his breath, and tried to calm his nerves a bit. "It'll do no good to go in there shaking like a leaf!" he said to himself. There was no sign of a fire, men, or animals. The area was lifeless except for the pale blue light coming from far above him. "It must not be the Patrol—they always use ponies but I have not heard or seen any. If it's the Scavengers, I'd have heard a lot of noise by now—they are anything but quiet," he thought to himself.

A great curiosity began to swell inside him, turning now to a desire to know. He carefully sneaked to the doorway. Still there were no signs of anyone else around. The old door was half-open; it was made of heavy oak nearly two feet thick. Its massive hinges were layered with rust. Despite its appearance, it was still solid, a formidable barrier if you had to get through it. At last taking a deep breath, he stepped inside. A blackness he'd seldom experienced surrounded him. For a moment fear swelled like a wave over him. Actually, he found his right arm was shaking quite by itself. That was unnerving to Marc, and he struggled to regain his self-control. He decided to turn on the torch and see what to do next.

Before he could do so, and aging voice said, "Come on up; I've been expecting you." It was so softly said, yet it had such a command value about it that Marc could not resist. He was just shocked. He muttered something reflexively, turned on the torch, and began climbing. The voice added with strong emphasis, "Do not touch anything on your way up."

It was no longer by curiosity or desire that Marc began the assent; it was as if some force beyond himself were totally compelling it. As he started up, the voice added from far above him, "And bring your friend with you." Marc blushed. Just what did he mean by that! He'd brought no one, heard no one, saw no one as he came here. He quickly turned around. As he glanced by the door, there was a form standing in the opening. Marc nearly dropped his torch; it was all he could do to keep from screaming! Once again, he reactively mumbled something that sounded like hello.

Then the familiar voice of Mindi came back. "It's me Marc—Mindi. What's going on here?" In hushed voices broken by gasps, Marc said he saw a blue light coming from Obelos Sud and came to investigate.

Then he calmed down. "What the heck are *you* doing here? This is no place for you."

"Watch it, Marc," came the sharp retort. "I was heading home and saw a blue light too. I went back to get you, but you weren't there. So I came myself. I rather figured you were ahead of me, but I didn't see you until you slipped in the door. I couldn't say anything in time, and besides I was afraid too."

"Come on up you two, and do not touch anything," came the voice from above.

It was Mindi's turn to start. She jerked sharply at the sound and grabbed Marc's arm, uncontrollably. "Who is that?"

"I don't know," he said. "I had just started up when it said bring your friend. I nearly fainted when I saw you there in the doorway."

"That's ok, love; come on; let's do as he asks. I don't think we have a choice," she replied. With his torch, they could see the circular stone stairs, ever rising. Side by side, they began climbing with their arms at their sides, for fear of touching anything. As they climbed, the torch lit the walls faintly.

They caught glimpses of strange forms, shapes, and creatures and men. A multitude of colors covered the walls; and there were many strange objects lying in perfectly carved nooks in the walls. Another time, another circumstance, they would have been content just to examine the walls. Now, however, they felt a strange compulsion to reach the voice; his commands had been forceful. Upwards they climbed, step after step, until at last they got to the platform at the top. There they stood, side by side, breathless, but intently looking forward.

Chapter II—Malazar, the Wizard

In front of them was a wide room entirely lit by a pale blue light coming from atop the wizard's staff. The aging voice of Malazar spoke first. "Welcome to Obelos Sud, my friends. Welcome." There was a hint of some great relief in his voice, as if some burden of mind had been eased somewhat. "I am known as Malazar, the Wizard, in these parts at least. Come have a seat, Marcos Blancas, son of Fredric, and you, my dear Mindi Francos, daughter of Samuel. Do not look so startled that I know your names, for am I not a wizard? To me, much of yourselves is known. Did I not know you would be here tonight? But come and sit—I will shut the windows. We do not need the confusions of others upon us tonight."

With that, he swiftly closed the heavy oaken shutters that barred the four large viewing windows on each side of the tower. Mindi studied the wizard intently as he went about the task. The oak shutters were three inches thick, at least, and quite heavy. He was an old man with both white hair and beard; the latter came down to his waist. He looked very old; yet as she watched, he was as spry and swift of movement as she was. Now and then, she observed that his face had the look of one who has an overwhelming, unbearable problem. Yet the impression seldom lingered, but kept flickering back.

Marc had sat down; all sorts of emotions were raging inside him. He felt very strange indeed. Pictures flashed through his mind as though in a dream. He felt both at home and comfortable, yet in a rage, ashamed, scared, and sick, simultaneously. Marc did his best to observe his surroundings, and in vain, he tried to control his mind and its imaginings. This phenomenon had never happened before; he was quite perplexed.

The wizard had now joined them at the large square table, made of a wood of which they were not familiar. It was highly polished with a sheen to it and was very smooth, but it felt extremely solid to the touch. Much to Marc's surprise, it was Mindi rather than the wizard who began the discussion. "I

10

see that you know of us. Let me tell you of yourself. You are an old man outwardly, whose years I cannot guess; you have traveled widely and on foot, I'd guess by your weather-stained cloak and well-worn shoes. Yet you have hidden from ordinary glances a strong body, and one that acts as though it were young. Indeed, I suspect you have little trouble on the road that you cannot handle. You also mask that you are agile. I suspect that I would have a challenge with you on the gym bars. Yet you are more aware than you let on. Further, I deduce that you have drawn us here on some purpose. You have and are wrestling with some major problem. Considering you are a wizard, I would guess that it concerns even more than Metro or the West Flats. But anymore I cannot discern."

Marc sat back quiet aghast. "How do you know all that, Mindi?" he blurted out.

"By observing the obvious, I'm afraid to say," interjected the wizard. Mindi grinned, and Marc tried to regain mastery of his thoughts and emotions. "There is much to learn and so little time. . ." Once again, Mindi caught a fleeting glimpse of that countenance of trouble. "I shall start with the way things are today. We have fallen into hard times. The Evil Ones, Scavengers as you call them, are increasing in numbers. They now threaten much of West Flats. Your Patrols do very little to stop them. Soon your suburbs will be unsafe, industries laid bare to the scourge. How long do you suppose it will be until Metro fall victim to the Evil One? Have you not seen the Scavengers being joined by your own citizens, particularly from Harlos? Things are grim. It is safe to say that you do not know your own peril."

"But I thought the attacks were just transitory ones," protested Marc, becoming even more troubled and upset.

"Yes, you all do! Can you not see where it will lead?" pleaded the wizard. Marc was now looking quite ill. Malazar noticed this and asked, "Marc, how do you feel right now; you do not look too well." Marc felt an immediate embarrassment and was at a loss. He'd only confided his inner thoughts before to Mindi. Here was this impetuous wizard whom he'd just met and who was now seeming to pry into his personal life. His face got red and he merely mumbled something.

11

Mindi, who had now been watching him closely, seemed to realize this, and she reached over and laid her hand on his. Questioningly, she said, "Marc?" However, she got no more said.

He brightened up and declared, "True, this is not the trouble—the trouble really is that I am quite at a loss to explain myself. I came here full of curiosity; now I don't even know what's going on with me."

The wizard sat down eyeing him intently, listening to his every word. "Tell me about it," he said softly, much interested.

"Well, the best I can say is I feel at home here; you know, it's like, well, comfortable, nice; like I belong somehow. However, I've never been here. Nevertheless, at the same time, I feel sick and scared. I'm afraid, but I don't even know from what. It's like I'm being overwhelmed by grief, shame, and guilt—but for what I do not know." His voice trailed into silence. For a moment, no one spoke.

Then, Malazar sat up and said kindly, "Thank you, Marc. I have learned much, though so very much more I have yet to know. Of the mind, I can tell you this; there are mental pictures of many things. Some are of your coming here tonight; others are somewhat beyond one's control. I have found that every feeling I've had that was ill to me, came ultimately from these pictures. When I have fully seen them, these feelings have left me wholly. They are like ghosts of a bye-gone day. When viewed under today's sun, they vanish. Yet, if they are not viewed, they are as rats locked in a dark closet, ever scratching to get out. We are all beings and perhaps not merely bodies. If this be so, some may wonder what have these beings been and what have they done? If pictures be true, then I have had many bodies before this one, and more yet shall I have. Truth may just be the exact time, form, and event." Then there was silence once again.

Marc took a strange comfort in his words, and for an unknown reason, a calm came upon him, and he relaxed for the first time since entering Obelos Sud. "Come," said Malazar, "I promised you a history, and a history you will get!"

"In the beginning, Isel was a barbarian waste land.

Then came the Mizzinti, the Great Wizards—twelve in number with Missar, their chief. They were the Great Wizards of old. It is said mountains would rise at their call and seas swell into tempests. I have learned that they operated by a carefully planned cause to produce a specific effect. In any case, to Isel they came to prepare a perfect world, a sane paradise. Twelve houses they built throughout the land. Each took a place and there they helped the folk to create their cities as fair jewels."

"To protect Isel, the Mizzinti created the Obelos as watch towers, the Guardians of Isel. For many ages, there was peace and happiness; and trade flourished even beyond these lands. The splendor of Isel was known far and wide."

"It was then the overt—the evil—first began. Some Mizzinti began to have desire—seeing other's creations as better than theirs. They began to view themselves as controllers of the people, dictators of all that occurred. It was seen as an effort to surpass the other in wealth, glory, fame, and beauty. Thus began the hostility between the Mizzinti. Of these, Karzam was the worst. He spread his seeds of distrust throughout Isel, until each of the twelve was quite separated from the rest, feeling theirs was the best. They forced their peoples to their will, in an attempt to best the neighboring wizards."

"Isel could not stand the strain for long, and the Battle of the Greats ensued. Thus, it was that the Great Ones began to war. As fate would have it, the people themselves did but little battle. And for the most part, it was confined to the Mizzinti themselves, battling each from their Obelos in feats of fire unseen before in Isel. It was then that Missar, seeing the truth of the war, summoned all Mizzinti unto him. He laid the bare truth of the battle before them. It was then that the Mizzinti did see, and before any could sway them otherwise, they destroyed themselves, suggesting that that would atone for their acts."

"With the passage of the Great Ones, darkness fell on Isel for many ages. The various lands, already being separate, soon forgot their neighbors, and the Dark Ages came on full. Hate and evil ruled."

"But from these dark times, visionaries in each land

slowly built anew, although now isolated from the others. West Flats was rebuilt by your time honored Phillip the Great. It was he who turned Metro once again into the great Merchant City."

"But the desert region, home of Karzam, has never recovered. It remained long in destruction, until recently. Some twenty-five years ago, Kahill, the Evil One, came, taking over all of the desert as his own. With him, he has brought the Scourge, the Scavengers, his slaves. He took over the tower of Obelos Cerban, but his mastery of wizardry is so far small. Strong enough it is to turn men and beasts into Scavengers. He and his powers are growing."

"Of this, I have not any great fear, but of another, yet unspoken, I do. Missar, the greatest of the Mizzinti, built the Orb, a wand for all the Obelos. From his tower, Obelos Magum, by use of the Orb, he could control all evil that approached Isel or that from within. The Orb that Missar created had no power over good. Evil, it can control as the Master of the Orb so chooses. A fearful weapon it is, when it is used by the good to keep evil at bay. It was through the use of the Orb that Isel was kept at peace for so long by the Mizzinti."

"Now suppose Kahill acquires the Orb! He is evil and can use the Orb to his purpose. He can cause, via the Orb, anything evil to do his bidding, which is evil. If anyone has any dark thoughts toward anyone or anything, then Kahill can control him! Do you know any man that does not have some hidden desire? Not done any deed he regrets, ever? Truly, Kahill could control all of Isel and maybe all the world."

"But do not worry too much, my friends," said the wizard, seeing the terror reflected in their eyes. "The Orb has not yet been found. Indeed, no one knows of its passing. There are no records, and no legends that I have ever seen tells what Missar did with the Orb."

"However, by possessing Obelos Cerban and having found out how to use its powers, Kahill has begun again what the Mizzinti began long ago. It is indeed bad times that we've come into!"

To all of this Marc and Mindi had listened intently. Both of them had had many pictures—like dreams—flashing by as he spoke. Even now, an anger filled Marc. "But what are we to do about the Evil One and the Scavengers? Something must be done!" he cried.

"Yes, yes," said the wizard with a troubled face.

Mindi saw that look again, and interrupted softly, "And this is your biggest worry, isn't it?"

"Yes, it is," he replied, his voice sinking to a whisper, "if only," and his voice trailed away; each was left to his own thoughts. The silence was broken quite unexpectedly. The ancient table on which they were leaning suddenly turned pale blue and became transparent. As if by magic, it became a viewing screen. Both Mindi and Marc jumped up quite startled. Only Malazar remained calm and peered into the screen. "Look," he said, "this is the wizard's tower. I asked you not to touch anything because things in here belonged to the Great Wizards. Who knows what magic is here. But this one I know; it's the 'Vishi' or viewer. Even now, it operates as of old—look there is the bottom of the tower and the door. There is what has activated it—one of your Patrols has come here."

All three gazed into the scene before them. Marc suddenly realized the danger, "Malazar, we left the door opened. If they come in here, we'll be arrested or worse. No one is allowed up here on penalty of death. In Metro, there is a great taboo on this place."

"Right you are," he said. Malazar stood up and said in a strange language, rather musically, "Umli umla bewalla." The oaken door far below shut. As they watched, the Patrol arrived, and in hushed, scared voices, they decided nothing was here and hurriedly left.

"So much for your Patrols," said Malazar. Then the table returned to its original form, and they again sat down.

"How did you do that?" asked Mindi curiously.

"Am I not a wizard?" he grinned. "I have journeyed far and wide, studying whatever scrolls I can find. Of legends, I have studied most. I have even viewed some parts of my hidden mind. I have become something of a lesser wizard, but I'm not yet a match for even Kahill, because he possesses power beyond mine, but, I think, not the wisdom. He is as a kid with a new toy."

"It is getting late. As I see it, the Mizzinti must correct

15

their error. They must assume responsibility for their error!" Malazar had reached an angry tone, cursing the Great Ones' foolishness. Instinctively, Mindi took the wizard's hand in hers and looked at him understandingly. It was as if far off memories were swelling into a tempest within Malazar's mind. He calmed down and looked lovingly at her.

"You are quite aware, my dear. In anger, one does not see. Thank you." He began again, "Kahill, the Evil One, must be stopped somehow. Isel must be protected. The Orb, if it exists, must not fall into his hands. We, also, must protect all the other Obelos, least they fall into his hands, giving him even more power. There is so much to do and so little time." Again, his voice trailed into silence. He looked at his two new friends, as if studying them.

Finally, he said, "You will both do."

"Even now I am needed up north. I fear that I may be too late in getting to Burly. Marcos, do what you can to make Metro safe from the Scourge. Guard the Obelos somehow. Prepare yourselves for wandering in the wild. In two months' time, I will meet you at the East Point Inn, by Feanor Bridge in East Flats. Be ready for journeys into the wild, but do leave the Flats guarded and protected as you can. Will you do this?" Now, the wizard felt at a loss; he didn't know whether they would accept the challenge. He looked at them.

Marc looked at Mindi—when their eyes met, they immediately smiled, and as if with one voice, said, "Of course, we will."

"Remember that to wander and travel in these times may mean becoming a slave to Kahill, or worse. It is no place for a woman," said the wizard half expecting the worst.

For once, Mindi did not retort; she merely said softly, "I have a strange compelling to do this. I know in my heart that I cannot refuse this task, whatever end it may have."

"Then, it's agreed," smiled the wizard. It seemed as if a great deal of pressure had been lifted from his mind. He seemed quite relieved. Even Marc noted it. "Thank you. Two months, then, East Point Inn, by Feanor Bridge. Now we must be off."

With that, all three left the room and went down the

long spiral stairs, peaceful in mind, tired, and hungry. Quietly and quickly, they left the Obelos and Malazar closed the door. They watched as he went northwards; against the dark sky, he looked very insignificant.

Arm in arm, they returned quickly to Bellview.

Chapter III—Of Doubts and Preparations

It was two a.m. when they arrived back at Bellview, both tired and hungry. Neither had said a word since the parting of the wizard. Each seemed lost in their own thoughts. Once safe inside, Marc lit the small parlor light. They hugged and embraced, and the tensions both felt melted away. "Man, I'm hungry," exclaimed Marc.

"Me too." Without any further words, Marc cooked some leftover pork, while Mindi got the table ready. Though no words were spoken, each of their actions blended, as if they had lived together for years. After eating, they went to bed. Mindi did not feel safe going home tonight. Marc longed for her company as well. Barely a half hour after their return, they were lying in bed, but not asleep. Marc was staring at the ceiling; his mind was perturbed at best. Mindi, perceiving this, gave him a back rub, and he relaxed. Then, Marc returned the favor.

It was nearly noon when Marc stretched and rose. As he dressed, he looked at Mindi still sleeping. "She **is** beautiful," thought Marc; and he leaned over and kissed her. Mindi smiled, and they spent a few tender minutes together.

At breakfast, Marc was very moody. "Are we going to believe this wizard or not? They're only legends—tales we tell our children. Yet, the Scavengers do seem more and more precocious. What am I, a mere merchant, to do against the Scourge? He should have gotten the Mayor or the Captains of the Patrols, not me. Merchants do not wander. I don't even know the roads beyond the Flats. Why me?"

Mindi just listened to him. She also had many reservations. Though she felt emancipated, at least compared to the women that she knew, to travel, to wander, as a woman in the wilderness—horrible even to think about. Was the old man right? What could she do? And just what did he mean about the mental pictures, yet unseen. What was he insinuating?

So in a troubled state of mind, they departed; Mindi

18

returning home; Marc, to the Exchange, where he ran his business.

It was a bright, cheerful day with large white clouds rolling in from the sea. The air was balmy, a nice Monday noon; Marc arrived hours later than normal. As he walked inside, his assistant, Henry, greeted him. "Morning chief. Well, what's got you by the tail—bad night, huh, too much spirits?"

"Oh cut it out," jabbed Marc, who was in an ill humor. "What have you got going today? Any news on the Flounder's fish deal?"

"No, boss, nothing yet. I'd guess we'll be hearing more about midweek—boat's in them."

"Ok." Marc entered his office, shut the door, and sat down behind his piles of papers and charts—the tools of his trade. Somehow, he just couldn't get his mind on it. His thoughts kept running back to last night. Finally, he closed his eyes, laid back and ran through all that happened. Two hours later, he woke with a start.

"Your tea, sir."

"Huh? Oh, yes—sit it there, Henry. Say, thanks a lot. I'm having a bad day. Thanks." Yawning heavily, he sipped his tea and mused. He spent ten minutes yawning. He felt much better now, more alert, and more awake. Something had been gnawing at him all this time. It was not the confrontation with the wizard; he could grant that part validity. At least the legends he knew agreed mostly. However, the way he had reacted inside the Obelos—that bothered him. He reviewed for the tenth time the reactions that night. Then, he had an idea. He had always been master of his reactions—except last night. Would it do it again, he wondered? Jumping up, he quickly left the office, telling Henry he was stopping for the day.

With quick steps, he determinedly headed home. "Hi, Sheeba," he said. The housemaid was busily fixing Monday's dinner. "I shan't be here long—just in and out, you know."

"Bless you, my boy. You sure are in a hurry."

"Yes, I know," and he gave her a friendly kiss on her forehead and left. She certainly was a pleasant sort, he mused, as he quickly walked through town. A few minutes later, he arrived at Dunky and the sea—"Poor town," he thought. Here

19

he could quickly get lost in a crowd of people. No one would see him leave by the eastern paths; and with any luck, he could sneak through the hills unseen and come upon the Obelos from the east. "If all went well, I'll not even be spotted," he thought.

Shortly, he arrived at the Obelos. It stood alone and towered loftily above him. Its outside bricks had a multicolored pattern, faded, and quite weathered. No one was around. He took a deep breath and sneaked around to the door. His heart pounded; he felt very tense. He pushed on the door. It did not open. Try as he might, the door remained solidly shut. He sat down in front of it to collect his wits. The balmy day he began to feel again; and he relaxed and found that he was surprisingly calm. He did have pictures flashing in his mind; pictures—as if memories of the past. Then, he remembered the wizard had said that the door opened by command. Marc pondered this, wondering what the command was.

It was late afternoon now; Marc calmly felt an urge to stand in front of the door. He put his hands on it. It felt good somehow. Suddenly without knowing how or why, he felt he should say "Amon begure" and did so. To his utter amazement, the door creaked and opened in front of him. "I wonder," was all he said to himself.

Grabbing his torches, and turning them on, he went into the Obelos. As he wandered through the tower, he felt a strange sense of familiarity here, rather as one does towards his home. The walls were gaily decorated with every color imaginable; there were objects of all shapes and sizes, even drawings of the countryside. A splendid drawing caught his eye. It was a sparkling city. Was that old Metro, he wondered? For over an hour, Marc wandered up and down the tower, marveling and wondering. He no longer felt afraid, but very curious. He remembered the wizard's warning not to touch anything and he did so.

He realized that evening was coming, and decided to leave; his experiment was fulfilled. He descended the stairs and stood in the entry way. He felt calm here, quite different from the night before. Many pictures flashed by in his mind.

These he was alert to now. Finally, with a big yawn and a sigh, he resolved to leave. There was a small ledge by the door. As he walked out, he instinctively grabbed the sword and sheath lying there, and was outside before he'd realized what he'd done. The door closed automatically.

"Now why did I do that—remember the wizard's warning. Oh well, now that I've got it, I'd best be getting back before I'm missed." He returned via the back hills and Dunky. All the way, he carried the sword under his clothes, away from prying eyes.

He arrived home to the smells of supper. "Dear Sheeba!" he thought, "Left everything ready for me." He washed up and dined a pleasant dinner, alone with his new sword lying on the table. While eating, he observed it. A clean silver and gold color predominated in swirling patterns. The large hilt was formed with many bulbous knobs, and the end had a large red jewel in it. The blade was short, about one foot long, quite small for a sword, jet silver and incredibly sharp. The hilt was of gold and embossed with strange runes, figures, and flowers on the knobs. "I shall call you Tiny," he chuckled to himself.

Just then, the doorbell rang; he got up but before he could get to the door, it opened and in bounced a now bubbly Mindi. "Hi,love!" She sprang up, hugged, and kissed him. He was quite surprised by the welcome but he loved it.

"Come on in and have some sup if you haven't already."

"Yes, I will. I'm famished!" came the reply, and they returned to the table. Marc saw Tiny on the table and got red in the face. Mindi also saw it and of course picked it up questioningly. She turned and saw his embarrassment. All she said was, "This didn't come from—it didn't, did it?"

Marc stammered out a weak "Yes."

With a look of excitement, she said, "Hey neat! Come on; tell me about it. It looks like you've been busy too."

Marc relaxed and was actually a bit pleased with himself. "Yes, you're right. I was terrible last night and now I'm not. That does deserve an explanation." With pleasure, he described how his day had gone. Mindi followed it with a great curiosity and had him go over several times the parts about the

21

pictures like old memories, the door words, and the sword grabbing.

When he had described it all to her satisfaction, she finally said, "Well done Marc, very well done. Mighty interesting. I wish I had been there."

"Hey, now it's your turn," he pointed out.

"Ok. Ok." With a big grin on her bright face, she pulled a card from her pocket. "See, I'm a student again at the Academy!"

Marc let out a laugh. It was totally unexpected and unimaginable—Mindi a student again. Jokingly, he added, "Ah my pretty, you've taken up business to give me a rival, eh?"

They both laughed and playfully hugged. "Well," She began in earnest, "as you know, I was perplexed last night. I met the challenge of my lifetime, and all I could do was waffle about it. Should I, shouldn't I—that sort of thing. I began wondering about what the wizard had meant about the dream pictures. His words rang true to me; I've been pondering their significance too. I decided to be logical about the whole thing. I'm sure not going to be the big defender of Metro. You know women are seen but not heard at the Mayor's office. I decided the only reasonable thing to do was to get more data. I visited the Academy and the Archives of Grenoble there. It took some digging; such ancient scrolls are long unused. Well, to my surprise, I did find a whole cache of bits and pieces. In order to take them out, I needed to be a student and have, of course, the right access code so no one will get curious. So you're looking at the Academy's newest student of history! I, then, checked out a bunch of these and took them home."

"Mom—she's a dream—said, 'Well, it's about time you took up something sensible.' And here I am. Things will be even better. Mom and Dad are going up to Hill View to visit Uncle John and Aunt Mary for a week. They do it every summer—to help them can food and for a change of pace. Mom's always telling Dad it's good for his health—to get some fresh air. So starting tomorrow, my place will be full of books, scrolls, and me. What do you have to say to that?" She grinned, obviously proud of her achievement.

"A very well done to you too," grinned Marc. He then

gave her a hug, "You are really terrific! Good thinking!" They discussed other events, and, as the evening wore on, Marc again approached the subject again. "You know, we do need a plan, a schedule, or something. I feel I'm going twenty ways at once."

After some discussion, it was agreed that Mindi would handle gathering of information and provisions at her place. It would be quite safe with no one there. Marc was to handle the acquisition of supplies and the fortifying of West Flats. Of the latter, though he did not tell Mindi, he had absolutely no idea of what was to be done.

In early June their enthusiasm sprang up anew. The ensuing days found Marc no closer to having any idea of how to protect Metro. In fact, he had given up the idea altogether, at least for a while. His days, he spent acquiring the necessities for wandering. Inexperienced though he was, Marc was not without connections. It was through the "appropriate" acquaintances that he'd built his business up. He'd always said, "All it takes is finding the key person to make it happen." He used his communication lines to their fullest; for one thing, he had decided—if he were to go wandering, then he'd go using the best gear.

His trouble was that he didn't know for sure what gear. After some analysis and discussions, Marc discovered the man who most likely would know, and he was surprised to find out it was Shannon Wayfar, a Mariner from Mari, as unlikely as that may seem at first.

Mari was a mountainous tip of Isel just across the Grenwald River from Metro, and then across the forbidding Beeblaca Mountains (a high rugged range of mountains virtually impassable). On the other side of these mountains was the heavily forested region called the Forest of Rainu. Beyond that was the fabled Ceeblu, the City of Mariners. It was more like one long slender city, nestled upon miles and miles of seashore.

The Mariners seldom remained on land for long. They preferred to live on their ships, the finest around. To places undreamed of in Metro, they'd sail and were a vital supply line for Metro. Shannon was a lean and lanky, tall Mariner, with fair skin and long yellow hair. As with all Mariners, Shannon would hardly ever set foot on land, especially at Metro's port.

It was at Gate Way Docks that Marc found the Sendoa and Shannon. As a child Marc had watched their boats come and go, and was even fascinated by them. Seeing the large white, three-masted Sendoa, lying as if ready to depart, filled him with wonder again. How could people live at sea all the time, and travel to such strange places?

Marc found Shannon on board, in the captain's quarters naturally. He was leaning back in his chair and puffing his calabash slowly. "Greetings Master Merchant. Your fame precedes you. How can I be of service?" He spoke, breaking the awkward silence.

Marc little knew just how to begin, so he tried, "Well, I've a mind to do some wandering these days and have need of equipment. I was told that you were the best authority in these parts. So, ah—here I am."

Shannon looked him over, up and down, long and hard, before he replied. Then in a coy fashion he said, "Merchants, especially Master Merchants, are not known for wandering. These are dangerous times on land, matey."

Marc was in a quandary. Very well did he see how it would look to strangers to see a merchant talking about wandering. Should he tell Shannon the whole purpose, some part of it, or try to come up with a plausible explanation?

As if sensing Marc's dismay, Shannon broke the awkward silence by a cheery "Ho—come now let's have some drink. Have ya tried Rones de Caracus? No, well come on then." Shannon quickly got up and fetched two oddly shaped mugs (dwarfish origin he later explained) and a tall brown bottle of spirits.

Marc gladly welcomed the change of subject and for a while forgot his circumstances. Shannon was an excellent host, and the Sendoa lacked nothing for an amiable party. One thing had caught his eye. Spread over a drawing table in the corner was a chart, for navigation, Marc assumed. Looking closer he found it was a map of Isel. Though the writing was foreign, Marc quickly recognized Metro.

"That's my bible", explained Shannon. "With this, I can

sail as I may and ever return." Marc noted that above the Flats was a region drawn with a few symbols, almost featureless. He guessed this was the great desert, Kalhari.

"So that's where those beasts come from," he muttered mostly to himself. He found his old frustrations of how to stop the Evil Ones returning. However, Shannon, who in spite acting carefree, had been watching him as closely as an unmarked shoal.

He heard the muttered remark and offered, "So you hate the Evil Ones too?"

"Damned right," blurted Marc. "They've got to be stopped." Shannon guessed from his sudden seriousness that Marc was truthful.

"Come Master Merchant, I'm satisfied; you've passed the test. Before we continue, I've a tale for you, in hopes you'll understand my concern." Marc was taken by surprise. Sitting at the big table again, Shannon relit his pipe and began. "It was nearly a year ago; I was off the coast of Enchendar, delivering a load of goods. The Scavengers, as you call them, had been only a rumor in fair Mari. That's all changed now. Under cloak of night, a herd of beasts, I call them—they no longer warrant to be called men—came down the coastline and into our city of Ceeblu. They pillaged and burned as much as they could. We are seamen not warriors, but long did we fight. At last, they were driven off in the light of day. The northern part of the city was laid bare. When I returned home, I discovered my house destroyed; and my beloved sister, Irene, had been killed, and her fair body chewed by the wolves. There and then, I swore revenge on the Evil One."

"Many days lengthened my desires but wisdom came. There are other's whose lands, as well, are being ravaged. So I have resolved to do all that I can to bring about the down fall of the Evil Ones."

Marc reached over, laid his hands on Shannon's shoulders, and softly spoke "I understand." Shannon raised his head up, and Marc saw the grief that he still carried. "I understand," he repeated.

Shannon sighed and replied, "Thanks, my grief is indeed deep; we were very close."

25

"My friend," Marc offered, "yes, she whom you loved is lost now, but morn not the past. Look to the present and future. Seek not after revenge—that is the way of the Evil One. Seek with me after the removal of the evil ones. A friend of mine, Malazar, the wizard, has told me much of these matters and of the minds of men."

"You know of the wizard too," broke in Shannon surprised at the mention of that name. "He is ever a friend of the Mariners and has an honored seat in the council of Mari."

Marc then explained some of what his plans were, of course, leaving out some parts, especially of the tower. Of Mindi, he said nothing, for if any evil should come of this meeting, he wanted it on his head only. Shannon was fully behind Marc now and agreed to help.

"We'll need supplies for two travelers", he explained, "both sets the same size. But what will you take in trade?"

"Well, you give me the supplies I need for trade, and I'll see they're exchanged for the trip's necessities. As for a payment for me, let it be my contribution to the quest."

They agreed; and later that day, bags of grain began to be loaded on board the Sendoa.

Mindi had not been idle; the library had been thoroughly covered. She'd acquired nearly twenty-five books and scrolls covering the history and legends of Isel. Some charts were hundreds of years old. Additionally, she acquired a number of references on edible plants and animals of the wild, both by Lord Thomas of Klee, the northernmost city of East Flats which bordered on the wild.

She spent afternoons, studying these, trying to put the pieces together. She felt as though knowledge of Isel was one gigantic puzzle. The mornings, however, she spent on her shopping sprees, as she afterwards referred to them. She combed Metro for provisions for the journey, acquiring always just the right thing here and there. Light weight, compact, long lasting yet nourishing was her tact for the food. Indeed, she had a way with food.

In the evening, Marc would invariably call on her. They didn't want to rouse suspicions nor set any ill rumors flying that would upset her parents. Marc insisted he only call in the

26

evening for a few hours. They would briefly fill each other in on the progress made. It is noted here that her kitchen now looked like a grocery shop. Then, in earnest, they would go over the scrolls and maps, memorizing as much as they could.

Chapter IV—The Hill View Affair

At least once a day, usually around noon, Marcos visited the local taverns in search of any news of the Scavengers. News travels fastest at the pubs, at least in Metro. The weekly paper only carried the bigger events. Even if he only got rumors, it was better than no information at all.

A week had now passed; and the main news that he had acquired, beyond facts he already knew, was that the attacks were getting more frequent and, even worse, getting bolder. This latter continued to wear on his mind.

It was early Sunday night, Marc and Mindi were out strolling on the Bellview grounds. Mindi was feeling uneasy and apprehensive. The stroll would do them both good, thought Marc; they had been getting a bit too engrossed in the details. Marc first noticed the dull red glow on the northern horizon. As they both stared wonderingly at it, the glow grew higher and brighter, far brighter than any northern lights ever seen at night. It seemed a long way off.

Suddenly Marc felt weak and nauseous; he had a realization of what it meant. Nervously, Mindi asked, "What's wrong Marc? What is it honey? What is it?"

He looked at her, holding her tightly; and, with a great effort, he said in a hushed voice, "It's Hill View. Oh god! It must be Hill View!" As he said it, he felt her body drop limp; and he held onto her.

In a minute, she recovered a bit and they sat down. "What can we do? Mom! Dad! What can we do?"

"Easy baby, easy. We will leave at once." Marc nudged her inside and sent her off to change clothes. Then he ran to the gardener's quarters, Bill Jacks. He had several ponies that Marc, on occasion, had used. Marc was pounding on the door before he regained some measure of composure—"Gotta borrow two ponies now—it's Hill View, man Hill View," he said gesturing northward.

Bill gasped and said, "Anything you say, Sir—anything!" He rushed to the stables only half dressed. Five minutes later,

Marc had returned with the ponies; Mindi was still shaken but ready to go. He grabbed his dueling sword off the wall and ushered Mindi out. As he passed by the end table, instinctively he grabbed the wizard's sword as well. They rode off northward as fast as their ponies could go.

Hill View was a good slow day's ride north of Metro. Most would travel there by cart. On speeding ponies, Marc hoped to get there in a few hours, if the beasts could last that far, but he had his doubts. West Flat ponies were of short stock conformation, used to pull carts as a rule. They were not noted for speed.

Neither said a word for some time, merely holding on and doing their best to move with the jerking ponies. Keeping in sync with the rapid pounding was quite a task. To get the best from the ponies, they tried to minimize rider interference.

As they rode, the ominous red glow seemed to be steadily growing. There was now enough light that the road was dimly visible. Marc guessed the glow was visible for at least one hundred miles, in all directions. By ten p.m., their ponies were dripping with sweat; and the leather was foaming. They were now walking, leading the ponies along to cool them down a bit. They were over half way there.

Mindi still had not said much at all; Marc, sensing how worried and tense she was, kept conversation short. He knew better than to try to say the usual words of false hope. "We'll do what we can, as we can." Mindi understood.

After half an hour, they were speeding along again. The ground was very flat from Metro north; Hill View was at the edge of the flats. Marc never figured out why it wasn't called the "Gate way to the hills"—that seemed more appropriate than "Gate way to the flats."

Four miles from Hill View, the sky was aflame; the ponies shied and refused to go forward. Hideous noises greeted their ears. Quickly they dismounted and unsaddled the ponies and gave them their heads. They drew their swords; Mindi used one of Marc's dueling swords; he, the other. Arm in arm, they went forward into the dreadful fracas.

Hill View was besieged; the entire eastern half of the city was in flames. Everywhere, people were running; some in terror flights; others, as if with purpose. Everyone was screaming. Here and there, they had to step over shaking bodies that were cowering behind the scattered trees. A small troupe passed by them. Marc tried to find out what had happened, but all he got was a look of cold horror from their silent faces.

On they walked. As they neared the city, the Scavengers appeared. The men were laughing in a bone-chilling manner. Marc's stomach was repulsed by it. Two men sat toying with swords over who got to cut up the victim before them first. Around the men were three wolves, or wargs, eyeing hungrily the proceedings and patiently waiting. Beyond the wargs was a pair of jackals slowly pacing in circles waiting for their chance. The smell in the air was so foul that Mindi held her breath as much as possible.

Marc charged forward, yelling "Aie" as loud as he could, waving his sword. The two Scavengers saw him and for a moment stood transfixed, as if some fear had hit them. Then quickly they turned their swords towards Marc and Mindi. They were no match for the duelists enraged. Ten seconds later, Mindi helped the man up. He was in such shock that he couldn't even speak, but Mindi saw his thanks in his eyes.

Marc lunged at the nearest warg, and the pack backed off. Then they went onward, and turning around, they saw the wargs devouring the two slain men. "Scavengers!" screamed Marc. Mindi gagged.

Within minutes, they hit the main body of Scavengers and were quickly out numbered. They stood back to back fighting off nearly twenty-five men shrieking. Their dueling swords flashing, they fought with a rage and passion the Scavengers had never seen. After ten men lay dead in a growing mound at their feet, the noisy beasts gave ground. Slowly, the two began to drive them backwards away from the city. At this point, they were joined by a group of Hill View guards, led by a tall man dressed in a weather stained, well-worn, grey cloak. He carried a large sword, Marc noted. The tall stranger seemed to be in command, and the pair was soon relieved to have guards standing beside them.

The stranger spoke only, "You are a pair of fair

warriors." They continued slaying the Scavengers before them. In about an hour, the melee had all but ended. The Scourge had been driven off. They had never had such a resistance to their will as had been shown by the lone pair of newcomers and the grey-clad stranger.

Yet, the wargs and jackals remained, making calculated dives here and there, grabbing, and hauling off the Scavenger's remains. The exhausted pair followed the guards back to the west half of town, to a temporary shelter house. They both collapsed on the floor. Mindi laid her head on Marc's chest, and for the first time began to cry softly. Marc too was moved.

About five a.m., an old lady came offering, "Have some ale miss and you too sir. You be need'n it." They thanked her and sat up.

Dawn had come. The eastern sky was a pale red. The fires had died down considerably. The hideous noises were gone. Scattered wailing had taken its place. "Come on," said Marc; and they left, heading for the east side, where Mindi's relatives had lived.

As they walked, they saw half a city destroyed—smoldering ruins of a once fair rural village. Bodies were scattered, lying dead or so wishing. The air was filled with smoke and filth. They arrived where her uncle's home used to be. Charred walls remained. Lying about the once wide green front yard were four bodies, heavily mutilated and chewed, but still recognizable. Mindi gasped and collapsed on Marc.

He, with effort, kept from vomiting; they both turned aside for a while. By eight a.m., the stranger in grey had organized a burial squad. It was decided to have a mass grave and memorial. By noon, seven hundred and sixteen bodies were buried under a huge mound just off the Old Caravan Road. A large plaque carried their names, including Samuel and Elizabeth Francos.

Around early afternoon, the heavily armed Patrols arrived from Metro. Marc and Mindi rode slowly by them, eyes down cast, heading homeward. Their first combat with the enemy was over at a heavy price. Between them, they'd totaled forty-one Scavengers.

They arrived at Bellview, neither having spoken. Once

safely inside, Mindi broke down and cried. He consoled her as best he could. Then together they slept soundly for ten hours.

They awoke as the sun was setting; and, without speaking, Mindi fixed up some food. They ate and cleaned up. Marc watched her closely while she was going about these chores for signs of what was going on with her. At best, they were out of communication.

Finally, Marc made her sit down and he took out his pipe. Lighting it, he said, "Now Mindi, it's time to talk. They are gone. You loved them, but they are no longer here. If Malazar is to be believed, they are not dead but have gone in search of new bodies. In that, there is some small comfort. The past is past, the present is here and now, the future will yet be. Dwell not in the past—on what might have been. They would not have wanted that. Do not seek to have them live on through you. You are you. They, they. Above all, let not hate fill your heart. Let us rather vow to end the evil at its source."

As she listened and brushed off tears, she knew that he spoke, as it should be. "I need to be able to face it is all," she said meekly when he was done. She put her hand on his and he held it warmly. They looked at each other for some time. Marc almost felt he could see strange pictures flashing by her head, but they just continued facing each other for some time, neither doing nor saying anything.

After easily an hour and some heavy yawns, a small smile began to grow on her face; a sparkle returned to her eyes. She said softly, "It is done. I have seen it all. I shall not be as mom. I am me. It is done." Then she leaned over, hugged Marc tightly and lovingly, and gave him a tender kiss. "Honey, I doubt if you fully realize what I have done here today. It is as Malazar claimed. There are mental pictures, which, if viewed, disappear. You have helped, perhaps even saved me. Thank you, but I will need help in carrying on."

"Of course," came the reply. In Marc, she could not have chosen better help. The Master Merchant easily and swiftly executed the personal matters of the late Francos. Utilizing his resources, he quickly handled the various aspects of the estate. He set up a self-sustaining format for the feed corn business that Mindi had inherited by allowing and forcing it to be at least slowly expanding. He put one of his best assistants in charge of it. Marc had insisted that she move into Bellview with him. It was now more socially acceptable—he being the closest to the family. This made their operation much smoother since they had to watch after one house only.

Mindi was very glad of the move because being alone in the empty house gave her a constant, foreboding reminder. She had set about the task of moving her belongings, their provisions, the scrolls, and books. Marc had kept an observant eye on her, but she showed none of the usual retrogression signs that others sometimes did when the loss would return in their minds. True, she was much more sullen, the old vitality, though there, was subdued.

Nevertheless, she had continued her cycles of gathering provisions and information.

Marc, after getting Mindi's house in order, had taken to going to the pubs for hours on end. West Flats was in an uproar of indignation, horror, and disgust. Some were afraid, Marc discovered; some angry. Everyone seemed to have different ideas of how to handle it. The Mayor's office took no official action to combat it. They did, however, send out the customary condolences to be expected in these times. Clearly, no one was doing anything about it.

The Hill View affair remained the topic of conversation for many weeks in Metro, and the story spread through all southern Isel. Many distant watchful eyes had seen the hideous fire.

Three days after the affair, Shannon returned; and, within an hour of docking at Gate Way, Marc was aboard. Shannon was enthusiastic. He'd made some great deals. Marc was amazed at the efficiency of his friend. Hardly anything was left to chance. Shannon, however, almost at once sensed that something was gravely wrong. He'd seen the red light at sea. He'd assumed it had a role in the trouble. "Something has happened, hasn't it Marc?" he said in an exploratory way.

"Well yes," he replied, "Got any more of that Rones?" They settled down at the table; and slowly, and at times angrily, Marc unveiled the recent events.

Shannon listened intently. "A bad business," he

repeated several times.

"Since then, we have had no attacks—only clouds of black birds circling high in the sky. My guess is that they did not expect such fierce resistance, or such losses of their numbers."

"Or unless they're staging," put in Shannon. "In any case, evil times have come."

"Well, you have been of great service to us," said Marc, changing the subject to brighten things. Mindi and I have decided you must come to Bellview for a dinner, just the three of us. Mindi insists. She is a good cook you know."

Much to his surprise, Shannon agreed. It was to be his third time ashore, ever, in Metro. Marc sent word on ahead while he and Shannon set to work to transport the gear to Bellview, Southview. Within the hour, a small caravan of "Ace Transporters" began the two-mile stretch from the docks to Southview, accompanied by the two men.

The streets of Metro were packed, as usual, with people moving goods. Buyers and sellers thronged in great crowds in Metro's Center for trade. Marc and his supplies merely blended with the masses. He was relieved to find no one noticed. They were riding two of the dwarfish ponies, and leading the third. Shannon had acquired the three from the dwarf lords in Khorizaba. They did not make either the swiftest or the nicest riding beasts, but they, like their dwarf masters, were strong and hardy. They were bred for rugged endurance, for use in the mines and mountains of the dwarves. No stronger or dependable ponies could be had anywhere. It would prove an excellent choice.

In an hour, they arrived at Bellview. Mindi stood on the porch waiting their arrival. She had on her long, flowing, white gown for the occasion. Against the blue sky, green grass, and reddish house, she shone like a silver star. Her long black hair, waving in the gentle June breeze, set a striking contrast. As they rode up, Shannon did not wait for an introduction. "Many treasures, fair lady, I have brought with me, but none that can match thee."

Mindi blushed; and Marc, realizing suddenly the truth of Shannon's words, gave the introduction. "Mindi, daughter of Samuel Francos, this is Shannon Wayfar, Prince Mariner of Mari."

"If all Mariners are as fair as thee, my lord, Mari I must see," Mindi returned the compliment. "Come in, dinner will be ready in an hour. Can we not see your treasures at once?" She was as excited as Marc.

The hour passed quickly. They sat amid piles of opened boxes and repeatedly acknowledged Shannon's choices. Besides the dwarf ponies, which Mindi named immediately as Blackie, White Foot, and Butterball, there were backpacks of various sizes of dwarfish origin. Shannon explained that they were light weight but rugged and were used to carry hundreds of pounds of ore from the mines. There was a mariner's stove and star labe. The latter, as was explained in detail, would serve as a navigational tool. Elvish water flasks, Burly made knives, cooking ware made by the fairies (lightweight and durable), and some rugged clothing made by the horsemen of Illanos rounded out his selections.

Shannon apologized for the clothes. "He'd said to get two sets both his size. Had I known his companion was one so fair, I would have brought things more fitting."

"Yes but," interjected Marc.

However, Mindi had the last word, "This is not going to be a pleasure trip; I'd feel more comfortable in the wild dressed as a man." Neither could discount her viewpoint.

There was also a coil of lightweight elfin rope and various torch lamps of Metro origin. Finally, Shannon pulled out the last two boxes. With a big grin, he proudly announced, "And here lies the best of the treasures." He opened the smaller package first. "Elfin shoes!" he announced.

They were of a shimmering pale green color with a pointed toe and sides that reached up over the ankles. "In a forest or on smooth ground, these will prove superior to anything in Isel!"

Mindi immediately had to try them out and, with many exclamations, agreed with him. The other box held pairs of Burly boots, a very rugged boot that proved feet saving in rough terrain. Then, they left the mess in the front room; and, led by a gracefully, flowing Mindi, they went onto the veranda for dinner. Mindi proved an excellent host, living up to the Francos's reputation of serving the most exquisite dinners in West Flats. There were eleven courses, altogether fitting she explained, under the circumstances. Their pretext, "It was too pretty to eat," did not last long. It was their turn to return the admiration flow.

Pushing aside an empty desert bowl, Shannon said, "An absolutely exquisite chef you have here. Truly enough to tempt us mariners to land!"

Marc added, "And one heck of a fighter too!" He grinned and gave her a loving hug. She beamed appreciatively.

The sun was now setting, and the sky was rosy against the green rolling hills of the East Range. The obelos stood away in the distance reflecting the last rays of the sun. Mindi was the first to speak as they all gazed into the distance. "Marc, why don't you fill Shannon in on all the events. I detect here an ally of honor and magnitude."

Marc blushed for a second, recalling how he had endeavored to tell him only enough to suffice. In matters of character, Marc implicitly trusted her observations. So if she thought Shannon should be trusted, he would only agree. Shannon listened intently to the tale. He displayed a keen interest in both what the wizard had to say about the mental pictures and the history and, in particular, the events at the Obelos. He'd had Marc repeat those parts several times.

Mindi remained silent, and while sipping her tea, watched his reactions closely. She almost never made a mistake when it came to sizing up the true nature of a person. She was keenly interested in Shannon. There was something about him. Maybe it was his noble attitude, but there was more to Shannon than he'd let on so far, anyway.

The discussion of Hill View brought a distinct lowering of his tone, from intensely interested. She detected that there was some hidden grief that Shannon was subduing. The answer was not long in coming. "My Lady," he began, "My deepest sympathy and understanding is due," and he bowed low and kissed her hand. "I also know something of grief at the hands of the Scavengers." Then he told her of the raid on Ceeblu and the loss of his sister, Irene.

Marc then continued the tale and brought him up to the present. They all sat quietly for some time watching the star-filled heavens and felt the gentle, balmy, sea breeze that had arisen.

Finally, Mindi probed a bit. "Shannon," she began fumbling for just the right way to put it, "there is still yet more about you than you've admitted. If I'm wrong, my apologies, but I did detect a keen interest in our adventures with the obelos—particularly with Marc's second visit and his reactions. You know something more in this area, I'd guess." As usual, she was spot on, and Shannon burst out laughing, relieving the tension that had been building.

"You have here Marc, indeed a treasure; she's also a wizard of minds!" Marc blushed and felt truly proud. "Yes," he went on, "you are indeed correct. Since you've told all, I shall likewise—though bear in mind, I've never spoke of this to a living soul."

They listened intently as he began his tale. "For years, as a boy, I lived and breathed by the sea, longing for I knew not what. There by the sea rises Obelos Wund, a splendor to behold. Yet it is ominous and foreboding. None ever go there. Well, I did, did it repeatedly. It held a strange fascination, like a power, over me. Your description, Marc, is particularly interesting; it does feel like 'home.' I searched all our records and scrolls for data on it. Finally, when I was sixteen, I found a collection of wizard scrolls. I tried them out on the door. Sure enough, one worked. I've explored the many splendors inside. The 'Vishi,' as Malazar called it, is known to me as the 'viewer.' By the hours, I'd stare into its visions of the world and sea. That chart you saw in my cabin, Marc, came from there. When I got older, I got my own boat and sailing I've being doing ever since. I still frequently visit the obelos—especially when storms are brewing. It gives much knowledge of them. I've used it many times for the good of all mariners. I've become the 'forecaster supreme,' it's said. It's strange about the sword, Marc, I also have one; more exactly, it's a cutlass. I always carry it on me."

With that, he leaned over and pulled a golden cutlass from under his shirt. It gleamed in the starlight. "It has done strange things in the battles I've seen; it seems to glow when it's being used." They marveled over the blade.

When they were done, Mindi leaned over and taking his hand in hers said softly, "Thank you."

They mused about other events for a while; then Shannon asked at last, "Well, now then, what is the plan?"

"Ah—uh—what plan?" was Marc's bungled response. He'd forgotten that he neither had a plan for protecting the obelos and Metro nor for getting underway. In these matters, Shannon proved no better than a good listener did. A warrior he was not. After much discussion, it was decided that Shannon would see that Obelos Wund was guarded and that supplies for the company would ever be at hand. He explained that whenever something was needed, they'd only have to come to the seashore and build a signal fire. Mariners would respond.

Marc and the Mariner arranged for a grain trade flow to be established. It felt very comfortable to know that help was always near at sea. It was a very late night before the Mariner finally returned to his ship. In the ensuing days, Mindi visited Shannon and took charge of ordering the gear and provisions. Inside of three days, the gear was all set and lay in readiness in a corner. Then she continued with her legends and maps crusade.

Marc visited the Mayor. He found Mr. Appletree, as usual, sympathetic with ears and apathetic on doing anything. "What can be done?" he'd repeated until Marc grew tired of it. Marc finally realized that if anything were to be done, he'd have to do it.

The Round could be fixed up, assuming he could find someone with the technological mastery to do it. As for the suburbs, he was at a loss. He confided his ideas in the other two members of the company. Thus, it was decided to rebuild the Round. Shannon said he knew just the half-man to do it. He'd left them with a riddle.

Meanwhile, Marc set about the task of determining how to defend the rest. It was after midnight one night, when Mindi found Marc sprawled over a map of Metro, asleep. "Honey, wake up, come to bed," She gently rubbed his neck.

"Huh—oh, it's late, isn't it?" Mindi noticed a bunch of hash marks in a great semicircle around Metro.

"What's this," she asked puzzled.

Marc yawned and said in jest, "It's Blancas's Hedge." Mindi looked at him, and he knew that she expected a full explanation. He had no other choice. So he gave her a back rub while he explained his idea of building a post hedge around the area. Armed with sufficient riders, it would give advanced warning of any attack, as well as a big delay for the enemy. To his amazement, she thought it might work.

The next day Marc set off to execute his plan. The Master Merchant began to operate in the craft he knew well. First step, find the opinion leaders of Metro defenses. Second, arrange a meeting. Thirdly, see them. Finally, let them sell the others and get it executed. With papers in hand, Marc entered the Civil Hall for a meeting with a dozen of Metro's most influential spokesmen.

He found them in a state of extreme concern over Metro's safety, yet without any clear idea of how to defend it. He found a receptive audience. Thus, it was barely an hour later that Marc found himself dictating specifications to several crews of engineer foremen.

The next two days saw a tremendous resurgence in self-pride of the citizens of Metro. They were building their defense! By unanimous choice, it was called Blancas's Hedge.

In two days' time, Shannon returned bearing his half-man. This time, both Marc and Mindi went to the docks to greet the incoming vessel. Shannon greeted them with a broad smile and introduced his friend. "This is Nache Thraindruil, son of Drain of old, Master Craftsman of Khorizaba."

With that, a stocky dwarf dressed in brightly colored finery, stepped forward and bowed low. "At your service, Master Merchant, and fairest lady of the land." They both accepted the compliment and were a little at a loss for words. They'd never seen a dwarf before, and felt a bit uncomfortable in talking to someone barely waist high.

Nache had a long white beard nearly to his knees. He was very stocky and muscular, even for a dwarf. His clothes had the typical zigzag swatches of colors. Dwarf designs invariably had this pattern. In fact, Nache presented himself in the best clothes he had. Dwarves were long unaccustomed to meeting the big people—let alone visit their land alone. He felt nervous and kept fumbling his belt. On it hung a big broad axe that gleamed silvery in the sunlight.

Shannon handled the awkwardness for all. "Come," he began. "This will be only the fourth time I've set foot on land in Metro. This is an occasion of magnitude. Long has it been since a dwarf ever set foot in the Flats. We are honored by the Master Builder of the dwarves. On such an occasion I, the Master Mariner, will go forth on land to honor him!"

Thus, it was that the four left the Sendoa and went to Bellview, quickly, avoiding the crowds. Seeing the rich gardens of Bellview, the ponies from his country, and his amiable hosts, he did relax.

Mindi took an immediate fancy to him. Seldom had he had such attention from one so beautiful, he kept saying. After exchanging news and the like, Marc took them on a royal tour of Metro. The citizens hearing of the arrival of the Master Builder, who was going to repair the Round, made the day a celebration in his honor. This he liked, for dwarves love such places of importance and attention.

They toured the Round. Nache kept muttering exclamations of this and that in his dwarfish tongue. He did seem pleased by the Round. Then, Marc took them to the Hedge, at least to the part that was built. Nache's comment was a stone wall was better but given the time, it would do—indeed it would. It was made of logs pointed sharply on their ends laid in a crisscross pattern, with points toward the wild. The Scavengers would be hard pressed to crawl over the eight-foot high barricade. Especially when riders would be riding alongside it, spaced a minute apart. Marc demonstrated. They all laughed while he took four minutes to pick his way over without getting poked.

Nache agreed to direct the rebuilding of the Round. Nache proved to be an amiable person and an exceptional builder. The Round was built in ancient days by hands unknown. Nache knew this once he looked at it. The Craftsman was something to behold and altogether fitting for the Round. Industrious was the word Mindi used to describe him. He'd be gone by daylight, returning by darkness. He seemed tireless beyond belief, ever humming a tune.

Metro put everything at his disposal. This twist suited Nache, and he felt both honored and proud at being selected. For his services, it might be noted here, three shiploads of grain were delivered to his city of Tulan in the mountains of Armagh.

As the days passed, both the Round and the Hedge grew, and at the end of June, both were done. The Mayor declared a holiday of celebration and thanks. Marc and Nache were to be the honored guests. So it was that for the first time in hundreds of years, a Master Merchant and a Master Builder dwarf were given places of honor, equally, by West Flats. Truly, a new day was dawning.

Chapter V—The Message

During the time Nache spent with them, they became excellent friends. Mindi was especially fond of him, and he was forever admiring her as a flower of faery. Not a single night passed without their hearing of a dwarf legend or song.

Marc had heard Nache humming quietly to himself every day as he worked. After they had finished dinner one night, Marc began, "Nache, every day, you incessantly hum something. I am dying of curiosity to hear what it is! Come on; sing it right now for us."

"Please," put in Mindi.

The dwarf's face got red, and he humbly explained, "We always sing while we work. I know many working songs, but it is hard to sing them when you're not working."

"Well then, why don't you just pretend you're working, and sing it," pleaded Mindi, full of curiosity as well.

Proudly, the gaily-colored dwarf stood up from the table, backed off a few feet. He picked up one of his hammers, planted his feet apart, and began swaying back and forth rhythmically. Soon with a stiff face, he began to hum. Finally, seeing they were really watching expectantly, he began to sing in an accented voice.

> (one of Nache's working songs)
> Bash and bang and build and moan;
> Ba—du—ba—du—ba—du—da
> Carve and cut and crash and groan;
> Ba—du—ba—du—ba—du—da
> Toil and sweat, we work all day;
> Done for Lost Ones and Alones,
> Come and see the wonders new.
> Ba—du—ba—du—ba—du—dum.

He explained that it was a "round"; when you got to dum, you slurred dum into bash and began all over. He demonstrated several times. Soon Marc and Mindi were swaying back and forth singing along. Finally, with all three laughing so hard, they had to quit, and all sat down. Nache felt proud.

Previously, Mindi resolved to permit their tale to be told in full to Nache. Hence, even though it was late, Marc painstakingly told their entire story, omitting nothing. Predictably, the dwarf queried some points, forcing Marc to dwell on certain parts, as had Shannon. Not until Marc was completely done, did Nache comment; for a dwarf would never interrupt a tale, except for clarification. If Mindi had some questions about his reactions, she didn't get a chance to air them. Just as soon as he indicated the end of the story, Nache commenced.

A dwarf loves tales and especially to discuss them. Nache was no exception. He clapped his hands in excitement and exclaimed, "Excellent, excellent Master Merchant!" It took both by surprise. He continued, "Long have I, Nache Thraindruil, sought those who can read the obelos! I myself am the Appointed One—the Kharanda—Tower Watcher. The position has long been in my family, last held by Drain, my father."

"Obelos Khander towers mightily in Tulan, high in the Armagh Mountains. For ages, we await the return of Belwain, the Great Wizard of Khorizaba. Stories and songs have been handed down through the endless ages of the splendor of Khorizaba under the hand of Belwain. He built the first cities in the mountains of which Tulan is the fairest. The Appointed Ones are the guardians of the tower until the time of Belwain's return. For the legends say:

From far above in Misty heights,
Mighty Mizzinti issue forth,
To conquer all our fears and foes;
Isel freed once more.

"In such times to Tulan, where the Mighty Yaca and Baca rivers join, to Obelos Khander will the Mizzinti return. Even now, evil lurks on our borders; though by all the powers in Khorizaba, none shall enter our kingdom. For fifty years, I have studied the lore and songs of the old. It shall be one day that these I pass along to my sons as they become the Appointed Ones. Yet to you I will tell truly, though to none,

43

not even a dwarf, have I openly spoke these words. I have had a feeling that the Appointed One's days are numbered. Belwain's return I sense I will see. Home you called it, but it is to us even more so, revered home, source of love. Yet, it is I who feel truly at home there. It is as if I belong. At first, I attributed it to my position. By long research and weary hours of searching, I discovered that no other Appointed One had such feelings.

"Then nearly thirty-five years ago, I sat outside the doors of the tower, and I felt the urge to swell with song. I sang happily of the old Mizzinti songs. It was as if I expected something. Well, the door did open unto me, Nache Thraindruil! To none other, save Belwain had it done so. Though blasphemy, it may be, may Belwain forgive me, I did enter. I have explored its mystic avenues, though I dared not touch anything. Many tales I can tell of its fair beauty, but alas, that would take years! This I've told no one."

Reaching under his belt, he produced the silver axe—"Kazab I call it. I removed it ages ago from its cradle within. Never has it failed me nor ever left my hand, though many battles were fought!" He lovingly patted it.

Mindi reached over and kissed him gently on his forehead. Nache blushed and got very red. He stammered, "Bless you my Lady."

She said decidedly, "Fate has certainly been with us. We began as two and are now four—five with Malazar. Our errand draws close. Thankful are we that you, Nache Thraindruil, are on our side."

"Yes, glad am I that there are others as I am," came the reply.

"I still have one question," she asked, "How old are you anyway?"

"One hundred fifty-two," came the reply.

Thus, it was that the company of questers now totaled five.

During the days, Mindi continued her studies of the lore. Marc now had little to do. Merchant that he was, he got the citizens themselves diligently to build the Hedge. He took to spending more time with Mindi, learning as well. His formal education had ceased beyond the edge of West Flats. It would prove time well spent.

One curious fact began to emerge among all the volumes she'd bring home. There were always several volumes concerning the fairies. It became very curious, when Marc recalled that in her childhood, she was forever telling him fairy tales.

It was around midnight one evening in late June. Marc was sitting back in his chair, books piled on his lap. He was watching her leaf through a volume intently. She blushed and felt funny. "It's on faeries isn't it?" He asked inquisitively.

"Yes," she blushed even more and made no further reply.

He used her tactics and said, "Come on now Mindi; there is something that you haven't fully talked about. It's as plain as your nose. It has something to do with faeries. You are quite fanatic on the subject. Remember all those stories you filled my ears with when we were young? Come on, what gives, precious?"

"Well, if you want to know, I really don't know what it is."

"Why not just tell me about it?"

"All right, you asked for it. I—I love fairies—everything about them. I always have. I read nearly everything I can find on them. Sometimes I feel the stories are familiar. Yet I've never heard them. Sometimes, sometimes I feel I can sing in the fairy tongue! Often times in the spring, I'd find myself singing in a language that is foreign to me! Fairy, I'd bet anything. Malazar's words I've heeded. My mind's full of fairies! Countless pictures, they're so beautiful, I wish I could share them with you. I have the strangest feeling that it will be so! I don't know what to make of it."

"Also, often times in my dreams I see a tower, a pale blue tower. I've never really seen one, you know. Of late, I keep seeing it when I sleep. Maybe I've just read too many stories, but I don't know. I feel a strange kinship with the fairies. You know as well as I do, I've never even seen one! Go ahead Marc and tell me—I'm crazy—I'm going batty. I'd believe you too. I'm so confused!" And with big tears swelling up in her eyes, she laid her head on his lap.

For a time, Marc said nothing, just caressed her head fondly. Then he raised her head—they looked straight at each other, seeing each other. He smiled and gently kissed her forehead. "There is more about you than the eye reveals, my Fairy Queen. If you are mad, then so am I. Let's be mad together, madly in love!" They hugged and embraced. Then, Marc went into his study and returned with an old yellowed paper. "I found this long ago when I was young. I was going to show you this, but at the time, I forgot. I just now remembered it." He read from the brittle aged pages.

The Waltz of the Faery Queen
I wandered out one evening bright
Into a forest enchanted,
Marvelous sights hoping to see,
As reddened sun pierced the branches.
Ah, mysterious dew that hangs
Dripping over the darkened floor
With patches of fleeting reality
Confuse my muddled brain.
Strange sights began creeping 'round me
Luring softly 'round hidden feet.
Fantastic forms drown the eyes, and
Feet, fearing to crush, moved no more.
The leaden air swamped my lungs
A weight too heavy to carry,
Laying down, mists flowed 'round me, as
I drifted into seeming sleep.

I awoke, or thought I did,
As dawn was slowly coming,
Gone was the mist; gone, the forms.
A thin morning haze filtering 'round me.
As early rays slanted thru trees,
Strange sounds drifted into my ears.
Not forest bending in the wind,
But soft music played on a string.

46

O curiosity you would come
"See what makes that morning music."
So off I rambled through the trees
To seek that enchanting music.
T'was not only strings I hear,
But a voice so happy, sang along.
Songs my wild fantasy begot,
A gaiety inviting trees to join.
Who could be the maker of such sounds
Was my only thought to answer.
And as I crept close to hear
I saw the Faery Queen.
She was what words can ne'er describe
Ah a happiness superior to a mortal's try,
Reflected in her carefree song
And flowed from her as there she danced.
T'was like a goddess standing there
Something impossible for man to touch
And I, cowered in a hole, fearing the wrath
Which sure would come should she see me.
But my fear was numbed by her song;
I began to feel her joy and
Wanted to sing and dance as well.
T'was then she saw me there.
Oh gods, the song will stop now,
For I have surely broken the spell.
To be the end of such happiness,
I deserve to be quite dead.
But lo, her music did not stop
And she came dancing to my side,
Without faltering, grabbed my hand
We both began to dance and sing.
O that river that flowed from her to me
Happiness gushed out from my heart
Oh tell me please what be your name?
I am called the Queen of Faery.

And we sat down among the morning's mist
Just me and the Faery Queen,
There in the golden fields in reddish rays
Within that enchanted wood.
Oh tell me wondrous being
Such love I have never seen.
Are you always this happy
To sing and dance all day?
O inquisitive soul, must you know
That such happiness can cover things
So sad, a life, most desperate one,
Even a life not worth living?
I am the daughter of Hecate,
Evil, vicious, destroyer of man.
Having to live with the evil she makes,
Can this phase you, naive little one?
So most desperate was I when the Caravan came
And Perseus on his shining horse rode by.
He stopped and talked, and then
Showed me the whole caravan's wares.
And all the tired dusty travelers
Welcomed me, saying join us for action;
See the world wide from our wagons.
All I said was "Take me away."

Oh gods, when the caravan rolled again
It left me behind.
Standing there in the dust,
Life disappeared in a blinding flash.
So now you see,
That happiness free
That flows from me
As I can just be.
But now, I've put tears in your eyes.
Ah my Faery Queen—you've shaken my heart
To see such a Queen who only happiness should see.

Oh come with me—let's be free.
My room walls surround me
And my dizzily spinning head
Now thinks only of food
As I try vainly to create, again.

When Marc finished, their hands met. She said softly, "I love you Marc," and kissed him, "There is more about you, Marc, than you let on."

The Round and Hedge now being completed, the company began looking for a way to depart on their journey. Nache agreed to join them. Nothing, he claimed, would separate them, especially from his fair lady, as he put it.

Now for the famous Master Merchant to one day announce that he is up and leaving Metro for parts unknown was unthinkable. The social uproar would rock Metro's foundations. It went against every fiber of the people and when the city most needed him, too. The three counseled many hours, but no useable idea developed. Nache even suggested Marc pretend to be killed, and they'd all sneak away. Somehow sneaking away seemed a poor choice.

On July 3, a special courier arrived at Southview looking for Marc. By the time he found him, half the city was alerted.

Special couriers were a rare event. It was usually an event of some importance. Marc was at his office when the courier arrived. "Marcos Blancas, Sir?" the tired travel-worn man said.

"Yes, that's me."

"I've a special letter for you, to be delivered to none but you sir." He reached into his pouch at his side and produced a brown stained envelope with his name scrawled in black ink.

Marc gave the man a tip and a thanks, and the man left. He left, but was snatched up by a group, taken into a pub, and given all the free spirits he could consume, but no information did he know, except that the letter came from East Flats. Not much news for the eager ears.

Marc opened the letter curiously, wondering who would send him a letter, Malazar? The signature was that of George

Bighollow.

"George. Oh yes, George," he thought, "My old Academy buddy—that's been six years now, more or less." He read on.

30 June

My Dearest Marc,

Forgive me for being so bold, but I am in the gravest need. In the days of the Academy, we were friends, and as one, I now call on you for assistance. I have heard rumors that by your valiant hand the tide was turned on the Scourge at Hill View, that you alone have caused the reconstruction of your ancient defense, and you have fortified Metro.

In East Flats, we have fared even worse at the hands of the Evil Ones. Farmers we are and a widely scattered people. Our lands are flat and the cities house our granaries—storehouses of the grains. Scavengers even now are raiding at will, destroying farmstead after farmstead. Our sheriffs are powerless to stop them.

I myself have moved to Hays to protect the granary as best I can. Merchant, you know the ramifications of what the loss of all East Flat granaries would be.

I know of no one else on whom to call. If these rumors are true and you have become a warrior, savior to your people, I beg of you to come to Hays. At the least, observe our plight and offer suggestions as you see fit. Our need is great. Hurry if you can.

If I have affronted you, the excuse must be the times we are in.

Yours truly, yet in need,

George Bighollow

When Marc had finished reading it, he stood up and yelled, "Yahoo!"

Henry came bursting into his office, "Anything wrong sir?"

He laughed, "No Henry, good news—no rather bad news. I will be leaving for an extended stay in East Flats. Prepare the necessary paper work. You'll be in change!"

"Yes Sir!" came the reply.

News of the courier had spread rapidly over the city. Thus, when Marc arrived at Bellview, he found a very anxious

Mindi, Nache, and Shannon waiting for him.

"I have it; I have it!" Marc carried on wildly enthusiastic. They went inside; and, leaning over each other's shoulders, they read the letter several times.

Nache spoke first, patting his axe handle lovingly, "The time has come."

"When do we go?" asked Mindi.

It was Shannon's counsel that they abided by. Hays was four full days' journey. It would be best to leave early the next day. That way the time on the road would be minimized.

Leaving them to get things ready at Bellview, Marc visited the Mayor's office and explained to both the council and the Mayor of the request he had received. They were all ears, as the saying goes in East Flats. There was some grumbling at the prospect of being without the only person who seemed to know what to do. Marc easily handled that one. Further, he explained that he would go accompanied by Nache, but no word did he speak of Mindi. That would have been a shock.

The news spread like wildfire. Certainly, there would be no chance of an unwatched exit from Metro. Marc then let it be known, to the right ears of course, that Mindi Francos was to leave to go visit with some of her relatives in Greenside until his return. So she was covered as well. He returned to Bellview by way of his office.

When he returned, he found all was in readiness. Mindi had done her job well, and it had taken the three of them only an hour to have it all ready. They discussed their plans for leaving. Marc and Nache would take Blackie and Whitefoot and as much gear as they could. The rest, they stowed on Butterball. They would leave at six o'clock in the morning. Mindi was to lead the pack pony through the back country northward to a point ten miles above Metro and wait for them. Marc and Nache would take the parade route through town and out onto the Old Caravan Road. If all went well, they would rendezvous at around noon.

Only Shannon felt uneasy about seemingly "everyone" knowing that Marc was going to Hays.

They had a solemn last meal together. Of the group,

only Nache seemed unaffected by the prospect of the journey's start. At last, Shannon took his leave and returned to his ship, and the rest retired to an uneasy sleep.

Chapter VI—Journey To Hays

Dawn of July 7 came, bringing a sky half filled with large fleece clouds, rose red. Silently the trio ate a hurried breakfast. All was made ready. Marc nervously made last minute inspections just to have something to do.

By six a.m., the ponies were loaded. On Butterball, they put the crossed arch saddle, designed for packing gear. Mindi intended to walk. The other two had riding saddles; both Marc and Nache would carry back packs and saddlebags. Both Mindi and Marc were dressed in the dark brown pants of the riders of Illanos, made of a rugged and durable leather. Their light cotton Metro plaid shirts were covered by the heavier woolen variety from East Flats. Covering them, from head to ankles, were the elfin cloaks, gray-green. With their hoods pulled up over their heads, they looked so much the same that Nache could only tell Mindi by her shoes. She had on her elfin slippers. Marc's choice was for the heavier Burly boots. Nache was similarly dressed with dark colored dwarf clothes and well worn, dark brown cloak.

They briefly went over the plan again, and it was time for Mindi to leave. She gave both a hug and kiss, and they said their farewells. Mindi picked up the lead rope and slowly walked off across the grounds of Bellview, slipping quietly away through the wet, dewy grass. She went due east almost to the ancient city before turning to the north. Marc watched her until she was only a small dot in a sea of rosy green. He longed to follow right then, but Nache brought him round, "Come it's time for us."

"Yes, Ok."

They put on their packs and mounted up; Nache on Whitefoot and Marc on Blackie. From the grounds, they slowly neck reined the ponies onto the road; and they began the slow clip-clop through the streets of Whitegate toward Metro.

It was not long before expectant crowds began to gather. By the time they got into Metro proper, great throngs had gathered. Indeed, the Mayor had called a holiday. There were cheers and much waving. Marc felt a growing sense of importance; Nache felt very proud, and he held his head high. They continued to meander slowly through the streets, waving and beaming. At last, they came to a big platform erected near Black Bone Gates in the Round. Marc was surprised. On top of the gaily-decorated stand stood the Mayor, the captains of the newly reorganized Patrols, and a number of the top merchants. Instinctively, they halted in front. Banners were flying from several poles, and people cheered. The Mayor waived his hands for silence, but it took nearly five minutes for the crowd to quiet down.

The Mayor began in a rehearsed fashion, "We are gathered together here today to honor Metro's finest, those who have served us in our hour of need. . ." (Big cheers went up halting the speech.)

"Today, we pay tribute to our Master Merchant, Marcos Blancas. (More cheers.) And we take special pride and honor in presenting a representative of a people long forgotten in Metro, Master Builder, Master Craftsman, Nache Thraindruil of the Dwarves." (More cheers and yells drowned his voice.)

Nache's face got red, but he sucked in his breath and threw his chest out as far as he could. Then, he bowed as low as he could in his saddle. There were more cheers and yelling.

Finally, the Mayor regained control, and continued, "Thanks to these two, Metro is reasonably safe. Now, as we have all heard, our friends, the farmers of East Flats, are in dire trouble and have asked for our aid and help. Today we send forth our best to aid our neighbors." (An uncontrollable round of cheers and yells began again.)

The Mayor tried to finish his speech over the din, "Let them bring honor to Metro." However, all was lost in the noise of celebration. The crowds began to swarm to the platform.

Realizing the potential danger, Marc nudged Blackie forward. Whether the Mayor was done or not, it was time to leave or be squashed. They trotted off waving and hoping that they'd make it through the gates. They did and were on their way once more. The waiving crowds of Black Bone were not nearly as large as Metro's.

Soon they waived to the last stragglers; and, looking

behind them, they could see the splendid city outlined against the blue sea behind her. It was quite picturesque, Marc felt. "Well, Nache, we're actually off. What do you think of all that?" Marc asked.

"Amazing, simply amazing!" came the reply. "I wish the dwarves could all have seen that. It makes for a new strong bond between our peoples. Perhaps after the evil is gone, more dwarves will be seen in your streets."

Then, as if each were lost in their own thoughts, they rode on in silence watching the country pass slowly. The Old Caravan Road went due north from Metro to Hill View. The entire land here was very flat, and the country was ever so slowly rising. Hill View marked the start of the foothills that eventually lead to the high mountains of the interior. The flat ground was relatively dry and covered with a sparse grass. The tall Beeblaca Mountains to the West in Mari forced most of the rainfall into the forests of Rainu, though some did get over the lofty peaks.

Time passed slowly; and, as the sun rose, they removed their cloaks. Nache hummed to himself. They rode slowly onward. They met no fellow travelers; the road was deserted, but the land was not entirely void. Here and there, they heard shepherd bells and saw small flocks of sheep grazing. They'd occasionally waive to a shepherd. They seldom waived back.

As noon approached, Marc began to doubt his wisdom of sending Mindi on ahead. What if they should miss each other at the rendezvous? Actually, there was no landmark to wait beside. All that was said was to meet ten miles north of Metro. That required timing. As it turned out, they both were about right, and it was the nature of the land that helped. Soon Marc saw two black specks far ahead. He relaxed and breathed a sigh of relief. Nache smiled. In a few minutes, the rendezvous was completed amid hugs and tales of the events.

Mindi's trip had been completely uneventful. She'd seen only some flocks of sheep and had steered a course wide of them. They ate a brief lunch and continued. This time Nache insisted on walking.

Their idea now was to veer northeastward and connect with Haskel Road by evening. Hopefully, they'd be in the hill country of the East Range by nightfall. That would give them some protection Marc thought. There were at least a few scattered trees there. Hot and dusty, they traveled on.

Finally, Nache broke the silence, when they were well off the Old Caravan Road. He happily announced, "I have written a song for the occasion. Want to hear it?"

"By all means," came the reply. Nache swayed his body in rhythm as he walked, he hummed a bit and began.

Clip clop the horses plop;
Foot foot upon the ground;
Trudging ever on.
Hours pass as miles roll by
Sun climbs and then goes down!
Onward ever on.
Star light it seems too bright;
Our hearts are all a flame;
To victory we do go.

Then he smiled and looked at the others. They applauded him heartily, and they all sang it through several times. It seemed to relieve their tensions and the weariness of such flat countryside.

In the early afternoon, that cheerfulness left them abruptly. Marc saw them first—a pack of black forms in the distance. They halted and watched the ever-closing dust clouds. Soon they recognized a pack of wild dogs that were out ravaging the land. Evidently, the Scavengers unleashed them. They drew their swords, and Nache, his axe. They spent ten tense minutes as the dogs noisily approached and watched them for a moment, glaring from a distance. Then, noisily they continued their southward running. In a few minutes, they were again black dots
on the green horizon.

"More evil is at work; I've not heard of wild dog packs in West Flats before," spoke Marc.

They determinedly continued their journey, with the sun now at their backs. Soon hills began to loom ahead, foothills of the East Range. In an hour, they hit the road. They felt much relieved when they found Haskel Road. It meant they were back on the map, about ten miles due east of Hill View. Here they stopped for an hour's rest. They were weary, having walked a good distance and saddle sore. Neither Marc nor Mindi were used to riding all day.

They rode for two more hours, intending to make camp around dusk. The ground was now steeply rolling. The hills rose nearly one hundred feet above the valleys. They were constantly going up and down; in a mile, there were nearly five rounded hills to go over—a sea of hills and basins. The rocky ground itself was covered with a tough sparse grass nearly a foot high. Trees were of the stunted oak variety and grew twisted and gnarled here and there. There was no good cover to be had. A dwarf might get some protection from one of the trees, but certainly not big folk. Dusk came early in the hills. The trio decided to camp in one of the endless basins, just off the road. Though they had met no one all day, they felt safer being a few hills away from the road.

Dusk was growing when they at last halted in a steep basin, three hills north of the road. Near the center stood an old gnarled oak tree. Here they made camp, tying the ponies to the tree with a long enough lead rope so they could graze. Marc made camp; Mindi got dinner; Nache gathered firewood. There was no water to be found. In the fading twilight, they relaxed and ate supper. Nache had a small fire going, both for light and to ward off the chilly night air. The sat huddled around the fire for a while, three dark figures in the night. The elfin cloaks blended into the night, as did the dwarf's, though not as readily.

Nache first noticed the noise of something walking nearby. At once, a fearful hush came on all three. The listened intensely. More stalking noises came from the hills nearby. They distinctly heard grunting sounds. They stared blankly at each other, wondering what was out there in the night. The noises sounded louder and were getting closer. Instinctively, Nache threw more wood on the fire, and drew Kazab, his axe, out from under his cloak. Marc and Mindi drew their dueling rapiers. The three stared into the darkness, waiting.

Soon dark shapes appeared on the hill tops around

them, small and black against the night sky. You could tell where they were by the absence of stars.

"Boars," screamed Mindi suddenly recognizing the shapes, "Wild boars!"

Quickly, the three moved around the fire in a triangle, backs to the fire, eyes straining to see in the darkness in front of them.

"Beware their tusks," said Nache, "they usually charge their prey. Stand still and wait to the last second, then jump aside and stab them. I'll chop them all before this night is over!" The boars cautiously approached.

With a wild squeal, one lunged straight for Marc. He stood frozen, wondering what would happen if he missed. As the beast got within the firelight, he could see the black, ugly thing. It had two white tusks protruding in a curved fashion from his snout. Marc aimed his sword; the point was very sharp for thrusting. He waited breathlessly.

"Now," yelled Nache.

Marc jumped to the left and thrust his sword forward. There was a hideous squeal and a heavy jolt that knocked him to the ground. He got up at once, and, pulling his sword out, exclaimed, "I'm OK!" He watched as Nache's axe flashed over the boar's head.

"Good going," he said, "for a merchant."

Soon several more set upon them, and then more and more. They seemed to flood into the basin. Marc and Mindi, eyes alert, kept jumping and thrusting. Some they missed; some they got, but the marvel was Nache. He seemed to be everywhere at once. Yelling in the dwarf tongue, he was moving here and there swinging Kazab right and left. Each swing brought a boar to its end. Nache and his axe seemed to be in a perfect harmony and full of action. He was ferocious; in three minutes time, he had already gotten ten boars to the other's five. Somehow, the boars kept coming Marc's direction repeatedly, and Mindi and Nache were constantly shifting around to help him out. They were sweating heavily now and tiring rapidly. Would the boars never end?

Just then, they saw a flash of light of a three-foot blade as it moved through the air. A loud squeal came as it hit it mark. Repeatedly, the sword flicked in the light. Help had come; they knew not who. In another minute, with twenty-three of their lot dead or dying, the pack broke off the attack, disappearing over the hills as fast as they had come.

The four stood by the fire gasping for several minutes. Then, the stranger said, "They're gone now and probably won't be back, Master merchant and company."

Marc gasped again, though not from the fight. "How do you know me, and who are you, and where did you come from?" he hastily asked between gasps.

"I'm a friend," said the stranger, finally catching his wind. "But let's clean up this mess first." Swiftly the two men and dwarf moved the bodies away from the camp area. Meanwhile, Mindi fixed some tea, and, when the men were done, they sat down by the fire to calm themselves. Mindi handed the stranger a cup, and he replied, "Thank you fair lady."

He had a rich deep voice, somehow noble, she thought, and familiar. "I'm known as 'The Drifter' in these parts. We first met at Hill View under the fire."

They both suddenly recognized him. Here was the strange guard dressed in a weather-worn, grey cloak who had been running things during the battle at Hill View.

"But I thought you were a guard or some such," protested Marc.

Drifter laughed, "No, I'm not a guard. I'm called Drifter because I drift and wander where I'm needed, like here tonight."

"But how did you know it was us, and where we were?" asked Mindi.

"It is unfortunate Master Merchant that your departure from Metro was so widely known. I'm afraid the Evil Ones know about it as well. When wandering in these times, it's best not to broadcast it widely. There are many prying ears around. I guessed that no good would come of it, and I came. A good thing I did."

Nache felt offended and protested, "We had the boars beat; trusty Kazab got many."

"Yes Master dwarf, you are a valiant fighter; I meant no

insult. There were more than enough wild boars to go around." That calmed Nache.

Then he announced, "Since I'm also going to Hays, I shall accompany you if you like. I fear that other Scavengers may try to stop you."

They didn't like the idea of a stranger joining them, but he had helped with the boars. Marc decided it by saying, "Well, truly another blade may just be of use; you are welcome Drifter."

"Thank you," came the reply. "I would suggest setting up guards so that we are not surprised; I will take the first watch," the Drifter said.

They were all too exhausted to do otherwise. Besides, he was right about a guard being needed. Then, they laid down on their blankets and quickly passed into a deep sleep. The Drifter choked the fire a bit, folded his cloak about him, leaned against the tree, and watched. There were no further events that night.

After laying down, Marc felt a comfort knowing there was a watch guard. The next thing he knew, the eastern sky was a pale red. Dawn had come. Suddenly Marc woke in a fright! He remembered Drifter. "Why didn't he wake me? Did he steal the ponies and leave us stranded?" Oh, he regretted he had ever gone to sleep. How careless, and on their first night! Quickly, Marc got up and looked around. There was Drifter, still sitting with his back against the tree.

"Sleep well, Merchant?" came the quiet question.

Marc fumbled out a reply and sat down. "I know," came the Drifter's voice again, "you probably wondered if I'd stolen all of your gear and killed the rest. Well I didn't. I've been standing watch all night. Nothing has stirred."

Marc looked around the sides of the basin. There were all the dead boars. The night before came back to him in a flash.

"Sickening isn't it. Evil usually is," Drifter continued.

"Wake the others; it's time we got moving. They won't want much breakfast, at least not here anyway."

Marc roused the others. They had reactions similar to Marc's when they first awoke, but there he sat, in exactly the same place by the tree. Marc insisted upon an explanation of why they didn't get a turn at watch.

Drifter replied, "Well, you all were very tired, and drifters are used to very little sleep in the wild. I figured you would need the rest. And now," he said, finally getting up and stretching to his full height over six feet, "Ah, that's better. It's time we get going. Time enough to eat later."

Mindi couldn't have said it better. Within ten minutes, they were back on the road again, heading east, all four walking and stretching.

As they walked along into the sunrise, Mindi began to feel more relaxed. She was glad to leave the slaughter hole behind. She asked, "Drifter, who are you exactly? You handle a sword extremely well."

"Tales cannot be told on empty stomachs," the Drifter suggested, "I will tell you as we eat some breakfast, if that is acceptable." They agreed. Provisions were made ready, and they munched as they walked along.

He began, "I'm known in these parts as the Drifter. The elves and dwarfs call me the Grey Ranger, as you may have guessed Nache."

Nache's face lit up with that, and he stopped and bowed so low his beard more than touched the ground. "Hail, Grey Ranger of afar, Nache Thraindruil, at your service." Then, to the others, he explained, "The Drifter is ever a friend of elf, dwarf and of men; a slayer of Yac's, the Scourge. We are indeed honored to have such company."

As they walked on, the Drifter felt inclined to speak. "Long have I and my people of the north country wandered throughout Isel, protecting people from the Evil One as we can. Though our numbers grow thin, each grows bolder and stronger. Little do the people of the south know of us, because we have spent our time keeping the evil locked inside the Quad. Now they are too strong for us and have broken out. Yet we still do what we can to help stop the Scavengers. Yes, I was at Hill View. I trailed the band there, but I could do nothing to stop them. However, I was able to rouse the town guards, and with your assistance as well, we drove them off."

"I wish I was there," broke in Nache, patting his axe.

"Yes, my friend, but there will be more Yac's to come, if you are on this journey."

Marc, who had been silent most of the time, asked what had been long on his mind. "I've heard only vague rumors about the enemy. Since you seem to have firsthand observations, can you tell me what they're like? What are we up against?"

"It is good that you've asked me during the day, I will tell you what I can. Scavengers is a general term. The Evil One has by treachery and lies and fear gotten many slaves to his will. Mostly there are four: jackals, wargs or wolves, goblins, and lean northern men that dwarves call Yac's."

"That's because of the foul noise they make," put in Nache.

The Drifter continued, "They work by night, since they rule and fight with fear as their mighty weapon. Seldom are they seen in daylight hours beyond their realm in the Quad. They are brutal beyond belief."

"We know," interjected Mindi with a sigh.

"The Dark Lord has been gathering his strength for a long time now," continued the Drifter. "His goal and aim I fear I do not know as yet, but it is evil. A few other dark things are far worse than these four. Of these, I will say nothing now. This is enough talk of them. Let's not darken the day any more." Indeed the sky was now fast becoming overcast and grey. They walked on in silence.

Around noon, they were tired and stopped for lunch. They had been going up and down since morning. The rest was needed. The sky had grown steadily darker during the morning and was now very grey. The Drifter was watching it. "Hey what's this?" he asked in a hushed voice.

Everyone looked up. Coming their way was a large flock of black birds. Ravens, Mindi guessed. "Ravens seldom flock like this," the Drifter explained worriedly. Then, he had everyone gather around the nearest oak. Better not to be seen by prying eyes—was his belief. They watched intently as the birds passed overhead. The omen was felt by all, but they guessed they had not been seen. "We must be more careful," he ordered. They hurriedly picked up their things and continued their journey.

The hills grew steadily higher and steeper. They hoped that the second night would be spent near the top of the East Range. It would only be two days journey from there to Hays. They pushed onward to reach the divide.

When dusk came, they were at about the right place, the Drifter guessed. The sky was very dark; and the weather threatening. Their guide suggested they move considerably off the road, which recalling the last night, they did. While Marc and Mindi set up camp and dinner, Nache and the Drifter collected wood and surveyed their position. They had a quiet, uneventful dinner around a small campfire. He'd explained that having no fire would be bad if they were attacked; but that a fire would also be bad, as it would give their location away. Considering the events of the night before, all wanted the fire.

The Drifter took the first watch; Nache the second; Marc the last. None had any events to record. They awoke on the third day to a black sky; rain was eminent. They hurriedly got on their way, trying to make as much distance as they could before the weather got bad. None wanted to spend a fifth night if it could be avoided.

Around midday, the rains came. However, they kept on going. At last, a welcome sight came, but they were so engrossed in trudging along that they almost passed it by. The hills had ended, and before them lay East Flats, a wide space of extremely flat land, many times larger than West Flats. At the Drifter's suggestion, they retreated into the hills off the road, for the hills offered better protection. They camped as before. This night, though, all were tired, footsore, hungry, and muddy. Without any ceremony, they ate and went to bed. The Drifter, as usual took the first watch.

He had not spoken to the company of many things. The Drifter guessed that, if they knew, they would be terrified into a panic—no need for that just yet. Perhaps he was wrong. If so, no need to worry them any further. He fell off into thoughts.

Around ten o'clock, as the fire barely flickered, a lone howl pierced the night stillness, coming from the north, several hills off. Another answered it from the south. Then another, and another. Within minutes, the hills were echoing the hideous howling of wargs. Everyone jumped up with a start. The Drifter threw a huge mound of wood onto the fire.

They put their gear out of the way. Nache took up a position in the south of the basin. There between two scraggly trees, a lead line had been tied for the three ponies. Kazab flickered silver rays in the now crackling blaze in front of the ponies. The Drifter took the northern spot; the fire behind him. Marc and Mindi took the flanks. The fire was roaring now.

Standing on the rim of their basin and encircling them stood a silent pack of wargs, fangs white with dripping slobber. They did not attack but stood there staring down into the basin. It did not take long to see why they did not charge the group, because shortly, Yacs began to appear among the wargs—twenty Scavenger men in all. There was a silent moment as each side stared at the other. Then the Yacs laughed and charged straight for Marc.

Five were making at him. Marc held his ground and took a deep breath; his dueling sword was ready. As the nearest one approached, Marc thrust his sword in one graceful, yet speedy, forward motion. The Yac collapsed; his belly, punctured.

Yelling, "Elidine", the Drifter cut off two them on the left, and like a black shadow, Nache appeared from the rear removing the legs of another Yac with one flash of silver. This gave Marc time to recover, and he began battling the fifth. The others had much to do; the Yacs now bore down on them from all sides.

They were forever laughing in a hideous, nauseous manner. Repeatedly, Elidine flashed, as it paused high in the air ready for its downward path. Repeatedly, the silver axe streaked from side to side.

Now the chief of the wargs began to thirst for battle, and he crept his way toward the fattest pony. Just as he was ready to grab a leg, Butterball began to stomp and kick wildly with his hind legs. The warg got the worst of that, and a moment later, there was a silver swish; the warg lay headless; the dark dwarf blended back into the shadows.

Ten Yacs lay dead, but again they charged. The odds

had been growing steadily against the defenders. Four more came down on Marc. Using his now proven thrust technique, he lunged into the first. The dueling sword broke with a snap. The others heard it. Instinctively, Marc hit the dirt and began rolling. He rolled out of the charge but into the fire. He let out a yell as he got singed. Elidine flashed; the axe flickered; and Mindi, leaping over the fire where March had been, thrust. All three groaned and were no more. Mark grabbed for Tiny. It felt strangely heavy. He held it up in two hands and continued to fight, yelling "Thanks."

"Good recovery," returned the Drifter.

Tiny was acting very strange in his hands. He noted that it began glowing red. The nearest Yac, seeing such a short sword charged him. Marc deflected his sword, but as Tiny hit the Yac's sword, there was a breaking sound accompanied by the noise of steam. The Yac's blade broke and had melted where Tiny touched it. Before the Yac could draw his knife, Marc thrust Tiny forward into his gut. The Yac screamed; from his belly, steam rose up with a loud hissing noise. Marc marveled, but continued the fight.

The odds were now getting close to even up; the Drifter called for Marc and Mindi to help him perform a charge to drive the rest back. It caught the Yacs off guard. Steam rose again, and Elidine flashed.

"Mighty strange sword you got there," yelled the Drifter.

The Yacs had broken into a route and, shortly, were seen no more. The trio turned around and headed for the fire. They saw two large wargs slinking up to the pony string from either side. Before they could yell, a dark form moved; silver swished in a huge sweeping arc; the wolves fell at once. "Nice swing for a dwarf," yelled Marc, grasping for air. They heard a breathy "Yes" from the dark.

The four stood around the fire, recovering. They were dripping with sweat and fighting for air for several minutes. Finally, the Drifter recovered sufficiently, "All Ok?"

"Yes" came the replies amid the heavy heaving.

He put more wood on the fire. Silently, like slinking ghosts, the wargs crept down from the rim. One by one, they grabbed the dead and dying Yacs, and, amid grunts and growls, dragged them up and over the rim. A hideous din of growling and fighting followed. The noise eventually gave way to the incessant yapping and yelping of the jackals. Then, all was silent as before, except the crackle of the blazing fire.

Mindi went to work on their gear; shortly she returned with a skin of water. "Here we go, it's a healthy mix I've concocted," she explained. They all drank heavily. It felt rejuvenating. In a few minutes, they were relaxed again and feeling like conversation.

They all wanted to see Marc's sword. They had seen it operating. Now it lay lightly in Marc's hand and was its normal gold and silver colors. The Drifter studied it closely, then asked "Nache, what do you make of it?"

Nache looked too. With an excited voice, he said, "It is not of dwarfish or elvish origin. It is too fancy for Burly men. See how the colors ebb and flow. I now of none who could build such a sword today." Nache had seen Marc's face and had said only the obvious. The Drifter was still not part of their group, he felt.

Marc merely protested, saying, "It's too damn short!" Then, they all demanded to see Elidine. It was a broad sword, nearly three inches wide, razor sharp on both edges. All the fighting had not even put a nick in it. They marveled at the big red ruby in the pommel.

Finally, Mindi said, "There is more to your sword than you have said."

The Drifter merely nodded and changed the topic. "You both need much sturdier swords. Dueling ones may be fine in West Flats, but they won't hold against the Evil Ones." Neither could disagree with that.

Then, they felt the heavy fatigue coming over them. Drifter again took his position against a tree. The rest slept soundly until morning.

They arose with the first light. Hurriedly they broke camp. None wanted to linger, remembering the hideous night. Only bits of bone, fur, and clothes amid the trampled stubble grass indicated what had occurred in the night. They quickly made the road and entered East Flats. Haskel Road was certainly no longer safe!

Soon the land became friendlier. Here and there, tended fields emerged; and, at last, small, adobe houses could be discerned scattered widely along the road. Farmers were at work in their fields, and the land was almost perfectly smooth as far as the eye could see. It felt different, but very friendly, overall. The troupe's spirits rose and they began discussing the events.

It was becoming apparent, especially to Marc, that they were somehow after him, especially. It disturbed him that the Scourge seemed always to know him. The Drifter would only agree that such was the case; he offered no explanation as to why.

By late afternoon, they could see Hays far off in the distance. Also, some riders were approaching them swiftly. Since the Drifter did not seem alarmed, the rest rather ignored them; they were hot, dirty, and exhausted. Eventually, the riders pulled up in front of them.

It was a sheriff and guards. The grey uniformed man began by saying, "Who goes here? I am the Sheriff."

Marc looking haggard and worn, made an effort to straighten up, and tiredly said, "I am Marcos, the Master Merchant of Metro. These are my companions Mindi Francos, Nache Thraindruil, and the Drifter. We have come to see George Bighollow."

The sheriff looked them over carefully, and said cautiously, "We have been expecting you, but you pick strange company with the Drifter. However, with your permission, we will escort you into Hays and to George's place."

Not much can be said of the remainder of the trip to Hays. The party was so fatigued that they paid little attention, and so they arrived in Hays, East Flats, on the eve of their fourth day on the road.

Chapter VII—Defense of Hays

It was suppertime. The Sheriff, now being safely inside the town, became more in control of things. He sat even straighter in the saddle, leading the procession through the streets. Marc grinned towards Mindi; she understood his glance. Soon, they stopped in front of a large adobe building with many windows. Lights were faintly shining out. In the fading light, they could read a large sign over the main doorway—"Dew Drop Inn— Proprietor George Bighollow." One of the guards hurried inside; the rest dismounted.

Soon a welcome face appeared in the doorway. "Marc! Oh, Marc! Am I glad you could come—come on in." George said, shaking Marc's hand vigorously. Then they briefly hugged.

Marc thought George looked much the same, except possibly a bit fatter. He said, "George I'd like you to meet Mindi Francos." She pulled her cloak back, smiled, and offered her hand. "And this is Nache Thraindruil of Khorizaba." Nache bowed low, his white beard touching the ground.

"At your service," he replied.

George saw their condition and suggested, "Come in. I've got some rooms reserved for you; bath water will be ready in five; the boys will bring in your gear." Hurriedly, he shouted, "Tom, their ponies; Sam, their things; Emily, you go tell Sharon to get three baths ready, now hurry up. My kids," he grinned. From his tone, Mindi could tell that he loved them greatly.

Marc kept looking around. He was going to introduce the Drifter, except he was nowhere to be seen. Mindi noticed his glances and asked what was wrong. Marc quickly explained that the Drifter was gone. None had noticed him slip away, apparently when they had entered the town.

George merely said, "He'll show up sooner or later, if you know what I mean. Come on inside."

The Dew Drop Inn was a very home-like place. It was the best inn in Hays, especially since George and Sharon recently took it over. George's unending optimism and the family's industrious help had made the Inn a very comfortable place to stay. The service was quite good.

Within minutes, the three found themselves in warm tubs, soaking and enjoying it immensely. George had planned well; they each had adjoining rooms with connecting doors. Marc had the best room in the inn, the Bridal Suite. After some laughs, he and Mindi swapped rooms.

The bath had rejuvenated more than their tired bodies. It seemed to have washed away the last traces of the evil events of late. Nache and Marc got into a playful towel-snapping romp while they waited for Mindi. In the middle of it, Sam came in and said timidly, "Begging your pardon, sir, but Dad says the food is ready any time you are." He watched the dwarf curiously. Nache felt amused.

Marc felt playful, "You ever see a Dwarf?"

"No sir," came the reserved reply.

Nache stood in front of the young boy; they were the same height. Sam looked in wonder at the dwarf. Nache had put on his finest clothes for the occasion, brightly colored reds, blues, and yellows formed in zigzag patterns. His white beard contrasted sharply.

All the boy could do was ask, "How old are you, sir?"

His eyes opened wide when Nache said proudly, "One hundred fifty-two years; we seldom live less than two hundred and fifty years, so I am yet young." Sam's mouth gaped.

Mindi came in to the room. "You guys ready?" They looked with amazement; she had on her long, white gown; and, to them, she looked especially beautiful. "It's the hazards of having a lady along on the trip," she said jokingly. Arm in arm, the three led by Sam went off to find supper.

The main hall had two sections, one was full of tables and chairs all made of roughhewn oak. (The walls and floor were, of course, hard packed dirt. Wooden pegs were imbedded in the walls for coat racks. The ceiling had several great timbers and, crosswise, sod. Grass actually grew on the roof.) The other section was open with only a few scattered tables. From the ceiling, numerous oil lanterns hung in patterns like wagon wheels.

By the time the three made their appearance, half of Hays had tried to get into the Inn. Good naturedly, George had controlled the situation by insisting the overflow crowd could come tomorrow. The barkeepers were kept busy. All eyes focused on the trio as they entered, and the noisy atmosphere became hushed. Marc sized up the scene rapidly.

George appeared apologetic, but Marc jumped up on a chair and said loudly, "Welcome, I'm Marcos Blancas, Master Merchant from Metro. With me is Mindi Francos of Metro; and my special assistant, the honored Master Builder of the dwarves, Nache Thraindruil." Marc in his silk, blue, merchant's suit, Mindi in her long, flowing gown, and Nache in his brightly colored, zigzag, dwarven finery made quite a sight. They all three bowed.

There was a loud round of cheers and applause. Marc accepted it with a show of his hands. They quieted down; he obviously had more to say. "As you know or guess, we three have fortified West Flats from the Scourge. We have been asked by George to see what can be done here. That is our purpose. However, we are tired and have not eaten since noon. We must eat."

With that, he stepped down, and the noisy group shouted and resumed the merrymaking. Sharon rushed up and began serving the dinner. "You must forgive them," she began while fixing the table. "There has been so little hope here; you are like a blessing to us all."

Mindi looked at her and said, "Thanks, we will do our best." Then they ate.

The food was excellent and well made, if simple. It was very nourishing, but not fancy as in the city. Sharon was an excellent chef; they ate for some time of various greens, soups, potatoes with gravy, and roast pig basted with eggs. Marc remembered how George always used to brag about the ale of East Flats. "Hey, how about some of that super ale you were always talking about?" he playfully ribbed George.

"Coming up," came the reply. The older two boys brought in three mugs. It was good, no doubt of that. George made it from the best of the corn crop each year. Quietly, Marc fumbled in his pocket. Then, with only a grin, he handed

George a big gold crown. George looked inquisitively at Marc; then, he remembered and laughed. Six years ago at the academy, Marc had bet him that his ale wouldn't stack up to some of Marc's wines. Marc obviously lost.

There were various farmers among those who had managed to acquire a seat this night at Dew Drop. Some were curious farmers whose lands lay nearby, but most were the city folk of Hays. A discerning eye could tell the difference; the rural dwellers' clothes showed signs of heavy wear. In fact, not much else separated them. The Agrarians were for the most part dark skinned and husky. Their outlook was almost uniformly conservative. They wore numerous varieties of dark colored, heavy cotton breeches that ended above their ankles. Without exception, all were barefoot. The woolen shirts were big and baggy and seldom tucked in. All wore their hair, predominately black, short, and stringy. The women, similarly, were plainly dressed, if not outright drab. The dresses, open at the neck, covered their upper arms, and fell fully below the waist; nearly every hue of brown was represented. The people of East Flats were farmers.

After they ate, the children amiably cleared the table. George and Sharon had been sitting with their guests and lovingly holding hands. George said, "How about some music?" Sharon blushed.

Mindi enthusiastically said, "That would be splendid, please do."

Sharon retrieved her zither from its case. It was very old and made of walnut. Then, sitting it on her lap, she began to play. Soon, the whole place was singing and clapping. Marc felt a sudden urge. He grabbed Mindi, and with a bow, they began to dance. Nache got excited as well, for the dwarves dearly love song and dance. When Marc had finished a round, he cut in. He barely reached her waist. It was comical and all began laughing, even Nache. When the song finished amid roars of laughter, including Nache's, he bowed low and thanked her. She bent over and kissed his forehead, smiling.

As the music began a slow lament, Marc and Mindi danced once more. Nache, to everyone's surprise, walked over to Emily, who was just turning thirteen, bowed low, and, in his

71

most formal voice, asked her if he could have this dance. She blushed and quickly looked at her mom, who nodded with a smile. Bubbling with excitement, she agreed.

They made a splendid pair; she could hardly contain her enthusiasm.

Finally, their tiredness could not be ignored any longer; and Marc and Mindi retired, thanking their hosts. He now knew why the Dew Drop Inn was the best.

Since dwarves are tireless, or seldom admit it, Nache stayed and danced for nearly two more hours and thoroughly enjoyed himself.

For the first time in four nights, they all slept in peace and comfort. They slept far into the morning, and they awoke refreshed and ready for action. Marc and George decided that the first order of business should be a guided tour of Hays and the surrounding countryside. Early afternoon found the trio with George and his eldest son Tom, in a buggy cart. Marc and Mindi sat in the rear, Nache and George in the middle seat, while Tom sat up front and drove.

Unlike Metro, with its curved streets, Hays was laid out with a surveyor's precision; all the streets were parallel and were exactly perpendicular to the crossroads. The streets were made of hardpan, hauled painstakingly from the north. There were no sidewalks, but the well-tended yards formed precise edges with the yellowish roadways. There were numerous hitching posts but very, very few trees. Houses were similar to each other. All patterned similarly to Dew Drop Inn: grey adobe walls with sodden doorways and window blockings.

The center square of Hays was the hub of city activities. In the exact middle was a pavilion—for square dances, George explained. One side of the square housed the Sheriff's offices and the courts. There was no ruler in East Flats; each area elected a Sheriff for a two-year term. His job was to enforce law and order. The laws, as George discussed, were made by group decision; but they always had to agree or at least not interfere with those of another area. Hence, the actual laws on the books were few. Farmers got along very well with each other.

The first actual stop on the tour was the Granaries.

Here the real wealth of East Flats was contained in rows upon rows of great, grey, adobe silos, called kavas. Kavas were cylindrical in shape, twelve feet across at the base; the domed roof stood a little over six feet tall. The double door system kept spillage and vermin to the minimum.

George estimated that Hays had around one hundred Kavas; but Tom interrupted, "Ninety six, Dad, I counted them."

Each town had a set of kavas. The grain flow pattern George explained. "Local farmers cart their grain to their nearest city. There it is stored and gradually carted to Pratt, the southern port. At Pratt, it would be exchanged via the mariners for other goods, particularly lumber. Just now, the kavas are only half-empty; normally they're nearly empty by this time. The Scourge has slowed down cartage to Pratt."

Located at the southeastern edge of the granary loomed the tall Obelos Pan. It dwarfed everything in the area. The trio had been glancing at it frequently and had hoped to ride by it. They had not said anything about it yet, because they did not know what the mood of the people was concerning it.

George explained that it was an ancient treasure of the past riding forward in time, a reminder of their history. Legends tell of Gregory, the Great, establishing the Agrarians in East Flats long ago. Marc mused that perhaps the life style had not changed since those days. George, obviously fascinated with the tower, told them a long story of Gregory and the founding of the great farms, as they returned to the inn.

Presently, they were all having a tankard of ale and lunch. Something had been on Marc's mind, or rather the absence of, was. He finally put the question to George. "One thing I've noticed, where are all the swords, weapons, and the like? I've hardly seen anyone carrying one."

George's face grimaced, "Few swords are there in the entire Flats!" That was a sobering thought. Silence prevailed for some time. George softly said, "You see our plight. We cannot even defend our kavas. Never before have we had the need." Marc felt discouraged. How could he ever hope to provide help, no weapons even!

Nache asked permission for Tom and Sam to be his assistants. Good naturedly, George consented. After lunch, Nache and the boys left on foot. Marc and George began lengthy conversations regarding old academy days and of current events. Bored, Mindi found Sharon and helped her with her chores.

That evening was much as it had been the night before, only the people had changed a bit. George had in another group—the ones who had had to be turned away the previous evening. Marc saw little difference though. Of the children in Hays, Tom and Sam were now greatly sought after by their friends, since word spread that they were Nache's helpers. Emily, too, was the envy of the younger girls; for several hours, they had met and exchanged giggles and small talk.

That night, Marc told briefly of the events of their journey. He, of course, omitted a few details, especially of the swords. There were many "oohs," "aahs," and much general concern.

The farmers were virtually hopeless. This brought on a general feeling of degradation. When he was done, the air felt stiff and massy. Only when Sharon struck up a tune and when the dwarf and Emily began dancing did the atmosphere become lighter once again.

In a few days, they had fully recovered from their trip, and Marc called for a council on what was to be done for East Flats. It was a grim-faced council at best. They had invited several local opinion leaders, including Sheriff Ebanizer and George. The meeting lasted only an hour. The only thing agree upon, for it was the only practical idea presented, was that George, Marc, Mindi, and Nache should be in charge of the defense. Nothing else useful came from it.

It was the morning of July 10, when the four found themselves alone in the Inn, staring down at the big maps George had laid on the table. It was the only complete map, George had said. Indeed, there was something queer about it. It was very ancient and yellowed with broken, cracked edges. Of its origin, George said little, save that he had updated it as need be.

There were strange letters written in various places.

George was going over the various landmarks, mud rivers, and all. However, Marc was not listening; he was lost in thought, and prone to doodling little circles with his charcoal pencil.

"Hey what are you doing?" Mindi interrupted him.

"Forgive me," he said rather embarrassed at what he'd done. He stood looking at his little circles. "Hum, I wonder," he pondered.

"If you've got something," Mindi pleaded, "tell us; more heads may help."

Rather than telling, he asked George in rapid fire, "How many adobe bricks can you make in a day?"

"500 more or less," George guessed.

"Got a lot of extra oil for lamps?"

"Oh yes, kegs worth; we ship it out to the rural districts."

"Rope, got any rope?" Marc was beginning to get excited.

"Yes, we make it ourselves here in East Flats."

"I need a pole." Marc said almost shouting, "A pole, George!" The others were beginning to get excited too.

"Come on, in the shed!"

They nearly ran outside to the grey shed where George stored supplies. Directly, George produced a pole about eight feet long and two inches in diameter. Marc had Nache chop a crude point on one end. Then, Marc wrapped a big rag round and round the pointed end, about two inches from its point. Then, he soaked it in the oil. He got a match from George and climbed up on the roof. They were guessing and staring in disbelief at Marc's childish manner. Marc was excited, he hoped, he hoped. He stood near the edge, nearly eight feet above the ground.

"Stand back," he yelled and lit the rags. The oil slowly flared. Then Marc yelled "Bonzii" and threw his fire spear down toward the ground. It flamed through the air and, with a thud, stuck in the ground roaring. They all began cheering excitedly. The fire spear worked.

"Brilliant," exclaimed George shaking his hand.

They put out the fire stick and went inside. Marc was now confident something could be done.

They gathered around the map and Marc explained his idea. The basic idea was to erect adobe platforms nearly vertical about eight feet high, accessible only by rope ladders that could be drawn up. Armed with sufficient fire spears and hay piles, the defenders could spear almost with impunity. Further, they could pitch burning hay on those below.

"If we could ring them around the city say twenty feet apart, the whole town could be protected," suggested Marc.

Nache added, "If you cut a trench, you can fill it with oil and light it. Wargs will never cross a fire lane."

They all were wild with glee, and holding hands, began to dance in a circle. Sharon came in running to see what was the matter, but George just grabbed her up and gave her a big kiss, shouting, "We've done it," and all five danced in circles.

The Master Builder drew up the specifications that afternoon while the rest worked on other details. The only problem was poles. Wood was scarce. Mindi handled that one by suggesting Shannon be contacted. It was agreed.

The next day, Nache and assistants began directing the placement and construction of the "fire towers," as they became known. George, Mindi, and Marc prepared to journey to Pratt to try to contact Shannon.

Nache found the farmers had a renewed hope and worked under his orders surprisingly well. He quickly was unable personally to keep up with all the action. Hatting up his two assistants, Tom and Sam, he kept the chief engineering in the hands of the small ones.

Indeed, Hays took on an atmosphere of a fair. Men, women, and children began to make the adobe bricks. The "quarry," as it was called, lay just north of the city. There dirt, grey clay, was dug, mixed with water into the finest mud mess you'd ever care to play in, then formed into bricks, and laid to cure in the sunshine. Nearly a thousand people were involved in the construction. The town pavilion had been turned into a giant feast area to serve the workers. Sharon had quickly taken charge of the eating arrangements. A new spirit of group participation in their common defense grew and mushroomed, as had not been seen in East Flats since the time of the Great Ones. In less than one week, there would be nearly one hundred thirty-fire towers in a giant circle surrounding Hays, the granary, and the obelos.

Of their journey to Pratt, little needs be said. It proved completely uneventful. George, at first, knew most of the farmers. They were constantly finding welcome doors as they rode southward. Jolly George, as he was known to those in the south along Mule Lane Two, made the excursion a happy one, quite unlike the trip to Hays.

There was little difference between the lands west of Hays and the lands on which they were now traveling to the south. Small grey farmsteads were scattered here and there across open fields of corn, beans, cotton, grains, and vegetables. There were scattered pastures, some with livestock grazing—mostly cows, pigs, and sheep. For much of the trip, George told them tales of Gregory the Great and the founding of the Farmers, until at last Marc had thought he had heard everything except a family tree of the Agrarians.

Pratt, they found, was similar to Hays but with two exceptions. The sizes of the granaries were at least four times that of Hays. Being the seaport and trade center of East Flats, there were more shops and more varied merchandise. They immediately went to the docks to locate mariners. With two inquiries, Marc found them and was soon leading his troupe on board the Lucky Lady.

The Captain was Erving Seafund. They exchanged greetings. Shannon, Marc, discovered had done his job well; Erving explained that he had been told to expect him and do whatever Marc desired. Soon George and Erving had reached an agreement, four boatloads of grain for two loads of poles. As usual among Merchants, they sealed the transaction with a toast.

Before they left Pratt, George wanted to visit some shops. He explained that he seldom passed this way lately and wanted to get Sharon a few surprises. Gaily, the trio did some shopping. Erving sent them word that the poles would arrive in two days. So they decided to wait and see to the northern transport of a part of them for Hays.

True to his word, Erving returned with two boatloads of poles, all nearly two inches in diameter and about eight feet long. The next day, the group traveled westward along the Great East Road. They had calculated it would be safer than the northern Haskel road. In five days, they arrived at Hays without incident. It was excellent timing, as Nache was putting the finishing touches on the fire towers. Two days after that, all was prepared, and a local holiday was declared.

The general feelings of degradation had vanished in Hays. The establishment of a defense had been the cause. With renewed interest in life, everyone began to organize into fire spear throwing defensive action groups, with a robustness of newfound life. Even the Drifter arriving with news of a group of Scavengers moving down from the north country did little to sway the festive atmosphere. It brought mainly boasts from the people.

The Drifter had arrived in mid-afternoon looking tired and worn. He sat down at a table in the nearly empty inn, and Sharon brought him some food. The others gathered around expectantly.

Finally, as though he was very tired, he began, "I've been away up North near the Burly border, checking on their movements. It seems that they are pretty well leaving West Flats alone for now. My compliments to Master Merchant and Master Builder."

They nodded.

"I gather from their movements of late, that they are shifting toward East Flats. I am only about eight hours ahead of one band heading this way. I suggest you carry your swords."

They explained the defense that was prepared for Hays. Nache complained, "We could have really built a wall if only there was decent rock."

"It may do, it just may," came the slow response from the Drifter. After eating, he went to bed. The others helped around the inn and made ready for the night's festivities.

Shortly after supper, it began. The center pavilion was turned into a large dance floor with a stage at one end. Music began flowing; people began arriving. The Sheriff was calling the shindig, as the fiddlers played. The farmers had a passion for square dancing; the music was practically continuous.

George and crew were kept busy serving tankards of ale, but occasionally George and Sharon took a turn on the floor.

Nache, as a favor to Emily, was taking turns with her girlfriends as well. He felt very happy and proud, as he danced with the young girls. All was going well. Around ten o'clock a horn blast blew from atop one of the fire towers.

Quickly, others followed it. Instantly, the music ceased; and the sheriff yelled, "To the towers men. Women and children get home fast, bolt the doors." The party was abruptly terminated.

Sharon frantically began to call her children; Mindi saw her panic and rushed to her side, "It's ok, Sharon. I'll help you."

Together, amid the wild clamor, they rounded up the kids; and Mindi, with sword drawn, escorted them back to the inn. Sharon was grateful for her aid and saw clearly for the first time the power that was Mindi.

As they got to the inn, the Drifter was just coming out, fastening his sword and belt. Mindi said, "Mind if I join you?"

"Nope, I'm honored. Let's head for the granary; that's the most likely target." He was precisely correct.

Meanwhile, George, Marc, and Nache had headed for the granary. Everywhere men were flocking for the towers and raising fire spears, blowing against the dark sky. George stopped by one particular kava; and, grinning, he produced a ten-foot heavy pole pointed at both ends. "I've been saving this one," he said.

Since George had no sword, Marc figured he could at least ram a Yac with it. Within minutes, every tower had torches blazing from their tops. It made quite a sight.

The Scavengers halted just beyond them for several minutes; they were actually quiet. They obviously did not expect such resistance and probably were a bit unnerved by what they saw.

Hays was entirely surrounded by Yacs. It was the biggest assemblage of the Scourge yet. Marc guessed that it was because West Flats was being heavily defended now. Nache pointed out that the Yacs were shifting to positions near the granary. They had guessed right about where the biggest blow would be aimed.

Suddenly, the Yacs began their hideous yelling, screaming, and laughing—intended to paralyze their victims with fear.

Marc held the three back saying, "George, let's see how they do defending themselves. If we are needed, we can attack."

It was a good idea. The people had to become self-dependent sometime.

At this time, the Drifter and Mindi arrived. She said quickly to George, "They're all home safe."

"Thanks," came the relieved response.

Just then, the noise peaked, and the Yacs charged waving their spears. As soon as they got within range, the farmers began wildly yelling and throwing the fire spears. They watched as the startled Yacs broke and retreated leaving behind several Yacs with burning bellies. Again, they charged and fire spears rained down like fireballs from heaven. This tactic was repeated four times with the Yacs retreating more and more. Many Yacs were felled and lay burning and screaming. Hopefully, it was unnerving the Yacs. However, the spear supply was running low.

This time the wargs began the attack; here and there, in slinking runs, they began to dart into the area of the granary. The men were ready for them. Quickly, the oil bags were loosened, and oil gushed down into the foot wide channels in the ground. Moments later, as the wargs began to splash across, the oil flared into a blaze. A hideous howling drowned out all of the other noises. Here and there, a flaming warg could be seen running, howling off into the distance.

The emotional tone level of the Yacs had changed from a cheerful expectation of an easy victory to an anger they'd seldom felt. The Drifter caught this change in tone, and ordered the rest to make ready for a charge. Yelling wildly, they came. Over fifty Yacs charged. The fire spears, now few, only stopped half, and the rest broke through. The group was ready.

The Yacs again yelling charged toward Marc who stood near the front. He tensed himself for the onslaught. To everyone's surprise, George stepped forward three feet and, holding his pole horizontally, charged the Yacs at the last minute. He met their charge head on, smashing them with his pole; it bent considerably under the strain of stopping six Yacs at once.

It suddenly became apparent how muscular George really was; they watched his body, not only take the impact, but also knock the six completely off their feet. Before they got up, Nache, as usual, seemed to be everywhere; quickly, with flashes of silver and yells of "Kazab", he beheaded them. Elidine flashed high in the air, and jabs and thrusts appeared here and there from Marc and Mindi.

Marc broke another dueling sword and was forced to use Tiny. Again, to his amazement and the Yacs horror, it grew heavy and glowed red. As the blade clanked into a tall Yac's spear, there was a searing melting sound, and a dismayed Yac gasped as Tiny dove into his belly, amid clouds of steam and hissing noises. He screamed in terror and ran wildly into the darkness.

George repeatedly, using his pole, smashed Yac's heads or knocked them to the ground. Then a huge Yac, probably their chief, dressed much fancier in a tunic of yellow and black squares, charged. Elidine flashed, and he crunched to the ground and did not move.

Within five minutes, it was all was over. The horns blew wildly, and Yacs and wargs routed, fleeing randomly in all directions. Breathing heavily, the friends relaxed and began congratulating each other.

Marc and Mindi walked back toward town. Just then, the Chief Yac, though wounded by the Drifter's blow, got up, raised his sword, and crept up to Marc's back. Before anyone could do anything, accompanied by a swishing sound, George's pole found its mark. The chief Yac's head, they later observed, was completely stoved in.

Soon amid the cheers atop all the fire towers, there came a hideous mournful, baying from a distance. Then all was quiet, before a spontaneous celebration began. Everywhere, the farmers were yelling and jumping and dancing—dancing wildly. Truly, they had blown their degradation; they had protected their city and were exuberant about having done so.

The tally was seventy-three Yacs dead versus one farmer who had a broken leg—he fell off a fire tower in his excitement over winning. The cheering went on far into the night.

The group, however, retired to the Inn for their own private celebration. The Master Merchant had done it again. At the Inn, Nache enthusiastically told the wild eyed attentive children all about the attack.

Sharon kissed Marc and said, "We thank you more deeply than you can ever know. It is as if you have given us renewed life. How can we ever repay you?"

"With a tankard of ale," broke in the Drifter.

"Coming up," said an exuberant George.

Before George could fetch any, Marc beat him to it, saying, "I owe you one."

They all laughed at that. It was a good celebration and a job well done.

The news of the huge success of Hay's fire towers spread rapidly throughout all of East Flats. With a pride they had not known for a long time, the people of Hays began to instruct those of the other towns. Indeed, so great was the enthusiasm, that the troupe themselves had very little to do in the ensuing days, except keep an observant eye on things.

The next morning as the group was eating breakfast, Nache's curiosity had now exceeded his capacity for holding it back.

He asked, "George, your pole, last night, did wonders. I would like to see it, if I may. Seldom have I seen a pole whose strength exceeds that of six Yacs!"

Now that he had mentioned it, the others were curious as well. George got embarrassed, but he produced it and laid it across the table. Nache at once examined it closely, speaking curiously to himself in the dwarf tongue. The others looked as well.

The pole was ruddy red in color, exceedingly smooth, and reflected light off its rounded surface. There was not a mark or blemish on it, or even a sign of the wood's grain.

Further, there wasn't even the faintest scratch from its use the night before.

Nache finally said, "This is a strange pole, a wood I have never heard of, Master George. No wood have I ever seen approaches this. What kind of timber is it?" The others concurred.

George's face got very red; he stammered something inaudible and nervously fidgeted his pants.

Sharon, who had been drying the cups at the bar, came over to her husband, took his hands in hers, and said softly, "George, I think it's time you shared your secret. These are our saviors truly; yet they come with ability, a power I have never seen here in East Flats. If you can't fully trust these, I wouldn't know who you could."

George seemed to feel reassured by her words and at last, spoke, "Yes, I'll tell you. The pole comes from within Obelos Pan." There was a complete silence.

Sharon finally broke it by saying, "In these matters, I'll leave you and see that you are not disturbed." She quickly left.

Nache excitedly climbed upon the table and sat cross—legged saying "A tale, a tale, Master George!"

George seemed much more relaxed now that his secret was made known. He spoke swiftly and confidently, yet as a man who is truly relieved to have gotten these matters openly displayed.

He explained that years ago he found that he had a strange fascination with Obelos Pan. He'd spend hours playing around its base, singing songs. One time, he had sung; and, to his amazement, the door opened. It operated by music. Inside, he had found many things, but mostly documents that told of the history of the Farmers. He had removed the pole as a weapon to fight off Scavengers, since he had none. When he was finished, he felt much lighter in spirit than he had in a very long time. To Sharon, only, he had confided his adventures there.

When he was done, Mindi reached across the table and taking his hand, said softly, "Thank you, George. Now it's our time to be truthful."

The others permitted their tales to be told as well. This

they did in spite of the Drifter's presence. They seemed to have forgotten him, actually. He had sat quietly throughout the proceedings saying nothing. When all had finished, George brought out a round of ale, proposing a toast to the group.

However, the Drifter arose and strode to the front. Suddenly, they realized that he was there and had heard all.

Before they could react, he said, "Hold the toast, Master Farmer, there is yet another story to be told—much to your liking," he said aside to Nache. They listened intently while he spoke.

"My name is really Stephen Steadford, Wanderer of Ocalla, home of the Guards. Some of my tale you already know, but of this, I have not spoken. In the days of the wizards, my people alone did battle the great evil unleashed by Karzam the Bad. It was mainly a battle of the Great Wizards, but we entered the Battle to keep the evil of Karzam contained within the Quad. Bravely we fought, though outnumbered. It is not known whether we would have been able to contain Karzam's brood, had the Wizards not departed from Isel, after the Great Battle. My people vowed to keep forever the evil of Karzam out of Isel and to protect the varied people as best we could. My people have, therefore, always been the wanderers, the Nomads of the North."

"We too have an obelos—Obelos Nord, it is called. The guardianship of the tower has been in the Steadford line for centuries. I became the twenty-third Protector of the Nord when my father Erroid was killed by the worst evil of the north. Long I vowed revenge but could not leave the obelos unprotected. Many years ago, I turned the guardianship temporarily over to my son Arthur, after his mother Sonya was killed in a Yac raid. My anger could no longer be contained."

"Before that time, I had a loving feeling toward my charge. Obelos Nord and I became inseparable; it was ever in my dreams. One day I was fondly passing my hands over the door, when it opened. I discovered that a hand pattern causes it to operate. I explored its dark, mystic interior. Much did I learn of the history of Ocalla and the Battle. Also, I learned much from the maps and charts of the paths and ways within the Quad. Elidine, I also took as mine from Obelos Nord. May

Wendell, the great Wizard, be proud of its use against the Scourge."

"With the passing of Sonya, my beloved, I began to wander as the rest of my people do, seeking ever a way to enter the Quad and put an end to the Evil One, but alas, I have never been able to get through; the entrances are heavily guarded at all times. Once I tried, but a hundred Yacs forced my retreat, though many were felled. Since then, I have been systematically following their movements, doing what I can to stop and deter them."

His voice trailed off as one who having succeeded in lesser goals had not yet achieved the main goal. Mindi took his hand and said softly, "Thank you, Master Wanderer. Your tale does much to dispel our doubts. For your double grief, we do understand."

"Thank you, my fairest lady," came the reply. "There is a bit more; I know Malazar. Indeed, he sought me out among the Wanderers. He has told me much of himself and his plans. We have had many councils. At the last one in early June, I was ordered to search for you and be of whatever assistance I could. At the time, I did not realize the full significance of his words. I do now. For if any in Isel have the ability to stop the Evil One, it is us. Now your toast George." They toasted many times and broke up to inspect how things were going.

The days passed, and there was much activity all across East Flats. Every city was rapidly building their fire towers. The poles had been transported from Pratt. The defense of East Flats was nearing completion. The Yacs were not heard of again for some time; their defeat at Hays had been an ominous one, damaging to their morale.

As the end of July rapidly approached, Marc realized that they must be off soon or they would miss their rendezvous with Malazar at East Point. They began to make their preparations, and George announced that he was coming with them.

However, they were hesitant; after all, he had a loving wife and three children to protect. Marc said he'd feel terrible taking George away from his family, especially if anything happened to George as a result.

However, Sharon settled the question. "To me, George is very special; truly I love him dearly, but he is more than a husband. He is himself first. Whatever he feels he must do, I too feel he must do. Other people in Isel are in need and yourselves as well. I will remain here seeing to the safety and comfort of the people of Hays; George must seek elsewhere. If the gods be with us, we will meet again and be as we are now, only more. If I were to hold him back, then I would no longer be a wife, but a slave master, no better than they."

When she finished, George had tears in his eyes. She spoke truthfully. All were moved, especially Mindi.

She said, "Sharon, thank you. Truly, you do have more wisdom in you than you let on. If all women could be as you, Isel would be glorious," and she kissed her.

That decided that, the questers now numbered seven including Malazar, wherever he was. They made ready to depart the next day, as time was growing short. George, late one night, made another trip to Obelos Pan. He put his pole back for safekeeping and acquired a small sword. "More useful in the wild," he explained.

Early the next morning, they departed with many farewells. The excuse they used was to inspect the other city's fire towers.

Chapter VIII—Retreat to Feanor Bridge

There was some discussion of the route they were to travel; clearly, there were two choices. Taking Haskel Road over to Murdoc and then south down Mule Lane Two offered the most cities, along with more possibilities of running into the Scavengers. Taking Mule Lane One down to the great East Road was townless and scenic with little chance of trouble. Since they had only three days left, it was decided to take the scenic route. They could not afford to be delayed.

As they rode along, they received cheers and welcomes from all the farmers. Many offers of "rest and have a bite" were turned down. They were constantly delayed.

Nache fairly well summed up their viewpoint, "Congratulations and thank you's are warranted, but this is getting out of hand." He yearned for some action.

The delay at Pratt was even worse. News of their trip had already arrived before them, and a day of celebration was called in their honor. This they discovered as they entered the town.

"Oh No!" exclaimed Mindi in dismay.

"Yuc!" said Nache, and then he said some more appropriate words in his own language.

The Drifter sighed, saying, "If it were me alone, I'd just disappear!"

Marc grinned and said, "Let me handle this one; just go along with me."

They agreed. Shortly, they arrived at Pratt Square filled with throngs of grateful well-wishers. Amid the cheering crowd, Marc walked, smiling, waving, and shaking a hand here and there. Finally, he made the center stage and greeted the Sheriff and other leaders, shaking their hands and being overly agreeable. Then he raised his hands up and got the crowd quiet.

He began, "Welcome all you wonderful people of Pratt. We, the Questers, all thank you for the great honor you do for us today. We are very pleased with everything." There was a round of applause and cheers.

He continued, "We have journeyed here with a purpose—to inspect your fire towers—to verify all is as it should be." Again, there was wild clapping and noise making.

He concluded, "Let there be a big celebration here today—we will mingle among you and visit with as many as we can, as we inspect your towers. Whatever happens, make this the brightest celebration ever in Pratt!"

He stepped down amid an even louder roar of applause and yells. He began making his way back to the others, shaking hands as he went.

"Ok, we break up here; each makes for a different fire tower on the east side of town. Shake hands, mingle, do your thing. Then, inspect quickly the tower, praise it and excuse yourselves to see the next. We'll meet at the tower nearest the road east and just leave."

They agreed and a slow hour later, they rendezvoused by the East Road tower, a bit worn out by all the well-wishers. Though they did loose precious time, Marc, to the amazement of the others, had pulled off the quickest possible departure without affronting anyone.

As they left Pratt behind them, the Drifter said with a chuckle, "I see why you're a Master Merchant!" They all laughed.

They continued until dark and made camp. So far, the only evil things seen were giant flocks of ravens flying overhead. They were tired and in need of a rest. The Drifter estimated they could still make their target and George concurred. The next day they hurried on to East Point, arriving around three miles from East Point proper. Here the country began to change. More and more trees appeared along with a heavier grass. They were getting close to the river.

Unfortunately, the East Point citizens would undoubtedly want to honor their guests, they assumed. This time, they could not afford to stop and have dinner. So the Drifter suggested that they bypass the town and head for the inn. All heartily agreed, and as darkness grew, the company walked through the open countryside, three miles north of East Point.

Drifter was the first to spot the trouble. Just north of their location, they saw flames lighting up the sky. It was a homestead, George reckoned. Since they did not want to be caught in the open, if it could be avoided, especially with the inn only miles away, determinedly, they picked up their pace and began to jog along, but they were not fast enough, and they ran squarely into the main band of Scavengers, who were on their way to try to wipe out East Point. There were a hundred Yacs at least.

All drew their swords, as Drifter yelled, "Run to the road; we must get there first!"

The Yacs stopped their march southwards and watched them briefly. Then, as if in sudden recognition of what the small band was, they yelled and gave pursuit, but their momentary stall was just enough to permit the company to make the road before the Yacs, forcing the Yacs to pursue them from behind on the road.

Laden as they were with their gear, they couldn't out run them. The Drifter took command and, about three miles from the inn, pulled the company under cover of a thicket of trees to get a brief rest.

"Ok," Drifter began, "Here's what we do. Marc, you and I will run rear guard; Nache you and Mindi take the ponies and the lead. Go down the road as fast as you can toward the inn. The road runs right by it. George, you watch the flanks. If any get by us, you pick them off. If anyone needs help just yell. Above all, let's don't get stopped. They'll swarm us like flies! Ok—here they come; our rest is done; **go!**"

Marc and Drifter charged at the oncoming Yacs, who, taken aback by their charge, temporarily halted. The two hastily turned around and caught up with the others. As the company ran on down the road, Drifter and Marc ducked behind trees and ambushed the lead Yacs. Repeatedly, Drifter kept pulling every stunt he could to slow the Yacs down.

Then, it happened again; as Marc thrust another Yac, his last dueling sword broke under the strain. He recovered and staggered to his feet. In front of him were five charging Yacs; Drifter was entertaining another group. Marc was on the spot. George saw Marc go down and slowed the ponies down.

As Marc got up, he drew Tiny. The five charged.

Marc felt anger and clutched the glowing sword with both hands. Without paying much attention, he said loudly, "Umla strenga."

Much to everyone's surprise, Tiny responded. There was a blinding flash of red flame; Tiny became a three foot long blade of fire, flaming brightly in the dark. In terror, the five Yacs broke off the charge; but too late, Tiny came down upon their backs. Blinding flashes of searing heat and smoke arose among their terror screams. Even the group attacking Drifter moved away in fear. Marc charged them, and they fled in a panic.

"Hurry," yelled Marc "Get going!"

They began running down the road again. The Yacs continued to press in on them, but, with Marc waving the flaming sword, they kept their distance.

As they ran, Drifter yelled for all to hear, "It's Andrill, the Fire Sword, Andrill come anew! Marc's got Andrill!"

Drifter now left Marc handling the rear and went forward to help guide the way to the inn. As they rounded the bend, they found the inn. It was now in ruins. It seems the Yacs had been here some time before, unbeknownst to the company. Doubt and fear hit the group as they stopped by their hoped-for sanctuary. The Yacs merely pulled back to see what they would do next, feeling sure that they had them now.

Secretly, the Scavengers broke into three parts, one flanking north, one flanking south, while the main band stopped gasping for air.

This was the first time that the company really felt a real sense of fear. Their sought after protection was gone. For a moment, they were confused. The Yac leader had anticipated this and now tried to ensure his success; he began talking to the group from a distance, in a coy, covert, sickeningly sweet manner. "Come my friends. Why do you flee and attack us? We mean you no harm. We are your friends. The Great One merely wants you to come and visit him. Why not stop this silly running, and let us accompany you to see the Lord?"

As he talked, a feeling of disgust and revulsion arose in the company; Mindi turned her head away. The Drifter paid little attention; he was not caught yet. His quick eyes, used to such plights, had seen the Yacs split into three groups. He guessed what they had in mind. In a minute, it would be all over unless he acted now.

Interrupting the breathy speech, he yelled, "Flee! Run on down the road! They are trying to surround us," and he took the lead.

George followed behind, then Nache and Mindi bringing the ponies. Marc, sword still flaming red, brought up the rear—now running—now dashing left and right.

Their action was just in time. As they passed a big oak tree, the three groups of Yacs rejoined, nearly surrounding Marc. Seeing the flaming sword, they hesitated from fear again. Still, the pack of Scavengers did not give up the chase and followed behind, ever watching Marc and his sword.

The Drifter was making for Feanor Bridge, less than a mile from the inn where it crossed the Kanandrul River, which flowed down from the mountains of the dwarves that separated East Flats from the heavy forests of Enchendar, the land of the Fairies. If they could reach the bridge, he felt they might be able to hold them off. Kanandrul's waters were cold and deep and fast-flowing; the bridge was small and little used. Very few ever crossed the bridge into Fairy Land, at least in these times. It was their only hope, for they could not last much longer. Even the ponies were well lathered and breathing heavily under the strain; but they did not balk even once.

The last quarter moon had risen; they could hear the dull rushing of the water ahead. Onwards they rushed headlong towards the bridge. As they came over a small rise, there below them lay the Kanandrul, the river of the dwarves. The road ran straight to Feanor Bridge, shimmering pale blue in the moon light. It was an ancient bridge, built, legends say, by the Fairies themselves. It was narrow and wooden; yet it did not weather nor show any signs of wear.

Drifter ran onto the bridge at once. However, both the ponies and Nache stopped dead in their tracks at the edge of the bridge.

"Ieee," cried Nache, "do you know what you are doing,

Drifter?"

As the others huddled around, Drifter said, between gasps for air, "Come on—this is the only way—ahead is Enchendar."

Nache, also gasping but very worried, cried again, "But legends say that those that enter never return. Dwarves never cross into Fairy Land; we are afraid; many creatures we have seen cross and none ever return. I say it is dangerous for us to cross. Let us rather stay and fight with our backs to the holy river Kanandrul."

Even the ponies seemed to share Nache's deep felt concern.

"But we cannot hold off a hundred," pleaded Drifter.

Mindi, who alone of the group felt calm and completely peaceful, said softly, yet still struggling for breath, "Nache, it is I, Mindi. I do understand your belief, deeply felt. There is no other choice; it's not our doom to perish here; ahead lies the unknown for you; but for me, it feels as a home; here you must trust me. Nay," she raised her voice so all could hear, "Nay, all of you. You must trust me; the good in you shall prevail. Trust me."

Into the hectic madness of their flight in the darkness, her words and commands pierced through the fear and, gently and surely, melted the emotion and effort. They found their ridges of anxiety ebbing and flowing away, leaving in its wake, a tranquil, calm, cleanness of heart and mind. Mindi kissed Nache on his forehead; and she raised her hands in the air and gently placed them on Butterball's neck and kissed him. Then, with only her hand on his neck, she led him gently across the bridge. Within two minutes, she had Nache and the other two ponies across. Marc was the last; alone in the middle of the bridge he stood, sword raised high in the night, a red flame flashing from its blade. He stood firmly and calmly there.

He was moved and said aloud, "For now, my sword shall cease to flame; but it will come again another day."

At that, he jumped across the rest of the bridge. Tiny's flame flicked and went out, returning to its normal color and size.

On the Enchendar side, hills and a heavy forest lay at

the edge of the river. Quickly, Mindi led them into the woods; and within minutes, they lay hidden in the dark woods, watching the bridge. Marc said, "Won't the Yacs cross as well?"

Mindi merely said, "Sh, watch and see."

The Yacs had seen them cross and were now at the bridge holding a conference. Their voices were hushed; they too, knew the peril that lay before them. At last, ten large Yacs crossed the bridge, while the rest waited to see what happened. Marc began to draw Tiny, but Mindi put her hand on his, restraining him. "Watch."

As the evil ones began to walk on the ground of Enchendar, Marc noticed that they seemed to slow down. Soon, they were ambling along, yawning heavily. Twenty-five feet into Enchendar, all ten Yacs were lying on the ground snoring heavily, oblivious to the world. Terror sprang into the rest of their group; and, in a panic route, the Yacs fled screaming into the distance. A deep quiet fell on the forest.

The company began to feel a bit drowsy as well, a sleep not due to their fatigue. They tried to walk along to get deeper into the forest for safety, but they were getting sleepier, merely ambling along. All, except Mindi, felt a peaceful, tranquil urge to just lay down and dream. Mindi suddenly realized this, halted the group, and stood before them. They looked at her standing amid the forest trees, moonlight filtering down in patches on her face and hair. She looked so beautiful, but she was very much awake and alert. Her eyes sparkled in the light.

She raised her hands towards the moon light and chanted softly, breaking the stillness of the woods.

"O fairest ones of all,
Whose forms we beg to see,
O light within the forest night,
Though we cannot see,
O brave guardians of Eos,
These are here, strong of heart,
O free their minds,
For good they be."

A sudden breeze rustled the leaves, like a breath of fresh air; and, as if coming out of a spell, all jerked and were wide-awake, though feeling amazingly refreshed.

"What happened?" asked George curiously, trying to figure out what had been occurring.

The Drifter seemed to grasp the situation quickly. He began, "We have entered Enchendar and the forest of Eos, land of the Fairies. It would appear that Evil is put to sleep as soon as it crosses into this land."

Then, they all looked at Mindi, suddenly realizing what she had just done. She beamed, radiating a happiness that was a delight to see.

The Drifter realizing her power said "Thank you, fair Lady." She nodded.

They made camp where they were, Mindi cautioned all to harm not even a tree in this land. They used Marc's torches instead of a fire. Dinner was very welcome, even if served cold.

Now in better spirits, they began to discuss the events. Chief among these was Marc's sword. Nache and the Drifter hounded Marc until he explained.

"I don't know what exactly I did—I just got mad and said something, though it was a foreign tongue to me. Tiny just responded."

The Drifter, who seemed well versed in these matters, told the tale of the sword. "In the days of the Mizzinti, Argos, the Great, created mighty Andrill, the Sword of Fire, to protect Isel from evil. Legends say in the wizard's hands, it would blaze like a star's fire; its touch would melt even rock. All foes of Isel, withdrew in fear as Andrill blazed above them. There is even a dwarven poem, which tells of Argos and Andrill coming to the aid of Belwain and slaying the Dragon, Cetus, who once ravaged their mountain lands. The elves have a song, which describes Argos and flaming Andrill, as seen at night from atop Obelos Sud. It is quite beautiful to hear. My friend, you do indeed bear a sword of old."

"Yes, but I'm not a wizard," Marc broke in, and then his voice faded off into silence.

Nache added, "We understand, Marc; we're all just borrowing our wizard's gear."

Then too, his voice trailed off into the quiet, for in his mind he was seeing pictures of far off Obelos Khander.

Mindi softly broke the hush, "It's time we rested."

They all laid down and slept. Each slept with a peace of mind and heart they had never felt before; and each had visions, dreams of old, as the night passed slowly into day.

Chapter IX—Of Fairies and Tales

The next morning, Marc woke by being pulled out of his dreams by Nache nudging him. "Look! Look! Look!" the dwarf said in excited whispers.

Sunlight filtered down through the trees softly lighting the forest bed where they lay sleeping. At the edge on a small rock sat the strangest little man Marc had ever seen. He was barely two feet tall at best, covered with green clothes head to foot, a black sparkling belt around his waist, and a funny green hat, that looked like leaves. Behind him on his back was a pair of silver translucent wings—not unlike those of a large fly. His facial features were round and bulbous. If Marc were to guess, he'd say it did have a smile on it. The eyes were unusually pale, bordering on transparent; so that when looking into his eyes, one would get the eerie feeling of gazing far beyond the eyes, into a "land between his head," as George later spoke of it. The group was quickly awakened to get their first look at a fairy. No one moved beyond sitting up to look at the little man.

Mindi smiled and said softly, "Hello, little one. We entered your country last night in an escape from the Evil Ones. I hope we haven't affronted your people in any way."

"Yes, I know; and no indeed," he said cheerfully, in a small, high-pitched voice, now smiling broadly. "I have been watching you for some time. I have disposed of the Yacs, as you call them; my sister, Lynn of the Pools, needed some more frogs. You are safe here; the evil you fled have themselves fled. Welcome to Enchendar, and my special welcome to the Forest of Eos. Prince Faedon, your servant." He stood up and bowed low.

Mindi then introduced the members of the party, each bowing as he had done.

"If you are ready," Faedon began, "I will take you before his regal majesty, King Faegor Finios and Queen Miranda. There you may explain yourselves. I have been commanded to bring you there myself; for in hundreds of years, very few have ever broken the spell that Faegor had placed on the woods, and never has there been five at once! Strange are the times, it is said. If you are ready, follow me. I shall walk so I do not lose you in these enchanted woods."

Mindi got up at once and began to follow him; Marc and Nache followed quickly, leaving Drifter and George to bring the ponies.

The forest was unlike anything they had ever seen. The trees were strange; though they had green leaves, the bark was fairly smooth and silver-brown so that they constantly reflected and flickered in the light, creating a twinkling, sparkling effect as though they were jewels. Mindi began a conversation with Faedon.

"Are not these called Elosir trees?"

"You are right," came a surprised answer.

They were leisurely following a small path that led through the shimmering trees. The little man said to Mindi, "I am the Prince of the Forest. I tend them and they respond to me. They told me of your presence at the bridge, and I watched you enter Eos Wood. They are very old, even older than me."

Then, they came to a fork in the path; one lead toward the right. To this one without a hesitation, Mindi turned, not even breaking stride.

Faedon watched her closely and asked, "My lady, do you know the way to Finiae City already?"

Mindi blushed and insisted she did not, but could not explain her actions.

As they walked along, the others began to discuss the absence of Malazar and of what should be done. No one had any real idea of either—but the Drifter was probably correct in suggesting he'd been delayed in Burly.

When the path again branched, Faedon immediately took the one to the left, but Mindi stopped and, in a funny, questioningly manner, asked him, "Don't we want the other one?"

Amazed, Faedon, said, "Yes, that is correct," and eyed her even more curiously.

They continued through the Enchanted Woods. Presently, they arrived at Finiae, the city of the fairies.

Finiae was actually laid out on four hilltops and a large

valley. Well-worn paths followed the valleys between the hills. Three hills lay in a line, and on the center one was the Royal Palace. The Palace was built with many pillars and arches; every color was represented, formed into streams that blended into one another. Squarely in the center, on a shiny post, stood a glowing ball that radiated a soft moon light on all.

Each of the other hills was filled with little houses barely waist high. The hill behind the Royal Hill was likewise covered by homes; and to the left of that hill was the Pool of Ian; and to the right, was Obelos Feos, towering pale blue to the heights. Directly in front of the Royal Palace was a large, flat area called the Royal Square. Faedon explained that here was where his majesty addressed strangers from time to time.

As they arrived, they found the air filled with the odor of sweet cherry blossoms; and they were expected. A fanfare announced Faedon's arrival, and the hills were alive with fairies, all watching curiously. The King and Queen were sitting on the steps of the Palace and appeared dressed for the occasion with various robes and crowns and many shades of purple.

They stopped on the Royal Square. The Prince stepped forward, bowed formally, and said, "I bring you the visitors, your lordship."

Faegor indicated to Faedon to begin; and he introduced them one by one. Faegor eyed each one closely; he was quite pudgy and had a bushy grey beard; and the gold crown on his head made him appear comical, but nothing escaped his eye.

To the dwarf he replied, "Beware his axe; there is a tale, but Master Dwarf do not use it in Eos."

To Marc he replied, "Long has it been since a Master Merchant has been here; that is itself a tale; yet you bear the Fire Sword of old. I do detect that there are many tales you may tell."

He continued similarly as they were introduced. Finally, he got to Mindi; Faedon had obviously been saving her until last.

The old fairy arose when she was presented and kissed her hand, saying, "And here is a flower like us, yet not one. She, alone, broke my spell; she knew the trees in Fairy tongue;

she knew the paths of Eos unto me. Rare is she indeed, perhaps a blossom long from home."

"Our friend, Shannon the Mariner, has said you may come; of this we are not surprised, but of the tales they have to tell—oh indeed—I'm excited to hear. Let me introduce my family and all bid you welcome. This is the Queen of the Fairies, Miranda."

She was beautiful beyond belief; her flows of love, all could sense, even Drifter.

"You've met my son Faedon, and these are my daughters: Fay—Princess of the children; Lynn—Princess of the pools; Melissa—Princess of all creatures." All three were quite lovely to behold. "And now let us have breakfast, for you must be hungry by now." They suddenly realized how truly he had spoken.

Then, the fairies all began to go into action at once; some began making music that, though softly done, moved the heart easily in ebbs and flows. Others, in a flash, produced large quantities of food; most was foreign to the guests, but it gave a renewed vitality seldom experienced in eating.

As they ate, Marc related to Faegor the various parts of his tale; and Nache, likewise, filled in here and there, impeccably demanding all relevant details be presented.

After breakfast, Faegor invited them to roam the lands and see such sights as desired. He bade them bathe in the pools, and the travelers soon found their every desire was fulfilled effortlessly. It was Fairyland.

Soon each was walking his own path around the city of Finiae, lost in his own thoughts and absorbing the incredible beauty. Mindi went off alone with Miranda, Queen of Faery.

From her first step on the bridge, Mindi had the feeling one has when he has arrived home after a long journey. She could not explain it. As she and Miranda strolled among the trees of Eos, she told Miranda of her feelings and emotions, of her strange knowings. Miranda listened to her every word, now sober, now smiling, ever reassuring, and encouraging.

When Mindi was done, Miranda said, "I do understand my child. If wisdom I may give, let it be two fold. First, it is important that you observe what you observe; never hesitate to do that. Secondly, the most knowledge there is, is simply certainty; certainty that something is or is not. I will not evaluate your mind and feelings for you; only you can do that, but it is safe to do that here in Enchendar. By way of help, rather, let me tell you the tale of Lenora. It is a tale of woe and sadness, yet of hope."

In the land of twisted trees, came the fair Lenora,
Wizard of love and of old,
There she dwelt and built a land, beautiful to be seen,
Shimmering trees—all of gold,
Pools and creeks and shores and peaks.
Gay Lenora gave to all, those that did believe,
A kingdom of admiration and respect,
Joy in living, being as one upon the path,
Her gift to us all, a timelessness, a speck,
With no start nor end, only now.
But others could not have such enduring love,
And sought to bring it to a close,
And she did end herself to keep our speck,
And we survive but ever grieve, that one so fair
Is lost from us, forever more.
The Great One came to us in tears,
Long he stayed and dwelt with us,
Shared our grief and we did his.
Timeless sadness never ending.
Then he spoke to end the loss.

In times to be will she return, unsought for,
In form quite new, to Eos, her gilded realm,
She will seek here for her loss.
With tower lit once more,
Find it as it was.
Until that day I trust to you,
This realm to keep, to guard.
Let no evil mar its presence.
Let it be as it was, as it is, as it shall be,
Unto the day of her arrival new.

To these ends, I do give this silver glow,
Moon beams, radiant power, yet still it gives.
No force be that can remove it,
Until its appointed task is finished.
Let it not bend to my will until this is done.
Though full of timeless woe, we did accept
Our charge, our gift, his hope, his love.
Ever more, we dwelt as he bode.
No evil shall enter, no change suggest,
Though forever more, we grieve for lost Lenora.

As she listened to Miranda's tale of old, Mindi felt many emotions; pictures flashed through her mind as if they were dreams. These she saw as they are. She yawned and yawned and yawned, becoming, all the while, more alert and awake. A strange calm grew steadily over Mindi; and, as Miranda finished, they shared words not spoken but felt.

Alone, Mindi found herself standing beside the door of the pale blue tower rising high above. She spoke ever so softly as a gentle summer's rain; and, with a serenity of mind she'd never known, Mindi entered; and the door closed behind her. That night the tall light of Eos would shine once more.

Later she reappeared amongst the fairies serenely glowing with life. She seemed to ebb and flow amongst her friends as was needed.

George had gone for a walk with Fay, who was known as the Fairy of Children. Fay had sought him in particular, sensing that, of all the visitors, he alone knew the joy that children bring. Hand in hand, they strolled through the many gardens and paths of Finiae. George was filled with a great sadness, but he endeavored to ask Fay, "If you are the Fairy of Children everywhere, why do you not come to them. Mine have never seen a fairy. But still they tell your tales."

Fay sensed his sadness, and he hers. She began, "We went abroad over all of Isel in the days of the wizards. Children would call; and we would be there, cheering hearts and strengthening minds. The little ones I hold dear, as they are the fruit that will seed, grow, and become tomorrow's lif, but in these dark times, few children call; they believe not. Of those who still do few can we visit because of the danger involved. Since the passing of our Lenora, there have been no new fairies. Though Miranda still speaks of her coming anew, I don't believe that our numbers will grow. In truth, they dwindle."

George understood her sadness and became lost in his own grief. For here in Eos, he discovered many pictures half unseen had come to view; and he had feelings from them; and he cried.

From the Garden of the Eternal Tulips, Mindi in her white gown gracefully came towards him, sensing his plight. As he saw her coming, she appeared to be enshrouded in a white glow of supreme serenity.

"My dear George, you are troubled—nay—grieved beyond words." Sitting beside him, she said in a voice that pierced through his grief, "Tell me what you see."

Accented by tears, he brokenly told her, "I see Pan, yet I see it no more. There is a group of us—I have done wrong— there is a flash, and I am no more." He yawned amid his tears.

Softly, she said, "Is there more?" There was a long pause, filled with much yawning.

Then, with a surprised look that turned into a grin, George said, "Hey—dying does not make it right!" He laughed as one who had not truly laughed for ages.

Mindi said "Thank you" and continued her walk.

George found Fay again and begged her to visit his children and wife and let them know he was all right. Fay could not refuse the exuberance and need of his request. That night four in Hays had a most unusual occurrence.

When Mindi came upon Nache, she found him in a terrible fit of anger, red in the face from yelling. He had gone off with Prince Faedon to examine the Elosir trees. Faedon had been describing their majestic beauty and their lineage of old, being living breathing creatures. Nache, at first, marveled about them; then, as more and more pictures flashed around his head, he became a bit hostile towards Faedon and trees, saying the dwarf scrubs were just as fair. He soon got into an uncontrollable rage, swearing these were not the best, insisting his were. The irate little man was stomping around insisting

Faedon take back his admiration for the Elosir, when Mindi came by him.

When Nache saw his "fair lady", her appearance was so commanding—more like a white radiance—he stopped abruptly and stared at her.

"Nache, I'm here and it's safe," she gently said, but, with so strong an intention, his little body fairly shook as he relaxed and became more calm. "Can you tell me whether this anger urge stems from Faedon or from somewhere else?"

Even as he spoke, a vivid dream-like picture had presented itself uncalled for by him, "No—Yes—I mean the images." He hugged her tightly, and she accepted it and sat down beside him.

"Tell me about it," she asked concernedly.

Reluctantly, he began to tell what he could. "I see the Armagh Mountains and strange cities, the ancient ones; they are beautiful beyond belief, with zigzag arches and angular lines of red stone and blue with scraggly, strong dwarfed trees that glow in the sun. Now I see a huge mountain and a tower; I am afraid and anger comes. I must not let it happen, I must not let it happen," he repeated over and over slowly.

Then, the anger subsided; and he saw flashes of scenes quite beautiful. This was followed by intense shame, and he described it as best he could. His occasional lapses into his own language did not seem to bother Mindi at all; she ever listened intently.

Then, Nache screamed; covering his eyes and head, he cried "The light! The light!" and began to shake. Then, he stopped all motion, and yawning, said in a rather embarrassed fashion, "It doesn't hide it, you know."

Mindi stroked his head lovingly and held him tight for a moment. Then, he began laughing and chuckling, while she beamed and broadly smiled.

"You know," he exclaimed, "I feel so good. For whatever you have done, I am eternally grateful and forever at your service, my lady."

"No, Nache, it was you who did it. Thank you for looking," and she kissed his forehead.

Then, exclaiming it was as if he had never even seen the

Elosir trees, he and Faedon went off to explore Eos wood.

Melissa, recognizing that Drifter, being a Nomad, had a substantial knowledge and love of the wild, had offered to show him the various animals and creatures that dwelled in Enchendar. Stephen would normally have eagerly accepted the offer, for little escaped his astute eyes in the wild. Yet for some unknown reason, he was in an ill humor; he couldn't concentrate and kept constantly remarking that he wished they could just get going on their way. Melissa tried in vain to interest him in the fauna she treasured so dearly, but to no avail.

Just as she was about to give up on him, Mindi joined them and asked, "Well, Drifter, are you picking up any useful information; I have never seen so many animals; they seem so tame."

"My doing," Melissa proudly interjected.

"Forgive me, ladies," Drifter said, eyes down cast, "Seldom, if ever, am I found to be in the company of two so fair; but I am not feeling well—I just wish we could get started again."

"He's been saying that all along," Melissa explained, "And you've only just arrived."

"Leave us for a minute, please," suggested Mindi, and she put her arm around Drifter's broad powerful shoulders. "Let's walk."

After going a little way, she could feel how tensed his body actually was; and so she asked him in a querying fashion, "Tell me, how do you feel?"

He shrugged his shoulders and mumbled something; the Drifter was not very communicative.

She tried again, "Have you felt this way before?"

As she said it, she felt his muscles tense and ripple throughout his body. "Yes" came the reply.

"Tell me about it," she commanded.

"Well, I've always felt like this—it comes and goes," he said moodily.

She asked him to close his eyes; and, then, she put the question to him, "What do you see—is there a memory or a picture there?" There was a long pause broken only by a yawn.

Slowly the Drifter began, "Well, yes, I see an obelos—Magum, I'd guess—and some tall mountains. I feel I want to reach out and touch them."

"Anything else going on there?"

There was a pause, which was followed by an almost total relaxation of Stephens body; Mindi caught him and kept him from a collapse. Yawning heavily, he spoke only, "So that's why—that's why I have been wandering."

He at once began to recover his composure and a smile broadened to a grin. He stopped her and squared her around, "Hey thanks. I never thought of that. What are you anyway?"

Mindi blushed and said cheerfully, "I'm just me, Mindi."

Together they strolled back to Melissa. He was now feeling great, and he and Melissa went off to examine the creatures of Eos. Mindi, waving bye, smiled as they receded into the woods, talking enthusiastically.

"It did not matter what he saw," Mindi mused, "As long as he saw it as it is."

Marc had not felt much like exploring Enchendar. He felt listless and moody. As far as he was concerned, it was an ill day. The party needed Malazar but no wizard. Where was he, what were they to do now? He was confused. He had, therefore, gone only to the pool in Finiae. He found Lynn was there; and they lay on the bank for some time, neither saying anything; but occasionally Marc would throw a leaf or twig into the clear blue water and gaze at the ripples.

"What should be done now? Could I single handedly kill the Evil Ones? What of Andrill? Was it the Fire Sword? Why do I know how to use it? Has all of this so far just been good luck? Malazar's luck? Am I a wizard? Was I a wizard? I don't want to be a wizard. But the evil must be ended; I have to end it; I can't end it. Maybe I should have let Malazar do it; he's the wizard. I'm only a merchant. I'm not a fighter; but I did do a good job of it; the Fire Sword stuff made me feel terrific. Is it really my obelos and sword?"

He was about to throw another leaf into the pool when someone held his arm back. He slowly rolled over to see Mindi smiling down at him.

"Oh, hi Mindi," he said in a monotone. Then he chuckled, saying, "I'll bet you know what's going on with me right now."

She lay down beside him, "Well I don't for sure, but it looks like some problem has got you; want to tell me about it?"

"Yes, I guess," and he told her of his confusion of thoughts which led seemingly in circles. "You see, I feel I'm being shoved back and forth. But that's not the only thing. What makes matters worse are these confounded images that I keep having."

"What about them," she inquired.

"They're probably just muddled illusions to add to my confusion, but they seem to be of an older age or what I think the older age might be." He glanced at her; but, since she looked quite interested, he continued, "I see men, glaring at men; I see armies marching—one is dwarven, I think. I seem to be watching—Mindi," he said a bit startled, "I'm getting the urge to fight on one side and then a big resistance to it—oh! You know, if you never make up your mind—decide—why, it stays unresolved—you get hung up or stopped there. Now that's interesting."

Mindi saw that he had how brightened up considerably; and they looked understandingly at each other for a moment. Then, Lynn joined them, and together they shared an afternoon exploring the beauty of the Pool of Ian.

The ensuing days passed rapidly. Mindi and Drifter spent many hours with Melissa, learning much of the kingdom she knew so well. George and Fay strolled often; neither seemed to run out of stories to tell nor did they lack eager ears for listening. The only event was Shannon's arrival; King Faegor had intuitively summoned him.

The summer was now in its ebb, when with renewed hearts and minds, Marc called for a council of the group. The First Council of Marc, to which it was there after referred, took place in the Royal Square; the topic, the quester's next action. Marc opened the affair by briefly describing the situation, which was more a series of unanswered questions than a synopsis.

"We have all, directly or otherwise, have accepted the

challenge of Malazar—to assist in the freeing of Isel from the Scourge. Thus far, we have followed his bidding; the Flats are temporarily defended. Of the next step, the wizard has not informed us. He has not appeared as was planned; thus, we do not know his fate, good or evil. We are now faced with deciding the next path we should follow. Do we wait for the wise one to send word; seek for the wise one; or design our own next action?"

Mindi rose and said, "As I see it, the first choice is do we stay in Enchendar in the bliss of forever or do we depart, to tarry no longer."

"Yes, My Lady," the Drifter began, rising in turn. "I agree fully, we must depart very soon; too long we have already delayed. For my part, I would suggest that we go abroad in quest of armies. Let us seek out those we can and form a united army to lead forth to crush the Evil Ones."

"You have the dwarves," Nache proclaimed, "I agree with Drifter; many armies of might we can obtain. The Scourge shall feel the pound and slash of the steel of Armagh. Say the word and all of Khorizaba will rise to your command."

There was a moment's pause; Marc looked at George. "I think it's too hopeless, too unsure, to go off in search of armies. If we take the dwarves from Khorizaba, what is then left to keep their lands from being overrun? The Quad has many sides—all need to be protected. Even if we acquire the armies, whither do we lead them, there are only four narrow passes into Kalhari. No, I vote we return to the Flats and guarantee an area of safety, like here; then await the return of Malazar for further council."

"And you Shannon, what have you to say," Marc spoke soberly.

"As for me, there is truth in all that's been said so far. We cannot hope to muster one army to charge the enemy; it may prove disastrous. I would suggest that we sail the seas in search of other lands and armies there, and by trade, to acquire their help and aid. This would surely make us stronger than the Evil Ones. Easily could we then overrun them. But another thing I have to say. Because I too feel my duty to the quest, I have decided with Faegor's help, to stay on land and see it through. When we're done, I will return to the sea, my love. Till then, my golden cutlass of Mari be raised alongside of yours."

A large round of applause followed this.

Then, Drifter said, "Marc, this is your council; you have had our views; but you have not told us yours. What say you?"

Marc looked at Mindi for a moment, in silence, and then slowly he rose and looked over his friends, then began.

"I feel a sense of duty—of obligation, even—to end the evil Scourge. The raising of armies will only cause delay of time; the enemy also is raising armies; I see only a bitter end of many lives in that direction. I do not like involving others in the fight. I feel it is somehow our fight, ours alone. We cannot stay here, that is doing nothing. The Flats, truly, are now defended; but the evil grows daily. There is no hope in returning and waiting, only despair, especially if Malazar does not come. We cannot afford to journey endlessly the seas, for as we do, our land is being destroyed. Also, I cannot condone bringing other unknown peoples into our affair, particularly if we have begun it ourselves, if that be true. I feel most strongly that it is our affair, and we must somehow handle it."

As he spoke, the others realized he was actually very correct; they had expressed their ideas but none really believed that theirs would really handle the situation. Marc's words, though striking all ideas down, did strike a note of truth in all. There was a large round of applause.

Then, Marc said, "Then we're in agreement on these points. Well done. Now we come at last to exactly what should we do next."

At this point the First Council of Marc, abruptly ended. Faedon came running into the Square. "Someone's just entered Enchendar from Feanor Bridge!"

At once, the entire company leaped to their feet and ran with Faedon down the paths of Eos toward the bridge. The common thought and hope—"Was it Malazar?"

As they came out of the trees near the bridge, they drew up short; in front of them stood a huge man with bulging muscles, large deer horn about his neck, clad in fur apparel head to foot, with a large grey-white dog standing beside him.

At his side was a sheathed, silver scimitar; and his bare, wounded, left chest had a large streak of dried blood on it.

Chapter X—The Water Boils

It was late at night when Malazar left Marc and Mindi at Obelos Sud. Though he was tired and hungry, he knew he absolutely must press onward, north toward Burly. He took the direct approach. Leaving the tower, he went due north, paralleling the edge of the East Range. It would cost him hours to cut back just to catch the road, which didn't make much difference in this flat country. Using his staff as a walking stick, he took as large a stride as he could do so efficiently.

He began to wonder whether his plan for the south had worked. True, the defenders of Isel were very few and, even now, very out-numbered. He could not be everywhere at once, so he had had to come to Metro for help. He wondered if he had succeeded; would they actually come through? Would they be successful? He felt confident that he had picked the right ones. After all, they were the only ones in all of Metro's thousands, who had responded to the obelos signal, but he was, still, only a merchant, whose lot in life is definitely not that of the types that the wizard needed. Had he aroused their inner-selves sufficiently? He thought so, but was not entirely certain.

Finally, he could not squelch his growling stomach any further; so he took a break and pulled out some dried food from his pouch. Sustaining, but not much more could be said of the dried Burly venison. Stretching and yawning, he watched the eastern sky grow pale in dawn's first rays, and with the disappearing stars, the old one started his lonely trek once more. He pressed onward all the day and far into the night. Ever since he hit the hills north of Hill View, his going was slower and required more effort. Finally, when he could go no further, he made a hasty camp and slept.

The rising sun found him hurriedly striding once more. Here and there, he came upon cold, abandoned campfires; his quick eyes rapidly identified the traces that the Yac inhabitants left behind. As he passed more and more of these old campsites, his worry and concern grew. Was he too late; had

Burly fallen? What of Vorag Boraski? He quickened his pace even further. By nightfall, he had reached the Old Caravan Road. Hesitatingly, he started down it. Time was pressing; he felt secrecy must give way to boldness. He hurried down the road.

For a few miles, all went well; but then he heard noises ahead. Quickly, he left the road and scrambled for cover behind a thicket of young oaks. He waited. A minute later, a company of Yacs appeared on the road, walking in threes— twelve all total. He waited until they'd passed him; and, then, he left the road and pushed on northeastwards, about a mile from the road. He pushed himself onward until nearly midnight, when he reached the edge of the Grenwald River. His legs would not take him further, and he hastily made camp, ate, and laid down to try to sleep.

Something caught his attention; he realized the night sounds had ceased; all was quiet. A stick broke not too far away. He leaped to his feet, grabbed his staff, and peered into the dark. He distinctly heard the hissing sound of breath being drawn in through clenched teeth. His grip on his staff tightened.

Then, a voice in the night said belittlingly, "Well, what have we here, boys—an old man, beyond his prime?"

This was followed by awful sounding laughter from all sides. Malazar's back was to the river, and he had to do something, so he raised his staff slowly and carefully and spoke very softly to it. He touched the ground in front of him. There was a flash, and a fire sprang forth, lighting up the glen. Instantly, he could see his foes; fifty Yacs had him surrounded on all three sides. They were taken aback by the flash and were shielding their eyes from the light.

Then, the biggest yelled, "Go get him boys; his light makes him even easier to see."

The Yacs stepped forward, closing in on the lone old man. Malazar instinctively began to back up ever so slowly, eyeing the group and holding his staff horizontally out in front of him.

This could not go on much longer. He knew he had to do something.

As his right foot splashed into the water, the leader, cackled, saying, "Oh, the old one has got his feet wet. Oh, oh. Shall we get him all wet? Maybe he can't swim. Wouldn't that be too bad?"

More snickering laughter followed. Slowly and carefully, Malazar spoke strange words that the Yacs did not understand. Having finished, the wizard raised his staff high into the air and yelled loudly, "What do you do with a stupid Yac? Boil them I say!" And he touched the water with his staff.

There came a blinding flash of flame, and the waters of the Grenwald steamed huge clouds of vapor everywhere. Within seconds, the whole glen was filled with a dense cloud of foggy steam. Visibility, nearly zero. Quietly, but swiftly, he walked up the bank and out of the glen amid the violent curses and yelling and screaming.

"The enemy knows I'm abroad now; I've left my mark. I must hurry."

Off he went again, following the river ever northward; and within a few hours, he reached Sudoor Bridge, just above Klee. Sudoor Bridge was an old bridge, and it had a well-worn appearance. The folk of Klee used to maintain it, but, with the passing of the years and the general decline of descent traffic, the bridge had been left to fend for itself. He stopped mid-way across and looked behind him. No one was after him.

"This has been an ill omen," he said to himself.

He breathed deeply and continued to cross the old planks. Once on the other side, the road went northward again, along the edge of the deep hilly forests of Burly and the gently rolling, grassy hills of Illanos. Instinctively, the wizard left the road and entered the deep, dark, forested land. He decided to continue along the forest, paralleling the road; it would provide cover.

Burly was an interesting land; it began, here in the south, with heavily forested, low hills that grew more dense, hilly and rocky the further north one went. The northern edge was actually the Quara Sud Mountain Range with tall ragged rocky peaks. The forest was extremely dense at the northern edge. Far to the east, the forest ended, as the Armagh Mountains rose to the highlands of the dwarves.

The forest was filled with large deciduous trees; some oaks were three feet in diameter. Maples, elms, and poplars were interspersed here and there; and groves of ash grew near the creek beds. The forest was the home of many wild animals, from big black bears to porcupines to a multitude of squirrels and rabbits. Here was the land of the Burly men—the greatest of the hunters. They were big men, usually over six feet tall, with a very heavyset frame. Burly men were always boasting of their feats of strength; it was usual for a hunter to barehanded wrestle a bear to gain the coveted fur. Crude, though they were, the hunters of Burly were honest, brave, and loyal, even unto death.

Malazar soon found moving through the hilly forest slower than he expected and was considering returning to the road for a while. After all, since the river episode, everything was quiet so far. However, dawn had come; and, as he rested, leaning against a tall oak, he realized how completely hungry and fatigued his body really was. Quickly, he flashed his staff and helped himself to a roasted rabbit meal. "After all," he said chuckling to himself, "being a wizard does have its advantages." Next, he scrapped some leaves into a pile and laid down to a much-needed sleep.

Amid the greenish towers, half-buried in last year's brown leaves, and nestled against a boulder, the wizard slept soundly as the day waned into dusk. Sometime after full dark, Malazar woke with a start; his body jerked and the leaves rustled. He heard a twig snap nearby. The forest was ominously silent; he could hear his own breath, but it was the crackling of the leaves that had made his whereabouts known.

A large pack of wargs were out foraging for their evening meal. Over a dozen were roaming helter-skelter through the deep woods, ever moving southward. One large wolf had cracked a twig not more than five hundred feet from the sleeping man. The keen hearing of the warg heard the leaves rustling and had growled softly, as if in acknowledgment. Quickly, the wizard leaped to his feet; he knew he had at most a minute to react. The growl was known to him. But was there more than one? Instinctively, he guessed more. His eyes probed the darkness for some cover, some protection. In the middle of the little hollow stood a tall white oak; quickly, he began climbing. As he got safely onto the lowest broad branch, the wargs appeared from all directions and swarmed into the area.

Seeing their prey already nearly had, they began to growl and howl loudly. Soon, over a dozen wargs were prowling in circles around the tree, occasionally making powerful lunges upward trying to get his feet. Unfortunately, for the wizard, the next branch up was out of his reach. To try might mean a slip and a gruesome fall into expectant teeth. He made his staff flame red hot; and, using it as a probe, jabbed here and there at the bolder ones leaping up at him. It was effective; the wargs stayed clear. A howling stalemate resulted. The wargs crouched down in a circle around the tree—red eyes blaring with fire, fangs dripping, voices growling. Eventually, he would have to come down; they were prepared to wait. He wondered how long he could stand on the branch without a slip. Ten minutes passed filled only with the wizard's taunts.

"A wizard is easier to tree than he is to eat, my friends. Fire, fire in the night burning brightly, such a fright. Ah my pretties, afraid of a little fire are you, such a shame." He kept his spirits as high as he could.

Ten more minutes passed when suddenly the forest shook with a bellowing blast from a Burly deer horn. Then, there came the sounds of what might seem an army, smashing, crashing through the woods from the north. Malazar made his flame brighter; and strained his eyes into the distance, as the wargs rose up expectantly. In less than a minute, a Burly scouting party charged into the hollow, bellowing loudly, brandishing their silver scimitars wildly before them. Malazar recognized Vorag immediately and yelled out a welcome. Six men charged with a ferocity akin to their brawny, burly nature.

As Vorag leapt down from the boulder under which the wizard had slept, one of the biggest wargs sprang through the air in a great leap, teeth bared straight for the big man's throat. Vorag met his challenge not with his scimitar held high in his left hand but with his clenched fist. In midair, the fist met its mark, accompanied by a loud crumbling and bone breaking sound. The warg spun around in the air and fell lifeless to the ground; his head was stove-in and neck broken. The pack fled wildly; but the other hunters felled five before the wolves disappeared.

"Verily, tis long ere we seeth a wizard in a tree. Art thou hurteth, my friend?"

As he climbed down, Malazar gratefully said, "Not a scratch. Mighty glad to see you, Vorag, the Bold Keeper."

They exchanged handclasps and shakes, although a bit too heartily for Malazar's taste. The others joined them, and all were rolling hearty laughter off their bellies. He quickly recognized the familiar faces of Fergus, Garth, Owen, Berman, and Olaf, and, then, the huge, grey mastiff, who had now come running back from chasing the wolves, Vorag's dog, Oran.

"Tis a good thing that we cameth on thee as we didst. Pray, Grey One, how comest thou here? Nary mind, tis well yea cometh, though late it be. Only two days past, we faileth at thy appointeth task. The Scourge didst overpower us with their numbers."

The wizard, dusting himself off, interrupted, "I feared I would be late. For this, I am truly sorry, but much news I think we have to share, but not here just now, for even a wizard can be scared."

"Verily, Verily, tis true, I hast overlooked thy plight. Come let us journey north toward my camp; t'will be comforts there."

And with that they quickly left the ill-fated hollow; Vorag, with Oran ever at his side, led the way through the forest with Malazar close behind. The rest followed in single file, all taking great strides through the woods, as was their nature. The men went quietly through the trees, which the wizard noted they rarely did. Vorag hurriedly explained that large armies of Yacs were on the move down the road.

Vorag, the Bold, was the Keeper of Obelos Bracken and its weapons. The Burly men had always been hunters, even of old. Unlike the other lands, here the obelos was an integral part of their social activities. The maintenance and guarding was under the care of the Keeper: both a title and a very high honor. It was passed down through generations of hunters. Vorag, the Bold, had assumed the title ten years ago for his impressive legacy of both bold and courageous feats.

Malazar had guessed that he was the strongest man in all of Burly. He was six feet six inches tall and weighed three hundred twenty pounds—all muscle. He had a big, bushy, black beard, straight, long, black hair, deep set, coal black eyes, and a hairy body. He was clad in bear fur; this was a great honor and indicative of bravery. To wear the bear, one had to kill the wild animal barehanded. Vorag carried the immense bow and silver scimitar of Obelos Bracken. Though centuries old and long used by the Keepers, they had never failed and had no mark upon them. The stout black arrows were always retrieved; in all this time, only one had ever gone amiss of its target. All the men wore heavy rugged boots made of various hides and skins.

Forever at his side was Oran, a great, grey mastiff, his hunting dog, nearly four feet tall, with large, white canines. Oran was exceedingly loyal and brave; the two were inseparable, and they worked together as a team.

Of the others, Fergus and Garth were twins; they were excellent fighters, clad similarly in deer hides and both six foot five inches tall. Fergus had reddish hair, while Garth's was browner. They carried heavy, oaken bows and silver, curved scimitars.

Owen was a beaver hunter and, therefore, clad in beaver pelts, but otherwise quite similar to the rest. Olaf was the heaviest of the group, nearly three hundred fifty pounds. His name was actually descriptive of his frame; even Vorag had a very hard time unseating him in contests. Berman, the Bear Friend, was the most unusual of the troop. Like Vorag, he wore the skin of bear, but he was more a keeper of bears. He had a rapport with them; alone of the hunters, Berman could walk into a bear's den and come out riding a friend, but he was ferocious in a fight.

Indeed Vorag had chosen his scouting party well. Malazar learned that two days ago, a large company of Yacs had burst through Kyder Pass, storming and overrunning the fortress at Greagon. Their aim was apparently to break out of the Quad, for they went on by Greagon. Though the hunters did their best, there were just too many Yacs to stop. Many had gotten by them. Malazar had hoped that the Burly men could contain the Evil Ones mostly within the desert regions. The lands of Burly stretched from Kyder Pass to Begrundi Pass and the whole length of the south wall of the mountain range called Quara Sud. The only places they could get out were the two passes at either end. Malazar had elicited their help in trying to keep the Evil Ones inside. Though Vorag told of the many brave deeds of those of Greagon, they had not been entirely successful, due mostly to sheer numbers.

Burly had only three small cities: Greagon in the west, Beregrin in the east, and Old Varg, the ancient city of the obelos, squarely in the middle between the rivers Beone East and Beone West. Each city had a lord who acted as governor of the city and surrounding lands. They settled disputes, officiated at festivities, and saw to the running of the towns. Lord Edmund ran Greagon; Lord Edward ran Beregrin; Lord Egmond ran Old Varg. All were renowned with fairness and integrity.

Vorag explained that, after the large group got by them, with Lord Edmund's permission, he formed his scouting party to follow the Yacs to learn of their plans. Malazar was informed that they had not gone in any great numbers towards the elves nor took the Wan Real spur road toward the horsemen. Almost all had gone southward. The wizard was both relieved and troubled; Marc would have a worse time than he had expected. Late that night, they arrived at the camp nestled among a thicket of huge trees deep in the forest. As they approached, Malazar saw the cheerful fire and recognized the Drifter, who was standing guard. There were welcome words, feasting, and much sharing of news, until nearly dawn, when they at last slept.

The next day dawned and the company rose early with only a little sleep. Malazar was deeply troubled and he spoke privately with Vorag and Drifter.

"It concerns me much that so large an army you spoke of is heading southward. Those that I have chosen to help us and to fortify the southern Flats are going to need time; they are little used to these actions. I did not expect these tidings, and I fear it might go ill with our new allies, but I must go north; there is worse evil there."

"Rest your mind, my friend," broke in the Drifter, "My work here is done. Long have I alone watched the doings of the Evil Ones. Now, they have gone south. To fulfill my duty, I must also go south. There I may follow them and give advanced aid or warning, as may be. I will be of little use here, my friends."

"Verily, they willst need an army to stoppeth the hoard that went yonder," Vorag added. "But we canst not affordeth to guard two lands; we hast not the numbers."

"You speak truthfully," the wizard spoke. "My mind will be relieved to know that you will be there watching. The two that you seek are the Master Merchant, Marcos Blancas, and a woman, Mindi Francos. Go with my blessing."

At that, the Drifter quickly gathered his things, hugged Vorag after their fashion, and departed. Silently, he disappeared into the woods.

"Now Vorag, we must make with all haste to Greagon."

"Verily, Verily," came the reply.

In a few minutes, the scouting party was again on the move, ever northward toward Greagon. They journeyed onward for two days, finally arriving near sunset at Greagon.

As they arrived, great horn blasts echoed through the hills and were dampened by the giant trees. The city of the western hunters was built of logs. Surrounding the city was the stockade—an eight foot high wall of six inch posts sharpened to a point at the tops. Jutting above the wall were numerous log guardhouses, each with small, window like openings, through which archers could loosen their arrows. There were two sets of gates: one to the north, one to the south. As they approached the city, the mammoth gates were opened; and many husky guards were about. Standing apart from the others, stood a tall man dressed in green, Lord Edmund, who had heard of their arrival and waited patiently for them. Inside the doors could be seen children playing in the dirt streets, having fun, oblivious to the arrival of one more scouting party. Edmund smiled when he saw Malazar was with them.

Raising his right hand, he said, "Hail to thee, Grey One,

and hail to thee, mighty scouts."

There ensued a hearty round of hand clasping and hugging, as was their custom. As soon as the children heard their lord speak of the Grey One, they dashed rapidly toward him. Soon he was besieged with many cries saying, "Grey One, showeth us thy fire tricks!" Malazar was known here! Malazar promised the kids a fire show after it got dark, and they gaily ran off to tell everyone else.

"I wisheth we hadst such enthusiastic words to telleth thee. I believest Vorag hath told thee of our failure to do thy bidding. We couldst not contain such numbers."

"Speak no more, my Lord," interrupted the wizard, "You have done well; it is no fault of yours. Bravely the deeds have been done here, as Vorag spoke. Against such numbers, there is no fault, but let us speak of these matters later in private council, for we are tired and have journeyed at the fastest pace."

"Forgive me, Grey One, thou dost speaketh truly. Breaketh open the barrels, men."

Actually, they did not need the latter words because already they were scrambling to grab the mugs and kegs. Soon everyone was eating and drinking merrily.

When it was sufficiently dark, Malazar collected the anxious children, and many of the older ones. He took them to the central, open area of town. Then, feeling as excited as the kids, he began to make various fire flames shoot skyward from his staff with many multitudes of colors. Everyone was pleased, even Malazar himself. At last, he ended and received a loud round of applause. Then, he, Lord Edmund, and Vorag retired to Edmund's Office Cabin.

It was constructed of one-foot diameter logs nearly ten feet tall and was of a square shape. Inside were tables and benches—also of split logs. On the walls were various skins and trophies. There was also a map of the city and of Burly.

Edmund told them the latest news, which amounted to two things. Not much had happened since the big, overrun battle many days ago. The best news yet, Beregrin had successfully contained the Evil One's push at Begrundi Pass. Malazar was pleased by this turn of events.

He began, "We have fared well so far—in some ways more than was expected, but now with the enemy loosened into the south, we must know of their plans. Indeed, it is imperative!"

"Truly thou speaketh my own thoughts," put in Vorag. "But how canst we find out this?"

There was a long pause; and Malazar said softly, "We must spy on them."

At this, Oran who had been lying quietly beside his master, pricked his ears, and raised his head, as if he understood as well.

Vorag laughed, "Prithee, tellest how? How? I lookest not like a Yac! Ho, ho, ho."

"I had in mind a small company to journey to Kyder Pass, even beyond if possible. There I myself will sneak in and spy, to learn what I can."

Obviously liking the idea, Vorag said decidedly, "And I, Vorag the Bold Keeper, willst accompany thee. A spy to be."

"That settles it; pick one or two more trusted men. We'll start at once, but we must use extreme caution; we can't be seen nor heard; there must be no trace of our presence—not felt nor heard. If we're discovered, the Evil One will only change the plans."

"Excellent," said Edmund, "I bid thee rest a while longer in mine house. I willst arrange a secret departure."

The others left, and the tired wizard lay on a bed in the corner and slept for a brief time, until Edmund returned.

It was now midnight; all were asleep except for the guards in the log guardhouses. All was quiet. The nearly full moon cast silver shadows through the trees onto the town of Greagon. Vorag had chosen Fergus and Garth to join them. Malazar found them by the gate waiting in the shadows. Exchanging nods and grins, the four quietly set off northward through the night forest.

North of Greagon, the hills grew steeper, higher, and much rockier, though still heavily forested. The pale moonlight gave a ghostly glow to the dark forest. It took a brave soul to wander through these woods at night. There were noises of startled rabbits scampering away and other scratching and prowling sounds. For Vorag, these were sweet music, for all knew very well what no sounds invariably meant in these times.

By dawn, they were near the Quara Mountains where the forest of Burly ended. On Malazar's advice, the four made camp at the edge of the forest where a tall mountain rose up, towering high above them. They merely had to parallel the mountain for two miles and they would hit the Old Caravan Road and Kyder Pass. They made camp here and slept, as they could, through the daylight hours. No words were spoken.

As the darkness began to fall once more, Malazar briefly outlined his plan. Garth was to remain at the camp. At the one-mile point, Fergus would stand guard. At the edge of the forest by the road, Vorag and Oran would wait. This would guarantee a safe retreat if things went ill. Alone, Malazar would go on the road to spy.

Quietly, they made their way, pains-takingly slowly, across the very rocky and rough terrain. Finally, Malazar and Vorag arrived at the road and pass. Here, the wizard changed his cloak, donning a dead Yac's. He entrusted his staff to Vorag, who insisted on entrusting to the Grey One his scimitar. The wizard took it and hid it under his ugly, stinking, black cloak. Yacs did have a foul odor. Then, as the moon again cast deep shadows on the pale scene below, Malazar crept slowly down out of the forest and hills onto the flat roadbed below. He was a quarter mile from the pass entrance, which was hidden because the road curved to his right. Slowly, the dark speck walked along the road to Kyder Pass.

As he rounded the bend, before him rose the mountains—like a monstrous, black wall—and, in front of him, towered two might, sheer, rock cliff; Tol Sear and Tol Glear, whose three thousand foot faces rose diagonally upward lost in the sky. They almost touched at their base; Kyder Pass was narrow, only ten feet wide. In other days, it was a splendor to behold; these times, it cast grave fears on those who dared to gaze upon it.

The Evil One had been at work. Sprawling on either side of the pass were dilapidated, crudely built houses, row upon row. "For the Guards," reflected the wizard. On Tol Sear, the northern wall, there was a ledge some hundred feet up. There were watchtowers and welcome gates constructed here in days gone by. He saw a light coming from the windows above him. Pacing back and forth across the entrance to the pass were two Yac guards. They had seen him and had paused briefly and, then, continued pacing. Evidently, the disguise was working, at least at night.

Slowly, he wandered up to the guards; and, when he got close, he said softly and as apathetically as possible, "Nothing brewing down there. All quiet here?"

"Yes, nothing moving, except you, for the last two hours. Can't see the reason for all of this either. We teached them Burly men a lesson they won't forget. They'll be guarding their families and all."

"Yes" said Malazar, "I recon they'll never bother us again."

About that time, a voice came from above, "Hey, everything ok down there?"

"Yes, all cool here," yelled one of the guards, "also up ahead too."

"Say, I didn't get your name, guard?"

Malazar thought quickly and said "Harry and yours?"

"Grugor," came the reply.

Then, the wizard said testingly, "I think I'll go up there and set a spell?" motioning upward toward the tall watchhouse.

"Yes, go ahead, but don't let the Captain see you. Fredgar's a mean one."

"I won't. Yell if anything comes up."

"Yes, ok."

Slowly, Malazar walked into the pass. There was a rope ladder dangling down. Quickly looking all around, he slowly climbed upward toward the old tower. Strange pictures flashed in his mind of a time when the walls were splendid and the ominous watchtower was a joy to behold. He yawned and continued.

At the top, the two guards greeted him; and he quickly said, "All cool up here?"

"Yes," came the reply.

"I just wanted to come up and sit a while; it's late."

"Yes ok," they said quietly, resuming their card playing. They were sitting around a table on which an oil lamp sat.

The building was made of granite blocks, which had now become weather worn and had lost not only their sharp edges but also the colors that had been given to them in the Elder Days. From the windows, the wizard gazed far off into the desert region. All was quiet and dark. He looked around in search of an idea. Suddenly he had one. A big, beer barrel stood in the corner.

"It's a shame," he began slowly, "that you can't have a little. It's such a boring, quiet night; and the stuff is so good."

That brought an immediate response, as calculated.

"Yes, it sure is!" the taller Yac began in earnest.

"Shut up," slobbered the other, "and play your cards! You know the captain don't allow it—someone's got to be alert up here, he says."

"I tell you what," said Malazar exploringly, "I ain't got much doing, I'll watch for you. It just isn't good fun playing cards without no drink."

"Oh, come on," pleaded the first.

"Look, if he's going to do the watching, who's gon'ta know anyhow?"

Shortly, Malazar was filling their mugs repeatedly. Once started, they lost no time in drinking. It wasn't long before they began to feel the effects.

Malazar, looking out the northern window, asked, "Hey, you guys know how many guys we sent southward the other day? I've been meaning to ask, but never got around to it."

"I recon it was nearly a thousand, what do you say?"

"Bout right, a hundr'd of 'em foul wargs went too, an a mass o jackals follered 'em through da pass."

"Not a bad army", Malazar muttered.

He looked carefully at the two Yac specimens before him. Here were two drunken men, becoming lost in a forgetful stupor. They were black mostly because of a distinct lack of baths. The dirt and filth was so thick, that in places, their bodies reacted with masses of pimples. They stank with a stench that grew with age. Their clothes were even blacker

123

than their bodies, and torn and tattered. They lacked the very customs that made men social. Yet, as he watched them guzzle and snort their own slobber with their beer, a feeling of pity came over the wizard. They were still men—though horribly debased and degraded. He could perceive that there was still a spiritual being there with some traces of good. Yet how could one become so criminal, so degraded? Pondering briefly, he gazed out the window off toward the central mountains.

"Any more coming?" He turned around and closely watched them.

They were getting quite drunk, however. From slurred snatches, the wizard learned that Kahill was now amassing a large army of several thousand, recalling his forces from the north and east, for an all-out drive through the profitable southern regions. He also learned of other evil things that may even surpass Kahill—up in the northern regions. Their words were so slurred he was unable to gather much more useful information from them. So he began to climb down. Too late.

Their captain was standing below and began yelling up at them. Malazar guessed they'd missed a report or so. He knew that they were too drunk to react appropriately. For sure, the captain would ask him about what was going on up there. How long could he hold his cover? Probably not long with the ferocity being displayed below him. Unfortunately, as he neared the ground, one of the drunken guards had leaned his head out and began to yell incoherently down. As he reached the bottom rung, he felt the strong clamp of a cold hand on his shoulder; he tensed instinctively.

"What in blazes is going on up there? Who are you; I don't remember seeing you on guard duty."

The wizard jumped off the rope and began yelling as if he were terribly excited about something.

"Over there, we saw them—over there! Sound alarms— charge, get them," Malazar cried, pointing to the hills and trees on the opposite side of the road from where Vorag was.

He didn't answer anything the captain said, but kept acting frantic and pointing.

"Over there, big men over there."

Quickly, the alarms sounded, echoing and piercing the

tranquil night. Hurriedly, Yacs came rushing out of their shacks, madly running about. Malazar kept pointing and yelling. Soon the Captain rushed in that direction issuing orders rapidly, and within a minute, Malazar found himself standing alone. The Yacs were swarming like soldier ants over the hills to the west. No one saw the dark form move to the east side and disappear into the forest.

Quickly, he met Vorag, changed cloaks, and swapped weapons.

"Verily, I thought thou hast met a bitter end."

"That was the only thing I could think of at the time. I guess it'll do; let's get out of here."

Quickly, yet quietly as panthers on the prowl, the two disappeared deep into the woods, later joining the other two and continuing together southward.

At daybreak, they were in the deepest areas of the forest. The air was thick and musty here. It only added to the wizard's burdens. Here they stopped; and, while Fergus and Garth went hunting, the other two made camp.

In a few minutes, the four were sitting round a campfire eating roasted rabbit. Malazar had not spoken yet of his adventure; and Vorag respected his silence. Finally, he looked around and saw Vorag with Oran lying quietly on his right leg, watching him expectantly.

"Forgive me, my friend, but I have heard such news that I have been at a loss to handle."

"Tis as I guessed."

The wizard told Vorag what he had learned of the army being readied.

"Tis evil news thee bringeth, but tis as I expecteth. An enemy doth not dwell on a victory; they chargeth forth. Burly men willst not let them pass, ere we hast all perished," Vorag said, smashing a log with his clenched fist.

"Relax my friend. I cannot permit your people to fight this Scourge alone. Isel must not be deprived of its mightiest hunters! We must have help, but there's scarcely a month to get it."

The slowly setting sun found the four men awake, refreshed, and breaking camp. The Grey One had obviously resolved something because he was once again more cheerful. Vorag, too, seemed in better spirits. Quickly, Malazar took Vorag aside and spoke hushedly and quickly.

"I am entrusting to you this charge. Return to Greagon and counsel Lord Edmund in all that we have learned. Prepare Burly for a great battle. I will go to the horsemen and the elves and seek assistance. I will return before the army drives out of the pass. Between us, the Evil Ones will encounter three armies! Farewell my friend," and he warmly clasped Vorag's arm.

In a hearty, deep voice, Vorag said, "This I shallst do; may thee goest in peace Grey One."

With this, they departed; three going south through the woods; and one solitary old man heading west toward the road.

Chapter XI—The Red and the Yellow

Daybreak found the old wizard among the trees at the edge of
the hilly forest, watching carefully the road below him. He
watched for nearly an hour and had seen no signs of the
enemy, or anyone for that matter. The Old Caravan Road was
deserted. Overhead, through breaks in the green ceiling, he
could see large, billowing, cumulus clouds easily floating along
on a cool, mid-June morning. Here he rested for another hour.
He was about fifteen leagues from the kingdom of the elves—
ten from the dark pass. The spur road to the lands of the
horsemen, the Wan Real, was fully thirty leagues further
south. The Old Caravan Road snaked its way southward,
paralleling the edge of the hills and forests of Burly.

Beyond the road rose the slowly rising, yellow-green,
grassy hills of Lanos Brillos, the northern part of Illanos. It
was a great sea of waving grass that ebbed and flowed in the
gentle breeze. The pale-green grass grew thick and nearly two
feet tall; great yellow seeds like wheat created a waving yellow
blend of color. The hills were not high but were broad; the
land would rise for nearly a mile, cresting in waving colors,
and descending as it rose. As far as Malazar could see, there
was no change in Lanos Brillos. The ground beneath the
undulating grass was made soft to the footstep by endless
seasons. There were no trees, except near the road where the
forest was encroaching slowly upon the grasslands. So the
wizard decided to travel along the road, with the forest ever on
his left, where he could vanish as the need arose.

He made very good time in this manner, and there is
little to relate of his journey; he encountered no one, except
occasional Yac scouting parties. In two days' time, he saw a
white form far in the distance; it grew tall as he neared it. Here
was the side road, the Wan Real. In olden days, the horsemen
had built a road to connect them with the rest of Isel. To
designate its beginning, they had built a horseshoe shaped
arch of white rock. As he approached closer, he could see the
white arch plainly. Under the arch was the beginning of their

road that lead to their capital city of Wancos. The arch was nearly twenty feet tall; and, everywhere, it was three feet thick. It was the only sign present. Wan Real made a startling contrast; its bed was made of laboriously crushed, white rock. The waving sea of green and yellow was sharply cut by the stripe of bright white. It had been a road of immense pride. At the arch, the lone figure paused for a while to rest and to eat. Ahead there would be no cover for many more leagues.

In the early afternoon, Malazar passed under the arch and began his trek down the Wan Real. He was a solitary figure in grey on a tiny, white strip in a vast waving sea of yellow-green. There was a difference though. The road exactly marked the breaking of the ground. To his right was Lanos Brillos, with its rolling hills; but to his left began the Lanos Vampus, which was flatter in nature. Here the hills were not as tall; hilltops were nearly five miles apart, but topography was the only difference to be seen.

At sundown, the lands of Illanos became particularly magnificent. The deep red glow cast ruddy shades on the sea of Illanos. The incredible beauty of the land did not pass Malazar; he paused a while, leaning in a bent fashion on his staff gazing at the country. The clean smell of the grass was rejuvenating to the mind and soul.

Here and there in the distance, a keen eye could detect the dark forms of the various herds that roamed virtually unmolested amid the splendor. There were herds of wild horses, deer, antelope, elk, bison, and of sheep. As the darkness came, the old one moved off the road, laid down in the soft grass, and slept as an infant in his mother's arms.

He awoke at dawn refreshed, and he watched the sunrise as he ate. All his senses were opened wide as they had the night before. He resumed his journey on the Wan Real, at peace amid the beauty around him.

Around noontime, he heard distinctly the far off sound of hoof beats. He stopped, turned around, and gazed into the distance, straining for a view of the distant black dots. He assumed that, since it were horses coming, they were the horsemen of Illanos. Since they were going his way, he relaxed and waited for them to catch up to him. Riding would make his trip all the faster and with much less effort. Within minutes, they approached him, and he could now distinguish the grey horses of Illanos. However, as they got close, they split up in a thunderous charge; and, before he could do anything, he was surrounded by the waves of horsemen.

He gasped and sucked in his breath. A wave of fear and terror, which began as a knot in his stomach, rapidly engulfed his whole body; he fought for self-control. They were not of Illanos, though the horses were. A small company of grotesque goblins surrounded him! The hideous, blue skinned, greasy, fat goblins were from the very bowls of the earth. He had last thought they were gone from Isel in the Olden Days. They had great horns protruding from their ugly heads; and their mouths were full of enormous teeth, broken and jagged. They were gruesome even to look at and stank horribly. Each carried blackish spears and equally black swords. The wizard found himself surrounded by spear points and much foul laughing and snickering. In addition to the eight, great, blue goblins, there was also a large Yac clad in a dirty, yellow and black checkered tunic. At once, the goblins began to chatter wildly in their own language, which sounded more like ugly clicking noises than words, but the largest one, also spoke the common tongue as well as the Yac. The latter spoke the first intelligible words.

"Well, what have we here, Umacka, a stranger in a strange land?" Umacka was apparently the chief goblin.

"Yah, a grey chicken, we can eat, but not much fat on 'em, Segor."

Segor, the solitary Yac, pressed his horse closer, and spoke, "Old man, if you don't want to be eaten, tell me who you are and what are you doing in our friend's land?"

Malazar nearly jumped when he heard that. "How could the men of Illanos even tolerate these vile creatures—what did he mean, friends?"

Malazar put on his old man identity and spoke in the feeblest voice possible, even dragging his words, "Eh, I can't hear you so well sonny. I'm only an old man, walking here toward Wancos. Did they say they wanted to know if I had any thing for them to eat? I don't, half-starved myself. I'm only an old man, barely able to walk sonny."

Umacka laughed and poked him, saying, "The old one can't even hear—thinks we want his food! Food he'll soon be!"

"Take pity on an old man," said Malazar dripping with sympathy and an imploring pity.

"Cool it, Umacka," barked Segor, "We'd better take him to the Emperor—that will look very good for us."

"Nay, I say eat him here. I'll not share a horse with the likes of him," protested Umacka.

Malazar knew goblins could not be touched by humanity for they seldom displayed any, even to their own kind. He was hoping to strike a buried cord of goodness that may yet remain in the tall Yac. Malazar continued his plead.

Fumbling with his food pouch he feebly said, "Do they want some food? I have some dried skunk here somewhere and some berries. Have pity on an old man."

Segor, though a chief of Yacs, still had a strain of compassion in him. He could not wantonly slay a feeble old man who couldn't even understand what was happening. He ordered the old man to climb up behind him. With jerking efforts, Malazar feebly tried to do so. The goblins grabbed him and plopped him up behind Segor, who felt mostly disgust. Swiftly the host of darkness galloped off toward Wancos, with the old man precariously hanging on to the Yac and his staff. For Malazar, it was a nightmare ride toward Wancos.

His mind was racing. What had happened in Illanos? How could the old horseman, King Alfonso Romes, ever befriend or even have such vile creatures on his land, let alone riding the fair horses of Illanos? What evil lay ahead? And what of the horrid goblins? Apparently, they had not all been destroyed ages ago. Were these the terrible creatures that the two drunken Yac guards had referred to? No. Still, things were even worse than he had imagined. Kahill's powers must have grown immensely to be able to control these fell beasts. He looked at the ugly, slimy goblins, sparsely dressed in what would pass as rags. Their hideous blue hides were thick, and only a good blow could find its mark. Their heads alone would create fear, even in the strongest of hearts. How many goblins were there?

Late at night, he was jolted back into the present by Segor, who had stopped his horse and had pushed him off, saying "We'll camp here."

The goblins lost little time in tearing up the grass, gathering up piles of dried, yesteryear's grass for a fire. Dinner was sickening to behold. The goblins produced a food sack of raw, spoiled meat and sat squatting around the fire, noisily gnawing away at human arms and legs. Malazar felt so nauseated he couldn't eat. Segor also seemed to be affected, and he stayed away by the horses until they were done and the fire nearly out. When he returned, he tied up Malazar, explaining that they didn't want their rabbit to get away. Despite his aching thighs and buttocks, made sore by the constant jolting of the wild ride, he managed to get a little sleep.

In the morning, he was thrown back up behind Segor. The nightmare ride continued much as before. Malazar estimated that they'd make Wancos by evening, for good or ill, though it would be hard to find something more ill than his current scene. The lands rolled by him with little change; it was a forever sea of grassland hills. To keep his mind off his present torment, he began to recall his last visit to the horsemen, some ten years ago.

The white Wan Real went in a straight line to the capital city of Wancos; the road lead straight to the mammoth wooden gates. The city was surrounded by a high, white, stone wall—a dike with giant, white, horseshoe-shaped arches and gates that corresponded to the cardinal directions. The dike was five feet tall; the blocks were three feet thick; and it encompassed some sixteen square miles of Wancos. The city itself was built on a hilltop and was dominated by the great Citadel Dias, which served as a combination of meeting place for the riders of Illanos, a fortress, and the imperial palace for the Lord of Illanos. It was a towering, angular, block building, entirely made of white stone slabs. The stone came from quarries, which were located by the seacoast. It made a truly magnificent sight—to ride over the sea of waving grass and gaze over the hilltop toward the brilliant city.

Nestled snugly around Citadel Dias were a large

number of small, stone houses in which many of the
inhabitants dwelled. Just beyond the smaller homes,
grasslands flowed to the dikes. Here the fabled horses of
Illanos were kept, ever ready. They were usually grey and had
a strong, sound conformation that provided both speed and
strength. In the days of the Great Ones, the Cavalry of Illanos
was held in awe throughout all of Isel.

Malazar recalled that the horsemen were led by Lord
Alfonso Romes, an elderly, noble warrior, both brave and bold.
As he remembered him, he was old, yet, nevertheless, still had
the integrity of youth, if not the vitality. He, gracefully, and
with noble honor, ruled the riders of Illanos with the
assistance of his children. Three, as Malazar recalled; Hector
the eldest, Hildaro, and Felipe the youngest. Ah fair Felipe, he
remembered, was quite a beautiful young girl of thirteen when
he last saw her; quite promising indeed. Virtually all the
people of Illanos were fair skinned, blonde, and exceptionally
beautiful. He and Hildaro had become good friends, and
Hildaro never seemed to tire of telling him of the legends of
the horsemen. Malazar thought he was rather a romantic.
Hector was always very aggressive, and Malazar had spent
very little time with him. He wondered how such a noble
family could have taken such evil allies, if the goblins spoke
truthfully.

It was late afternoon as they came galloping, pounding
to the top of another long, low hill, horses sweating heavily.
When they reached the top, the group was blinded by the
bright, unexpected flash of light from the city of Wancos
ahead. The horses broke stride; and the goblin riders, who
hated light anyway, nearly fell off, cursing and swearing
constantly. Segor covered his eyes and had the least reaction.
They spent a few seconds recovering from the shock and rode
onward.

Down the hill, they charged straight toward the eastern
arch and gate in the dike, as welcoming horns sounded from
the bastions in the wall. Malazar's spirits sank even further,
and they galloped under the ancient arch and headed for the
Citadel Dias. Then, through the big gates of the palace and into
the Chamber of Meetings, they clamored. The meeting hall

was huge, for horsemen always counciled with their steeds, a tradition dating from the old days. Once inside, they halted abruptly; and stable boys ran to hold the lathered, panting horses. The group dismounted.

Umacka said gruffly, "We come to see the Emperor now."

Segor added, "Tell him we bring a trespasser for his amusement."

Immediately, one of the guards rushed off; and the group went to the watering trough and slobbered water over their bodies and faces, grunting and making other foul noises that echoed, magnified in the large, tall ceiling chamber, lit by a multitude of torches.

The meeting chamber, Malazar observed, was now dirty and decaying. It had once been the place of honor where the proud and free horsemen gathered. Even ten years ago, it was sparkling clean and filled one with awe, a sense of responsibility, but now it had been allowed to deteriorate. "Things must have gone ill here," thought the wizard.

Presently, the royal entourage entered; the new king strode in, dressed in the plush apparel that Alfonso used to wear.

"Hail to thee, Umacka, Chief of the Goblins and to thee Segor, Captain of the Imperial Men; welcome to the Horse Hall."

As the young king stepped forward to shake hands, Malazar hid as much of his face as he could, leaned heavily on his staff, and carefully examined the reigning ruler. It was Hector! Malazar began to think uncontrollably, "What happened to Alfonso? Probably died. Why does Hector defile his past heritage? He was an ambitious youth. Best I better not be recognized."

Suddenly, Malazar heard Segor above the background of discussion, "And my Liege, we have captured a spy, a traitor, on thy lands. Truly, he was heading here, for some evil purpose against thee, my noble Horse Lord."

With that, gruff, blue hands, sparing no courtesy, threw Malazar across the floor at Hector's feet.

"Arise traitor and state your name before the Lord of

these Lands and your purpose for coming here."

There was a note of curiosity imbedded in the angry tone. The wizard, acting old and feeble, struggled to his feet hanging onto his staff as if he expected to fall over at any moment.

"Please, your lordship, have pity on an old man. I'm no spy, just an old man. I came walking through your lands to see the fabled horsemen once before I pass away. Have pity on one so decrepit."

"He lies," screamed Umacka, lunging forward, "Let us eat him."

Hector waved him off saying, "I have no time to root the truth out of this one now. Throw him in the dungeons. Maybe he'll come around to reason. For your service, my friend, I thank you. It is yet another example of the good faith between our peoples. Now, Umacka and Segor, come into my chambers; we have much to discuss on our services. Guards, throw this spy into the dungeons. Come on."

Hector led the two off through a set of doors deeper into the Citadel Dias, while a pair of strong arms fairly lifted the old one off his feet and dragged him off down the corridor to the dungeon.

As they rounded a corner and were out of hearing of the rest, Malazar threw himself free, straightened up, and began walking on his own, saying gruffly, "I can walk."

He recognized his guard; it was Philippe, a tall man, who still had his same job, he remembered. Years ago, it was a post of honor among the horsemen—guard of the Lord of Illanos. Malazar picked up the man's sadness; for once out of sight of the main chamber, he too had changed. His arms had gone limp.

"Forgive me, ancient one; I do this to you most unwillingly. In other times, the revered Lord wouldn't have treated one so crudely. But times have changed; we now have a tyrant. I'll do what I can in the court for you. Anyone can see you have done no deed against us."

"Thank you," came the reply, "Yes, I see times have changed."

Philippe was startled at this and looked long at the old

one. Malazar could not discern whether he was recognized or not.

They were now descending a long stairs into the depths of the Citadel. Far underground were the dungeons, seldom used of old. Now, however, they had become more popular with Hector's rule. Shortly, Philippe came upon the jailer and briefly told him what had happened. Malazar immediately recognized Fernando even in the failing light of the depths. He was an old man now himself and, under Alfonso, used to be the Lord Rider's private guard, and, often times, councilor. Apparently, he had been removed. To become a jailer was obviously a serious disgrace for one so noble and trustworthy. He also recognized Malazar immediately; his eyes sparkled with knowingness; yet he said nothing, merely ushered him to an isolated cell over in one corner.

Fernando whispered to Malazar as he locked the door, "I'll be back shortly."

Heavy clanking sounds followed and then receding footsteps and then an oppressive silence and darkness.

Now, Malazar knew he could leave at once; no door could long bar his way, but he needed data, and Fernando may be able to help him; so the wizard contented himself by creating a dull green glow atop his staff, propped it up in a corner, and paced back and forth, reflecting on the events of the recent past.

He didn't have to wait long; shortly Fernando returned and bought him some food and drink. Together they shook hands and exchanged welcomes. The noble horseman apologized for the treatment he'd received; but Malazar, detecting the degradation, did not let him dwell on it.

"Truly Fernando, this situation is an affront to you; Alfonso would never have tolerated it, but come, you must tell me what has happened to Illanos; such evil is terrible."

Fernando sighed, as one under a great burden of torment, and began to tell the tale of woe.

"It began eight years ago. The Honored Lord had gone hunting the wild bison; alas, his age could no longer endure such trials; and he fell from Sirloin, his fiery steed. He had broken his neck and died. Bless his soul. May he rest in peace.

For days, even Sirloin hung his head in mourning. Hector, at once, took over the rule, being the first-born son. We did not disagree. From the beginning, he had a wild uncontrollable streak in him; and, when he got ill of temper, even I could not handle him. Things grew slowly worse. He fought long with Hildaro and Felipe. Then, the Evil Ones from the desert began raiding on our eastern borders. Hector himself rode in answer to the challenge. He returned changed. My own guess is that he saw such things that made him greatly afraid, though he has ever been loath to speak of it."

"Shortly thereafter, he began to speak of the good in the desert ones. Until at last, he brought some of their filthy lot to Wancos. Two years ago, there was a council here with some dozen of the Yacs and an equal of the filthy ones. My protests proved too harsh, and I was retired to my job here in disgrace, but an even worse disgrace has befallen the riders of Illanos. For now, we are the allies of the horrid ones. Even today, they are arranging a horse trade; I have learned Hector intends to trade a thousand Illanos steeds to the foul ones. May the gods forgive such an ill fate for the honored horsemen! Here in the city of the revered Obelos Yllos of Bernardo, our founder, tis evil times that we disgrace both him and ourselves. Yet to Hector's might, none in Wancos dare to challenge openly; his anger is deadly. There are a few of us that still honor the true of Illanos."

"You mean there is none that are against him? That is bad indeed, but what of Hildaro and Felipe? They were not like Hector at all; they could not tolerate such desecration of Illanos honor!" Malazar asked searchingly.

A light appeared in the sullen, downcast, old man's face. He brightened up considerably and said warmly, "They are the hope of Illanos still, but we must talk in whispers of this. Hildaro is much like his father, and, by the legends, of even Bernardo the Great. He saw that he could do nothing in Wancos to handle Hector, so he moved to Uvalde, our port. There he has raised an army of revolt. Many of our people have, in secret, gone there to be free and help. You have seen the Red of Hector; yet our hope does ever go to the Yellow of Hildaro. Although he never talks of revolution, many of us expect a civil war to begin. Few like Hector; he rules by power alone. Daily the Yellow become stronger. I sense Hector sees this, and I fear he may be even today bargaining horses for an army of Evil Ones to come and put an end to the Yellow. Of this, I'm mortally afraid. Hildaro represents the last stand of the horsemen to regain their honor."

"Now Felipe has become a beautiful woman, like her mother; but she too is at war with Hector. She has become a spy as I. Hector is envious of her beauty and still permits her to live in Dias. She uses this as a cover to pry out the plans of the Red."

But the old man could tell no more, because they heard soft footsteps coming their way. Malazar quickly extinguished his green glow. They waited.

Soon they heard a whispered voice, "Fernando, where are you? It is me."

Fernando at once got up and ushered her inside; Malazar again caused his staff to glow. In the green glow, he saw a grey-cloaked form that endeavored to look beggarly, but Malazar saw the beauty within at once.

"Felipe," he said and warmly rushed over and hugged her; and, after a moment, she looked up; tears were in her eyes.

"You have come, noble one. I'm so grateful." She held him tight for some time.

Then, he bade her sit and holding her hands comforted her, "There is yet hope my dear, while the faith and honor of Bernardo still lies in the hearts of Illanos."

She took courage in his words and relaxed. "I heard that an old man had been captured while coming here. I didn't know it was you, but I had to find out. Does Hector know it's you?"

"No, I have not revealed myself to him. I thought better of it at the time. It proved a wise council."

"Hildaro must know of this at once. He'll want to see you and may come here even."

"No, I think that is not best. There's much evil about," said the wizard. "I'll go to him, for I have learned all that I can here. Let us go."

Malazar was surprised to see the efficient spy network the two had erected. Within ten minutes, everything was arranged. In three hours, it would be dark, and the best time to leave in secret.

Felipe explained that Hildaro was something of a wizard himself, for he had known, somehow, of all the secret passageways through the citadel and town. When their need arose, he had shown the two how to get around Wancos unseen. The hidden ways were long unused and had a heavy layer of dust in them. Hildaro never spoke of how he came to know of their existence. If Malazar had guessed, he spoke no word.

Just after dark, three forms crept through the hidden ways of Dias and with an amazing efficiency. Soon, there were three cloaked riders leaving Wancos, riding over the dark sea of grass with only the rushing noise of horse legs against the grass, breaking the still night sounds.

Uvalde, their port city, lay two days ride to the west. The three rode hard and fast, pushing their steeds to their limit, pausing only when it was necessary. They spoke little on the journey, but two were filled with newfound hope.

Late the next afternoon, they rode to the top of one of the endless hills, and quickly reigned in. A panorama of exquisite beauty stretched before them. The waving sea of green ended abruptly with huge white cliffs, and a blue sea of water stretched as far as the eye could see. Amid this rose the city of Uvalde, patterned much like Wancos and built of white stone blocks. It was built in three tiers, the bluff, the cliff side, and the beach. Surrounding Uvalde in a great semi-circle was a white dike similar to that of Wancos.

As they rode up, six horsemen, dressed in bright yellow tunics, rode out to meet them. They were carrying the axillones of Illanos. The axillone was a long spear with an axe blade about six inches from the point. The brightly colored weapons were held forward and upward, blade slicing the air before the galloping riders. In front of their chests were the familiar multi-colored rectangular shields with yellows predominating.

This was the welcome that Malazar was familiar with

one symbolizing strength, valor, and honor. The three waited, and soon the enthusiastic young horsemen had quickly pulled up in front of them. Their faces were fair to look upon and all carried the smiles of welcome.

Felipe threw off her dark cloak, revealing the noble woman she was, and proudly spoke, "Here we welcome to Illanos the great Grey One, Malazar of Old. Let the hills resound with the sounds of honor and welcome fitting to so great a guest of the horsemen!"

The leader of the guards signaled with his axillone, and the hills were filled with great blasts of the Illanos' horns of welcome. As the echoes passed away, they rode through the solitary arch into Uvalde, the port of Illanos.

They quickly rode through the streets and slowly descended the great switchbacks that led down the cliffs to the lower tier. The city was overflowing with people, many who had fled Wancos. He learned that the population of Uvalde was growing daily. All about them people were waving and cheering. There was life and vitality here in the last stronghold of the riders.

Within minutes, they halted in front of a large, white building, little different from the others. Here Hildaro and Felipe had established their home in exile.

As they dismounted, Hildaro came to the doorway; he paused and stared; then, he cried, "Malazar, it's you. We are indeed blessed! Come in! Come in! The Horsemen are truly honored this day." They embraced as old friends and cheerfully entered the Romes villa by the sea.

Hildaro Romes was young and stood tall. He was fair of skin and had short yellow hair. His frame was not that of a fighter, but more that of an artist. What his home lacked in grandeur of Dias, it more than made up in aesthetic qualities. The west side had large balconies that overlooked the sea. You could stand on the white ledge and watch the sea pounding on the beach below. Or you could go downstairs and rest your feet in the soft wet sand.

For some time, the weary travelers bathed in the clean waters and ate heartily of the vast array of fresh seafood. At last refreshed in mind and body, the four gathered around a table on the balcony, and Malazar was brought fully up to date with the events of Illanos. Malazar asked for a moment of silence in honor of the late Alfonso. Then, Hildaro began once more.

"Malazar, our current state is perilous, hanging on the thread of a grass spider. I have long expected Hector had been plotting to remove all traces of rebellion against his will. We are called the Yellow Ones; he, the Red. Though I have never spoken of a rebellion, the loyal riders are ever talking of it. My heart desires no such fight. Never has a horseman of Illanos raised a weapon against another rider of Illanos, but the people are becoming more desperate. Soon I may no longer be able to restrain them, even though I have been elected their leader and spokesman. Even now, they are gathering their crossbows and axillones. If war it becomes, I'll be powerless to prevent it. Yet something must be done and soon."

"Yes," said Malazar, "I fear very soon, perhaps before the day is ended. Fernando and I heard of the current plans. The goblins and Yacs are here to arrange a horse trade. Though we didn't hear what Hector was to gain, I feel it can only be the use of an army of the Scourge. Against both combined, Uvalde will be in dire trouble. We must act at once."

"Truly," Hildaro sighed. "It can't be avoided further, but I was prepared for this." He looked at each one squarely and stood up and said, "I have a truth to tell you that I have not yet revealed, even to my honored sister." They all looked at him; she in awe and wonder, for he seemed to grow taller and stronger somehow.

"For good or ill, I, Hildaro Romes, have entered our father's tower, Obelos Yllos. There I learned of the secret ways of the Citadel and of many other things. I have brought the golden saber and axillone of our wizard, Bernardo, to use them to regain the honor and trust that the riders have lost."

Felipe and Fernando were aghast— mouths open in wonder, as Hildaro produced the ancient weapons from their hiding place in a cabinet.

"Here is the golden saber, Conzone, and the silver axillone of Bernardo, the Great Wizard." They shone brightly in the sun. "Once more, they will be used to bring honor to Illanos."

Then, he retrieved a package from behind a chair in the corner. It was wrapped in a tattered old cloak. He unwrapped it, and standing with his side to the setting sun, revealed the Shield of Bernardo. As the cover came off, a brilliant flash of golden red filled the room, nearly blinding them. The ancient wizard's shield was gilded and covered with jewels. Though it remained light in weight, no sword or lance had ever pierced it nor even marred its brazen, glowing surface.

As Hildaro held the shield aloft, he appeared to their eyes as one transformed into the mightiest of riders.

Fernando fell on his knees saying, "Truly, my Lord, we shall regain that which has been lost." And he wept for joy.

Felipe was breathless, her nerves tingling with sheer joy. She wanted to scream from happiness, yet restrained herself.

Malazar merely cocked his head sideways, eyeing Hildaro closely and said, "Very well done, Lord of Illanos."

Then, amid a barrage of questions, Hildaro returned them to their hiding places. Felipe and Fernando talked excitedly with Hildaro for some time, getting him to tell them of the obelos. Of what they learned from him, here will be mentioned only that its doors opened to the soft sound of his horn.

After the excitement and joy of his revealment had subsided, they returned to the discussion of what was to be done. Here Malazar proved a wise council.

"Neither of us desires to charge, army to army. There yet may be another way." He paused thoughtfully. Then, he spoke, breaking the silence, "It may yet by possible. If we can get those within Wancos onto our side, then there will be no army to battle."

"Yes, but how do we do that," implored Fernando, "I do know many that are in secret on the side of the Yellow, but still Hector does have support from the Red."

"True, true, but perhaps the Red may yet become Yellow."

"Let us make use of Hildaro's gifts. Let it be known far

141

and wide that not only are the true horsemen of Illanos riding to retake their capital city and honor, but also that the armor of the Great Wizard will lead the charge, as if in a second coming of the wizard. If we make a great importance out of this, a great tide will flow our way. Still, one more deed can be done, if your sister has the heart to do. If she may, she can lead me back into Wancos. There we can spread the word that the horsemen of Illanos are coming to regain all, and tell the tales of the mighty armor of old arisen anew. This may just leave Hector standing alone."

"You know my heart," Felipe said, "I will gladly lead you. Also, if the evil ones are yet there, you have a score to settle, am I not correct?"

The old wizard had a wry smile on his face, "Yes I certainly do! It will be my pleasure."

Thus, the Ride of Resurrection, as it was thereafter called, was established. Malazar and Felipe left at once; Hildaro was to follow in twenty-four hours. The army would appear in two days at Wancos. As they left on horseback, the two began to hear wild yelling and cheering, as the people of Uvalde heard of the incredible news that their great wizard's armor was to lead the resurrection of Illanos.

Malazar had guessed right, and Felipe did her job well. Within hours of their return to Wancos, they heard hushed whispers all over the city. Malazar grew very confident. Nevertheless, they remained within the shadows of Wancos.

The next day, she led the wizard through the hidden ways to Hector's chambers. Then, he asked her to go to the tallest balcony in the citadel and to watch the spectacle. She willingly did so. When he was alone he began his final actions. Hector was still entertaining his guests; he chuckled to himself when he saw the ugly, blue faces.

Umacka and Segor were with Hector in his private study and were bickering over a map, when, to their amazement, the secret wall moved open and out stepped the familiar old man. The door shut behind him. There were grunts and cries, but Malazar ignored them. He raised his staff, and it burst into a red flame.

"Hear yea, traitor of the Horsemen. The day of

142

reckoning has come to thee."

The two Evil Ones shrank back under the flame. Hector cowered and screamed for his guards. None came.

"Hector, to evil you have sunk and nearly destroyed Illanos. Today the Ride of Resurrection comes."

Suddenly, distant hills began echoing the horn blasts of the army. The sound was utterly deafening, and the two fled the room.

"Come with me to see thy doom!" He led a trembling Hector onto the balcony. It was an incredible sight! The hills surrounding Wancos were entirely covered with the riders of Yellow. Before the western gate sat Hildaro on his steed. From his shield came the blast of fiery yellow flame that only the wizard's shield could generate. The flash nearly blinded onlooker's eyes. Few dared to confront Hildaro directly. It was as if Bernardo the Great had arisen from the dead. Now, echoing horn blasts arose from the city; and great crowds emerged through the open gates and swarmed into the hills to join them. Next to Hildaro rode Fernando, who had proudly regained his honored place. No one spoke or moved. Hector began to scream and writhe in utter terror.

Then, Malazar raised his staff high into the air, and caused a great ball of golden flame to flash blinding all. Everywhere people stood motionless. There came, as if in answer, a flash of gold from the shield of Hildaro. Slowly, Hildaro and Fernando rode amid the people through the gates and into the citadel.

Shortly he appeared beside Hector and Malazar, high on the balcony. Felipe, who had been watching, joined them. Then Malazar spoke in a commanding voice of which few even knew he was capable.

"Today the horsemen of Illanos have retrieved their honor; the Ride of Resurrection has succeeded. You are a free people once more and by your own hand. I, Malazar, do ask you to welcome and honor your leader and Lord, the holder of Bernardo's armor—Hildaro Romes."

Then, there came wild shouting and cheering, and everywhere great horn blasts echoed through the hills. Before anyone could decide what to do with him, Hector, in his terror or madness, leaped from the balcony to his death.

Hildaro's only comment to Felipe was, "I only wish that would make amends, but alas that is not the answer." She understood, and glanced at Malazar, but the wizard had disappeared.

He had gone after the Evil Ones. They had tried to escape. However, they had not been permitted to leave the building. Malazar found them running through the dungeons searching for a hidden way out and to escape from the blinding light above.

"So you dared to play with a wizard did you—an old man to torment?"

The Yac was terrified and was shaking uncontrollably, but the goblins felt enraged, and the six charged the wizard. A great blast of flames was followed by hideous screams of pain, and the goblins were no more. The Yac fell on the ground screaming and yelling in violent fear. Malazar looked at him and felt compassion for a soul so tormented.

He gently laid his hand on his shaking shoulders and said softly, "It's ok; no harm will befall you."

Slowly, the violent trembling subsided, and Malazar helped him into a cell. The Yac welcomed it and, with eyes full of awe, fear, and wonder, gazed up at the old man. Then, Malazar returned to the others, telling them that the goblins were no more, but the Yac had been spared and that no harm should come to him—if he behaved.

Then, Malazar ushered Hildaro into the Meeting Chamber. He bade him sit on the lord's regal seat, and the joyous people rode and walked into the room. They beheld their rightful Lord seated with the fire of their ancient ones at his feet. Beside him, his fair sister stood proudly and, on his right, stood old Fernando, as he had done for his father. The Meeting Chamber was packed, and others strained to get in to see as well. It was a great day of celebration throughout Illanos.

They had much to do in the ensuing days, but the citadel was purged of its blackness and stains by a newfound jubilation. Great feasts were held for seven days straight. Finally, Malazar and Hildaro held a private conference when order had been brought to Wancos once more.

The wizard told him of the plight of Isel and of the coming army and Burly's need. Hildaro agreed and insisted that the riders join in the defense of Isel. It would take a few weeks to get all in readiness; so Hildaro suggested that by the second week of July, the Riders of Illanos would appear near Kyder Pass to join the Burly men. He himself would lead them forth.

That evening, he made a speech to all, telling of the peril that lay on their border. They were unanimously behind Hildaro. He was to leave his sister, Felipe, temporarily in charge during his absence. The next morning, Malazar departed with many farewells. He rode off down Wan Real on a grey steed given to him as a token of their unending friendship. For him, it meant a less toilsome journey. Besides, time was running out. He had to gather sufficient armies to stop the Evil Ones.

Chapter XII—The Splendor of Eldamar

Malazar rode hard for several hours eastward along the Wan Real. Then, he slowed his horse to a walk. The rapidly greying sky seemed to grow closer to the ocean of green, pierced by the striking, white path before him. Soon the eerie colors darkened; and lightning flashed from cloud to cloud, while amid the endless hills, a lone rider on a grey bent forward for protection from the rains. He turned the grey to the left, and headed due northeast, while all around him the glistening grass flowed in random circles around the horse's feet. The rains pelted down, driven hard by the easterly winds; the grey's tail hung dripping between her hind legs. He continued onward and marveled at the beauty of the wet land. Within an hour, the rains ceased; and the clouds parted leaving everything drenched.

However, the Grey One didn't stop or falter in his direction, even though there were no landmarks to guide him. He traveled with only a few stops for the next two days. By the end of the second day, a dark mass appeared on the horizon and steadily grew in size. Soon, he could see the tall mountains of Quara Sud; and he made straight toward the two immense cliffs that formed Kyder Pass. Finally, tired and saddle weary, he reached the Old Caravan Road, having cut at least two days off his journey's time. Though he was now around ten leagues from the pass proper, he detected no signs of the enemy. He continued on the road. Soon, he came to an unmarked junction, where another joined the Old Caravan Road. It was in decay—overgrown here and there by bushes and grass. However, it was a road. In days gone by, it had had better care. Slowly, the wizard urged his mare to the left onto Valmar Bypass, the road to the elves. More properly, though, Valmar, built ages ago by the elves, ran northward on the east edge of their lands separating Eldamar from the rugged Quara Wund Mountains and eventually joining other northern roads at the western edge of Isel by Chooe Pass, the northwest entrance to the desert region.

Here and there, he found signs of abandoned campfires, but no recent traces could be discerned. He continued along Valmar until late at night. Clouds had formed and blocked the waning moon; travel would be difficult on the abandoned road, so he took shelter under the leaves of a large fir tree, but he dared not sleep soundly and spent a restless, weary night. At dawn, he continued his way and soon heard the roar of waterfalls some distance ahead of him. He quickened his pace, and shortly he trotted into an open dale and reigned in the mare.

Before him were the rapids and the beginnings of the great river, Cuero, which separated the horsemen from Eldamar, the lands of the elves. On the south side of the valley were a number of large fir and spruce trees. which gradually turned to aspens by the water's edge. These white barked trees grew on either side of the river, but on the north side, they yielded to a heavy dark forest of deciduous trees set very close together. A man on horseback would find it almost impossible to ride through the close trees. Even on foot, the going would be strenuous and dark.

He stopped his horse mid-stream, and dismounted. While the grey drank her fill, he filled his water pouch and, then, slowly led the mare to the other side. As he bent over, he felt as if eyes were upon him, but when he looked, there was nothing to be seen. He mounted, and he gazed eastward at the towering jagged peaks of Quara Wund. Silently, he counted the peaks; then, he slowly rode onwards keeping watch on all sides and counting the peaks as he passed them. They were roughly ten leagues from him; and, since the elves had no road directly to any of their cities, he could only find them by careful directions. He was heading for the largest elfin city, Silvere; at the sixty-ninth peak, he would turn and ride straight west.

From time to time, that strange feeling of being watched came over him. He looked rapidly around at first, then very coyly, but he saw nothing amiss. Birds were noisily going about their lives ignoring him. Occasionally squirrels chattered as he passed their trees. A deer broke and ran in front of him. Nothing seemed out of place. Nevertheless, he continually strained his senses and kept the mare going northwards. After dusk, he stopped and made a small camp. It would be no use trying to cover more miles that night, since the sky was completely overcast. Besides, he was very weary. He was now deep within the area of elves and had not seen a trace of the scavengers since crossing the Cuero River. A fire he now permitted himself; and, quickly, he relaxed and fell into a deep, long needed sleep.

It proved to be a strange sleep. For hours, he felt he heard singing from soft, gentle, high-pitched voices. The elves, he sensed. During the night, the clouds parted, and he rose at dawn. As he rubbed off the effects of the night, he scouted around, but to his dismay, did not find any signs of visitors. He ate quickly, mounted, and continued his northerly ride.

To his right the craggy mountains varied little, rising tall jagged and ominous; he continued his count. On his left, there was also little change. The large oak and maple trees grew large and very dense. A few feet inside the forest, the light failed, and it was ominous and forbidding, but in a much more gentler fashion than the peaks. All that day, the orange granite continued to rise ever upwards like spires to the sky. The only thing that seemed to change much was the feeling of being watched; it continued to grow. Malazar noted that it was more of a merely being noticed feeling than one of eminent danger. The feeling had a rather comfortable and friendly aspect to it. Finally, the sixty-ninth peak was at his right. The late afternoon sun had turned the granite into a mass of glowing orange lines. The forest was too dark to travel at night, even for a wizard. Again, he made camp and spent the night, which passed, as had the previous one, except the music was irresistibly strong and beautiful.

After a meager breakfast, he put a halter on the mare. He could not ride through these woods. Actually, it was a trick to lead a horse through the dense tangled woods. Briars, thickets of wild berries struggled for the bare land between the giant trees. Everywhere vines grew skyward blocking the easier paths. Malazar made his way very slowly, twisting and turning and ducking the undergrowth. He doggedly kept at it and indeed made surprisingly good headway. Soon, he felt encouraged; ahead the darkness was diminishing; the forest was opening up. Just as his spirits began to rise, he heard soft singing all around him—a chorus of soft voices singing in a tongue that seemed to be of the forest itself. He stopped and listened.

Soon, there came a loud "Hail Cidithir. Elf friend. Hail to thee!"

Ahead of him, clad in a forest-green cloak, stood a young elf. Malazar stared at him for a moment and in recognition said questioningly "Aubrey?"

"Yes, that's me," came the reply.

Malazar rushed forward, held his right hand up, palm forward, and met the elf's hand. Palms touching, they made the familiar gestures of meeting—elf fashion.

"We would be honored if you would join us at our fire circle," Aubrey said.

Malazar agreed; he knew much of the ways of the elves. This had to be done, willingly or not. No one entered Eldamar without their consent, man or beast.

As they walked through the ever-widening forest, Malazar asked his friend, "I heard singing the last two nights. Do you know of it?"

Aubrey's eyes twinkled; his face beamed and grinned widely. "Yes, we sang of our love of the forest and animals and of our friendship for you. We stood guard over you. But, by our Master's orders, elves are not allowed to greet anyone on the road, but only those who enter the forest of Viniere—only those who enter Eldamar. My scouts first found you down by the Cuero and have followed you hence. Ah, here we are. Come have a seat and let us talk."

Aubrey had brought his guest into a small clearing; the yellow of the forest floor was broken by deep shadows from the tall wide trees. Amid the tufts of grass and greenish moss, the elves had arranged a large circle of weather worn, granite stones of a sharp orangish hue. In the center lay the blackened remains of campfires; a small stack of firewood lay neatly nearby. The elf motioned the wizard to the largest seat, while another elf led his mare to graze just beyond the ring. Quickly, the seats were filled; and Malazar found he had an interested audience.

Elfin bodies seldom reach the stature of men; the wizard was well over a foot taller than Aubrey was. They had small, thin bodies with a pale green skin tone that contrasted with their black or yellow hair. Elves had no facial hair. Their lightweight frames were built for incredible endurance; and, when an elf walked, he could not be heard. They seemed to float on the leaves of the forest lawn, barely bending the soft leaves. Once Malazar had seen an elf crossing a snowfield and was intrigued by the almost imperceptible foot tracks. Elfin senses seemed to be greatly enhanced.

He had learned much about elves from his close friend Elwine, who was easily able to distinguish exact form and identity of things at least twenty miles away. Elwine was not exactly sure how far he could "see" but it was a distance. In the woods of Eldamar, a crack of a twig could be discerned for miles—the maker known at once to these elves. As he sat, he became aware of the multiplicity of fragrances of the forest, aromatic scents flowing together, yet distinct. Pine, oak, ash, jasmine, decaying leaves, dewy moss, all were incredibly sharp in a collage of marvelous smells. He wondered if it was just the Viniere Woods or if his own sense of smell had grown.

Their voices were high pitched, but mellow, and always had musical quality about them. When they spoke in their own tongue, though their words would be foreign, a listener would become entranced by the sounds into a sheer aesthetic ecstasy ; and a feeling, sensing, understanding, would ebb and flow through his very beingness. Their singing, which they were extremely fond of doing, would transport one to incredible heights of insatiable delight.

Even to gaze upon their bodies filled one with awe and admiration of the sense of perfection they exuded. To confront their faces would be sufficient to dumbfound the naive. About their forehead was a clear, white light—a brightness formed as if from uniformly spaced, giant diamonds, forever sparkling. At night, the sight of a elf would astound even the hardiest of souls. Truly, here was a race of gods or near gods in the woodland paradise of Eldamar.

Malazar had noted that the size or amount of light varied from elf to elf. It seemed to be related to the power and ability of the being. Master Mandell and Mistress Celina, the elfin Lord and Lady, seemed to be the brightest he had seen, though their children, Elwine, Aubrey, Lana, and Ellena, were very similar to their parents. Their sparkling radiance greatly exceeded that of the other elves, but in all, there was a supreme vitality of life.

Aubrey began the conference, "Welcome Cidithir, elf friend. May the blessing of the Varina be ever on you."

Then, as was the elfish custom, he began to chant in the elfish tongue; and a musical air filled the glen. Malazar listened with supreme pleasure, his mind echoed with snatches of pictures of far off Varina, the fatherland of the elves, of the beauty and splendor of days no longer seen in Isel, and of the enchantments of Eldamar. He reflected on his elf name, Cidithir, given to him years ago by Master Mandell. To be called elf friend was indeed a treasured honor; for, in all these years, it had been given to a select few: several Mariners, several wanderers from Ocalla, and Malazar.

When Aubrey was done some ten minutes later, Malazar stood, bowed low, and said, "Thank you Aubrey, Prince among elves. I have come to see the Lord himself on a quest most urgent; haste is needed."

He saw that his sense of urgency didn't communicate to the timeless ones; he saw it was useless to try to get Aubrey to see his view, so he asked, "And where is my elf brother, my dearest friend, Prince Elwine?"

Malazar had inadvertently touched a troubled sore, for the glow faded from his face at once.

"Oh Cidithir, the times are bad; nay, decaying some say. Elwine has become a renegade. Against all of our begging and pleading, he chose to journey—to travel to other lands. He, alone of the elves, has been the first ever to leave Eldamar against the orders of Ancient Balmir, who long ago sealed our borders. Elwine has caused a deep hurt with our father and mother."

"Wisdom lies in many places and comes in many forms. Pray, do not lose all hope for Elwine, for he, as you, is great, and yet wise," Malazar solemnly suggested.

"You speak, even as I had dared think of it. I truly hope

this be true. I, we, deeply treasure our brother." He paused briefly, and then resumed, "He has been gone now nearly two of your years, though daily we mourn of his loss. Yet, if his words were true, his arrival should be soon now. When he left, he bid me watch and guard our family; and he told me that he would return in two great seasons—two of your years. Because the time is near, I have kept close watch for him; but yet no sign have I seen." He paused uncomfortably.

The wizard discerned this and said, "Yet there is more, is there not Aubrey?"

"Yes, it is as though I can feel his presence, growing closer. I can't see or hear him; but daily the feeling of Elwine's presence grows in my heart. I can't be sure of it; maybe it's my own desire to see him return."

"Ah my friend, never doubt your own perception or make less of it. Trust yourself, as I do. I will await his expected return as well."

"Thank you, Cidithir. You are indeed well named, elf friend." He brightened up considerably. "Come, let us journey to Silvere and speak with the Master of Elves and his Lady."

With that, the welcome council adjourned. Aubrey and two others were to accompany the wizard through the forest of Viniere to the largest city of the elves.

Together, they began to walk the unmarked paths of the woods. The yellow afternoon sun filtered through the tall trees, casting elusive shadows on the soft bed beneath their feet. The elves were full of song, and the air was filled with a multitude of fragrances. As they walked, the wizard felt surges of ecstasy flowing through his entire beingness.

The path was exceedingly winding; it never seemed to go in a straight line, as Malazar would have wished. The elves were seldom in a hurry and loved to walk in Eldamar. Thus, their ways were made nearly double in length by the many twists and turns. Yet, they did make forward progress, even if it was exceedingly slow to Malazar.

Time was, for the Elves, like the passing of water down a stream, endless. Aubrey was in his early manhood and, as nearly as he could tell, was approaching his hundredth year. Malazar had guessed that Mandell and Celina were more like six thousand years old; and Elohir, the ancient one, nearly ten. Elohir was the only elf that still lived who had come to Isel and Eldamar at the time of the Great Wizard's Creation. Thus, the elves had a very different viewpoint on time.

For them, a full year's passing was a small importance, being as a ripple on the sea. Though they marked the seasons in their songs, they seldom heeded them. The climate of Eldamar was forever balmy—never hot nor exceedingly cold. To hurry meant to them, something must be done within some ten years; extreme haste, maybe a year. They celebrated the coming and departing of the animals of the forest; the life span of the trees they sung of often in songs. The shifting seashore, the lowering of hills, and the erosion of the mountains were real to them and spoken of often. He felt the beautiful sadness of the isolation of the elves from other peoples. The life of a horseman was a bare fleeting moment to them. Their loneliness was immeasurable, bordering upon unreality.

In two days, they at last came upon the biggest city of the elves, Silvere, where Master Mandell and the Lady Celina dwelt, amid the ancient silver trees, the Dionti. As the small party neared the city, the forest began to change ever so gracefully. At first scattered here and there a lone Dionti grew in sharp contrast with the oaks, yet blending as if it belonged. The Dionti had been brought from Varina across the sea by the first elves to settle in Isel. Haldir of old had carried the golden seeds with him, and they had grown, multiplied, and now covered a wide area around Silvere. The Dionti trees had a smooth, soft bark that had a shiny, silver hue. As the sun shone on them, they sparkled and created ever-changing patterns of light. Their leaves were large and forever green. Every five of the Isel years, the trees produced large, yellow blossoms, filling the city with a nectar unsurpassed. Then, they produced golden seeds, which the elves guarded closely and planted in select places, but it was by moonlight that the Dionti were supreme. Shimmering shades of silver hues glancing here and there transformed the forest and town into an aesthetic paradise of beauty for all one's senses.

The houses were, at first glance, quite similar in nature to those of men, except for the indescribable sense of form, color, and luminescence. Each house was distinct, a model of beauty and grace that denoted the dweller. Pale shades of color that shimmered in the light of night or day transformed the house into a shimmering mirage of unreality. The elves greatly treasured the results of their handiwork; and their craft with wood was unequaled; each stood as an architect's model of perfection. As glimmering Silvere came into their view, Aubrey burst into jubilant song, and even Malazar felt a sweep of immense admiration and respect for the elfin city. In the exact center, the home of the elf Lord and Lady stood more refulgent and brilliant that all others.

On their porch, Mandell and Celina waited, radiant and expectant of their guests. If of years it is possible to say of elves, their marks could be seen on his face. Clad in pale green, they stood erect and a feeling of immense nobility and power radiated from him. By contrast, Celina, dressed in white, glistening robes, flowed both love and harmony.

She spoke first, raising her hand to meet his, "Welcome, Cidithir, ever friend of the elves. We are honored by your visit."

He met her soft warm hand and slowly moved them together as if of one beingness. Similarly, Mandell welcomed him. The ensuing hours of welcoming and feasting were such that words cannot express, save only that the ecstasy and true bliss were such that all the fears and woes of ordinary men would be long forgotten, like dim reflections of a distant past. As the evening came, the city grew in splendor; the crescent moonbeams shimmered, glowed, and glistened, shimmering in an endless stream of forms and hues.

Yet, Cidithir was a wizard; and, at last, in late evening, he managed to get Mandell alone in his study to hear his words of council. Briefly, the wizard told the Master of the Elves the situation with the Scavengers and the perilous state of all Isel. The Lord listened respectfully to all that he had to tell.

Finally, the wizard came to his request, "What I have come here for is to ask you to send an army of elves southward to assist Burly and Illanos to stop the massive drive of the Evil One and contain him within the Quad still. There is little time before the armies of evil will be pouring through Kyder Pass, sweeping a path of destruction before them. With the three armies, we may be able to halt and end that drive. Will you help us?"

Mandell let out a long sigh of one torn in two and said in a voice both beautiful yet sad, "Nay, Cidithir. I cannot by the oaths of Balmir. Even my son, Elwine, has chosen to defy me and has become a renegade and traitor to that oath."

He could feel the anger rise in the wizard.

"Let us step outside and drink together; and I will tell you the full tale of Eldamar, both fair and sad. Then, you may understand the words of my council. To none save elf has this full tale been spoken."

He followed the old one outside and together sat amid the shimmering, luminous visions and sipped the wine of the elves, that tingled and excited the sense of taste, leaving one wholly alert and awake. The old elf began now chanting, now speaking, now singing in a voice both beautiful to hear, yet filled with the sadness of the endless centuries. He paused now and then as if trying to get the right translation into the common tongue. The wizard listened keenly, acquiring knowledge he long wished to know. Elwine had told him some pieces of it; but, for the most part, it was new to him, and it explained many of his questions and puzzlements concerning his favorite people. They talked far into the night. Here is the tale of Mandell, as told to Malazar.

In the beginning, there was only Malena,
But not forever,
She, the great wizard of the blessed days,
Was both bold and fair,
The Mother of Eldamar.
She came to Isel, here to build for all to see,
The second splendor of the Elves.
Long she toiled with loving hands.
Her dream, she caused to be
The splendor of Eldamar.
Here she built the fabled Selerie,
(Obelos for all to see)

Towering far above towards misty heights,
Glowing ever far above the trees,
The beacon of Eldamar.
Then she, Mother Malena, put to sea
Sailed to Varina across the times
And brought a hundred Balee Elves
Here to dwell and with her to share,
The First Ones of Eldamar.
The left behind in Varina,
City of the God's most high,
Their lives and homes, here to build.
To expand the dominion of the elves
The kingdom of Eldamar.
Twas called Yhana, the period of the Sun,
When endless work and toil,
Built with beauty ever more to be
In the forest of Dionti,
The magnificient of Eldamar.
Here they raised the city Elgladore to shore the North
Tasayre by the sea to love and dream
And with majesty surpassing all, Silvere
In the forest of Viniere,
The dwellers of Eldamar.
But there were others in adjacent lands
Similar to Malena,
Their creations they did wrought as they chose
Other splendors to behold,
The others beyond Eldamar.
And in the period of the Sun, interchange
Amongst did begin and grow
Swelling to trading, seeing, and in sharing
Treasures to and from the elves
The visitors of Eldamar.
Chief among the hundred of Balee
Were Haldir the ruler, leader of elves,
And Balmir the bold warrior of old

And Elohir the bringer, grower of Dionti,
The Greatest of Eldamar.
Under Malena, Mother Supreme,
Our cities grew in splendor and in glory.
Our numbers raised ten-fold strong
All was fair and keen to sense.
Ah, our Malena of Eldamar.
So ends Yhana, the period of the sun and happiness.
Dark days fell hard on us
Brought on by the Nameless One,
Upset so great in size and shape —
A massive unmock of all our treasures
And even of Malena too.
Ever coy with words of hate and fire
Did he seek to destroy —
Doubt and rebellion and disbelief
That this could ever be in the lands of the free.
Yet he strove and fought by words and deeds,
Other's love, belief, and trust,
He did by greed and pride
In the minds of men forever
Destroyed the Land of Eldamar.
Visitors came no more, our borders shrank;
Malena and elves deeply grieved
That guards were placed at Viniere's edge
For attackers, cursing, swearing, defiling came
To efface fair Eldamar.
But her power ever great, did leave us
Seeking to end the waste.
To confront the evil at its source
And so she fought the Great Battle
Hoping to save Eldamar.
Dark Dharna, days of Sundering and of Loss
Heavy weighed upon our hearts
Evil's fiery blast consumed her
And took her from us

No more, Malena of Eldamar.
Oh greatest sorrow from which no end can come
Consumed us all forever more
Doomed to life eternal, bearing always
Amid the splendor, our great loss,
So Beautiful, Sad, oh Eldamar.
Full of timeless gloom, Balmir
Rose to console and to rule,
And we our borders under oath
Sealed shut, none to pass
As we isolated Eldamar.
With great eternal mourning, the Dharna Ended.
So began the Tirna, the Sad lamentful years,
Too great was our loss to bear.
Thus began the Exodus of Seven Hundred
Led by Haldir and Balmir
Saying farewell to Eldamar.
Led by two now old beyond measure,
They sailed westward to Varina,
Leaving Elohir and those
That could not bear double loss.
The Sundering of Eldamar.
In the days of Tirna, the son of Elohir, Mandell,
Began his rule, as father tended only Dionti,
And into darkened times brought four,
Of which Elwine is eldest.
Sad children of Eldamar.

The will of elf dulled and growth was slow
And ever borders remained closed.
As flowing days swiftly flew,
Bringing no relief, no joy
Eternal sadness of Eldamar.
But then the Mari, Mariners arrived
And influence spread in Tasayre
To them our doors we opened

Beginning anew, but not as old
Joyless rebirth of Eldamar.
Thru them we renewed our trade
Seeking to spread goodwill once more
And so through hopeless years we grew
Till again we number tenfold
The current of Eldamar.
And here we are in present time
The Living Dead of Eldamar.

Radiant filtered moonbeams reflected silver hues from the tall Dionti trees, sending shimmering rays flickering onto the walls of the elvish homes, as, joyless and without hope, the Master Elf finished his translation.

"I have only given the main ideas, Cidithir, for in our tongue, the story would take five hours to tell. I trust this will guide your understanding of our plight. You see, our survival as ourselves, though finite, vastly exceeds any other people of Isel. Elohir, though senile as it seems, is near his ten thousandth of your years; even my own Elwine approaches his two thousandth year. All of our personal needs are satisfied fully here in Eldamar. Our families prosper; even today, we approach the original tenfold. By our history, and our oath, we are separated forever from others; our borders are still closed. You see my friend, time for us is a vicissitude. You have known me for most of your life, long it seems; but for me, your acquaintance is as a brief summer's rain shower, seen and then gone. We are both blessed with a beauty supreme and yet doomed to an eternal sadness. I cannot give you an army."

"However," he said in a commanding voice and standing straight and tall, "I give you my solemn oath that any evil that enters our lands will never leave alive. On that you may be certain."

Then, he sat down and resumed his slumped, dejected posture.

Malazar had listened carefully as one who is both thirsty for knowledge and as an antagonist debater, ever searching for the fatal flaw. Instinctively, he saw the error of omitting mankind from their lives. However, he was so overcome with the heavy reality and truth of the old one's tale, no rebuttal came to him.

"Though I do not agree with your view, Master Mandell, I do understand your position; and I respect your view and your right to that view."

"That is all I can ask," came the reply.

Both men sat silently engrossed in their private thoughts for some time.

Then, Malazar raised another question that had been bothering him since his meeting with Aubrey, "What of Elwine, your eldest? Aubrey says that he has left Eldamar."

"A man can raise his sons with honor and pride, sharing what wisdom he can, but he cannot determine either their minds or actions. Elwine has chosen the life of a renegade. He has broken Balmir's oath and has sought knowledge beyond our lands. He is on his own now, wandering I know not where. We do not consider him evil or think ill of him, and will welcome his return. By severing the oath, he has, by our rules, relinquished all possibilities of becoming the Master of Elves, when I step down. That now falls on Aubrey, who ever has loved these woods, guards them as his own children. Aubrey claims that Elwine shall return soon now, but of that, I know naught. I know my son's mind no longer, but I still love him dearly. I shall retire now. Good evening, Grey One."

With that he rose, bowed, and entered his door, leaving Malazar still sitting in deep thought on his porch.

Barely two weeks remained before the attack that he knew would come. If it were not squelched utterly, Isel would soon be laid bare, making his self-appointed task even more difficult to achieve. He pondered his options far into the night. He resolved only that he should await Elwine. And he retired.

Like ripples on a pond, the days passed swiftly; and, upon the morning of the fourth day since he reached Silvere, Aubrey came to him very excited.

"Cidithir! Cidithir! He comes! I feel he comes even now. I am going to meet Elwine. Do you wish to join me?"

"Yes, Yes," came the reply, moving from a slow apathy toward the exuberance expressed by the elf. "Yes I do!"

160

At once, he grabbed his cloak, staff, and pouch and joined Aubrey. Quickly, the two left Silvere, and were rapidly moving through the forest, with a speed, the wizard noted, not usually displayed by an elf.

Now the elf trail from Silvere to Tasayre, by the sea, passed through the heart of Viniere Woods. The path was named Bindal, the bent one; it lived up to its name. Though only some thirty leagues distant, the ever twisting winding path totaled some sixty leagues! The elves were never in a hurry; and, this way, they could enjoy more fully Viniere, spending twice the time in the majestic woods. However, so great was Aubrey's desire to see his brother that, to the wizard's surprise, Aubrey was constantly leaving the well-worn path, making as nearly as he could in a direct line towards the port city, Tasayre. In fact, Aubrey was running!

Together, they were the picture of contrasts. Malazar lumbered along, leaves, and twigs continually crushing, cracking under his heavy tread, branches forcibly moved as he ran through the trees. In front of him, the elf's feet made only the slightest crumple on the forest bed; and with the agility only found in elves, his body leaned in all directions, as he avoided all branches from the trees he loved. He was a tireless runner, and soon slowed down to accommodate the laboring wizard, who, though in good shape himself, was no match for Aubrey.

The elf could have made the journey in half a day, yet he was content to make Tasayre the next morning to accommodate his friend. Malazar found that the elf, trusting his senses, had felt Elwine's return by sea. Both had been surprised by that. From time to time, the runners took short rests; and Aubrey bade Cidithir drink with him from his hide flask. It contained the elfish nectar, Solerae, a pale green liquid that completely refreshes the senses and rejuvenates the body.

In this manner, they continued until nightfall. By starlight and later the waning moon, they hiked, somewhat more slowly. At dawn, Malazar could smell the ocean in the air; and mid-morning the trees grew thinner; and the roar of the sea on the coast could be heard. At last, Tasayre rose before them, nestled at the edge of the forest on the sandy beach. Here, no Dionti grew, but oak, ash, and maple.

Tasayre was a brownish city with many graceful lines made, hewn, and carved from the stately trees that grew here. Rows and rows of houses were set back to back. None had a rear door, only a front one. Abutting against the rear and side were other houses. One side and row faced the sea; one, the woods. The land sloped sharply seaward; and each row stood taller than the neighbor did, so all could see easily the endless waves stretching ever westward toward Varina, it is said. Aubrey explained that everyone had both a sea view house and a forest one. That way they could enjoy both. As the ordered rows of houses fell below them toward the sea, Malazar could see many ships docked, moored to giant posts set in the deep blue waters. Most were small, and made of a brown wood with stylish elfin carvings, but near the center rose a large three masted schooner made of a whitish wood. He instantly recognized it—the Sendoa, the Mariner's.

There were many elves moving about the streets; and, with wonder, they watched as Aubrey and Malazar fairly flew by them heading for the dock. The elf was now singing in his own tongue. Malazar shared his excitement. Quickly, they commandeered a dingy and paddled swiftly toward the great boat, some thousand yards offshore.

"He's on deck by the main mast; can you see him waving?"

Malazar strained his eyes. He could see a form there. Soon they had a joyful reunion on board the Sendoa.

Once aboard, Aubrey and Elwine immediately joined their right hands making the flowing patterns of elfish tradition and then hugged each other, talking excitedly. The brothers looked remarkably similar, except Elwine was slightly taller and leaner. The biggest difference was the glow that radiated from Elwine's forehead. It was startling. It was as if a great, clear jewel was centered on his forehead with a ring of lesser ones around his head. His radiance was exceptionally brilliant. Aubrey noticed that it had grown immensely brighter since Elwine had left, and he was very curious about it.

Malazar first shook hands with Shannon Wayfar, who was cheerfully standing beside Elwine. Then he greeted and hugged his elf friend of many years.

After all the greetings finished, Elwine said, "Now, I've got someone else for you to meet; I have also named him Elf Friend; and he is due all the honor of that title. Let me present Tse Tse Wauli from the jungles of Winianie."

A small, very dark brown skinned warrior stepped forward shyly from the background. He had thick, oily, black hair, a broad grin, and wore a leopard loincloth about his waist. On his back was slung a blowgun. His hand carried a slender, sharp spear. His coal black eyes shone with excitement.

"Glad-honored-to-see-you," he said brokenly in the common tongue.

Aubrey, after the fashion of the elves, give him a royal welcome to Eldamar, leaving him even more in wonder and awe; and his shyness increased. Malazar's welcome was more mundane and to his liking; and he had an immediate fondness for him. Elwine explained that Tse Tse had saved his life in the jungles, that they had become great friends, and that the full story would have to wait, for it was a long tale. All agreed; and, at Shannon's offer, went below to his cabin.

There, amid round of toasts, they shared various items of news. Malazar heard of Marc and Mindi—that they had fortified Metro, had just recently established a defense for Hays and the Granaries, and were rapidly working on the defense of the other towns.

Late that afternoon, a messenger looking for Aubrey interrupted them. His news was ill. A party of goblins and a few Yacs had crossed the Cuero River into Eldamar. Aubrey bid all goodbye and was off at once to see to the defense. They learned later that he arrived on the scene in just over eleven hours and that none of the Evil Ones ever left Eldamar.

Shannon also took his leave saying that he was needed elsewhere. By evening, the remaining three were seeing the sights of Tasayre. The quaint houses with the delicate, carved, ornate architecture greatly impressed Tse Tse, who explained his people lived in raised, grass huts. The next day, they set off for Silvere together.

Though Tse Tse was a bit smaller than Elwine and very

different in form, he was equally at home in a forest. Malazar quickly discerned that Tse Tse could only be seen when he so wished, blending imperceptibly with the trees. Together they were a pair, mused the wizard. Before long, Elwine unfolded their tale, interspersed frequently with descriptions of the forest sights.

The elf explained that ever since Malazar's last visit, he had the growing concern of a doom falling over Eldamar; it had grown almost into a fear. He felt he must know what was happening in order to be effective in handling whatever was to come. He could find no one who either sensed what he did or who could go with him. Thus, he had resolved to set out alone.

Fortunately, the White Ranger, Drifter, had passed through Viniere and had happily taken him along for company. The Drifter had shown him a good deal of western Burly and part of Illanos, but they then returned northwards. The Drifter had an urgent message from Edmund of Burly to deliver to the other nomads. He explained how they had followed Valmar Road as it passed the edge of Witchachooie Marsh and of the growing number of evil things there. The Drifter had remarked that, before long, the nomads might become isolated from the rest because they were becoming unable to contain the growing goblin forces near Chooe Pass. The Drifter took him to Umatila, the City of the Wanderers; and he had seen Obelos Nord, a bleak white finger rising skyward amid the desolate hills of Ocalla.

"Then, since the Drifter had urgent business back in Burly, we parted ways. I attempted to visit the ancient home of the wizards, the Ruenzorti. As you know, I am forever thirsty for knowledge of them. I tried first the southern Banto Road, but horror of horrors lies there guarding all. A monster I have never known lurks there; and, by all the stealth I possess, I escaped. The northern Banta Road I tried next, but it was similarly guarded. So for the time being, I let my desire to see that realm pass and traversed the Wilderlands to the north. I came into a jungle land not mentioned in any lore. I have called it Anuir, a truly strange place! It is a jungle, yes, but it contains beasts that are mammoth in stature though not enemies. The whole area is filled with their massive bulks! One was huge, grey with a long nose that touches the ground, an Oliphat I believe. Others had huge horns on their nose; others, massive antlers—if that's what they were. Many strange creatures. Then, I hit the northern part of the Old Caravan Road and traveled south down it toward the Quad."

"But I still had my attention on those marvelous beasts, and I became waylaid by a party of Yacs—nearly thirty I guess. The bow of Elwine, from the Obelos of Elves, they had never seen. Into action I went and in a flash had spent nearly all of my arrows, with nearly half lying dead or so doomed. Whether or not by Malena's sword alone I could have handled the remainder I do not know. I doubt it, but in my dark need, Tse Tse came. Here I will let him tell of his deeds."

The small brown man shyly and in broken words began where his friend had paused.

"I hear noise—Yacs me think; I go at once. We of Winianie—hates them. I had my blowgun from Obelos with me. Sees Elwine—oh fastest shooter of arrows, I ever see! See also—he in trouble—elf I never see before. I shot fastly with my darts—dipped in manioc poison of jungle."

Elwine interrupted to say, "Tse Tse is the finest dart shooter ever! Very, very fast," and he good naturedly patted him on the back.

He stammered and blushed proudly, though it was hard to see.

"Yes and me got the rest of Yacs—foul beasts. We got us thirty Evil Ones!"

"You are both brave and worthy companions, my friends, good work!" said the wizard.

"Then, Tse Tse took me to his camp, Paomoho, and we became good friends."

"He fits very well in jungle—elf does well in my jungle," put in the little man.

The elf continued, "He showed me around his lands, and I met his people. Though primitive, I found them, none the less, a bold and brave people."

"Yes, and we were fascinated by elf—never seen one who glows!" Tse Tse inserted.

"We talked of many things. They were very, very

worried about the Evil Ones. For years, they have been flowing in increasing numbers out of the north and through their jungle. Seldom would they leave the road, though. Now things are getting worse. Horrible goblins have no fear, and they trample and destroy everything in their path. His people are having a very difficult time handling them. Their thick hides are hard to penetrate with a dart. Even spears sometimes break as they pierce home to their mark. So Tse Tse has been looking for help. Though he is not a chief, his words are listened to, for he has entered their Obelos Jund."

Here, Tse Tse broke in again. "Yes, Yes I am Master of Tower now. I go in many times. Here are our wizard's tools," and he proudly showed them the gilded blowgun, a sparkling knife, and a spear—light in weight, yet of a strange blackish metal that could not be bent.

He explained that Obelos Jund was a tall tower rising far above the jungle top. Its base was encrusted with a multitude of vines reaching upward to the treetops. He then told them the story handed down through the ages by word of mouth. It was the tale of Pali, their great wizard and the founding of the safe, jungle camps amid the harshness of the jungle by the sea. In these times, the Mariners had come and trade had begun with other lands. Indeed, Shannon had stopped at their port camp of Poli and had brought them back by sea to Tasayre, but their talk was interrupted by great gasps of awe and wonder from Tse Tse, for they approached Silvere amid the Dionti trees. The little man, far from home, could only gasp at the incredible beauty before his eyes as the sun was setting behind them.

Indeed, his timidity only grew amid the splendor of Silvere and the warm welcome of Master Mandell and Lady Celina and the crowds of glowing, radiant elves that lived here. He grinned, smiled, and nodded at everything. He spoke very little at first, but what he did say made a significant impression.

For in his greeting to the elf Master, he said humbly, "When I come here, I grieve for my people—the evil comes upon us. Now I grieve more deep for elf. Worse than loss of my people would be elf's."

He had communicated to Mandell. Not only had he said that a foreigner truly appreciated the elves and their land, but also that other people were in great danger as well. However, Elwine alone saw the impression they had made on his father. They spent another day showing Tse Tse the area and, then, left him in the company of Ellena, his sister. She happily continued his tour, while Malazar and Elwine held council among themselves.

Cidithir began, "Elwine I have waited for your return; we have a formidable problem."

His explanation of the southern situation and of impending peril of attack brought mainly nods and acknowledging grunts from the elf, whose countenance had shifted gradually to intensely serious.

"Yes, I presumed they would launch a major offensive. The sheer number flowing to his service from the north suggests the harsh reality of the peril. We do have a problem; you now know Mandell's position. You see, that is the very reason I journeyed beyond our borders. I had to establish some form of reality of all mankind beyond just elves. This I have done so, and it has broadened my viewpoint as well as yielding new friends. The fight of Burly men and horsemen, I fear, will go poorly without the aid of the speeding arrows of the elves, but Mandell would not allow such to occur. So Master Wizard, the resolution of our problem is simply to get the Elf Master to change his mind!"

Malazar discouragingly said, "And that's no easy task!"

Both had grown very serious, under the delightful Dionti trees. Elfish singing filled the long silence. Neither spoke for many minutes. Elwine suddenly jerked and rose up before his companion, a large smile appeared, ever growing.

Laughing he said, "Grey one, how can we hope to solve a problem when we're both so serious about it. After all, it is only a problem! I'm going to join my friends and gaily sing for a while. I haven't done so for two years. Come, Cidithir, let go of your worries; and merrily we'll solve it."

Malazar knew he was right on this one; but he urged his friend to go on ahead of him. Elwine needed no encouragement and soon another voice joined the perpetual music that filled the woods of Silvere. Malazar couldn't relax his hold over the problem and thoughtfully paced through the forest in circles.

In a short while, a bubbling elf interrupted his thirtieth circuit.

"Whoa there wizard, you are making a new path in our woods. It goes nowhere! Come on. I have solved it."

And he led a disbelieving wizard through Silvere to Obelos Furd. The tower still shimmered with a luster that could not be dimmed by mere time alone.

When they stood before the mighty door, the elf explained, "We need only to expand Mandell's viewpoint. Now what in all Eldamar could do that? Well, only the Vishi could! Isn't that a great idea?"

Malazar's stern face began to soften; the enthusiasm of his friend was having its effect. He recalled their days, many years before, when he and Elwine had stood before the door trying to get inside. He recalled the elf had sung nearly a hundred songs before they got the right one. He remembered the excitement they shared as they explored its wonders.

"But Elwine," he protested, "have you forgotten, that we were unable to get the Obelos operating? Our songs did not cause the proper effect then. How can we hope to do better now?"

"Elohir!" came the quick response. "Elohir is the oldest elf. He surely must know many songs of old. It's worth a try at least."

Malazar agreed; and, while Malazar sang the entrance words and entered to see what he could do now, Elwine gaily ran off in search of the ancient elf.

Elohir was the only remaining elf from the original few that Malena, the Great Wizard, had brought from Varina. He was the revered father of the Dionti trees; and, though now very old, he still spent his days beneath their boughs. His body was so worn that he could move about only with the greatest of efforts. These days, the other elves left him pretty much by himself because he seemed to always be off in some other time and place, but he was always singing softly to himself. Elwine found him beneath his trees as usual. He sat down beside him. He could almost feel the old one's years. It was several minutes before Elohir opened his eyes and gazed at him, as if from some far off place and time.

Then, slowly he said, "Elwine Eldaras, son of Mandell and Celina. You were only a boy when you last sat here beside me. We sang the songs of old."

"Yes, Ancient One. I remember. I now have a need that only you Elohir, First One of Eldamar, can fulfill."

"I, master elf, I? What can one so old do for you, my child?" Elohir said, his keenness of mind pierced through the veil of senility.

"You knew Malena. I want to know her through the ancient songs. Did you ever hear her singing? Those I most want to know. Can you teach me, Elohir?"

The years melted from his face; eyes sparkling, he leaned back against the silver trunk. His radiance, dulled by the years, now grew slowly brighter. He began to softly sing and chant. Elwine listened and joined him. On and on, they sang beneath the Dionti tree. Elwine's mind was carried back through untold ages to the days of splendor and of Malena. It was as if Elohir and he had stepped gently back into another age, another time. One voice, then joined by another, joyfully sang far into the night. Elwine noticed how full of life the aged elf had become. It had been a long, long time since Elohir had shared those the songs from the Yhana.

Malazar had learned much since the last time he'd been atop the elfin Obelos. He applied all that he now knew, endeavoring to get Obelos Furd operational. He achieved control over the door and had, after many unsuccessful attempts, gotten the cover off the Vishi, the viewer, but he had gotten no further. Exhausted, he'd laid his head on the table viewer and had drifted into an ill sleep.

The gentle voice of Elwine singing at the base of the tower woke him from his apathy. Singing in his own tongue, the elf began to climb the circular stairs that lead ever upwards. As he climbed, the walls became luminescent and shimmering with varied colors blending in great slashes and swirls, and as he passed, they remained lit and oscillating.

Malazar sensed this and intensely watched. Soon the walls around the top platform began to swirl and glow as well, as onto the platform came the elfin singer. Though barely perceptible, the song changed into a gentle chant, and the four massive windows burst open. The wizard had been using his staff as a torch. Now that the walls were glowing, he extinguished its blue glow.

Elwine stood before the great dark cylinder that hung directly above the center of the little room. He sang again, but all Malazar could grasp was the name Malena, repeated several times. Then, there came a blast of exquisite blue light from the cylinder. The beacon of Eldamar glowed brightly once more. The startled wizard covered his eyes at first; and, then in awe, he slowly uncovered them, and joined Elwine who was now gazing out the southern window down on top of the Dionti and Silvere. They were immensely beautiful reflecting now a bluish hue long unseen in Eldamar. Together, they enjoyed a view of the elf city as it used to be, as it was made to be. Both stood speechless. They saw the grandeur of Malena's creation.

Finally, Elwine spoke. "As I came here, I received news from our southern borders. The time has come. Armies of goblins, Yacs and wargs have flooded out of Kyder Pass; they have invaded our forest."

Then again, they both gazed, as the beauty below them washed their very beingness clean of fears and woes.

Presently, Malazar detected footsteps climbing slowly upwards.

"Elwine, someone comes."

"Yes, I have known it for some time. It is Mandell. Our lord has seen the light—he comes. Listen; do you hear any voices."

"No!" came the startled reply.

"You hear no singing! All elves are now silent and waiting. Does Malena come again?"

Presently, the trembling body of Mandell appeared at the top of the stairs.

"Elwine—you—Cidithir—I might have guessed!"

"No, not I," said Malazar sternly. "In this deed, I have

no part."

"Come father, this is my doing," Elwine said, in a soft, gentle, yet commanding tone; and he led his father to the table and the Vishi. "The time has come."

Then, he sang once more; and, as he sang, the table turned translucent and visions appeared.

Scarcely breaking the song, Elwine said, "Here is the recent past, noble leader of elves." As he continued, Mandell and Malazar gazed at the images that flowed before their eyes.

"Metro," mused the wizard.

They saw the slaughter of Hill View, the many of Metro rebuilding the Mound, the building and defense of the Hedge. Other images flashed; they saw the Dew Drop Inn and merry making, the fire tower in defense. Images of Khorizaba flashed amid others of Burly and Illanos.

Then, Elwine said softly, "The present," and resumed his songs. Now the viewer turned darkish and showed huge armies of Yacs screaming, yelling, issuing forth from Kyder Pass; the besieged forts of Greagon; a black mass of goblins issuing into Eldamar, destroying every living thing in their path. The screen now flashed bright with hundreds of Illanos' grey horses in a thunderous charge across the Lanos Brillos.

Then, Elwine said softly, "The future that may or may not yet be." Now the screen turned reddish and hideous images of blood-splattered bodies lay in large piles and mounds; Metro rose in flames. Other images flashed—too gruesome to describe. Then, Eldamar flashed before them. Goblins were felling Dionti, smashing, burning, and looting Silvere.

Crying and sobbing loudly, Mandell screamed, "Enough, Enough, Enough!" He ran down the stairs as fast as he could. Elwine ceased his song and the Vishi returned to its table form. There was a tear in Elwine's eye.

"I hated to hit him so hard; but the need is upon us. We have won; his mind is changed. Let us go."

Malazar and Elwine slowly descended the stairs. Once outside in the darkness, Malazar looked at his friend. His staff fell to the ground! He stared in amazement. The elf's white radiance about his head had grown immense! It exceeded

Mandell's now by at least tenfold. Elwine was now so brilliant that Malazar could barely look at his face.

At that moment, Elohir came hobbling through the Dionti leaning heavily on his walking stick. One hand, he held forward—out in front of him. When he came to where they were standing by the door, he stopped and gazed long upon Elwine. The tremendous brilliance did not seem to deflect his sight.

He said only one word questioningly, "Malena?"

Elwine put his arms around the oldest of the elves, and long they hugged; but no more was said. Then, he helped the old one back to his house and tree. Malazar could even sense the tremendous feeling of eternal peace that had engulfed Elohir.

As they propped him against his tree, Elwine said only "Thank's Elohir." And he slept.

The two hurried towards the center of Silvere. Already sounds of a commotion could be heard. When they arrived, they found that Mandell had already commanded the elves to war, setting forth new policy. The air was filled with songs of joy and of war.

Elwine watched and then said, "We must hurry and get our gear. The elf army will be off very shortly now; Mandell will lead the mighty army of the elves to join Aubrey in the south. Let us hurry."

They quickly gathered their gear and a rather confused Tse Tse. Elwine took a pouch, his golden bow, and silver sword. Malazar retrieved his sword, pouch, and his grey mare. In minutes, they rejoined the growing army of elves, explaining hurriedly to Tse Tse.

Within minutes, Mandell ordered the march. The Master of the Elves took the lead, with Elwine on his right, and Cidithir and Tse Tse riding double upon his left. They fairly flew through the forest, intending first to relieve the besieged Aubrey. A new day began the fourth era of the elves.

Chapter XIII—Of Fire, Logs, and Light

After Malazar had left, Vorag met with Lord Edmund. Insisting Greagon must not fall, Edmund counciled for further defenses and for more manpower. Duly, he sent Garth and Fergus to Beregrin via Old Varg to both inform the Lords of the wizard's finding and to acquire as many men as they could spare.

In the days that followed, Greagon was a hive of activity. Edmund, whose task was to further fortify the walls, led one group of builders. Shifts were organized around the clock, as Greagon sprang to life with the constant noise of chipping axes, thunderous crashes of felled trees, and the endless thumping of the heavy hammers driving posts. Within a week, the entire wall around the city was doubled. Even the great doors were heavily reinforced.

Meanwhile, Vorag led another group of the robust men. Their task was to create Edmund's Line, as it was to be known. His plan, built on Vorag's original idea, was to lay a trench line across Burly; it was to stretch from the road to several miles beyond Greagon. First, trees were felled in a straight path, nearly twenty feet wide. Next, the ground was mounded nearly six feet high, no small task in the boulder-strewn area. Finally, the downed trees were formed into interlocking units, laid on the top, and secured. After a week's continuous labor by many men, a ten-mile long barrier was established.

In order to be abreast of developments, Lord Edmund, in agreement with Vorag, sent out scouting parties. They established watch points north of Kyder Pass, by the Cuero River, in the rolling lands of Illanos, and in the northwestern corner of Burly just out of the way of the pass. Their function was to provide advanced warnings of impending attack.

While the men were busy with the construction, the women and children were not idle. They worked in shifts as well, providing needed meals. Others, especially the children, labored on the construction of spears. The smithy provided iron formed heads, and the children did the actual construction. Finally, a few endeavored to store up provisions in the event of a siege on the city.

When the week's labors ended, a group of two hundred warriors arrived from Old Varg and the surrounding areas. It was a very welcome sight. Added to Greagon's five hundred, it yielded a sizeable army of seven hundred, powerful, Burly men.

The ensuing days were spent mainly on spear building and training exercises. Repeatedly, Vorag drilled his men. He and Edmund realized their nebulous position. Edmund's Line could be flanked at either end, especially easy by the road. Here, they expected the biggest thrust. How long could seven hundred men hold the ten-mile line? Their men, if all on the line, would be spaced seventy-five feet apart! So organization was vitally crucial. At the more remote sections, sentinels stood with runners at hand. If a treat came there, the runners, who were composed mainly of children, would be sent for men. In this way, their force could be concentrated as needed.

Also of importance was loss of men due to wounds or worse. Vorag relentlessly stressed how crucial that was, for every man lost would be seriously felt. He cautioned for brave deeds—but no heroics—no one-man stands.

During this time, the spear pile had grown into the thousands, and now efforts were spent on utilizing the smaller branches to construct arrows and bows. They were placed in armory piles periodically along the trenches and within the city gates.

The first of August dawned with still no news of an attack. For a week now, the only reports that came to Edmund were those indicating a massive build-up of the enemy. Otherwise, all was quiet. Even the Yac sorties had virtually ended. The late summer had come bringing heavy heat and humidity to the forest. The air felt so thick that Vorag swore he could cut it with his scimitar. This day was no exception. The wind was calm and the heat, great. Even walking produced balls of sweat dripping down the men's hairy chests. The mood in Greagon was both solemn and concerned. Even Vorag was in an ill humor and spent the day lying with Oran against a great oak tree outside the wall.

Dusk brought no relief, no wind. The moon was new, and the hazy sky permitted few stars to be seen. Shortly after full dark, the scouting parties returned excitedly. Great deep horn blasts echoed through the trees; they yelled, "The attack! The attack! It cometh!" Edmund with Vorag and Oran at his side heard the reports from the breathless scouts. A large army had issued forth from Kyder Pass—a sea of Scavengers.

Above all the commotion, Vorag bellowed, "The hour of need cometh, to your stations. Tis our hour of glory!"

As planned, Lord Edmund took command of Greagon's defenses while Vorag took the Line. Vorag had chosen three captains: Berman had the Eastern flank of the line deep within Burly; Owen held the middle; Olaf took the east flank, by the road. Vorag joined Olaf; he expected the worst.

The men drew their arms and stood ready, waiting. Some nervous, some calm, some fingered their scimitars.

"Vorag, I standeth not this confounded waiting," declared Olaf to his friend, as he paced back and forth near the edge of the woods.

"Patience, my friend, patience," and Vorag laid his broad hand across his massive shoulders, "Thy time cometh soon."

For an anxious hour they waited. All the forest became uncommonly quiet. The silence grew ominous and foreboding. The hot air hung motionless; not a leaf stirred. Then, they saw a dull red glow in the northern sky above the trees. The familiar hideous laughter began to filter through the forest; swords were drawn; arrows strung. Soon, the first wave of the Scavengers was upon them, screaming, yelling, and laughing.

Yacs, goblins, wargs, and jackals issued from the narrow Kyder Pass as a great fire was lit. Now like a swarming mass of fire ants, they marched forward carrying red torches, blazing brightly in the still, hot night. The main army of goblins headed northward towards Eldamar, while the Yacs mainly swarmed southwards towards Burly. The wargs amassed in packs and went in various directions. Indeed, Kahill had assembled an army some five thousand strong. His big disadvantage was mobility. To get so many through the narrow, sheer walled pass required many hours. Dawn still found the last spewing forth.

The Yacs' plan was to swarm and devour Greagon; they expected some resistance but had no knowledge of Edmund's Line. When the Yacs encountered the line, they instinctively held back. When Vorag first saw the endless line of torches among the trees, his orders were for archers. The great mammoth bows of Burly twanged here and there; one by one, the heavy arrows found their marks; and cries were heard all along the line from the road down towards Greagon. It did not take the Yacs long to discover that they were easy targets; and, shortly, the dark night closed in on the forest as torches went out. Waiting began, while the Yacs, scattered in the woods, surveyed this unexpected obstacle. Per Vorag's orders, little happened through the night, save the twang of a bow here and there. He planned to save their strength and supplies.

Sunrise cast an orange hue on everything, reflecting in the heavy haze—now added to by the dust that was scattered by thousands of feet. The daylight brought understanding to the confused Yacs. As far as the eye could see lay the Burly men's line. Then they charged in force both at the western flank and at the center section closest to Greagon. They swarmed in herds over the great hunters, sending a large group away to the east. Clearly, the Yacs felt the wall to be little hindrance and had pushed on deep into Burly heading for Old Varg, leaving three-fourths of their force to mop up Greagon. In an almost suicidal wave, they stormed Edmund's Line.

Fierce was the resistance; arrows flew and a multitude of heavy spears sunk deep into laugh-less chests. The air became filled with their hideous yelling, flying shafts, and great bellowing horn blasts. Dust rose thick and heavy. Now swords and scimitars crashed and clanked. Swiftly runners carried orders up and down the line. Just as the Scourge was about to break through, reinforcements appeared closing the gap. Slowly the line grew in height with the dead or dying filthy bodies. Yet wave after wave of heinous Yacs charged— trampling, squashing their fallen. Here and there, wargs lunged over the line. Most felt the sharp impact of the Burly shafts in their necks or sides.

By noon, it was clearly a standoff, much to the dismay of the Scourge. The line bulged with the battered, bruised, and trampled. During the respite, Vorag gave the order to pile all the Evil Ones on the far side of the line, making the wall even more difficult to penetrate. Several hundred Yacs and wargs had been slain. Things had gone well for Burly; only fifteen were wounded; none slain so far. During the lull, they took courage and began yelling boasts and insults to the Evil Ones, taunting them; invariably woe befell those that answered the boasts.

Ever on Vorag's mind was the whereabouts of those that had flanked eastwards. The line would fall at once, if they charged from the rear. They had, however, chosen Old Varg as their target, underestimating the barrier that remained.

As they waited, Vorag gently mended a small gash that Oran received from a warg, who crossed the barrier and did not find a greeting arrow, but rather the canines of Oran. Over a dozen wargs had their throats laid bare by the ferocious dog.

As the afternoon wore on hot and tepid—only occasional sorties were launched by the enemy. Even though they were great hunters, they still needed the time to rest up after the morning's intense slaughter. Sunset came and still no major advance came from the Evil Ones.

"I liketh this not, Olaf," said Vorag worriedly. "They shouldst charge; yet, they waiteth, why?"

"Me thinketh they waiteth upon some fell happening," Olaf proposed.

"Verily, thy view must be so."

Stunned by the ferocity of their opponents, the Yacs withdrew and waited for the arrival of their strongest weapon. These moved slowly compared to the Yacs. Just after sunset, they came. Vorag and crew heard a wild clamor, a hugh commotion among their enemies. They instinctively tensed.

Soon they felt their forest shake and heard the telltale sound slowly drawing near.

Boom. Boom. Boom.

All the crying and yelling of the Yacs and howls of the wolves did not cover the dull earth shaking booms that were more easily felt than heard. Closer the sounds of doom approached the line by the road. Soon, the nervous hunters, heard amid the din, the sound of great trees cracking like toothpicks in a giant's hand.

Boom. Boom. Boom.

"What doom bringst these Evil Ones?" queried Olaf.

No one dared to answer him. They stood silent lost in their own imaginings of the foreboding booms that came ever nearer.

The ominous thunder now approached the area where the main force of the Yacs was located, and the wild yelling ceased! Clearly, the makers of the thunder cast a fear on the Evil Ones! Silence prevailed broken only by the thunderous boom, ever drawing nearer.

Boom. Boom. Boom.

Instinctively, the men began to slowly step backwards.

Then, the voice of Vorag broke the silence, "Holdst thy places men—at least till we seeth the makers."

Unwillingly, the men stopped their slow retreat; none save Vorag and Oran stepped forward.

Suddenly the large oak trees across the clearing from Vorag snapped like twigs, and there in the twilight stood the huge, grey form of a great cave troll! He stood nearly ten feet tall with a massive set of curled horns protruding from his head. His skin was all dark grey and was almost like stone. At once, the Burly men responded. Seeing their foe dispelled their doubts.

A rain of arrows flew but bounced off his thick skin. The troll only bellowed, and the forest shook. Vorag grabbed the heaviest spear; and, with a running heave, flung it with all his body behind it straight towards the troll's belly. A dull thud resounded; the sharp point broke; it had no effect! Fortunately, the troll could move only very slowly because of his great weight. Though with little hope, the hunters joined Vorag and threw spears as they could, ever retreating. Soon the boom of the troll's feet upon the ground were answered— another appeared, then another. In all, five great cave trolls slowly made their way towards the withdrawing, dismayed hunters. Finally, the Yacs appeared, though silent still, fully a thousand yards behind their ultimate weapons.

Vorag took command and ordered an organized retreat. Brave fighters, the Burly men followed his commands, and kept the fall back orderly, endeavoring still to pierce the nearest troll with a spear. Vorag had a sinking feeling in his stomach, as he envisioned Greagon trying to hold these at bay, but he had no choice but to retreat.

All that night, the ominous sounds of doom drew closer and closer to Greagon.

Boom. Boom. Boom.

Piercing the silent, humid night, the sounds of doom rang in every heart and mind—no matter how brave. Frantic efforts were begun on the walls around the ill-fated city to strengthen them. Everywhere people talked in hushed whispers. Endless booms slowly growing louder brought the accursed tidings.

Boom. Boom. Boom.

Edmund realized they were trapped. His heart fell at the thought of the wanton destruction of the women and children. Yet, he was powerless to divert it. If they withdrew into the forest, they'd surely become entangled with the large party of Yacs that had flanked them. Where could they go? Everywhere that they went would only find them temporary safety.

Boom. Boom. Boom.

The growing sounds drew him out of thought once more. Vorag and the last of the guards had retreated into the walls. The massive gates were shut and barred with giant logs that took ten men to lift into place. Fortified Greagon was now extremely over crowded; there had never been such a mighty assemblage of Burly force in so small a space, ever! Yet as the specters of death drew closer, none took heart in the defense.

Olaf probably spoke for all, "Verily, Vorag, I liketh this not; I feeleth like a fish in a net!" Then, all became silent, lost in their own inward reflections of the fate that was to come.

Boom. Boom. Boom.

The dawn came. The haze-reddened orb cast long bloody shadows down the abandoned line, ending on five, huge, dark grey hulks that seemed to absorb all its light. From the many ledges along the reinforced west walls, the figures of

179

doom could now be seen moving ceaselessly towards them. Vorag still had not given up hope. He suddenly called Olaf to help him. Both men worked furiously and feverishly. Time was running out. At last, the first of the great trolls had reached the west gate. His head peered over the top of the logs, horrible to behold. He bellowed in a low, deep voice that shook the very ground and began pushing on the gate. The great hinges creaked; the cross logs moaned and grated. But it held. The Yacs had gathered in a large mass some two thousand feet beyond the walls. Now they began laughing, encouraging their Evil Ones to smash the great gate.

Vorag called twenty men to his aid. He had constructed a bow of immense proportions. It had been a young tree, nearly eight inches thick. Ten men held the bow in place; ten more pulled on the massive rope; all grunted and strained heavily. Others saw the weapon and rushed to assist. Now, another troll had joined the first troll; together, they had brought up a huge tree—nearly two feet in size. A hideous crashing sound came from the gate, followed by a terrible grating and buckling. The massive gate fractured and splintered with a sickening sound.

Quickly, Vorag put a six-inch log into the drawn bow, pointed end forward. Then, as the remnants of the gate fell away leaving the great troll fully seen, he yelled "Now!" The mammoth bow straightened, hurling its monstrous projectile forward, while the force of the bow knocked all the men to the ground. "Uuphff," came the deep cry of agony, as the log projectile penetrated deep into his chest. The impact knocked the troll onto his back, and green ooze gurgled out, foaming as it touched the ground. The other retreated.

At that instant, the thunderous roar of thousands of hoofs rolled towards Greagon along with a multitude of bugle-like horn blasts. A moment later, down the abandoned defense line galloped a thousand horsemen from Illanos. Hildaro was at the point. The early morning sun reflected off the great shield of Bernardo; Axillones tipped in blinding flashes of blades. The Yacs screamed in double terror, and, blinded by the red flashes, panicked, and ran in all directions. Soon amid the rising dust cloud, myriad gleams sparkled off the riders' swiftly moving sabers and thrusted Axillones.

Vorag yelled, "Malazar! Charge!"

He need not have; for with double renewed hope, the great hunters had already poured through the gate and over the troll whose body had already turned to stone.

It was a wild melee; with the wildly galloping riders' sabers slashing, the hunters' scimitars flashing, and a noise deafening to the senses. Horn blasts followed horn blasts. In all directions, in a mass confusion were Yacs, wargs, riders, and the hunters. Oran and Vorag were an unbeatable team; as Vorag clashed swords with a Yac, Oran would cleverly dive in and tear open a leg; and, while so distracted, the silver scimitar would remove its head. Within an hour, the slaughter was mostly over. Here and there, an unlucky Yac was discovered and laid to rest.

Hildaro ended off and rode into Greagon, and Vorag joined him.

"Greetings, Master Horse Man. Thee cometh just in time," he said gasping for air.

"Hildaro Romes of Illanos, at your service and rescue," and he dismounted, and heartily shook hands with Vorag and Edmund, who had just arrived to welcome him. "Malazar said to hurry; I fear we were almost too late."

"Aye, goodst timing, Lord of Illanos."

"But where ist the Grey One? I hast not seen his mark," queried Vorag.

"He had left us weeks ago to seek the aid of elves. We came as fast as we could."

Lord Edmund heartily shook his hand and embarrassed him saying, "Forever willst the mighty hunters of Burly be at your service! The service thou hast done for us ist great beyond words."

"Let us be united bold hunters, and together we will drive the Scourge from Isel!"

Then, the three and Oran made their way to Edmund's cabin, exchanged further words of thanks and news, and shared many welcomed rounds of ale.

The rest of the day was spent bringing order to the chaos of war. The dead bodies of the Evil Ones were piled in a huge mound, together with their implements of war; and a great fire burned there for two days. In the fracas, another cave troll had been felled by a lance of Alfredero. The unexpected force of the blow had broken his shoulder in several places. However, by evening he was up and about and widely honored for his deed. Of the other three, there was little news. The blinding flashes of Bernardo's shield had struck such fear into them that they had fled down Edmund's Line and disappeared deep into Burly. At least eight hundred Yacs and wargs had been killed; while only fifty-two hunters, thirty-three horsemen, and ten horses had died. It had been an ugly slaughter; a grim victory at best.

During the night, Vorag, Edmund, and Hildaro held a brief council, while their men drank heavily in celebration. Hildaro warned that this was only a small part of the total force they had seen coming from Kyder Pass. He was extremely worried for the safety of his horses. In the woods, they would be a disadvantage and an easy prey, even for wargs. Thus, they decided to keep strong garrison of guards round the clock and, accordingly, shifts were established. All got some well-needed rest that night, but none had any relief from the excessive heat and dank humidity. Still no wind came, and during the night, the Yacs reformed and were joined with the remainder of their armies; they prepared for another battle at dawn.

As the sun rose ruddy in the eastern sky, Vorag who had not slept all night, but had stood all watches, blew his horn loudly. Shortly a hundred horns and bugles bellowed in answer. All were aroused and ran for their posts. Across the Line stood quietly nearly two thousand Yacs and hundreds of smaller goblins—almost twice the sum of the horsemen and hunters. When the horn blasts ended, a large Yac in a yellow tunic and grey helm stepped forward and began the telltale hideous laugh. Its sick sound echoed through the woods and was quickly joined by the host in an unnerving clamor. However, the Yac who began it laughed no more; a Burly shaft ended his days. This time, the fight was much more orderly. The Burly men spread out along the Line, and the horsemen galloped up and down the line fighting as needed. Scimitars flashed, bows twanged, sabers slashed. Then, the wargs, long held back, entered. This time, few archers could be spared for wolves alone; and soon they were across the line.

Furthermore, Hildaro rode to Vorag's side yelling "Look yonder!"

To Vorag's utter dismay, he saw charging through the woods hundreds and hundreds of the larger sized goblins!

He yelled loudly, "Fall back," and Hildaro sounded the horn of retreat.

On the western end of the Line, many were lost before the retreat could be effective. Once more, the mighty hunters were forced back towards an overcrowded fortress. Again, the tide had flowed to the enemy.

It had not taken the elves long to journey from Silvere to the southeastern corner of Eldamar. Having resolved to action, they went in great haste. The gray mare carrying Malazar and Tse Tse thundered and galloped through the trees, bending now to the right, now to the left, as she skillfully chose a path with her riders in mind. Such was the influence of the elves within their wood. Never before had Malazar seen the elves in such determined action. Usually they'd consume several days meandering through their woods, but this day, they moved so swiftly that one could only glimpse flashes of radiant glows as they sped from tree to tree. Viewed from the air, a golden glow swept through the forest below; and the only sound came from the mare.

Aubrey had intercepted the great goblin army as soon as they crossed the Cuero. As the Evil Ones numbered in the thousands, he was forced into a delaying strategy. Stealthily, he and his few would come upon their foe's flanks and loosen a rain of carefully aimed arrows. In ten seconds, each would shoot ten goblins; their hands a blur. In a flash, they would disappear. Angry cursing goblins would see no one, and yell and defile even more. Everything in their path they destroyed as they pushed ever though the dense, dark borderline of trees. After two hours of pillaging the woods, Aubrey could slow them no longer; and they broke through into the main part of the forest, where the sun shone sparkling through the trees.

Here the elf prince and his men were forced into stronger resistive tactics, for, otherwise, the evil goblins would move rapidly into their sacred realm. Here and there, in front of the host, the elves, though only a handful, darted amongst the trees, appearing and loosening a rain of elfin arrows at the leading foul beasts. Their movements had convinced the Evil Ones that a large number of the accursed elves were before them; and they slowed their pace considerable, endeavoring to pick off the elves as they appeared. However, vain and frustrating was their reward; the ancient people were just too swift within their own lands.

However, the goblins were making considerable headway despite the valiant efforts of Aubrey and his mere handful of guards. Periodically that afternoon, he received badly needed reinforcements as other elves began arriving from their guard places nearby. By sunset, the great host of destruction had pushed deep into Eldamar and were now twenty miles deep into Viniere Woods. As the darkness grew, the goblins began to light large fires; and some, carrying burning torches, began to expand their zone.

Then, everyone heard the sounds of a lone horse galloping towards the glen. Soon the incredible music of thousands reached Aubrey's ears; and he, too, began to sing. Cries of agony arose from the despicable host and they stomped around, covering their ears; they detested the beauty. From the northwest there came a fast moving, yellowish glow—the light of a thousand elves; a blazing white light led the way.

As they approached, even Aubrey stood motionless in awe at the sight before him. Elwine, his brother, radiant beyond measure, shone far brighter than the morning star. Beside him, though not as brilliant, strode the tall and proud leader, Mandell. Galloping to keep pace came Cidithir and the stranger, Tse Tse. Following them came the largest war party of elves ever seen in Eldamar. Their combined luminance reflecting from below gave an unearthly light to the forest. Cries of fear and utter dismay came from the instinctively retreating goblin host, but to no avail.

Swift were the elves, and within moments, the huge

army of destruction was surrounded in the glen. In the queer light, Malazar could see their ugly forms and the terror on their faces. At Mandell's command, a rain of silver arrows fell among the host. Wave after wave flew. Swords ringed, and then the elves charged into battle. Elwine, Malazar, and Tse Tse joined as a team, while Aubrey and Mandell took over-all command of the attack.

Never had the goblins of darkness seen such light, such power, as the trio came forth into battle. The wizard's staff fired brightly—its blue flames leaping forward. Tse Tse's blowgun flashed golden rays in the light, while elfin blades rang and glowed before the host. With skillful short "puffs," small black darts flew to their marks. The long, slender points penetrated deep; and the jungle poison, so carefully prepared from the manioc plant, swiftly felled its host. After getting fifty and having no more darts, the brown man used his spear to continue his toll.

As the two elfin blades of Malazar and Elwine clashed into the black blades of the ugly ones, horrid rending noises were heard. The black, goblin blades broke, followed always by startled cries and screams of terror as glowing blades penetrated foul skins.

Never had the goblins faced such opposition to their will, and in a frenzied panic, the condensed crowd broke through the elfin ring and ran head long through the trees down the blackened path they had made—back to the Cuero River. Only a half hour after it began, the forest sang with praise of victory. Fully eight hundred foul goblins lay dead— most in a giant mound at the center of the camp circle. Yet over a thousand had fled southwards. For now, the elves let them flee, for they had over fifty of their fair folk who needed cures after the battle.

Mandell ordered fires to be lit, and all that night, the elves piled the dead foes into a massive mound of filth. Then, with his staff, Malazar caused a great burning; the winds carried the thick, foul, black smoke high up over the Quara Wund—deep into the desert regions. It was noted by prying eyes. Other elves tended their fallen. Only five elfin fires had been prematurely extinguished. Elwine came and tended his fallen comrades. Later his sister, Lana, came with a group of elfin women. She knew from her brother that she was needed and had come at once. Mandell commanded the five slain to be carried in honor to Tasayre, given the high ceremony, and cast afloat in the seas—there to return to Varina. The wounded he sent back to Silvere under the constant attendance of Lana, and to each, Elwine personally tended their wounds, for it seemed his touch brought renewed life. Thus, the night passed.

Dawn came casting a pale light on the freed woods. Yet the vision was that of foul destruction. The fair forest had been blackened and destroyed in a wide path. Stretching before them lay a dark swath of wanton wrack and ruin. Blackened ground lay naked and bared, despoiled beyond belief. Softly a song of grieving arose, as the fair elves viewed the effect of their enemy. Elwine arose amid the wailing. As his hands rose, a stillness of expectancy fell upon them.

He spoke, "Grievous is the wound to Eldamar, forest of Viniere. Though had we not acted in haste, the more would be our grief. I, Elwine Eldaras, declare that from now on, no living thing shall grow on these defiled grounds. Around this path, Viniere will grow and prosper as of old, but long will it be ere plant or grass grows on the blackened earth. It shall be called 'Emlil e smar de Shil estril'—the Eternal Mark of Evil Destroyed. All of you are praised and honored for deeds done here, but we owe a special thanks to two elf friends who fought beside us. To Cidithir and to Tse Tse Wauli, our eternal thanks, elf friends!"

To both's embarrassment, especially Tse Tse's, a thousand voices began to sing, praising their deeds.

Next, Mandell called a council of the wise, for here he had a choice to make. "Cidithir," he began, "Long have you counciled an old man; ever truly—though sometimes not accepted. Here we have reached a turning point. We cannot send forth all elves from Eldamar. The risk is just too great. Some must go, but some must stay. Hear me, my sons. I have chosen to stay in Eldamar for now and guarantee its safety. With me will be three hundred. Elwine, your mind is already clear to me—you shall lead the elves forth in my place, but you

Aubrey, the choice is yours to go or to stay."

There was a moment's silence as Aubrey quickly looked at Elwine, at his father, and at the forest. Then, he spoke, "I am the Prince of the Forest. My duty lies here, but others need our aid. My father, you are old, but not so beyond hope as you suggest. However, my decision shall be to remain and assist the repairing of Viniere and to guard our homes, but my brother, if you have the need, send for me, and I shall come."

"It is decided then," and Mandell rose, "Let us be off on our tasks at once. I do feel that the need of others is extremely urgent. Waste no time my son, and farewell Elwine."

The council ended, and Elwine led six hundred elves down the black path in haste. Malazar and Tse Tse once again rode the mare, for swiftly the elves flew along the blackened trail towards the Cuero River. It might be noted here that Tse Tse spent his time among his fallen prey, gathering his darts, and making them ready for use once more.

Vorag and Hildaro had gotten their men and horses safely into the stockade. They, with two hundred hunters and riders on foot, had formed into a great wedge protruding from the nearly repaired gate of Greagon. Hildaro marveled at the great strength of Vorag, who stood beside him. It seemed to him that any one of these hunters was like three of his horsemen, when not astride their steeds. The wedge proved a strong defense, and growing mound of foul bodies was beginning to form a good wall of protection. Indeed, the two began to be an effective team. As an enemy charged forward, Hildaro flashed his shield, and, while temporally blinded, Vorag sliced. The mound before them at the point of the wedge was huge. They stood fast at the point, dripping heavy sweat from the hot, noonday sun. "How long could they last," Hildaro began to wonder.

Shortly after noon, a white glow appeared way down the abandoned Line. Above the din of battle, high-pitched voices were heard singing in a strange tongue. Within minutes, the elves were upon the flanks of the host of goblins, Yacs, and wargs. The jackals, which had no desire for fight, ran off from their dining.

Dismayed again, the enemy began to retreat and give way, while both Vorag and Hildaro looked in awe and wonder at the leader of the elves, whose glow was almost painful to behold. Neither had seen an elf! Here were hundreds. Then, they saw Malazar and yelled to him. Meanwhile, the other Burly men charged once more from the stockade; the horsemen mounted and charged, giving the wedge fighters a needed rest. Malazar rode up, and he and Tse Tse dismounted. Elwine came too, and they all exchanged greetings and introductions. Then, the five charged forth into battle as a group. Wherever they turned, none dared stand before them.

Though the army of Kahill was more than double the defenders, they were barely a match for the three united. The heavy air began to take its toll on those fiends of darkness, long unused to such humidity. By late afternoon, the foul host had been beaten significantly and were ever yielding ground, and always before the five. By late afternoon, the bash and clank of swords died down. The host had begun a retreat towards Kyder Pass. Quickly, the horsemen broke out of line, and rode hard and relentlessly, forcing the retreat towards the pass, slaying any that tried another route. Exhausted, the five ceased their forward press, slowly picked their way over bodies of the slain, and made their way back to Greagon.

It was then that the massive, grey, stone bodies caught their attention.

"What evil have we here?" said Malazar.

"Great cave troll cometh and almost proveth our undoing," Vorag explained.

Hildaro broke in, "Three escaped us and headed deep into Burly."

"Mighty are the deeds of the hunters and riders," spoke Elwine.

"Drink and tale, please," put in an excited Tse Tse.

"Verily, Verily," laughed the husky man in a sweat-soaked bear cloth, "Tis many tales we shallst hear, ere this night endeth!"

Edmund had not been lax, and they found he had arranged a great feast and drink. The grounds within Greagon had been cleared and great stockpiles of food and kegs of ale were waiting. Then, the six began the greatest feast ever held in Burly, and it continued throughout the night. However, after the tales were aired to everyone's fill, and with bellies stuffed, Malazar called his four aside for a council.

"Things have gone well here, but there yet remains much to be done. The renegades must be hunted down. I fear that the dawn will bring more battles at the pass. In truth, men, a few can hold the pass from hundreds. There is yet an obstacle before us. We know not where the trolls went; doom will follow their paths. What of Begrundi Pass? Did armies issue forth from that area? If so, what of your brothers and the dwarves? Forsooth, much yet remains to be done here."

"Yet, I'm now way overdue far in the south." (Several present suddenly remembered.) "I was to meet our help from the South of Isel on August 1. I'm many days late, and many shall pass ere I can start, and even more ere I can get there. They aren't without guidance, but such delay will only go ill, I fear. Thus, I have a choice to make."

Vorag had been following the wizard closely, recalling his earlier conversations. He interrupted the Grey One, "Nay, thy services be needeth here, wizard. I shall fetcheth our companions hither. You spoketh of the inn in East Flats before. Verily, thou needst a Burly man to guideth thy feet through these woods. If evil awaiteth in the flat land, a Burly man be worth many in strength."

Elwine added, "Then, great hunter, take with you several of my elves. They will learn of your woods, and should you find news of man or beast, send them back one by one, for you'll find none swifter in woods than my people."

"Thank thee, I wouldst welcome their company; I may learneth much from their high voices."

The Grey One spoke, much relieved, "Thank you, Vorag, my mind is much relieved; I know I shall be needed at the pass. Now let us rest a while; we will need our strength tomorrow. The pass will not fall easily."

They adjourned, and Malazar quickly told Vorag where he was to meet the others. Elwine brought ten elves to accompany the great hunter. In late evening, Vorag, with Oran at his side and with elves around him, began their journey through the depths of the stony, Burly forest. The others slept soundly.

Just as Vorag left the stockade gates, Berman approached him quietly, "Mayst I have a word with thee, Vorag," he softly queried, eyeing the elves with him.

"Of course, of course. What dost thee wanteth?"

"I seeth thee heading into the deep wood. I didst calleth upon my bears to followeth the three great ones. They hast not reported back yet. So be aware Vorag. Harmeth not any bear before thee."

"Well doneth, Berman. Verily, no hair willst I or the elves harmeth on thy bears. Perhaps, they willst guide us to the trolls."

With that, Berman quietly slipped away. The elves marveled and quietly discussed the words amongst themselves. The small troop slipped noiselessly through the trees and over the boulder-strewn ground into the night.

Chapter XIV—Journey Under Fire

Late that night, Vorag with the company of ten elves led by Elador actually got underway. As they left the stockade behind them, the dark forest slowly closed around them. They went quietly and without ceremony. Though the area was Vorag's backyard, to the elves, it loomed dark and massive, ominous yet exciting. For them, this was more like an exploration into some unknown forest full of wonders to behold, but the knowledge that the Yacs were somewhere out here in the darkness, coupled with the unfamiliarity of the woods, restrained their exuberance. The elves were content to follow Vorag quietly, but their ever-roving eyes viewed everything possible. They were heading a bit south of due east; Vorag intentionally did not follow the eastward path that the Yacs had taken days ago.

An hour from Greagon, the great forest became alive once more; battle had not reached its ugly hand this far; and the woods was teeming with wildlife, noisily declaring their lives. Above the continuous drone of the crickets, the saw-stroked croak of tree frogs burst forth in random patterns. The occasional chatter of squirrels blended. Now and then, the distant cry of a lone fox or the yap of a coyote on the prowl rose sharply above the background for a single measure of discord. The elves excitedly listened and began to whisper among themselves. Their forests had nowhere this much activity—this abundance of creatures of the night.

Their going was very slow, however. The forest was steadily growing thicker; the undergrowth, denser. Overhead, heavy foliage permitted little light to penetrate to the rocky mossy floor. The forest was very dark, even to the elves that could see much better than their guide could. He made up for this with familiarity. Nevertheless, progress was mostly a slow careful march with occasional stumbles. Oran roamed from side to side in front of Vorag.

Since they had left the fortification, they found no sign of any person, only the animals. Their spirits had grown and all were cheerful, as if on a playful romp. Suddenly, breaking in on their pleasure, there came a crashing, crushing sound ahead of them. Instinctively, all stopped and stood still, ears straining for sounds above the nighttime symphony. Something definitely was approaching them. Oran whined by his master's side. Elador drew his short sword slowly and quietly; the others did likewise, following their leader's example. Seconds later, Vorag drew his great curved scimitar and bent nearly double, straining for further awareness of what was before them. He motioned them forward and carefully led them creeping forward. They came to a small open area filled with large boulders, some nearly four feet wide. Quickly, they all took cover among the boulder field, and waited.

Shortly from the opposite end of the small rocky glen, a large black mass loomed. As if sensing them, it paused; then, it rose up to a massive height. Vaguely, they could perceive its huge black outline, blacker than the dark trees behind it. With awkward steps, it ever so slowly lumbered their way. The large form stopped close to the boulder where Vorag crouched, and they heard a distinct sniffing sound. Recognizing the sound, Vorag slowly revealed himself, but his tensed body remained so. Oran crouched on his belly. A low, bellowing grunt issued from the tall bear that looked at Vorag closely. Dropping to all fours, the big, dark grey bear continued his slow walk past Vorag. Then, he stood up and sniffed, as the elves stared in wonder at their first bear in the wild. Indeed, the elves and the big bear exchanged sniffs of confused wonder. Neither side indicated harm, and shortly the bear again dropped onto all fours, and continued on his way. In a minute, he was gone, leaving those behind talking excitedly.

Vorag declared, "Well, Elador, that be'st Beoral, the great, grey bear. What thinkest thou of Burly's mightiest? Beoral is the largest bear that I knowst of!"

BElador and the elves were talking rapidly with many exclamations in their own tongue, and the hunter only caught an occasional "Wow."

They rested here for a time; the elves were in no mood to go further just yet. Elador explained that they had never seen so huge a bear and were adding him to their songs. After an hour's rest, the elves seemed to have gotten Beoral added appropriately, and they continued their slow journey for another hour. At this time, weariness had fallen on all; and they made a small camp—mostly gathering leaves into a soft odor-full bed. They slept till dawn.

The hazy, ruddy rays filtered through the thick leaves and boughs, casting long dark shadows along the stony forest floor. The elves now could see clearly the rough beauty of the Burly woods. The tall, wide based trees were primarily deciduous: oak for the most part, with scattered maple, elms, and locust. The heavily stoned floor was covered by an endless bed of moss and grass and ancient decayed leaves—a myriad blend of greens and browns contrasted with the dull orange boulders covered with grey and reddish lichen circlets. The air was thick and had a very humid, musty odor that weighed heavily in the lungs. The elves ate cakes of way-bread while constantly surveying all within sight. Vorag munched upon some dried venison and, at last, began their march.

As the elves strode along, they began to chant sweet measures softly, as they now had added another sense perception. Vorag sensed their joy and awe and led them slowly at first. Indeed, it was the first visit of elfin folk to the depths of Burly in countless thousands of years, and the hunter felt a pride in his lands.

After an hour had passed, Elador spoke quickly to Vorag, "Something approaches from our rear; it comes swiftly—crashing as it goes. Perhaps it is another of your great bears."

Vorag halted and strained to hear; then he laid his ear on a large boulder and listened.

Slowly rising up, he exclaimed, "Verily, elfin ears hast magic about them. Thou spokest truthfully. A bear cometh." Then, he saw the look of a hopeful expectancy upon their golden faces and with a loud laugh he exclaimed, "Yea, we shalst await the bear. You shalst see another, but remember, harmeth not a hair upon their bodies!"

Gaily, the elves awaited the arrival of the bear.

Though they were prepared to see another of Burly's

great creatures, they were not ready for what sprang suddenly into the open between the trees behind them. Sitting astride Beoral, the great grey, clinging to his thick grey fur was Berman! The bear was making all possible speed. As he entered the little clearing where the elves were awaiting him, he slowed quickly and stopped, making loud sniffing sounds. Then, he let out a low growl of recognition and continued bearing his friend forward.

Berman saw Vorag and yelled, "Hail Vorag, Berman cometh!"

They exchanged hearty welcomes, while the elves, which at first were speechless, rapidly began to discuss the latest event. Elves were forever friends of animals and had always held a strange power over them, stemming from a mutual admiration and respect, but they had seldom, if ever, seen such in other people. Yet, here a great Burly hunter had ridden upon the back of the largest bear they'd ever seen.

"What bringst thou hither and such a pace?"

Slowly, as if choosing his words, Berman spoke, "I cameth to warn thee and thy friends. Beoral cameth to me with the news. Ahead layth the trolls. Beoral and several others hath found the beasts. The others are following them. My friend saith thy path leadst to the dark ones. So I cameth both to telleth thee of thy danger and to joineth and assisteth, my friends. I cometh not of single hand; I commandeth the bears. Beoral liketh not the destruction of his lands. The big fury ones hath declared battle, and Beoral seeketh my council."

"Then, let us accompany thee; there be more hands for fighting," declared Vorag.

Their discussion was sharply interrupted by the grey one, who rose up tall and let out a deep moaning groan, that echoed among the trees. The unexpectedness of this sharp bark caused the elves to jerk and a few even drew their swords.

Merrily raising his hand toward Beoral, Berman said, "He sayeth we must hasten now."

Berman and his friend led the way over the stony ground and through the large trees while Vorag and the elves followed. Oran now stayed very close to his friend. Even as they ran, the elves began to talk rapidly of the marvelous event they'd witnessed. Elador asked Vorag all about Berman. The elves were truly impressed by this relatively quiet and mild mannered great hunter. By the time they stopped for a brief rest, they surrounded the bear man and plied him with questions. A friendship was made that would last for a long time, at least for Berman. Neither seemed to tire of relating their experiences with their animal friends. Indeed, Berman afterwards received the title of elf friend, though at the time he didn't realize its significance. Berman permitted the elves to pet and rub Beoral, who trusted him implicitly. Though he was not used to having any person other than the hunter touch him, to the elfin touch, he quickly responded; and a friendship grew. After an hours rest, they continued their journey moving as swiftly as possible.

Occasionally, Beoral would stop, rise up, and issue a great yowl from his wide jaws. By late afternoon, a faint far off answer returned. They were getting close. The ground was now slowly rising in the far distance; through northern breaks in the trees, the Quara Sud range rose reflecting the orange rays of late afternoon. Here the ground became stony and increasingly filled with boulders, which rose taller than men. As they scrambled over the rough terrain, one by one, bears began to join Beoral. As they moved in close to the big one, they eyed the elves suspiciously, but accepted them. Soon the sheer number of wild animals overwhelmed the elves, unused to so many at once. Even Vorag grew a bit uneasy, and he and the elves dropped behind a ways. There, surrounded by at least twenty bears of greys, browns, and blacks, strode Berman— confident and at peace.

They moved up a narrow, rocky wash; the noise from Beoral's crew became loud and very close. The wash ended at a little ridge. Here Beoral and Berman halted; all around, the company could hear bears growling.

Berman turned to Vorag and quietly said, "Waiteth here," and he, Beoral, and a few others quickly and stealthily climbed the ridge and disappeared from view.

The elves began to whisper among themselves, much impressed with the events so far. Yet, Vorag and Elador felt a bit uneasy, surrounded by the kings of beasts; they respected the power of the furry beasts. While each would be able to face one alone; the throng, they could not do so comfortably. Vorag impatiently fingered the hilt of his scimitar, hoping Berman would return quickly. To his wish, he did. The hunter soon appeared alone atop the small ridge motioning them to join him. They needed no second invitation.

From the top of the tree-lined ridge, they found themselves looking down another wash; large shadows lay before them in the late afternoon sun. The wash was deep, nearly a hundred feet at its lowest spot, around a quarter mile distant. Countless bears roamed on the ridges on either side. Beoral had gathered all within range.

Down in the valley were nearly a thousand Yacs, hiding here and there among the boulder strewn gully floor. However, three distinct grey shapes loomed near the point. Unmistakable were the cave trolls, even in the failing light. Berman quickly explained that the bears had been roused by the wanton destruction of both a pair of cubs and of the forest. They sought revenge. Beoral had held off the charge because he was leery of the number of enemy below and had been content to box the Scourge into the gully. There was no escape now, for he had sealed the other end as well. He'd gathered over a hundred bears. Vorag guessed that, at these odds, the Scavengers would be the victors still, though at a tremendous cost. Still, the trolls continued to be the major problem, and the Yacs seemed contented to stay right where they were. It was a standoff for the time being. The watchers continued to watch.

The sun became oblong and ruddy, sinking between the darkening leaves. A first quarter moon cast pale, yellow shades into the gully. Dimly, the Scourge below could be seen. Then suddenly the ground shook with a boom. It was followed by a monotonous asynchronous rhythm of doom.

Boom. Boom. Boom.

The cave trolls decided to break through; the Yacs remained watching their weapon do its work. Cheers, wild yelling, and hooting arose from the black depths of the gully, but the bears returned with great bellowing yowls and howls, shattering the night, drowning the foul noise below. Slowly the bears amassed on all sides of the gully near the ridge where the men stood. The trolls slowly lumbered their way climbing ever toward them. Soon a few Yacs formed a shabby line some distance behind the grey trolls. Berman drew his scimitar and knife. Instinctively, Vorag and the elves did likewise. Berman cautiously climbed his way downward toward the doom, eyes forward. The others spread out and followed closely behind him.

At about a thousand yards, Beoral stood and and let out a tremendous blast; and, suddenly from all sides near the front, the bears charged head long down the valley to meet the doom. The hunters, brandishing their great curved scimitars that flickered in the moonlight, and the elves, whose sparkling foreheads radiated like their swords, charged as well. The ferocity of the charge totally freaked the Yacs, who screamed and fled into hiding in the black depths with the others, leaving the three trolls standing alone to confront the charging masses.

If Berman was worried about his furry friends being injured or destroyed by the three giants, he needn't have. At least ten ferocious, angry bears attacked each troll. Though an eight-foot giant troll could easily slay a single bear, confronting dozens proved their undoing. They hit the trolls full force. Towering crashes echoed through the trees, and the ground shook from their falls. The bears were on top of them at once, gnashing, mashing, and tearing at them. The trolls were so slow of movement, compared to their attackers, that their wild blows usually went amiss of their marks, but when they hit, a poor bear would be sent sprawling, moaning in pain. The noise was deafening; the elves had stopped and were holding their ears with their hands. In less than five gruesome minutes, the fight was over.

Three mangled, de-limbed trolls lay destroyed in the gully. Around them, two bears lay never to walk again, but another ten were badly smashed. Almost as quickly as they charged, the bears romped back up to their posts upon the ridge, while Berman and Beoral assisted the injured bears up to the place where the men had stood atop the ridge. Below in the gully, there was complete silence. A stench of utter fear and terror rose from the thick air below. Berman, assisted by the elves, tended the wounded. The hurting bears, though straining against every animal instinct, permitted assistance to be given. They seemed to relax considerably whenever they felt the touch of the hunter or of the elves. After that, two big brown bears appeared and escorted them off into the depths of Burly.

The party quickly counseled; all felt that the bears should not charge the Yacs because of the sheer numbers involved. They were now immediately north of Old Varg by some twenty leagues. Berman suggested that the bears chould attempt to hold them at bay or at the worst delay their movements until further assistance could come. The others agreed; and three elves, led by Maliro, who had been the most impressed by the bears, agreed to stay with Berman. Elamir agreed to return to Greagon with the news; while Vorag and the remaining six elves said farewell and continued their southeastern journey. And as the small party said farewell and left, they raised their voices in song, creating music of the great deeds of the bears. They continued their march in the moonlit woods. Upon leaving the bears, Oran seemed greatly relieved and began his forward roaming.

That night passed without further events and similarly for the next day. Only passing creatures and occasional deer marked the passage of time. By late afternoon, the forest's dense undergrowth began to yield to a grassier, mossier bed and was welcomed by all.

Presently, Elador put his hand on Vorag and stopped him, whispering, "Someone comes."

By now Vorag had learned to trust these keen perceptions of the fair folk. Quickly, the band dispersed among the trees and waited. Soon even Vorag could hear the tramp of approaching feet.

Then, he laughed loudly and yelled, "Over here!"

The noise now became rather loud and hurried. Swiftly, three Burly men appeared in the small clearing where Vorag stood.

"Hail to thee, Mighty Vorag," the taller leader of the scouting party said in greeting.

"Hail master Kelvin and crew. What bringst thou hither?"

"We scoutheth for Old Varg. Rumors sayeth the scourge nears."

At this point, the six elves reappeared from behind various oaks; and Kelvin stopped and stared, eyes wide with wonder.

Vorag laughed heartily and said, laying his big hand on Kelvin's shoulders, "These be elfin folk, who have saveth Greagon."

And he introduced them one by one to almost speechless hunters. Then, they spend an hour relaying various news. Vorag was anxious to get underway, especially when Kelvin told of the dangers befalling Beregrin. Elador decided to send three elves—with Ellidine as their leader—to accompany Kelvin and friends to Old Varg. There they could more fully relate the news and return to Elwine with whatever news they could get.

Once again, Vorag exchanged farewells; and he, Elador, and the two remaining elves continued on their way—but now heading east-northeast toward Beregrin. Kelvin, Ellidine and the others headed mostly southward to the Burly capital city to seek aid for Berman.

Now that there was some moon available, Vorag's party traveled as swiftly as possible. They took to sleeping very late at night. In this manner, the four spent the next two days of their trek across Burly. By the third noon, the distinct noise of scattered battles could be heard in the forest, which had been growing steadily quieter. Instinctively, they quickened their pace. Presently, the noise of a local clash could be clearly heard.

Elador said he felt someone was in trouble, and Vorag fumbled for his horn slung over his back. Slowing his pace slightly, he blew a loud, deep blast on the war horn; three times the forest echoed. Answering blasts came from close at hand, and the four and Oran ran headlong—crashing through the forest, making as much noise as they could.

They rushed through a clearing to find three Burly men in great peril, surrounded by nearly twenty, foul Yacs closing in for the jubilant kill. But the thrashing, crashing noise behind them pulled their attention off their prey. The four rushed out into the clearing, waving their swords in the bright sunlight, throwing blinding flashes of rays this way and that. Vorag and Oran did not even break their stride, but continued their headlong charge taking four Yacs flat footed and ending their joy permanently. The elves were more gracious in their movements and attacked with a beauty and grace deadly to behold; six Yacs lay dead in a very few seconds. With half their numbers slain by this awesome charge, the others fled screaming. And hastily, the group exchanged hearty thank-yous and greetings.

Neil was the leader of this ill fated sortie; he stood a bit shorter than Vorag, clad in rabbit and with blazing, curly, long red hair. After some discussion about the marvelous elves, Neil led the way towards Beregrin, relating the ill situation that had befallen them.

While they traveled northward, the story unfolded. Vorag learned that Kahill had launched a minor offensive at Begrundi Pass on the eastern side of Burly. However, he had sent only a thousand Yacs and a few wargs through the pass. At first, the Burly men had held the Scourge at bay; but at last their overwhelming numbers broke through; and the Scavengers rushed down the Great East Road. However, every time they attempted a push into Burly, the hunters, led by Edmond, had repelled them. Then, the Evil Ones had pushed further eastward toward the Armagh Mountains. By great luck, the dwarves responded; and wave after wave of the half-men had charged forth. The Scavengers were now being constrained by Burly on the west and the dwarves on the east. But they had taken complete control of the road, pushing far south to the Kanandrul River and Enchendar Woods. The river, the Yacs did not cross, for fear of the land and the fairies. The problem was the long boundary line that Burly had to hold with only some five hundred men—impossible against a thousand.

The dwarves had a better position with only some ten leagues of heavy mountain passes to defend. The dwarves' line had held fast. But the Burly side had not fared so well. Indeed, over such distances, the Scourge could and did break through repeatedly, sending small forces southwestward as desired. At present, Beregrin was more or less under siege. Parties of hunters could leave, if they chose to fight their way out. In order to protect the city, most of the men had to be recalled, leaving now only a few large scouting parties abroad. Neil said that Beregrin was now in its second week of siege, but doing remarkably well and not in any real danger of falling, yet. How long it could hold on to life, he could not guess.

They spend that night resting. Neil did not dare a fire; and, though cramped, the undergrowth did offer some cover from the eyes of marauding bands of Yacs. The further north they had come, the more troubled Vorag had become. By nightfall, he was in quite an ill humor. While they rested, Elador took him aside and queried him.

"Vorag, elf friend, all day I have sensed that you are troubled greatly. It cannot be just the news we've heard, for it goes much better here than the west. It may help you to talk of the problem."

Vorag looked into the shining face of the noble elf beside him, and he sighed and said, "Verily, thou speaketh truly." He paused and explained, "Malazar hath given me orders to fulfill. They lieth far to the south. Yet my lands, my city, lieth in grave peril. I am torn between the two."

His voice faded off into the silence. The elf also was silent, yet he understood.

Then he suggested, "I and my two will go to Beregrin and do what we can. I can send one back and bring reinforcements in from Greagon. If you go south, you will be able to do Malazar's bidding, and you may be able to return with an army from the south to relieve Beregrin."

"Verily, that doth handle the forces!" Vorag grinned. Elador saw that his friend was greatly relieved.

It was agreed, and the two friends shook on the bargain. Quickly, he announced his plans to Neil, who could not refuse them, save only to repeat the dangers ahead to the south.

Vorag hugged Elador and pronounced, "I be off, but I shall returneth with force for Beregrin!"

He and Oran quickly gathered their gear and set off on

the moonlit night heading southward with Oran ever roaming in front of his master.

The hunter was now on his own, but this was what he was accustomed to for most of his life. Oran provided all the companionship that he needed in the wild. Together, they journeyed for most of the night, stopping two hours before dawn for a brief rest. They had so far managed to avoid the Yac parties. The next day, they were deep in the woods of southern Burly. Here, there were only rare traces of the Scourge. At last, the roar of water grew among the cheerful sounds of the woods. Presently, the two came upon the rushing waters of Beone East. Wide and cold, the river swiftly flowed through a boulder-filled bed, going from the northernmost creeks of Burly to end in the great Kanandrul River far to the south. It was a wild river, and crossing was risky due to the swift gushes that flowed around the rock masses.

The pair paused for an hour, refreshing themselves on its eastern bank. Oran drank deeply from its cold, clear waters. The might hunter lifted his dog and, carrying Oran in his right arm, waded into the river. It took a strong body to fight both the treacherous, white waters and the cold. By the time Vorag reached the west bank, he was shivering and completely wet. Oran too. So Vorag kindled a fire to warm and dry them.

While his friend warmed himself by the small fire, Oran shook himself dry, sending a shower of drops over everything around him. Laughing, the big man began to wrestle playfully with the big mastiff; and, for a short while, each forgot entirely the many burdens they carried and were engrossed solely in play. Then with big leaps and bounds, Oran disappeared among the trees, while the hunter huddled around the fire. Shortly, Oran, with eyes bright, lay his offering before his friend.

"Good boy, good boy!" he exclaimed, "Tis a good idea."

He quickly prepared the rabbit, putting it on a stick. Oran lay down nearby, watching it slowly cook. Later in the afternoon, they shared a hot meal.

They got underway shortly after that, now heading due south. Old Yac campfires steadily became more abundant. Still no signs of the Scourge appeared. Some of the sites were only a day or two old, the hunter guessed. Apparently, there was little to restrain them down in the south of Burly. Around sunset, the thinning trees at last yielded. Before the two lay a few small hills of grass and, beyond that, lay an immense area of sky with a very flat, grey land. They paused and watched the western sun slowly sink—the long shadows melting into a grey sea of darkness, yielding only to the rising moonlight.

While stooping and petting Oran on his side, the hunter said softly to Oran, "Nearly full moon tonight, old boy. Twill maketh our way a bit easier. Tis a strange land we enter now. East Flats. Malazar saith they be down by the sea, but we best be careful—on our guard. Cometh."

The lone, dark figure of a huge man swiftly passing over the flat ground stood out sharply, while the great mastiff roamed from side to side, ever before him. They were in a huge empty space filled only with endless sky and stubble grass—shadowy figures moving.

Late that night, a red glow appeared on the southern horizon; it steadily grew for nearly a half hour. Oran whined softly as Vorag halted and knelt beside his friend, stroking him firmly.

"It looketh like battle ahead, old fellow," he offered. "We'd best not fighteth this one; we not be known in these lands."

Carefully steering slightly eastward of the glow, they warily continued their journey. An hour later, the noise of battle became audible. They could hear the continuous racket of laughing, yelling Yacs, the howling of wargs, and the jackal cries above the din. Murdoc was besieged by a host of the Scourge that had slipped through eastern Burly. As they drew closer, the source of the red flames took the hunter by surprise, and crouching low in the grass, they watched curiously. Great grey, dark towers with flames on top formed a great circle around the town; here and there, as the Scavengers drew too close, a rain of flames fell devouring, amid hideous screams of the luckless Yacs and wargs.

Together the pair lay in the grass some five miles from Murdoc—dark shapes among the grass, watching closely. Slowly the brilliancy of the defense grew upon the great hunter, as he realized there was hardly a tree here—only flat, grassy, grey fields. The Scavengers were beginning to route; quickly the pair clambered to their feet, jogging south as rapidly as they could. It wouldn't do to get cornered by the retreating swarm. As they hurried south and a bit east, the Scavengers were swarming in a great fan northward. Some were getting close now. They broke into a run, just as some Yacs had spotted their forms moving in the pale moonlight. He heard a hue and cry rise among some of the nearer Yacs; and the two ran now as fast as they could, putting all their attention on making the maximum forward progress. Swiftly southeast, they moved; even more swiftly, some twenty Yacs endeavored to cut them off.

Against the lean runners of Kahill, the heavy Burly man couldn't hope to outdistance them. His thought was simply to pull far enough southward before battling the Evil Ones, so that the main body of the Scourge would lie far to the north. The Yacs were now closing in rapidly, running toward him from his right, a mere thousand yards separating them. He pushed onward for a little longer and was significantly south of Murdoc. At last, he halted and leaned on his knees and caught his breath; Oran panted heavily as well. Together, they awaited the arrival of battle once more. His second plan was now executed; he and Oran would be rested slightly before the running Yacs attacked; he hoped for a slight advantage.

Some twenty Yacs, in glee now, since their major target had repulsed them, charged rapidly, feeling here was a prey they could certainly get. The lead Yac slowed a bit as he approached the big man and dog, giving five of his buddies time to catch up. Then, the six charged the lone hunter full force. Vorag drew and raised his silver scimitar high in the air. It flickered and shone in the moonlight. As the six charged, using two hands in one mighty down sweeping slash of the great curved blade, he sliced through the onslaught of foul smelling, sweating filth. Three were headless, two bellies were laid open and the other lost a sword arm. The forward rush of their swords, however, continued just long enough to reach the great hunter. A foul blackish sword hit him broadside in the left shoulder, while another's long edge landed on his right chest slicing his bare flesh. The other blades fell around him. Oran lunged and ripped open the armless one's throat. While Vorag inspected his chest, Oran put the finishing touches to the others, who were shrieking wildly clasping their scrawny bellies.

Another dozen Yacs drew up short of the battle scene and warily eyed the event. Vorag growled and made ferocious noises not unlike his enemy and brandished the great curved scimitar wildly in the air above him, casting moonbeam reflections toward them. As suddenly as they had come, they turned around and left in a slow jog. They had apparently had enough and had no heart left even to try attacking so wild a hunter, being after the more docile farmers.

Without further thought, Vorag and Oran continued slowly southward. Though both were exhausted and fatigued, they continued for several hours, before resting beside a small, bubbling spring. Though it was only inches across, it was cool, clear, and refreshing. Here, Vorag bathed his wounds, and together, they ate a small meal, before dozing for several hours until daybreak.

The bleeding had ceased now, and the wound was not deep and was clean. Vorag knew it would heal swiftly, but they could not afford to waste any more time. So they hurriedly continued their southward journey; fatigue and lack of sleep were beginning to have their effects on the two.

By the light of day, they could see small farmsteads scattered randomly across the vast, flat, prairie land. Here and there grew great fields of grains, and cornfields rose tall around them. They steered clear of the homes; strangers, he assumed, would not be so welcome in these times. Abandoned Yac campsites more frequently appeared—barren, blackened areas on the prairie. Warily, they continued for several more hours.

By early afternoon, a blackened path appeared ominously before them running southward. It was week's old and occasional green sprouts pushed their way valiantly up through the charred ground. Loathe they were to follow it—but it was going their direction as far as either could discern. Nevertheless, the two continued their journey, traveling just to the right of the black path, their feet treading upon the healthy greenery.

They traveled the rest of that day without further incident, stopping only when necessity so demanded. By nightfall, large, white, cumulus clouds dotted the deep blue sky; and the air became more humid and balmy, refreshing to breathe. They allowed themselves a few hours rest in the early evening and continued onward just after eleven o'clock. Here and there, small Yac scouting parties roamed, but these were few and offered no resistance to their progress. The hunter guessed that they spent their days hiding in captured homesteads. He felt relieved that they had chosen to give the sod homes a wide berth.

Daybreak found the two staggering along, very weary and nearly spent. Ahead lay the town of East Point. He knew he would at last have to enter a town to inquire about the travelers he was to locate for Malazar. Around nine a.m., the farmers of East Point saw a strange sight: a pair of tired, dirty travelers came walking down the streets of their town. One was a huge grayish mastiff; the other, the biggest, most muscular man they had ever seen, clad in a bear cloth with dried blood on a bare chest and long, clumpy, dirty hair. Both looked exhausted. Everywhere, people stood and stared at their visitors.

Eventually, the sheriff appeared and stopped him for questioning. Briefly, Vorag told eager ears who he was, told about the fight at Murdoc, and asked where did they serve ale. The sheriff accepted his story, mostly because they had already heard of Murdoc's battle from pony riders that had arrived earlier that morning.

Shortly, the fatigued hunter found himself sitting in a sod house—a pub called the Tall Field's Inn. The amazed innkeeper, Sam Gromberry, was kept busy filling Vorag's mug. Finally, he just brought the entire keg. Vorag laughed heartily and drank his thirst, giving the still surprised innkeeper some Burly tokens. After Vorag told many eager ears some things about Burly, the innkeeper proudly kept the tokens; they remained a showpiece for quite some time.

Vorag found he soon had an audience, as the small inn

rapidly filled to capacity. Poor Sam was busier than he ever had been, but he serviced his benefactors constantly. Oran had more bowls of food than he could consume in three days. Soon, the place became noisy and loud as Vorag related stories for which eager ears secretly yearned.

Vorag had no difficulty in gathering data about the travelers for which he was searching. The hero of the flats, Marcos Blancas and party, were seen a few weeks ago in Pratt, heading toward East Point to inspect their Fire Towers. He learned there was a big Yac attack, and no one knew if the party had come. Most had figured that since they had totally repelled the onslaught, the Master Defender and troop decided they didn't need to inspect their towers. What had become of them, no one really knew. No trace had been found. He also learned that East Point Inn by Feanor Bridge had been burned to the ground days before the company's expected arrival at East Point.

Having heard what he needed and having the place roaring with laughter, boasting, and in general good spirits, the big hunter and Oran took their leave quietly and quickly walked down the streets and turned eastward onto the Great East Road.

The ale and food had temporarily stalled off the growing fatigue, and the two made the ruins of the inn in short order. Here the two stopped and began a hunter's inspection of the area. Man and dog seemed to roam randomly over the ruins and general area. They came together somewhat beyond the inn. Here the hunter paused and knelt studying the signs on the soft dirt road.

"Oran looketh here. I seeth many Yac tracks, yet also others. Here lieth a tiny pair, dwarf perhaps, here ponies."

His dog panting seemed to nod his head in agreement.

"Very few travelers useth this road. Cometh," and he began to follow the road.

He was bent nearly double and constantly pointed and mumbled to himself, as they slowly followed the trail. In less than an hour, the two painstakingly arrived at Feanor Bridge with its sparkling, radiant hues of blue forms.

Here they halted, "Many tracks confused here. I loseth

the trail. Whither didst they go?"

He paused silently surveying the ground.

"Searcheth Oran, searcheth old boy."

He spoke to his dog, which actually already had his nose to the ground sniffing here and there. Carefully, the two went northward along the roaring river, finding no signs, retraced their steps and went southward below the road. Then, they returned to the bridge. It was nearly noon.

"No signs old boy, no signs. Must not goeth up or down the river. No signs goeth back toward the town."

Carefully, he inspected the bridge, but no mark of any kind, even age, did he detect on it.

"Tis a strange bridge, Oran. No sign of age or wear lieth upon it! Yonder lieth a strange land, spoken of in tales of olden days. Few entereth; even fewer leaveth!"

The big man sighed; a great weariness grew rapidly upon him. The strenuous journey with little sleep had taken its toll. Even Oran hung his head.

At last, Vorag mustered, "Let us checketh on the other side for tracks."

Slowly, the tired two crossed the bluish bridge into the enchanted woods. It was rather long, rising in a curved arch of planks with a three-foot wooden guardrail on each side. Through the zig-zag supporting slats, the great river Kanandrul flowed noisily to the sea.

Immediately on the other side, the two closely scoured the ground. Here the signs were unmistakable. Clear in the long unused path were signs of three ponies, a small set of feet, and several larger ones. Also unmistakable were numerous Yac footprints. These, he noticed ended abruptly. For a short distance, the two followed the trail, and after it led off into the trees with no more sign of Yacs, Vorag felt relieved. He and Oran lay down amid the grass and the unusual trees, feeling more at home than they had for days. All was peaceful. Together, they closed their eyes and rested. Oran laid his head on his master's lap. Vorag rested against a tree. Time and dreams passed.

Chapter XV—The Charge of the Seven

For some time, the lone hunter and companion rested under the eaves of Eos Woods. Both felt a strange tranquility slowly creeping through their very beingness, but they had no urge to resist it. Shortly, Oran's keen ears pricked and stood upright; he lifted his head curiously. Soon Vorag also heard approaching footsteps; he got up and planted both feet in readiness, hand upon the hilt of his scimitar. The growing trample along the path before him indicated a carefree, hurrying attitude. He waited inquisitively.

Presently, the company of questers led by Prince Faedon appeared on the path before the hunter. They stopped short and stared in wonder at the Burly man. Nache mumbled something about their guest being a Burly man.

In contract, the Drifter smiled and strode forward shaking him heartily, exclaiming, "Vorag! Oran! Vorag, it's you! You're a long way from home! Any news of Malazar?" Then, he saw the speechless faces of everyone else and paused.

Shannon also stepped up and welcomed his Burly trader. "Let me introduce the company to you," Shannon began, the diplomat in him arising to the occasion. "Let me present Vorag Boraski, the Bold Keeper of Burly, and his faithful companion Oran. This is Prince Faedon of Enchendar—in whose forest we now stand, by his leave."

The short fairy stepped forward and bowed low in greeting.

Vorag stared in complete wonder! "Verily! Verily! Thou art a fairy! Thee existeth!" he heartily proclaimed. "We thinketh thou liveth only in legends, but it's not true!" Oran continued to eye the prince. He had never seen a people smaller than himself, and he was both excited and terribly curious.

Shannon continued, "This is George Bighollow, Farmer of East Flats, otherwise Innkeeper." George bowed, being rather taken aback by the huge size of the man before him.

"This is Mindi Francos, Lady of Metro or perhaps," he

added coyly, "a wizard of many things—maybe even of Fairies."

She blushed and smiled; but Vorag was taken totally off his guard by her radiance and beauty. He blushed heavily and embarrassedly blurted, "Thou—thou art the fairest I—I hath seen!" He glanced both at her and at the ground in front of him.

"And this is our leader in these dark times, Marcos Blancas, Master Merchant of Metro, who now carries the Fire Sword, Andrill." Marc stepped forward and shook his hand, but was a bit overwhelmed by the heartiness of the big man's shake.

"And last, but certainly not least of our company, this is Nache Thraindruil, Master Builder of the Dwarves of Khorizaba."

The dwarf stepped forward and, planting both feet firmly, bowed low; his beard touched the ground. "I and the Dwarves are at your service Great Hunter."

"Verily thou beest the company I searcheth for," he proclaimed in relief both because the introductions had been concluded and he had found those whom he sought. "In truth, I cometh from Malazar by his order. He couldst not be spared from his tasks and sendeth me to bring thee unto him. Much news I bringeth for thy eager ears and much haste be needeth."

Prince Faedon interrupted, "If I may add a caution, the power of Enchendar does not extend much beyond our borders. This is not the place to discuss events, for we are not safe from prying eyes. Let us return to Finiae at once."

"True," said Marc. "True, let's go." Ill memories were returning of their flight across the nearby bridge.

Prince Faedon again led the way down the paths through Eos Woods, while the company followed close behind. The Drifter and the hunter brought up the rear. The latter and his dog continually observed the forest and hills as they walked—marveling that a forest could be this beautiful and yet not be rugged as his homeland. With renewed hope, all returned in excellent spirits.

As they arrived at the Royal Square in front of the

Palace, King Faegor and his queen, Miranda, expectantly sat on the jeweled thrones. Prince Faedon quickly presented the newcomers. The King welcomed him briefly and eyed the dog closely. Then, he introduced Miranda and his three daughters. Each curtsied in the proper fashion before their guests and stood behind their parents on the steps. Except Melissa, she gracefully approached Oran, her hands outreaching. Oran eyed her closely and with great curiosity, being almost twice as tall as she was. Melissa touched him and then stroked him lovingly. The big dog relaxed considerably, and she hopped on his back and scratched his ears.

"I'll be responsible for this one father," she gaily stated.

Vorag in disbelief said, "Truly this be the land of Fairies! Never hath Oran consented to a rider or to a stranger, without word from me!"

"I am a princess of living creatures," came the understanding response.

Miranda, who had been silent, now arose and stepped forward facing the giant.

"Mighty hunter, I can see that you are wounded—slightly, I would guess, but hurt nevertheless. Before we do you the disservice of plying you with hours of questions, let us give thee much deserved rest. Lynn, take this noble hunter to the Pool of Ian. There let him bathe in your waters a while. We can discuss events later."

None would disagree with her, and Lynn stepped shyly forward, but so great was their size difference, that Vorag began a hearty laugh while he held out his little finger. Soon the rest saw the humor, and everyone laughed as well at the dichotomy. Then Lynn flew up onto his shoulder, resting as light as a feather, and led him off to her pool. Instinctively, Oran followed his Master, and Melissa rode atop the Mastiff.

While the others milled around the square discussing the events and the council results, Vorag was taken to the Pool of Ian. Lynn bade him to go for a swim. He lingered on the bank—embarrassed and fiddling his hilt and horn strap.

At last he spoke, "Truly, I art a bit confused. I—I swimeth not, and doest I undress here?"

Lynn quickly saw his bewilderment and laughed, "No,

you need not undress; just leave your gear here; the waters of Ian will clean your fur as well. It's not deep at this end. I'll see you do not get in too deep. Now in you go!"

He laid his scimitar and sheath, pack, and horn in a pile on the green bank. Carefully, he stepped forward. Suddenly, he stopped and removed his big heavy boots. He gently put one foot into the dark waters and then the other. The waters of Ian felt strangely warm and soothing. Soon, he was splashing and lying in the shallow end. Melissa bid Oran join him, and the great dog playfully splashed into the water, showering the two girls. The two wrestled and played for some time. Then, both laid down in the waters and just relaxed.

The Pool of Ian had life giving, restoring, healing properties. The two, almost at once, began to feel the fatigue slowly drain from their tired, sore bodies. After some time, Vorag arose and noticed his wound. It was gone! No trace, not even a scar remained. He stood speechless, staring down at his chest.

Lynn quietly spoke, "We can do much, but not beyond our borders." The exhaustion has also been washed away with the dirt.

The impressed hunter could only mutter in awe, "Thanketh thee, thanketh thee."

The hunter got out and Lynn caused a large towel to appear before the speechless giant. Alone in the pool, Oran now noticed the frogs croaking. He stared long at them and soon let out a low growl of seeming recognition. Melissa spoke to him, and he quieted down and came to her.

She explained, "Oran's senses are keen indeed; they speak truly."

Vorag missed her meaning, and Melissa and Oran went for a walk in hilly Finiae, while hungry Vorag rejoined his companions, now ready for conversation.

At the Royal Square, he found the others were eating a lunch spread on little yellow tables. Without further words, he joined them at once.

It was a long luncheon. Vorag found he had an eager audience, and he talked long of the events in Burly. Throughout, Mindi watched him closely; and Nache kept interrupting with exclamations. Marc asked few questions, but pondered all he had to say. The Drifter kept asking for details here and there; they seemed to be great friends.

When he told of the tramp of doom, everyone fell silent—even the forest lay still. Such was the evil of the great, cave trolls. Vorag continued his tale and told of Beoral and of the besieging of Beregrin. When he came to the latter events, Nache couldn't keep still. He kept interjecting constantly.

He had stood up and excitedly swayed from side to side. "Yes, the Dwarves are ever the friends of the Burly men. Yes, we fight again. Yacs will know the blades of Khorizaba!"

After several hours, he finished his tales by telling them about the wonders of the Pool of Ian. Mindi was the first to reply. "I sense here another. Indeed, he is the Keeper of the Burly obelos. You shall now hear our tale more fully."

"Verily, I wisheth to know more of this Fire Sword. Hath the legends of old cometh true?"

Marc then told him of their adventures in more detail, especially of the obelos' events. As he came to the parts played by others, he had them continue the tale. At last, he finished the story by telling him of Andrill's fiery appearance during their flight across Feanor Bridge. Then came a round of many questions and answers.

Marc ended by stating, "The resolve of this company is to end the reign of the Evil One. We are prepared to journey to that end."

"The time cometh then. I prayst we canst leave for Beregrin soon. I feeleth an ill day for Burly."

At this point, King Faegor arose and spoke once more, "Great be the deeds done beyond Enchendar so far, and even more mighty are they that yet will be. Alas, our fairy kingdom has no army to offer, for in greatest peril only can we cross the river or forest's edge. But—but two gifts I will bestow. One for your leader. He alone may have visions of things that yet may be in the mirror of the Pool of Ian. You must be brave of heart to look. Though I know not what you will see, good or bad, you shall have the chance to view, if you so choose."

Marc, a bit bewildered by this statement, rose and accompanied Lynn to her pool.

Faegor spoke again. "The second gift of the fairies shall go to Mindi, who is fairy of heart."

She stood in honor awaiting his words.

"Thrice thee shall have the power to restore life by the touch of your hand. Thrice. Beyond that I cannot say!"

She thanked him as was fitting, but her wide eyes never left his. Her mind was racing over his words and her mental pictures. The others were at a loss to say anything, so great was the gift.

Meanwhile, Lynn led Marc away; he was a bit confused and worried. Did he have the strength for visions? She waved her hand across the pool; the ripples died; a dark sheen appeared on the still waters. She bade him to gaze into its waters and see what he may. He knelt alone beside the dark waters and peered into its blackish depths. He wondered what would happen.

Slowly, a fear grew over him and a form appeared on the water's surface. A tall obelos appeared, lit by the noonday sun coming from the left. It was a yellow and black checkered tower. The origin of the fear came from atop the tower. As the image grew stronger so did the fear. Around the base of the tower, he saw endless sand dunes. Then, he realized that he was looking at the tower from far off—through a dark, rounded arch. The image flickered, and, once again, he saw only the dark waters of Ian. He felt an overwhelming terror. He lingered by the pool. Again an image formed. He beheld a golden, glowing woman of immense beauty and radiance dressed in white robes, her right hand out stretched towards him. At once, his fear blew away, and he was filled with an awe and deep respect. Somehow, she was familiar.

Then, the pool went dark. He paused, but no more images came. He stood up and looked around. There was Lynn way off to the left by a tree.

"Done? Come," she said, and he spoke no words.

When he joined the others, he still said nothing and, though besieged with questions about his visions, still he said nothing. Mindi noticed how pale he was. He caught her glance and stood staring at her for a long minute. Then, as if waking up, he jerked, rubbed his face in his hands, and stretched.

"I do not understand what I saw. It filled me with fear. I shall tell you later. We must make ready to assist Vorag and Beregrin."

Quickly the ponies were packed with the gear, and the company ate a hurried supper before starting. They bid the fairies farewell, and Prince Faedon led them through the paths of Eos to their northern border. By sunset, the company stood at the edge of Enchendar.

Before them rushed the Kanandrul River once more, but here it was shallow and very wide. No bridge was needed. Ahead they saw, twisting and turning, the dusty, dry road that led north to Beregrin. In the distance far to the right rose the mighty Armagh Mountains, home of the Dwarves. Nache incessantly explained this fact. Before them were low hills and scattered trees. Further off in the distance rose a darkish mass—the forest of Burly.

They said farewell to Prince Faedon, and Mindi kissed him gently. He blushed and smiled. With splashes, the company of seven plus animals waded the cool shallows of the great river and soon were trudging along the dry dirt road as twilight waned.

Immediately, the Drifter's head was downward, and he pointed out the telltale signs of Yacs. Vorag, Oran, and the Drifter led the party northward. Marc, Nache, and Mindi followed, leading the ponies, while George and Shannon brought up the rear. Soon the keen eyes of the Drifter discerned fresh signs.

Quietly, he halted the company and whispered, "Careful, Yacs are before us. See, these prints are fresh. Be alert and quiet."

Nache unfastened the clasp that held his axe to his belt. Others felt for their swords. Taking a deep breath, Marc urged Blackie forward. They continued moving north in the growing darkness.

The expectant company made their way slowly forward on the road. Shortly after nine, the gibbous moon rose high in the east. The night sounds were only broken by the quiet trudging of their feet upon the dry, clay roadbed. Shannon had brought more supplies to Enchendar; and now both he and

George wore forest green, elfin shoes with pointed toes. George had protested wearing shoes; he'd gone barefoot all his life, but Vorag had pointed out that his feet would get brutalized in the rocky forest. So he'd consented to wear the elfin slippers. They were so light that he was hardly aware of their presence. Marc and Mindi also wore theirs. Nache still stumped along in his stubby, dwarf boots.

Around ten, Drifter halted the group. Marc handed Mindi Blackie's lead rope and joined the two in front. Vorag pointed out the sign of a flickering light among the gathering trees ahead. A Yac watch point, he guessed. The hunter suggested they should encircle them, while the Drifter suggested he spy them out first.

Whether this debate would have been resolved or not, George came rushing forward, "Look behind us, Yacs!"

They turned around and saw yellow flames far behind them on the road. A faint yelling could be heard. Drifter lay down and put his ear to the ground. All were silent.

Then, he quickly rose, saying "They're on to us; they're running."

Marc calmly said, "That settles it; we will charge, making all possible speed. Let us sweep through whatever lays before us as fast as we can. Let them join the others at our rear. Let us charge."

This was more to Vorag's liking, and he quickly drew his silver scimitar.

Drifter had the last word, "Let us do this orderly. Marc, you take the front point with Andrill. Vorag and I will be slightly behind you and at your side. Nache, you and George take a pony on either side of Mindi and guard the flanks. Keep close together. Shannon you bring up the rear; if you need help, just yell—I'll fall back, but keep together at all costs!"

The company drew their weapons and took their places. Marc yelled, "Go," and they started off at a jog. Marc increased their pace. Though Nache did his best, and said no word, Mindi saw that he could not keep up so fast a pace. She ordered him up on Blackie. So strong was her intention that Nache did not hesitate.

Once astride a pony bred for dwarf use, Mindi called

out to Marc, "Faster, Nache's aboard."

He increased the pace to a slow run. The road twisted and turned before them, avoiding the low hills.

The light grew steadily before them, yet they made no sound, save running feet. As Marc rounded the bend, the Yac campfire lay squarely before him. Sitting around it were a half a dozen Yacs, who were now aroused by the sound of running feet. As soon as they got within the light of the fire, Marc raised Tiny high and muttered to himself. Suddenly to both Vorag's and the startled Scavenger's utter bewilderment, Tiny flashed red, extended to three feet, and burst into flames. Carrying the awesome banner forward, Marc charged straight at the staggering Evil Ones.

Vorag and Drifter, yelling "Elidine," were right beside him. The nearest Yac drew his sword and had it up as Marc arrived. With a two handed swinging arc, Andrill cut a flaming path; the blackish blade smoked and broke instantly. Amid fumes of smoke and stench, the Yac's head rolled off. As Vorag passed by, a silver flash arched through the fire light; a Yac was cut open as he stood gaping. George stabbed another, and Shannon de-limbed the last as he passed. They ran on into the darkness of the road and forest beyond the fire.

"Well done! All ok?" yelled Marc, as he slowed them down to a comfortable jog.

They continued their hurried pace for several hours and then took a short rest. In a similar fashion, by this time, they had run through two more enemy watch fires. The Scavengers would certainly that know they were abroad; very clear was their trail. The Burly woods had now become dense so Vorag led them off the road. They had a two-hour rest, while hidden in the thickets of eastern Burly. Their trailing enemies had fallen far behind. Indeed, they had left an ill omen in their wake, and the rest was much needed by all, save Nache, who crept back to the road to stand guard for the others.

The waning moon now stood high overhead; only a few clouds blocked the starry heavens, but the dark leaves above let only a few beacons shine. The company ate and drank a little and relaxed, leaning against the trees, but they remained as silent as possible under the shadowing cover. The southeastern part of Burly had become a no-man's land of rising hills; scattered boulders lay everywhere. The country had become increasingly stony, with piles of leaves collecting in the shallow spots.

In one of these soft depressions, filled with the accumulation of leaves, lay Mindi, elfin cloak pulled around her. She lay on her back, hood drawn around her head. Far above her, dark shapes swayed in the gentle breeze. As the canopy of dark green rustled, occasional star beams fell on her face. The beauty of the forest at night had been steadily growing in her mind. She felt as though she could just reach up and touch the swaying forms; she could feel or sense the gentle breeze.

George had similar sensations; he had never been in a wild forest. "Enchendar was enchanted so it didn't quite count," he'd said. As he lay with senses probing, he listened for the night sounds but few animals stirred. "Probably the times," he mused. He decided that a forest was a nice, wonderful place to visit, but there was no cropland! In a flash of insight, he glimpsed how harsh survival would be for a pure hunting people and was glad to be a farmer.

Meanwhile, the others, leaning against a large, orange-hued boulder that was covered with green lichen circles, were quietly discussing their approximate position and how best to make for Beregrin.

The peaceful respite was abruptly ended by the thumping of scurrying dwarven boots coming towards them. At once the Drifter arose, likewise Marc and Vorag, but Oran, Mindi, George, and Shannon remained where they lay, only propping their heads on an arm, listening and looking for Nache. Shortly he appeared running swiftly and noisily towards them.

"What's up, Nache?" the Drifter whispered, as he came into their small camp, "You certainly make a lot of noise in a forest!"

"Battle—a battle is near. A strange one. Come and hear," said the deep breathing and worried dwarf, who had already loosened his axe.

Quickly, the four of them hurried back to the road,

while the others began to break camp and get the gear and ponies ready. They reached the dusty ribbon of road where Nache had stood guard duty. While the others listened, the Drifter laid his ear on the dry ground of the road, straining for the distant sounds. They had grown louder now.

"Verily, it doth sound of clashing shield!" spoke the amazed hunter.

"Yes," the Drifter said rising and brushing himself off. "There is a battle going on—off northwards. Armor seems to be involved, curious," his voice trailed off as he became lost in thought.

With growing recognition, a small voice suddenly yelled, "Dwarves!"

The others jumped in reaction to Nache's startling shout.

"Right," replied Drifter.

"What's the matter?" Mindi said, leading Butterball from the forest onto the road followed by the others.

Nache excitedly said, "Dwarves are ahead of us—in a great battle. Let us go help! Kazab will join them!" He flashed his silver axe through the air.

"Careful with that axe," cautioned Drifter, "Let's go; we may be needed."

Nache needed no further invitation, and he climbed aboard Blackie. The group was off as before, jogging at first, then increasing to a run. Dust clouds rose behind them; and trees moved past them, as they raced northwards on the curving road that remained fairly flat, needling its way around the base of the hills. The clatter of swords on shields steadily rose. Soon the noise of battle was distinct. Yac laughing and shrieking could be easily heard. Nache worked himself into a frantic fit, having nothing to do but ride, and he angrily swore and cursed the Scourge.

Vorag pulled his horn around to his front and raised it to his lips. Breaking stride momentarily, be blew a great, deep, bellowing blast that resounded loudly through the forest night. Thrice he blew the sound of assistance. All drew their weapons; they increased their speed into a head long run.

The twisting road now rose for a distance as they

climbed up a ridge. Below the ridge lay the valley of the Blayborne Wash; it fell from the Armagh Mountains down to the Beone East. As they reached the ridge top, they could see the battlefield below, lit by many torchlights of the Scourge; some the trees had been set aflame as well. Huddled into a small circle near the creek around several tall oaks was a band of a dozen dwarves. Their bright silvery shields flashed in the moon and fire light. Mail clad bodies glimmered and axes flashed. They were surrounded by nearly two dozen large Yacs screaming, laughing, and bashing their swords on the beleaguered dwarves. From the bush on the left, another group of some dozen was running to assist in the destruction of the half-men. Several wargs paced just beyond the Yacs' rear line. Scattered foul bodies lay about the small dale and a few small dwarves also.

Reaching the crest, Marc held Tiny aloft and spoke to it. Even as Tiny flared into existence, Vorag again blew a voluminous, deep blast, and the company raced down the hillside toward the battle. Whether it was the sound of the Burly horn or the sight of a flaming sword coming at them, the Yacs momentarily broke their attack and looked at the ridge. The arriving group stopped in their tracks. Like a great rush of wind, the flaming sword bore down upon them, the Scourge turned away from the dwarves to meet this new challenge, ill prepared.

The company charged at great speed straight into the middle of the band of Scavengers. Andrill swished a flaming arc through the air, and several heads rolled, accompanied by steaming, searing noises, and screaming in last-instant terror. Elidine rose and fell repeatedly, and the curved scimitar flashed in figure eight patterns slicing deeply its targets. The dwarf opened several bellies as he rode by in a flash. The company halted near the dwarves and turned around to face the Yacs just in time to see a grayish form fly through the air, knocking a Yac to the ground, with a gushing tearing sound. Oran was at work.

Nache yelled to the Dwarves, "Nache Thraindruil and Company to your rescue!"

He dismounted and rushed toward the evil host, who

had now backed off to the west, joining the new comers. Mindi quickly grabbed the lead ropes of the ponies and stood near a tree guarding them. The dwarves, recovering from the sudden shock of so powerful a charge, rushed forward to assist the company.

As one reached Mindi, she commanded, "Guard these ponies," and she ran forward into the line. For now a battleline had formed.

The company of seven stood facing the Scavengers with dwarves falling into line on either end. Only Oran continued his random attacks nearby. The ferocity and power and the incredible sight of the awesome weapons brandished by the newcomers had unnerved the Scavengers considerably, and they continually gave ground, retreating slowly towards the woods.

Then Marc yelled "Forth Andrill!" The fiery line rushed the Yacs. Blow upon blow fell. Swords clashed; shields bashed, but none could stand before Andrill, and no one could stay the force of the scimitar's blow or Elidine's. Dwarf axes sliced bellies open and heads rolled. Shannon's cutlass continued to chop. Mindi gracefully thrust her point here and there meeting bellies squarely. The seven disposed of all the Yacs in their vicinity and broke into teams, surrounding the remaining Yacs on either end of the line. In less than fifteen minutes, Andrill flared for the last time and went out.

The battle was over; forty Yacs lay beaten in the dust and rocks. No warg walked; Oran saw to that. Only one dwarf had suffered a slash in this round. Instinctively, they made their way back to the creek where they had first come upon the surrounded half-men, and there they rested, drank, and splashed from the stream. Cold, grey light was in the sky as the first light of dawn began to appear in the eastern sky, high above the mountains.

All the while, Nache talked incessantly in the dwarf tongue, first to one dwarf and then to another, as if time was coming to an abrupt end. The others of the company had now sufficiently recovered, aided both by the cool, clean waters flowing down from the tall mountains, and by the growing dawn, with now rapidly swelling, pink shades. They milled around feeling rather awkward.

Mindi finally handled the situation, "Nache? Nache come; it's time for introductions to your friends."

He stopped short and saw the others were rather impatiently waiting on him, and the dwarves were as well. Actually, they had formed into two distinct groups—each facing the other. Nache found himself in the center—all eyes were upon him. This he enjoyed immensely. Using the common tongue, he began in a dignified manner, "We have rescued from certain doom a dwarf scouting party led by Broom."

Here a young dwarf clad in yellowish mail, a silver helm (with ear-pieces and a spike on top), and carrying a round silver shield stepped forward, bowing as low as he could. His youthful ruddy complexion and brown hair and beard contrasted sharply with the half-revealed, bright red and yellow swatches of color—his tunic. He stood in typical black boots, seemingly oversized and fluffy, that reached nearly up to his knees.

"We are deeply in your debt and at your service," he pronounced.

Nache interrupted to state, "He is the Fourth Captain of the Second Kunthzar of Khorizaba. That is, we have three armies—Kunthzar. The Second is led by Aaron from the Yaca side of Khorizaba."

Here Droom interrupted Nache, "Yes, Aaron sent us three days ago to spy and to learn the plans of the enemy, but we lost four before you arrived. Many thanks. We are in your debt," he repeated and bowed again.

Then, Nache introduced the members of the company one by one, describing the nature and armament each bore. There was a good deal of mumbling among the dwarf party on each. When Marc and Andrill were announced, the talk really became noisy, and Marc spent five minutes answering questions regarding it. The dwarves were very excited about the return of the legendary Fire Sword.

Finally, Nache introduced Mindi. "Here is my fair lady, Mindi," and she, feeling a bit haughty just then, stepped forward and threw her hood back and revealed as much of her womanhood as possible.

It had its effect; there was much oohing and aahing among the surprised dwarves. She enjoyed it.

Then, Nache began to introduce the dwarves rapidly, "This is Kolo, Bolo, Orti, Doru, Borti, Kula, Movin, Immy, Bimmy, Timmy, ..."

Mindi cut him off laughingly, "Whoa there, not so fast. I can't remember who's who at this rate."

He grinned, and his face blushed a bit; he repeated more slowly with each in turn stepping forward and bowing with the ever familiar, "At your service." Nearly all gazed first at Marc, but lingered on Mindi. The men—they were understandable—but such a beautiful woman they could not grasp and remained in awe.

Then Vorag suggested, "Pray Master Droom, wilst thee and thy men accompanyth us to Beregrin—least other evil befalleth thee?"

However, Marc had been thinking now for several minutes, and having resolved a matter, spoke. "Let us take council with Droom. I have a plan, but let us move up stream a ways; there is too much foulness here."

All agreed with both points and quickly moved into another dale some distance to the east. The sky now cleared with the first golden, ruddy rays of the new day. The company plus Droom sat in a circle on the soft moss and grass; between them trickled the babbling rivulet of Blayborne Wash.

Quickly Marc outlined the situation here in East Burly. Vorag added a little from time to time. They were on their way to assist the besieged town.

"With some assistance, the Scourge may yet be driven from these lands back from whence they come. If the armies of the dwarves can sweep from the east to Beregrin, whilst we from the south, and the hunters from the west, Beregrin can be rescued, and the Evil Ones driven northward."

Droom, obviously delighted with the plan, stood smiling broadly, and said loudly, "It shall be done! The Second Kunthzar of Khorizaba shall flood from Armagh, ere this day is ended! But first we shall attend the fallen." Marc and Droom shook hands sealing the pact.

Soon the sounds of chopping axe blades filled the early morning air. They quickly buried their four in a mound of rocks and trees. Nache explained that the location was chosen so the fallen ones could always be in sight of their homeland— the Armagh Mountains. Leaving the industrious little men, the company prepared to continue their northward trek. Bidding the dwarves farewell, they gained the road and walked onwards. The rising dew of morning filled the air with the fragrant odors of the Burly forest. The sky had cleared and the sun shone brightly in the dark blue field. It was to be another stifling hot, Burly summer day.

The morning passed uneventful filled only with the endless dirt path, hot muggy air, and flying insects. This seemed to be their day; and the pests were out in droves, bombarding the sweating travelers, occasionally drowning in a pool of sweat. Though the sun was now high, the road seemed to darken with every step. Towering trees grew thicker; underbrush, more dense; there was a dark canopy overhead. Only an occasional struggling sunbeam could penetrate the greenery. The shafts of sudden rays shone sharply through the leaden air in contrast to the dim shades of grey-green. The toiling company had entered the denser part of the Burly woods in the height of summer. By noon, all needed a break, and they paused for nearly an hour by a small creek.

The afternoon dragged on unrelenting in its baking heat. Far above them, the leafy trees seemed to absorb all the heat, radiating it to all below. The forest was cooking at a slow simmer. No trace of wind could be felt or seen. They bore ever onwards.

No traces of Scavengers appeared. Whether the heat had cooked them as Nache liked to suggest, or whether they were scared by their coming, or whether all were away attacking Burly, none could say for sure. By night fall, tempers began to flare. Nache and George were the first to show signs of heat exhaustion. The half-man, unused to this climate, had taken to cursing and tried vainly to chop down the forest. At this point, Marc insisted they take a long supper break. George had dived into the creek and drunk so much water that he became ill. So while the others handled the camp setup for dinner, Mindi tended the two. She had both lying down and was moping their heads when Marc called for dinner, but none had much appetite, save Vorag and Oran.

Nightfall brought welcome relieve; Nache and George finally cooled down, and everyone was now splashing in the shallow creek. It washed the clammy skins clean, and all seemed refreshed, so much in fact, that now they were hungry. So a second dinner was served, as the one hour rest pushed into its fifth hour. They were all talking, were in better spirits, and ready to resume, when Oran began to whine softly and rub Vorag's leg.

"Husheth!" the hunter commanded, "Oran heareth something. We be'st too loud!"

A hush fell at once; everyone strained to hear what the mastiff had detected.

Far off the heavy stamp of feet could be heard drawing closer.

"Tis friend. A hunter," Vorag announced, and all relaxed, but quickly got their gear stowed.

Vorag and Drifter agreed that it would be useful to meet whoever it was. They lacked news. Vorag pointed out that only a few of the company might be able to trample through the woods especially at night. Neither wanted to risk separation.

"Tis only one choice that remaineth!" The hunter blew a loud blast on his horn. Resounding echos came in a cacophony. Faintly, all heard the answering horn, slightly lower in pitch. The forest was treated with a horn symphony for nearly ten minutes. Loud and soft, yet not so soft. Finally, the answering blast was nearly equal to Vorag's, and presently a cautious band of Burly hunters appeared.

Vorag and Oran stepped forward in instant recognition and hearty greetings were voluminously exchanged. It was Neil and six companions. The company heard him tell Vorag that they were out rounding up men, for Beregrin was about to fall. Neil, noticing Vorag was not alone, became silent at once. Vorag laughed and led them to the company. Moonbeams filtered down from the treetops. To the mighty hunters, Vorag's troupe appeared very, very, strange—almost unreal, clad in elfin cloaks. One by one, Vorag introduced the company and briefly told of their adventures so far.

Mindi watched Neil carefully, this being only her second example of the great hunters. She noticed he seemed awfully nervous and pale. Surely, they didn't have that effect. At last, she could contain herself no longer and interrupted the men.

"Neil, you are pale and distraught. We are being unkind hosts. Come sit by our creek, and let us get you something to eat. Then you can tell us what has you so frightened."

Her observation was precisely correct, and he jerked, as he understood her remarks; but he willingly accompanied her, and though not hungry, did drink long and hard. His men did likewise. She kept the conversation light and non-significant.

At last, he seemed calmer, so she ventured to ask him what the trouble was.

"Tis not for ears so fair to heareth, but times be bad. Beregrin ist besieged and wilst falleth soon. The Scourge hath brought an awesome weapon. Three days past, we heareth a sound never heard before—a doom of foot falls. Oh so slowly, they cameth ever towards the city. We scouteth for the makers. Horrible ones. Three great cave trolls cometh. Lord Edward ordered them stopped, but nought ceaseth their plod of doom to Beregrin. By morning they shalst arrive." Tears were in his eyes, and he could continue no longer.

Mindi put her arms around the weeping hunter and comforted him. "There is hope yet Neil," she spoke softly.

He rose up and gazed into her face lit by moonbeams filtered through the forest above. "We bear the Fire Sword," she whispered.

Neil looked at Vorag, "Beest this so?" he asked, rising up full of wonder.

"Verily, Marc beareth the Fire Sword, Andrill, of old. Others beareth Mizzinti blades of yore."

In awe, Neil backed away from the group as did his fellow companions, as the actual reality, the identity, of the company became clear to them. The great hunters were familiar with the story legends of the early days passed down by word of mouth. Here before their eyes, the old tales took new life. Their eyes glanced from member to member of the company, perceiving both the person and their weapons. The strangeness of the party seemed to amplify for Neil; in awe, he slowly stepped back as if afraid to be so close to ones of such power. He stood speechless and limp.

Mindi, aware of the growing separation and where that could lead, smiled and stepped forward, taking Neil's hand and pulled him back into the group.

"Oh come on Neil, we don't bite," she ribbed. "Do we really look like wizards or more like just plain folks, huh?"

Slowly he agreed, "Well, for a moment, I thoughtest thee—well—I saweth thou differently! But thy touch seemeth as it shouldst."

He blushed when he saw what he had just said and hastily added, "I meanst no offense, by Lady. Thinkst me not too forward."

"No offense, Neil, I—we understand. In these times, help comes in many forms. We are here to do what we can however we can."

He seemed satisfied that he was not in the company of some ethereal gods, but was still a bit uneasy.

The Drifter who had been growing uneasy for several minutes now had begun to pace in small circles and finally said, "I hate to break up this friendly reunion, but I feel we must get moving. Beregrin is in peril; it would be foolish to delay longer."

"Verily, thou speaketh what hath been my thought," Vorag added.

"Yes, my axe thirsts for heads to roll," Nache exclaimed, patting his axe handle lovingly.

Without further remarks, they gathered up their things, clamored to the road, fell into a semblance of order, and continued their fateful northern trek.

As they walked, Marc discussed their position with Vorag and Drifter. Agreement was reached; if they pushed on rapidly through the night, the first rays of morning would fall upon the besieged city as they arrived. Vorag indicated that the pattern of the trolls at Greagon would probably make dawn the hour of doom. Thus, the company began a slow jog on the dim, dusty road. Once again, Nache climbed aboard Blackie, for it would be of little use for him to expend all his energies just to keep up with the others. They trotted on through the night of little event.

Slowly, tree after tree passed by the group, mile after mile in the warm August night. They found no Scavengers on the prowl that night. The Drifter mused that it meant they were preparing for a big attack soon. They increased their pace slightly, running on and on into the dark night in the depths of the Burly forest.

As he bounced along on Blackie, the dwarf watched the dark canopy above him. Here and there, small openings allowed the twinkle of stars to meet his eyes. Quickly, the heavenly fire would be eclipsed and another would appear as a lone jewel against a dark sky. Long he gazed upwards. All of a sudden, the dwarf woke from the half-hypnotic trance he'd been in, for he realized the dark sky was now a very pale blue!

"Dawn," he cried aloud.

Startled by his outburst, the others halted, breathing hurriedly and deep, gazing upwards. The forest itself showed little difference from where they had begun that night. Drifter and Marc called for a break, and together on the road, they collapsed for a much-needed rest. Nache scampered about eating a meal such as he could fix. After resting and recovering their labored breathing, the others extinguished a great thirst, and then hunger.

As Mindi afterwards spoke of it, it was just after finishing a morning desert that the horns of doom commenced. Low pitched and earth shaking came the voice of eminent doom to all.

Boom. Boom. Boom.

Casting heavy fear into the hunters, calling ill memories to Vorag's mind, leaving incomprehensible bewilderment into the others, the ominous sounds continued relentlessly.

Boom. Boom. Boom.

"God, are we too late?" Marc nearly screamed.

"Nay, Beregrin layeth yonder a mile," Vorag nervously replied, his mind flashing with pictures of Edmund's Line, the frantic efforts to build the greatest bow ever, the crashing gate, and the ugly towering figure.

"Forward," yelled Marc, "Blow your horns!"

Hastily they threw their gear onto the ponies, and the company, in disarray, ran full speed down the road. Both Vorag and Neil blew long, loud blasts on their horns, but rather halfheartedly.

Chapter XVI—The Battle of Beregrin

Unceasingly came the impending noise of doom, now rapidly becoming louder.

Boom. Boom. Boom.

The hideous cries from a thousand Yacs reached their ears, casting chills down their spines. A multitude of answering horn blasts echoed just over a small ridge.

Nache, who had been looking ahead and around, having little else to contribute on the run, first noticed the multitudes of silver flashes coming from far to the right on the nearest of the hills that rose relentlessly to the Armagh Mountains. The rising sun reflected ruddy rays from the tops of many spears and off shields and mail.

Nache yelled, "The dwarves! The dwarves come!"

The others looked where he was wildly pointing, and the sight of glimmering flashes filled them with renewed hope. Repeatedly, the two hunters blew great blasts. The forest echoed with their sounds. Repeatedly answerings came, and above the cries, the voice of doom continued to speak the sound of destruction.

Beregrin was a walled city, like Greagon, and was normally the home of some seven hundred. It lay nestled in a small dale bounded on both the north and south by two small ridges. Through the middle of the dale and the city ran a small creek called the Wade. Large, stony hills rose to the east, each one higher than the last, for some twenty leagues to the Armagh heights. Whereas Greagon's walls were vertical posts set deep in the ground, Beregrin's were constructed of logs lain horizontally. Uniformly spaced were massive vertical posts to hold the log stack. Holes were neatly placed in the wall for the archers to fire. Two great gates provided access from both north and south. The walls rose to six feet and small guardhouses rose above the walls in all four corners. In addition, a giant walkway and a pair of guardhouses stood connected above the northern gate. Inside the walls were many log cabins each adjacent to the next.

It was a beautiful sight to see as one reached the ridge top under ordinary circumstances, but this day, horror greeted the chargers atop the ridge. Below they saw the impending destruction. Three great cave trolls from the north were nearly down the northern ridge, heading for the gate. Inside packed elbow to elbow were hundreds of the hunters brandishing bows and scimitars. Rains of arrows uselessly bounced off the tough, grey hides of the trolls. Swarming down the ridge were rows upon rows of Scavengers; a hundred wargs prowled on the ridge top. The sea of Yacs remained just outside of bow range waiting for the gate's destruction by their champions. Far to their right, the company saw the shining half-men flowing in waves over the hills a half mile off.

Nache yelled, "Yes, Aaron! Yes, the Second Kunthzar comes!"

Vorag cried loudly, "The gates, the gates."

The company with renewed vigor charged as fast as they could down the hill, weapons drawn. Marc again raised Tiny in the air before him, held it in both hands, and spoke softly and hurriedly to himself. Amid cries of utter disbelief from Neil and friends, Andrill rose to its full length and burst into giant, red flames, roaring upwards. Vorag brandished his silver scimitar high in the air and headed straight toward the trolls, followed by Marc and Drifter yelling, "Forth Elidine." The others of the company followed likewise waving their swords in the air—content just to yell. Neil and the hunters were taken completely off their guard and totally unnerved by the incredible sight of the entire company's charge. So Mindi yelled, "Watch the Ponies," and charged as well.

The Scourge was likewise startled by the blazing, ferocious charge, and a hush fell on them. The bash and clash of the dwarf noise of arrival was now heard and cries of dismay followed.

Vorag smashed head long into the lead troll, whose massive hulk was only six feet from the gate, scimitar thrust forward as he hit with all his force. The wizard's scimitar bent but did not break or dull, but it afflicted only a surface slice upon the troll's chest. The force of the impact caused the troll to step backwards to avoid being toppled, but Vorag bounced like a ball off the huge solid hulk. For days afterwards, his whole body would ache from that blow.

Marc slowed as he watched the great hunter collide and be repelled. Then, without reflection or thinking, he stepped squarely before the evil monster and swung the flaming sword in downwards arc passing through the belly area of the tall troll. As the blade hit, Marc's arms felt a jolt so strong his arms nearly gave. He held on tightly, but Andrill was nearly jerked from him. Pain of shock racked his arms but he held on. As the blade met the foul, grey belly, a dark smoke, and foul spray of foam issued in a searing cloud nearly obliterating from sight the fiery flames. An earth shattering bellow racked the ground, and the very walls of Beregrin shook. The troll grasped his belly as foaming goo bubbled and flowed out, creating a giant, foul, grey cloud. He tottered and crashed to the ground. The tremor knocked Marc's feet out from under him, and arms shaking violently in pain, he fell to the ground as well. After a pause amid the bellowing roars of pain from the fallen troll, he scrambled to his feet holding Andrill away from him so he wouldn't be burned. He walked towards the next troll.

The dwarves had now arrived from the east and had fallen on the Yac's left flank, and the sounds of battle reached Marc's ears. He saw his company charging by him into the Yacs behind the trolls, while on his left the Burly men were running to the right flank of the Scourge. Grimacing, he knew he had two more foes. Again, he struck with all his might. The second fell as the first one, but the force wrenched Andrill from his aching arms, and he collapsed on the ground. The noise of battle rose like a hideous din to his ears. He tried to rise but his strength was failing him.

The third troll began to take action. Slow as he was, he made for his fallen opponent. Marc saw him getting closer. The giant feet grew nearer. He had to get up or be trampled under those feet. Vorag rushed to his aid and again drove his scimitar into the troll's belly but to no avail; it could not penetrate the foul skin that was created in another time and place by a power greater than the scimitar's. The troll cast the huge hunter aside, and Marc struggled shakily to his knees.

With all his might, he forced his aching arms to grasp the sword blazing on the ground.

Limply he held it before him, but could not get to his feet. The troll neared and Marc watched as the great one raised both his clenched hands high into the air. He intended to smash Marc as one does an ant. As the troll leaned forward to deliver the blow, Marc thrust Andrill up and forward meeting the belly of the cave troll. Deep it drove amid a violent, jerking, and retching. Marc held on and withdrew the blade. The giant arms fell mid-blow, and he grasped, instead, his searing, gushing belly in the pain of flaming light. He tottered and collapsed; Marc did likewise. The ground thundered as the troll smashed to the ground. The force caused Marc's body to rise nearly a foot into the air; he remembered the sensation of floating; then the ground hit him hard. That was the last thing he remembered of the Great Battle of Beregrin.

Vorag struggled to his feet, picked up Marc, and swiftly carried him towards the gate. At once, a group of women came and took the fallen warrior from him. They carried him into the city and gave him care. Meanwhile the great hunter retrieved Andrill, which lay blazing in the dirt. Very, very carefully he touched its hilt. It did not burn him. He picked Andrill up and carried it back to the wall. There he placed it high in a crack. The Flaming Sword continued to flare for all to see.

In the center of the Yac swarm, the four Yac chieftains stood commanding their forces. It was here that the more robust Yacs had gathered. These elite guards were dressed in yellow and black checkered tunics. All the Scavengers stayed well beyond bowshot from the wall, but most had crude, hide covered shields. The chief's were metallic. It was into this group that the others in the company charged.

Drifter and Shannon on either end with George, Nache, and Mindi in the center. Together they formed an impressive line. Swords bashed into shields and swords. Fierce was their attack, and equally fierce was the resistance. Though dismayed by the destruction of their trolls, the chieftains were far from routed. They fought with a passion.

Repeatedly, Elidine crashed down upon the black metal

shield of one captain. Elidine did not blunt nor crack. Finally, the shield was so smashed that the bearer discarded it, fending Drifter's blows with his sword. No dark blade could withstand the force of Elidine, and with a loud crack, the Yac held only a hilt as Drifter's next blow met its soft mark; that chief died. Dismay filled his eyes, even in death.

George found that he and Nache got along well as a team. He was a terrible fighter with a log. He had grabbed a log, and as the guards rushed him, he'd cleverly pivoted the log in such a fashion as to knock the attacker off balance. And while he fought to regain it, Kazab flashed in a big arc. Then, they'd go after the next.

Shannon was an old hand with his golden cutlass, a veteran of many pirate attempts at sea. Of all of the questers, he was the most lean and agile. While Drifter bashed and parried, yellow hair flashing, Shannon would dart cleverly in all directions and very effectively throw his opponent off guard or out of step. Only then did his short cutlass swiftly flash, squarely to the central chest—usually the point dove deep there.

Mindi assisted Nache and parried with others. Yacs were unused to the fine art of dueling, and with left arm raised and right moving swiftly, she would drive her opponent anywhere she chose. At the appropriate instant, her whole body extended in a great, thrust lunge and just as quickly, resumed its former position, leaving a neat, clean, punctured body gasping.

Within an half an hour, both the Burly men and the dwarves of Aaron had pushed the line of Yacs toward the center. Now they were effectively bunched together, and there was no danger of being flanked. Indeed, the toll of the two was astounding; many Yacs lay dead or dying in scattered piles in the early morning sun.

The largest chief now bore down hard upon Mindi, for he realized that she was a woman. Hideous, evil purposes and intentions rose in his mind, and he wanted her for himself. He was ferocious and unrelenting in his attack; she gave way continually. Nache tried to intervene and was thrown off by the blow of his shield. He struggled to his feet and ran to her side. She parried blow for blow, but his heavy sword could not be handled by her dueling sword. The dwarf's stomach sank when he heard the telltale snap. He knew that her blade had been broken, and he dashed between the two opponents. Kazab slashed widely. So ferocious came the axe that, for an instant, the gloating gleam of victory left his face. With great effort he stopped bash after bash, waiting. For eventually, he thought, this half-man would tire, and he could easily gain his prize. He grinned at her, revealing his ugly yellowed teeth, many missing.

Though Nache's strength was finally ebbing, he pushed his body ever on. He couldn't let his fair lady down. Suddenly, he knew not why, the Yac screamed and covered his face—it was contorted by wild terror. He had never seen such in any living creature. It was a terror beyond Nache's capacity to describe, even if given sufficient time to do so. Without a pause, he placed his axe swing deep into the chief's belly, but then the little man just stared. Blood and guts poured out; the Yac took no notice of it; he seemed frozen—rigid. Curiously, Nache pushed him with his axe; he fell over; his body held that rigid pose unto death. Nache could scarcely believe his eyes; then he turned around to see if his lady was all right. It was an amazed dwarf! He saw a hideous fanged face for an instant, which quickly melted into his beloved Mindi's.

In a moment, she spoke, "It's ok, Nache. We did him in together."

His eyes opened wide, Nache blurted, "Nay, nay. What magic! For a second I thought I saw a monster. What happened to the Evil One? I'd swear he died not from my slit but from terror!"

Mindi laid her hand on his shoulders, and said in a tranquil voice, "I allowed him to see what his mind most feared. It was not real. It was what he, in the depths of his darkest beingness, most feared. It was his own image that I showed him. He saw in me his own demon."

Nache looked very amazed and bowed lower than ever saying, "Forever at your service, my lady, my wizard!"

She accepted his offer and replied, "You can be as well— just do as you feel, but come; let us work together. I have lost my sword."

Together they raced back to the slowly receding battleline. Nache stood in front of Mindi who stood motionless and weaponless. Yet as the attackers came upon the pair, they beheld an individual terror, and the wizard's axe swung in greater and greater swings. Finally, Kazab flew through the air to its mark. By the battle's end, Nache had regained a long lost skill. Kazab would fly through the air many feet, always shattering through to its mark; then it would continue its swing, returning to its master's waiting hand. He was wild with excitement, exclaiming he never knew his axe could fly. Mindi smiled.

The brilliant midmorning's sun climbed high in the clear sky, as if watching the battle below. The company had gained the northern ridge. With the combined forces of men and dwarves, they were driving the Yacs down the other side. Drifter urged all to keep them constrained on either side so they would be forced to retreat on the road. He, himself, drove relentlessly forward heading the point on the road.

Soon the slow retreat gained momentum and gradually became an orderly route. The combined forces drove the remaining Yacs back down the road from which they came, mile after mile. Vorag had joined them. The hunters blew blast upon blast. By afternoon, the towering cliffs of Begrundi Pass loomed in the distance—like two dark slabs. On either side the giant orange-hued mountains loomed—ragged, tall, and forbidding. The only entrance was the pass.

The sight of the pass brought renewed hope to the challengers and relief to the Yac force, already cut in half. The Scavengers hope lay in achieving the singular protection of its narrow way. The hunters halted just outside, dwarfed by the immense size of the Quara Sud. Here they rejoiced, and all blew blast after blast in the loudest volume they could muster. The roar of victory was deafening to behold. Mindi and the dwarves covered their painful ears. Yet Vorag and crew blew mightily the trumpets of the conquerors.

Suddenly as if in answer to their challenge, the ground began shaking violently; the noise had set off an avalanche far above in the Quara Sud heights. They ran back quickly amid a shower of rocks. The earth gave one great moaning groan, and the rocks that formed the sides of the pass cracked and crumbled, hurling giant boulders and slabs into the valley of the pass.

In a minute, the trembling ground stood still, and an enormous dust cloud rose steadily upwards. Then there was silence! One by one, the men picked themselves up and dusted themselves off. The Drifter yelled at the top of his voice, "Three Cheers! The pass has been closed! The pass has been closed!"

Wild cheering ensued as the joy of victory was released once again. Tired and exhausted, they dragged their way slowly back down the road to Beregrin.

The dwarves were thorough on their return trip. Each of the fallen was deftly beheaded; they wanted to make sure. Vorag suddenly realized Oran had been missing since his headlong charge into the trolls. He became very worried and looked around to see if the rest of the company were still walking. They were all together exchanging comments from time to time. As they reached the northern ridge before Beregrin, Vorag found Oran waiting for him. He was panting heavily, as exhausted as the rest, and had numerous, bleeding cuts—none serious. Then Vorag noticed the incredible pile of wargs. The hunters counted them later. Oran had ripped open twenty-six of the wolves! Proudly the mastiff limped home beside his master.

In the scorching heat of the late August sun, the slain Yac bodies had already begun to decay. As the company and armies began the descent of the northern ridge to Beregrin, the nauseating stench of hundreds became overwhelming. Some were gasping; some covered their noses with cloths. As the company reacted to the stench, the Drifter came upon those that Nache and Mindi had felled. There lay the chief captain whose terror-stricken face lay frozen for all time, formed as it had when he fell.

"What magic is this?" he proclaimed, halting and pondering the wretched face in agony beyond words.

The others came up and were equally dumbfounded. There lay Mindi's broken blade as well. Suddenly, all eyes turned on the two.

Mindi merely said, "Oh nothing boys."

But Nache, proud of his lady, spoke for her, "Here is a wizard as well. Her sword broke under the onslaught of the great one. Alas, I was cast aside by his power., but when he beheld her, he saw her not, but thatwhich he dreaded most to see. It was in his mind. See here are my chops, but he was dead before I hit!"

The others looked long at her wonderingly. Then, Nache proudly showed others nearby. He explained, "Mindi showed me that my axe could do more. I have learned to throw it. It flies true, cleaves heads, and returns to my hand. See, here are some examples." He rushed about pointing out faces cloven by his blade. The others marveled at this.

Vorag began laughing, "Verily, thou art a full-man. No longer doth thy chops sunderuth bellies—but heads, like a hunter." He stooped and shook his hand vigorously—a bit too strong for the dwarf, yet he enjoyed it.

They continued towards the walls. Suddenly Mindi saw the Fire Sword. Blazing still, it protruded from a crack in a wall where Vorag had inserted it in the morning. A sinking feeling swept through their stomachs. All had forgotten Marc! He had not rejoined them.

Vorag quickly spoke, "Nay he dost not lie slain. I foundeth him unconscious beside the third troll he fell. I carrieth him inside the walls, and the women careth for him."

In spite of the sweltering heat and exhaustion, they all rushed forward into the city. Vorag quickly let them to the house of healing, and they clamored inside noisily and in haste. Mindi was most concerned. He lay in a bed of soft furs. Reddish rays of the late afternoon sun came through the windows. The room was stifling and hot; no breeze entered. By his head, an old lady fanned his body and had wet rags on his head and arms. Some children were tending the rags and buckets. He lay stripped to the waist and his body was fiery red, extremely hot.

"He gaineth not his senses yet. I feareth he be'st too hot. Fever rageth all day. It becometh worse, and speaketh strange tongue."

Mindi knelt by his head and gently touched his head. It was very hot. She felt his chest and arms. His reddened arms were swollen and so hot. She felt her stomach knot. Tears came into her eyes briefly. Indeed the others were all down cast and fought back their tears. Unable to do so, one by one, they left the room, desiring to be alone for a while. Pictures began flashing in her mind as she laid her head on him. She stopped crying and stood erect, and threw off her cloak, revealing the woman she was. The old nurse backed away in surprise.

Then, facing the situation, she laid her hand on his forehead and raised her left hand towards the sun, and spoke a solitary word of command. Suddenly, a cool wind blew in through the window. At once, the old one noticed Marc stirred. Her mouth open in disbelief; she saw the red skin rapidly return to its normal color; his eyes flickered and opened, gazing upon Mindi. Then, he raised himself up, and they held each other tightly for some moments.

To her amazement, Marc got up, stretched, and exclaimed, "Have I been sleeping long? I feel so refreshed!"

Mindi said, "The battle is over. You were hurt. How do you feel?"

He cringed; she knew he was recalling.

With a pained face of concern he asked, "The others— are they all right?"

She smiled and said that they were, and she put her arm around him. They walked out of the room leaving the old nurse gasping still. Outside the others full of grief were milling around. They all started visibly when the two appeared.

Nache spoke first crying, "You're—you're not dead?"

Marc laughed, "No my friend not dead—very much alive. I feel great! Hey, we have much to discuss. I fear I've missed all the fun!"

Lord Edward came in at this point, and, glancing at the surprised faces staring at Marc, fumbled, and said, "I cometh to honor the bearer of the Fire Sword."

But diplomatically Marc fended him off saying, "True Lord, the sword has done its deed, but I'm not the only one who has done deeds of praise."

He glanced purposely at his comrades. "Not the least, these here have feats of bravery and honor to tell, but forget not your own or the dwarves. With so many feats to recognize, I would suggest a celebration is more in order. What say you?"

Marc had deftly removed himself as the single source and put the reward where it rightfully belonged—on all. Edward could not disagree. He left to arrange the event.

Vorag then led the group to a room where he stayed from time to time when he was in Beregrin. For a long time, they drank and exchanged stories. That night the cool breeze brought a heavy thunderstorm that cleansed the woods and those that dwelled here.

Chapter XVII—The Second Council of Marc

Grossly overcrowded, Beregrin played host that night to everyone. The torrential rain demanded all take shelter. The dwarves seemed much impressed by the novelty of spending the night in log cabins in lieu of their halls of hard stone. Eager and relieved, everyone slept soundly. Edward had placed only a few guards on duty. With the refreshing dawn, slowly each arose in high spirits with cleanup the first order of business. This was accomplished swiftly by noon.

The Yacs were gathered into a huge mound upon the northern ridge. There the foul flesh was burned, forming a huge, black cloud that rose high into the clear blue sky. The fallen hunters were buried in a large mound beneath the eaves of their great forest, just west of Beregrin. Thereafter, moss alone grew, and it became known as the Green Mound. The slain dwarves were buried in their armor and mail. Axes were lain upon their chests. Industriously, their kin created a mound of stone blocks over their fallen ones. The chosen sight was a clearing east of Beregrin where the Armagh Mountains rose tall in the distance. Their resting place became known as Krasdul, and the hunters forever honored the burial site as their own. Lord Edward ordered the three trolls, who had turned to stone, carried to the crumbled pass. There they were stood erect—silent sentinels to the land of evil.

By afternoon, dwarves and hunters, now finished with their tasks, joined in company, holding a great feast in honor of all the brave deeds. Far into the night, the celebration continued with many, many tales exchanged. A strong companionship was formed between the tall, Burly hunters and the stubby, stout dwarves.

Lord Edward had, at various times, sent the elves to Old Varg and Greagon with news of the evil befalling Beregrin. So no elf was present when the Great Northern Battle raged. However, by afternoon, Elador and two others arrived with news from the west. They were extremely surprised by the sight. Having seen the black cloud, they came upon the city fearing the worst. Wild merrymaking of huge and small people greeted their eyes and ears. With only a brief explanation of Aaron and the battle, they were taken wide-eyed before Lord Edward, Aaron, and the company.

This was a time of many meetings, old and new, plus the exchange of tales. For many, it was the first elf ever seen; for others, the renewal of an old friendship, and for all, especially Nache, a time for tales. Dwarves excelled in this latter.

The elves stared in wonder at the members of the company as their stories were told. Elador, for whom time was endless, felt overwhelmed—far, far too much, too fast! It was late night before all had been told.

Elador delivered a message from Greagon. Malazar had successfully shored the western area and was now marching towards the host of Yacs that remained north of Old Varg. They had eluded the bears' trap and were ranging down toward the Obelos City of Burly. Malazar said for Edward to hold on; he would arrive as rapidly as possible.

Around one a.m., Lord Edward decided upon a plan. At dawn, Vorag would lead all that could be spared westward. With any luck, the Yacs would be caught in a vice and driven forever from Burly. Everyone agreed, and the word was spread. Elador sent his two elf companions off as fast as possible to carry word to Malazar and Elwine. Merry frolicking was still to be heard, as the company retired for the night. All felt very relaxed and at peace. The end of the Scourge was clearly at hand and do-able. At dawn, the horns of Beregrin sounded, and a great army of hunters and dwarves, led by Vorag and company, left Beregrin heading due west.

Malazar had not been idle after sending Vorag off to meet Marc and the rest in his place. Daybreak found him near Kyder Pass pacing back and forth. The Yacs and goblins had retreated to the pass. There they fortified and found renewed strength. At first, the Burly men charged forward trying to smash through, but were turned back by a rain of spears, axes, and arrows. Later Hildaro, shield blazing and Axillone shinning, led a charge of swift horsemen in an attempt to smash their way through. But to no avail. Hiding behind their shields, they were forced back as well; many had foul shafts protruding. Horses were lost.

Actually, the best weapon turned out to be the elves. Elwine led them forth in a peculiar manner. All were armed only with bows and full quivers. They rushed the pass with quick, elfin speed, moving like a greenish glow—a flash of light. The Yacs were slow to respond compared to the lightning elfin speed. Large quantities of the Scavengers rose up and proceeded to lift spear and bend bows. However, Elwine was faster. Using all their elfin speed, his archers loosened their entire quivers into the sluggish, blackish targets. Compared to the elves, the Scourge worked in slow motion. Many, many of the foul ones fell before the rush. Eventually, Elwine had to retreat, arrowless. Having fired all their arrows, the elves now had to make new ones.

Thus, the pattern was set for that day. Hours were spent with the hunters and riders gathering shafts, while elves worked furiously to create more arrows. Then, another strike upon the Yacs would ensue. Five minutes later, it was back to arrow making. By late afternoon, the Yacs had discovered their pattern and now remained hidden; only a few elfin arrows found a mark. Thus, three, slow, agonizing days passed.

The fourth dawn, Elwine found Malazar near the pass; he had not slept. Elwine found the wizard angry. Actually, Malazar was almost in a rage. The grey one stomped about yelling in a strange tongue. Elwine questioned the wizard and got him antagonistic and then bored. Tse Tse and Hildaro came upon the two and, seeing Elwine's approach, greatly assisted the elf in pulling the wizard out of a hateful anger, which would serve no purpose.

"If only I had the Orb of old, I could smash these Evil Ones!" Malazar lamented, "I don't know where it is. Have we not searched all the elfin records, Elwine, and found no trace of it?"

Tse Tse queried him about the Orb. Malazar became interested and briefly told him of the Orb and the abilities that the holder would get via the glowing ball. Using it, one can control all evil. Tse Tse explained that there was nothing like that in his obelos; likewise, Hildaro said that the horsemen's obelos did not contain such a thing, but records did tell of its use in the ancient days.

Finally, Tse Tse spoke up once again. "In my lands, if Tiger comes—eats those in village—we set forth—make great noise—Tiger runs. We chase him to cage—we capture him—then carry him far away. Here Tiger is captured already. Can we find way—close his gate—maybe logs of great trees?"

There was a moment of silence. Elwine was estimating how many logs it would take and how quickly they could be felled. Hildaro was planning how to use horsepower to move them.

Suddenly, Malazar rose and stood to his full height; a large smile appeared between his parted lips, hidden by grey hair.

"My friend, you have done it. I have a plan. Come." Quickly he left the rocky glen and headed down to the road. "Call all of our guards hither. Let none stand closer than this to the pass."

The order was dispatched, and men came rushing back. This did not go unnoticed by the enemy who carefully raised their heads above the boulders, wondering what was going on now. When all had retired to a safe distance, Malazar, who had been silently watching, said only in a commanding tone, "Am I not a wizard?" Without waiting for a response, he stepped forward onto the road.

The Evil Ones saw a lone, old man clad in grey, hobbling slowly down the road towards them. As he drew close, several goblins, who knew no pity for any living creature—even their own kind—stood up and raised both spears and bows. At once, Malazar threw off his cloak, stood erect, and revealed a brilliant whiteness he'd long concealed. The startling contrast created confusion among the goblins who hated the white and light.

Malazar raised his staff high into the air. From the up-reaching end, fire erupted in brilliant, white flames. Then giant bolts of lightning flashed—arced across the space and struck the mountain walls. Repeatedly, the bolts blazed; each time there came claps of thunder so loud that the men and elves fell to their knees, covering their ears from the voluminous peals of thunder. Repeatedly, the roars came, louder and louder. Yacs screamed and ran through the pass into the desert beyond to escape the awesome noise.

Soon answering roars thundered from the very earth itself. Small boulders fell; larger ones dislodged and cascaded downwards. The guard tower that he'd used to spy from high on the side of the pass shattered, and block by block, fell to the ground. Giant slabs of rocks broke loose, rumbled downwards, gained speed, and crashed thunderously into the narrow pass. The noise from the wizard's staff was dwarfed by the earth itself.

Giant clouds of orangish dust and gravel rose slowly upwards engulfing all light. The pass and walls faded from view, as the thundering noise continued. The puffy, billowing cloud of destruction rapidly engulfed the lone figure on the road. Elwine, who had been staring in wonder, was roused from the hypnotic effect of the event by the sudden realization that Malazar had disappeared, engulfed by his own cloud. Quickly, the glowing elf sped down the hill and disappeared into the orange cloud of rock dust. Moments later, he reappeared, helped now by his two friends, dragging a coughing wizard behind him.

Hildaro yelled above the dying noise, "Well done, wizard! Well done!"

They watched the dust cloud subside, and by late afternoon, all could see the destruction that the mountain had created. Kyder Pass lay blocked, covered by rubble and great boulders. Lord Edmund guessed that given a year, Burly men could reopen the pass. That night, a few guards were stationed nearby, but no one expected further trouble to issue from Kyder Pass.

Periodically, elf runners arrived bearing tidings. Malazar seemed particularly moved by the assistance of the bears, for he was then freed from the immediate worry of those that had swarmed into the heart of the forest, but the eve of the closure of Kyder Pass, one of Elador's runners arrived

bearing the sobering news of Beregrin's eminent doom. Late
that night while the noise of celebrations resounded among
the three peoples, Malazar with Elwine, Tse Tse, Hildaro, and
Lord Edmund held a council. All agreed that Beregrin needed
immediate assistance. Hildaro suggested they ride south
through East Flats, flanking Burly, for the horsemen would
have great difficulties in the dense woods. However, should
they go through the woods, the Yacs before them would have
to be handled, and the bears relieved. In the end, Malazar
decided that they would go eastwards through Burly; they
would leave at dawn. Word was sent to the warriors; the noise
gradually faded, and the night sounds grew.

The rising sun was heralded by loud, deep, horn blasts
from the city walls, and just beyond, answering higher pitched
horns of the riders resounded. All prepared for the great trek
eastwards. Nearly five hundred Burly men would accompany
an equal number of elves and horsemen. The grey steeds now
bore provisions for the most part; the riders were forced to
lead their mounts on foot, a cause for much grumbling. The
hunters led the way bearing due east, picking a trail the horses
could manage. Elves followed—their keen eyes observing all
that passed. The men of Illanos brought up the rear, carefully
leading their uncomplaining, but stumbling horses.

All that day, they moved forward, but progress was
slow. The great hunters felt they were snails, while the elves
were quite content, admiring the woods. Stately ancient trees
rose high above the stony, boulder-ridden lands. A deep green
moss covered their northern sides, while the northern faces of
rock were lichen covered. Tufts of a coarse grass grew
tenaciously between the smaller rocks, and brush abounded.
Great vines grew twisted and gnarled, spiraling upwards to
branches far above. Bracken and thorn bushes infested the
ground, fighting the boulder fields for life. The foliage grew
dense and deep green, and by late afternoon, the direct light
nearly failed as the forest grew dark and ominous. The air
grew steadily heavy and humid. No air stirred; the day was
hot.

Two days passed with little change; spirits steadily
lowered, especially for the horsemen. They felt a growing

uneasiness for the forest, which seemed to grow close around them like a coffin. Breathing became difficult. Even their horses became unnerved and were shying and balking occasionally. Only the elves remained ever curious. The elfin runners had been dispatched several days before to let Berman know they were coming, but now they had returned with evil news. One night, the Yacs had secretly rushed northwards breaking through the lines and had gone in a great circle around the bears and were again loose in the forests, presumably heading for Old Varg in the south-central region.

Malazar now feared that their sweep through Burly might miss the Scavengers all together, and since Old Varg had sent many of its forces to Greagon's aid, it would be in poor shape to handle a thousand of the Scourge. His worries doubled. After a brief council, the combined army of fifteen hundred men reached a clever plan. Their forces were divided into small teams, five of each people per team. Each band of fifteen would go forward as a group. Each team was spaced a thousand feet apart and in a north-south line, stretching southward for nearly seven leagues. Also, a number of elfin runners were sent even deeper to the south, just in case the twenty mile, sweeping line of men should miss the Yac host. Contact was to be announced by horn blast.

The marching wall of men continued their show progress forward in a great sweep through Burly. Several more days passed with only the signs of abandoned campfires of the Scourge discovered. Elador now returned from Beregrin and found Malazar near the central section of the line. His news was well received, and elf runners were sent north and south bearing the tale of the rescue of Beregrin by the hands of the Seven and the Dwarves under Aaron. The good news was welcomed heartily by all, for they realized now the end was at hand. Before them lay the battered remains of the Evil One's army. Malazar quickly saw that, if those of Beregrin came from the east in a similar sweep, the Yacs would be caught in the center of a giant trap and easily handled. Quickly he sent the tireless elf back to Beregrin. He was glad to have the speed of elves, and Elwine was proud of the service his people were giving.

The next day from a mile south of Malazar, the Burly horns began to blast joined by the trill of Illanos. In a chorus of sound, more and more horns joined. Rapidly the northern edge of the line shifted southwards.

One of the teams headed by Garth had come upon the flank of the Yac hosts. Both were surprised, but the horn blasts had disabused the Yac forces from attacking as a team. An unending wall of horn blasts greeted their surprised ears. They retreated before the noise, but could not find the end of the line of sound. They feared that a huge army had descended upon them stretching endless through the forest. They fled rapidly before the marching wall of sound. Malazar kept his line moving after them, permitting no attacks. He knew if they discovered the thinness of their forces, they could easily burst through and escape. Slowly but surely, the line shortened while pursuing the Scourge, and for two more days, the Yacs steadily retreated before the wall of sound, which had shrunk in length to less than five miles long.

On the third day and to the utter dismay of the Evil Ones, answering blasts came before them also in a long line piercing the woods. Their cries of horror rose above the trumpeting, as they clumped into a large blackish mass, trembling in fear, trapped between two mighty armies of endless sound. By noon, the advancing armies had them surrounded in a great circle. The Scourge had taken refuge on a large, boulder ridden, hilltop, and the advancing armies had stopped nearly a thousand yards off on either side. On one hilltop, stood Malazar and his group, and on an opposite one, stood the Seven. Before them, lay nearly a thousand black forms in tattered, yellow clothes.

Slowly Malazar stepped forward alone; he raised his staff and flames leaped skyward. A hush fell across the forest.

In a loud commanding voice he spoke, "Thy doom is at hand! All others of your armies are gone. We have come for you. You have two choices: surrender, throw down your arms, or stand to meet your certain doom."

Several trembling Yacs threw down their spears, hastily tore off their sword belts, and rushed forwards, but several spears flew from within the black host. The runners, crying aloud, fell.

A hoarse voice cried, "That be our answer!"

Suddenly, Malazar caused a great light flash, and thunder pealed from his staff. Elwine and the others rushed to Malazar's side, waving their swords. Here and there, sunlight reflected brilliantly from Hildaro's shield, blinding those who dared to look. Horn blasts echoed continuously.

From the western side, Marc drew Tiny, and it grew and flamed. The Seven charged forward from their side. Swiftly the circle shrank into close combat. Malazar and company blazed a path into the Scourge and charged up the hill of the Scavengers. The Evil Ones fled in terror; those that dared fell before them. Likewise, Marc and company rushed the hilltop from the east with similar effect. The two met on the enemy's hilltop. The light and power of the united group was blinding— all fled down the hill in utter terror into the waiting blades below. The battle was swift and sure. In minutes, order was restored—not a single Scavenger breathed. A chorus of victory filled the forest, heard as far away as Old Varg. For the company, it was a joyous reunion and meeting of new friends.

Vorag later named the battle field "Hill of Doom," for, from that day forward, not a single plant ever grew; it remained a bare hill in the heart of the dark, Burly woods. The rest of the day was spent in celebration and the making of friends. Not in many, many ages were hunter, rider, elf, and dwarf together, united as one army. There was much to commemorate, much to triumph—fanfare and banners were everywhere.

The next day, the people parted. Neil led those of Beregrin and the Dwarves eastward to their lands, while Garth and Fergus did likewise for those of Greagon and of Illanos and of Eldamar, while Vorag led the other Burly men back to Old Varg, joined by the rest of the company. The time was enthusiastically passed, for each had their opportunity to tell eager ears their adventures in the great war. By the time the forest thinned and the whitish stone and log city of Old Varg appeared atop a distant hill, each of the company had their turn, while the others learned and marveled.

Of note here is the discovery Tse Tse had made at the

Hill of Doom. There he'd run completely out of darts with many more opponents remaining. Upset, he had swore a curse, and vainly blew hard, but empty air through his golden tube. He had shockingly found the right combinations, for to both his and the charging Yac's utter disbelief, a great, narrow flame flashed forth, incinerating the Evil One's face amid his shrieks and cloud of foul-burning flesh and hair. Due in part to his smaller stature, Nache had taken an immediate liking to Tse Tse.

The hunters of Old Varg and the company of the eleven arrived; they received a royal welcome. The usual trumpeting horns, bright, flying banners, and cheering people greeted the arrival. Again, celebration became the order of the day. Malazar couldn't refuse Lord Egmond's requests for his company's attendance at the festivities. Everyone spent a very enjoyable afternoon in the heat of the late, Burly summer.

By late afternoon, Malazar had managed to get his company away from the events and had followed Vorag to Obelos Bracken, near the southern edge of the city. Here, Malazar called for a council.

Greys, whites, and browns blended into a tall, blocked spiral; Obelos Bracken stood towering above the rest of the forest. Near its base, moss and vines fought for control of its surface, but the rock wall won out some twenty feet above the ground. The group sat on stones upon the moss covered ground near its base. Westward, the sky was red with the setting sun; a cool breeze had come out of the south. Shannon could almost smell the very distant sea.

The wizard opened the conference speaking in a commanding tone. "The tide of war has now turned to our favor. Against great odds, we have saved the days of southern Isel. Both passes now stand blocked and guarded. Quara Mountains are the jail's walls, for an army cannot scale them in sufficient numbers to do battle. To each one of you, I extend my thanks and praise for a job well done. We have come very like the Mizzinti of old." Here he paused, reflecting.

Drifter rose and added, "Yes, as Malazar has said, great deeds have been done. True. Still there is more to be done. The northern passes are not closed and stand wide open. No armies lie there in waiting for the Scourge. Even now the remaining hosts of Kahill could pour forth and easily destroy Ocalla of the Nomads."

Tse Tse jumped up and injected, "My home too—jungle lies unguarded. Evil Ones come and go in northern wilds—my jungle not safe."

Elwine, head lowered merely added, "The lands of elves and also of Dwarves lie awaiting as well. How long can we hold off such evil force? Especially if Kahill rebuilds his might?"

Nache grunted his approval.

Elwine continued, "Drifter, as well as I, knows of the terrible blackness that has entered Witchachooie Marsh in the north of my country. Some say it is bewitched; lights glow in the seeping, slimy bogs. Moreover, I have seen a foe more deadly than any we've seen yet. This foul thing lives in the northern abandoned lands that used to be the ancient wizard's home."

Malazar also added, "True and from whence came the great trolls—that remains a mystery! They come from the ancient days, but how many do they number? Easily, if slowly, they could clear the passes. Without the magic Orb of the Old Wizard, we would again have to send our peoples to war. Without the Orb we are doomed to everlasting pestilence!"

At this point, the conference broke down—everyone talking at once to any who would listen. The disordered discussion grew in volume. Soon Nache was excitedly swinging his axe, slicing imagined foes, driving home his point to Tse Tse. The confusion continued for nearly a half an hour, by which time everyone was talking, whether anyone cared to listen or not. Some were yelling; some boasting, but Marc had grown quiet.

He looked around at his companions who were talking wildly, but pointlessly; they were getting nowhere! He rubbed his face in his hands, and then slowly, he rose and yelled, but failed to get anyone's attention—beyond Mindi's. The growing dusk was pierced by the brilliant flames of Andrill. Marc energized Tiny and stood tall and impressive. The others hushed at once and looked wonderingly at him. He extinguished Tiny and shielded the blade. He began in a stern voice.

"This is silly—stupid! We are getting absolutely nowhere! Now let's look at the facts! One, the rest of the evil in Isel must fall. That's obvious. I don't wish for further lives of any people to be taken. Now we know the southern passes are obstructed; we can't enter Kalhari that way. The northern passes are obviously guarded. From Malazar's and Elwine's stories, we know for a fact that against even a few, three armies cannot break through a pass—let alone us. We are now aware of further evils abroad in the north. Whether these are controlled by Kahill or not, we do not know. Yet they are certainly evil. Now however each of us may put it, it is our job, our duty, to handle Isel's impending doom. This we feel in different ways"

"So far we have been aided by our peoples, and many of them have fallen in the defense of Isel. Valiant have been all their efforts against overwhelming odds. As Elwine would say, years and years of songs are now needed to tell of all the events and deeds done by all. But now against the evil that remains, we can't ask our peoples to battle. They are tired, torn, battered, and wounded. Survival deeds: harvesting in the south, storage of venison here—these now must be done—and done in great haste or more will die in hunger's call. No, the fight must now be carried by us. I say that it is our responsibility to do so—maybe it comes from our past deeds of old. However the past goes, now is the time for us to continue to handle the evil ourselves!"

Malazar arose and spoke softly, "Thank you Marc. A wizard can at times forget his own councils! You speak truly and justly. As I see the situation, we must find the ancient Orb, if we are ever to handle the situation. For if Kahill gets the orb, all will be most certainly lost!"

To this last statement, there was much murmured agreements and comments. Then, clad in her white dress, Mindi, who had for the most part remained silent through the conference, rose. In the center of the group, Malazar had placed his staff—glowing bluish, casting shadows on the encircled friends. In the flickering, pale light, her sight was impressive; instantly she commanded undivided attention.

Soft were her words and slowly given.

"Consider a man and his people. Suppose that man commits some injury, some dark deed, some crime towards his people. He knows he has just done something he should not have. From this point forward, he can travel one of two roads. Ordinarily, the man will lament and feel guilty and shame for his actions. He will blame himself or he can blame others. Tis the fault of the sun or the god's or some such. Most often he will seek to have a reason for the bad deed. Some justification. For notice, if he has a reason, if there were some justification, even if it comes *after* his deed, then in part, the severity of his act is lessened. Or so he would like to believe. From here, the picture of our man is not pretty to behold. He sinks into a grief, an apathy. He can now lament his woes for sympathy. Even worse, since the act is now 'justified' in his mind—the scales being balanced—he can now commit further ill actions of destruction or worse against his people. He ill-uses the name of responsibility for the actions he has done. However, he *can* rectify the damage done."

There was silence, and she quietly sat down.

The flickering, blue light continued to cast illusive shadows on the members of the council. Each was pondering his own thoughts. Marc then continued. His voice was more relaxed than normal. Malazar seemed deeply troubled. Lines of age grew deep upon his brow.

"Each of us knows fully of Malazar's council on these mental pictures that seem to react upon us. Now myself, I have undergone intense changes! Three months ago, I was being Master Merchant, quiet, content in Metro. Since then, I have had many strange pictures flash, and some of these I have carefully viewed. Now if pictures are true, though I have my doubts, then perhaps I was a Mizzinti of Metro. For what else could explain my trials at Obelos Sud, acquiring Andrill, and commanding its use? Though I'm not originally a leader of men in Metro, to say nothing of leading an army to war, yet I have second naturedly done so without question."

"Then there are the visions I have had of places yet unseen and horrors there of a yesterday. True once viewed, as Malazar foretold, these pictures ceased to affect me, and my ability grows. Yet still I wonder, am I a wizard of old? If true, then—Oh Gods! Have I ever done something I shouldn't have? Look at all the thousands that lay dead because of self-destruction! It is little wonder that man will tend to take the route of blame and regret. For how does one face his acts? Yet I have seen whither that other route has lead—just look where Isel is today. We have nearly lost the whole area!"

"Nay, I say if wizard I be, then now is the time for me to take responsibility for my past actions. By this, I mean I have not only the willingness but also the ability to be the cause in these matters. However, am I a wizard or not? I still haven't resolved that one. Many of you feel as I do on this personal matter. Well, I say to you and everyone else, including me and you, Malazar: What the crap? It doesn't matter at all! The past is past; t'will be no more! The present is here now. The future of Isel lies before us. Whether we be wizards or not—that is totally irrelevant. That is my conclusion. Totally irrelevant!"

"You see, together as a group, we are the most powerful assemblage in Isel. Each of us is mighty, perhaps the most able of his people. Who else has any—any chance better than we do? Who else? I say it is our duty here and now to our families and people to do everything in our power to end totally the reign of the Evil Ones. No matter what the cost to us. For if we fail, countless thousands lesser than us in ability lie doomed to an eventual slavery or death!"

Marc found himself fairly yelling at his point, and he finished and quickly sat down. Then, he noticed the effects he had been creating. Mindi had caught them all and later filled him in on them. Malazar was loudly yawning and quite heavily.

Drifter at once commented, "Marc, you speak to the mark. I don't know of this wizard stuff; maybe it's just all in the mind, but you are precisely correct—that it's the present that matters—that counts."

"Thee speaketh for me, as well," exclaimed Vorag heartily.

Quickly others agreed. Malazar, who had finished a great yawn, arose and took control once more.

"Marc and Mindi, great are your councils—greater than

254

your aged wizard's. I had become lost in the past there, but you have spoken precisely; the present is all that, in the end, that matters. It is what we do here and now that is truly important. Now quickly, let's review the situation with the Orb. I know by personal inspection that it doesn't lay in the obelos of Metro, of the elves, and of the Burly men here. Can any of you others remember seeing anything that resembles the glowing Orb within the obelos of your lands?"

There was a moment of silence and then a sporadic round of "no's".

"Conclusion: if it is stored in an obelos, then only two remain, Obelos Magum of the great wizard and Obelos Cerban now held by Kahill. Now if Kahill found it, he certainly wouldn't have lost the war here in the south! So it is safe to assume that he does not know of the Orb—yet. It most likely does not lie in Cerban, though unless we inspect it ourselves, we can't be entirely free of doubt. Powerful as we are, we can't top an obelos made by the great Mizzinti! We must have the Orb. Thus, I conclude: we must journey to the plains of Serengreti of Ruenzorti. If evil lies there, it must be toppled. We must check Obelos Magum."

No one disagreed with that. However, Nache and Drifter raised a final point. They were squarely in the middle of Isel, should they go east or west? Nache urged them to pass through Tulan, while Drifter insisted on Ocalla.

However, Malazar resolved it swiftly saying, "We will go west first, for there lay known evils of magnitude beyond the hands of lesser men to handle. Nache and Tse Tse, if fate will have it, our return shall be through your lands."

This was satisfactory to all. They all returned to the city, which had now gone to sleep. There they joined the inhabitants. Thus ended the Second Council of Marc.

Chapter XVIII—Eleven Companions—an Interlude

Fiery, the late August sun rose blazing hot above the forest darkness. Steadily it climbed in the deep blue, cloudless sky. Though the company had agreed to depart at dawn, only Malazar and a few husky guards saw the ruddy display. The rest overslept. Fatigue had had its effect. Each awoke, startled by having overslept, and was apologetic, but Malazar understood. Mindi rose early. Rubbing traces of sleep from her face, she stepped outside the rapidly warming cabin. Nearby, the wizard and Elwine were sitting in the shade of the log cabin. Though her hair was disheveled from the night and her clothes ridged and ruffled, her beauty was still striking and did not go unnoticed.

"Fair is the gem from the south. Good morning," the elf said in admiration, beckoning her towards them.

Mindi always felt particularly loving when she awoke; and she appreciated the compliment, recalling the sense of love, security, and playfulness she shared with Marc. They were fond of snuggling in the early morning hours; Marc had called her his "playful puppy." At these times, both were especially full of life and livingness. Whether it was the way the elf spoke or his radiant countenance, she could not tell, but he reminded her of Marc.

Playfully, she bounced over to the two, announcing, "The others are asleep yet. The trip has exhausted bodies, but minds are keener."

Elwine, a bit shorter than Mindi, rose with a broad smile on his clear face, met her out reaching hands gently with his, and lowered her to the ground where he had been sitting.

"Nay Mindi, you don't look like one dragging herself forth under great effort to face a new day; more like a golden flower opening its pedals to the rosy warmth of the morning sun."

She gave him a loving, squeezing hug, returning his

flow.

Malazar merely grumbled at all of this playfulness.

Mindi, smiling, tugged at his beard, "And you old bearded one, you need to find yourself someone to cuddle. Say do they make female wizards?" she asked half-jokingly, half serious.

A twinkle—a sparkle—briefly appeared in his eyes, as if memories gone by flashed in his mind. A smile came on his weathered face; and he replied, "There is time enough for that, my dear."

Just then, George came half staggering out of a nearby doorway cringing in the bright sunlight. "Oh, sorry I'm late. I fear I'm a bit tired still. Food, where is the food?"

Malazar pointed.

"Oh, ok. Say," he continued after a brief pause, as he awoke more fully, "should we not spend some time here getting provisions ready? We do have a fair number of mouths to feed."

"Agreed," came the response, "Go eat." Rising and turning to the others, the wizard said, "Brief be my respite this morning. I have words to speak to Egmond ere we depart. Enjoy the dawn while you can." The fleeting twinkle in his eyes was now replaced by one of sternness—one full of concern. Quickly he left heading for the Lord's cabin.

Elwine and Mindi talked on into the morning. He discovered in her a purpose akin to his own—finding and sharing beauty. They quickly became very close friends. Nearly an hour later, Marc strolled outside, shirtless and shoeless. Seeing the two in the shade, he smiled and joined them.

"You two make quite a pair!" he proclaimed as he sat down on the dry dirt beside them. "I don't know about you two, but I feel incredibly peaceful this morning."

Mindi leaned over and kissed him. He blushed a bit by the suddenness of her flow.

"You two are like the flower and the bee," Elwine grinned, but Marc interrupted him.

"Who's the flower and who's the bee?" They all laughed. Then, Elwine showed the two how to greet elves, the traditional gentle touching of hands and fingertips and the following motions. Both were impressed by the joy it transferred, heightening by sense of touch, the closeness of the two.

By now the others had also arisen, so the trio adjourned. Mindi had to change clothes and supervise the gathering of provisions. Nache insisted upon packing the ponies. Tse Tse was ever at the dwarf's side, learning much from his new friend. The distance from home and from those left behind seemed to affect Shannon and George the most. George was understandably a bit homesick for Sharon and his kids, for he was very fond of having excited children pestering him. Shannon, farther from the sea than he had ever been in his life, kept breathing deeply, yearning for a trace of salt air.

By noon, the ponies were packed and the group assembled. Hildaro had consented to have his steed, Nada, used as a packhorse as well. If the others went on foot, so would he, although he hoped that somehow once beyond the forest, he could acquire horses for the others. Then, as they walked through the gates of Old Varg, the hunters' horns blared in their honor. Quickly Vorag led them westward. Soon the quiet forest surrounded them once again.

The day was hot and muggy, but the forest here in the south was less dense; the going was easier for man and beast. Vorag had suggested that they journey straight west to the Old Caravan Road. Though longer than a direct line to Greagon, it would be much faster. As the hot afternoon wore on, the small chatter died down. Everyone became lost in his own private thoughts, as they tramped onwards through the humid forest. Vorag, Oran, and Malazar led the way. Behind them came Elwine and Hildaro with Nada. Next came Nache and Tse Tse leading Blackie and Whitefoot, then Marc and Mindi leading Butterball. Trailing were Drifter, Shannon, and George. All were sweating and the pace was slow.

Mindi began reflecting upon her morning. She had an opportunity to visit with the women of Burly, while handling the provisions. She didn't like what she had seen. "Big Berthas" she had dubbed them. Equally as massive in bulk as the hunters, the women were all geared to a subservient role. They tended the cabins, did the cleaning, sweeping, and caring for the young. However, it was their relationships to men that had raised her ire. They were subservient. Drunk, loud boisterous men took to shoving and bossing them around. They were forced to tend to their wishes constantly. She felt that it was a very demeaning role. The structure back in Metro was detestable, but not as bad as here. In the city, she would be expected to do the usual duties, washing, cooking, and the like. Also open to her was the life of a socialite—a privilege of the more wealthy families, but the life style of parading in fancy clothes and tea parties left her cold. The more she pondered what she felt was the plight of the Burly women, the angrier she became. Suddenly, she realized that she was angry.

"Damn, I should follow my own advice—in anger you seldom see truth." She calmed down a bit by noticing the trees in the distance. Here and there, a brown squirrel darted higher into its tree escaping the noisy passage of the company.

Again, she reviewed the Burly life. She began to understand. It was a harsh life. Survival was difficult at best. No food was grown. Everything had to be hunted or gathered. Much time was spent by the men far from home acquiring food that would have to carry everyone through the bitter winters. The men depended utterly on the women maintaining the home cabins in their absence. If the men did not exert themselves to the utmost, all would go hungry later on. Neither sex had, then, any time for the finer aesthetics of life. Hence, their crudity. It was a harsh survival; each needed the strengths of the other to live. One case of infidelity on either's side would spell certain starvation for many. Mindi relaxed now and became quite bored. Certainly their life style was justified and useful, but—but. However, it was not for her. She walked on a little further, and then the curious thought hit her so unexpected that she jumped. "What were dwarf women like?" Marc looked at her curiously, but she did not respond. They continued through the forest.

By late evening, a breeze came up and was welcomed by all. The night was spent in a small glen filled with a soft bed of leaves. Little else occurred during the next three days as the company slowly moved across southern Burly. During this time, the biggest event was bath break, when they crossed the

Beone West. Late in the afternoon of the third day as the sun ducked behind fleecy puffs of clouds, the forest abruptly ended. They came at last upon the Old Caravan Road and, on the other side, the grass seas of Illanos.

Everyone halted and stared at the incredible sight before them. Tears of joy filled Hildaro's eyes, as he welcomed all to the lands of everlasting grass, home of the proud horsemen. After nearly a month of heavy, dense forest, the vast wide-open space with no obstacle rising above the grass was a cheerful, welcome sight.

The sight had raised everyone's spirits and eagerly they followed the road northward. A breeze was continuously blowing from the grasslands, bringing with it all the fragrances of the vast meadows. Hildaro found he had a captive audience, as everyone, save Malazar, was eager for stories about his lands. Compared to their slow journey in the forest, they now made considerable progress in spite of constant conversation.

The fourth night of their trek was spent sleeping upon beds of soft grass. Welcome indeed.

The following day passed as the afternoon before. However, by late afternoon, a white form appeared far in front of them. Elwine was the first to announce it.

"Look there. I see the white arch and wall."

Hildaro's response came swiftly, "True and keen be the eyes of the elves. It is the white arch—the Gateway to Illanos. The Wan Real begins there and leads towards our white capital of Wancos. It was built ages ago in the Days of Splendor."

Eagerly they quickened their pace and within the hour arrived at the brilliant white gateway. Nache excitedly walked its length and examined every detail closely, speaking excitedly in his own tongue. Tse Tse followed him, while the dwarf pointed out the incredible construction details to his brown skin friend. The Drifter merely sat down and leaned his back against the arch. Others stood beneath it and stared far off. Before them the crushed, white rock road lay in a brilliant contrast to the rolling hills of waving green. The Wan Real was perfectly straight, heading due west.

Suddenly, Drifter got up excitedly. "Horses come. A

thundering horde of riders." He explained that he felt the earth shaking as he had rested against the arch. Elwine climbed the wall and covered his forehead with his long slender fingers, gazing into the distance.

"I see a white dust cloud. There are thirty riders in all. They carry long spears with axes at the points."

"Axillones," interjected Hildaro.

"They are clad in brown clothes. The lead rider carries none. They are five miles away, I'd guess."

Soon the others could see the small, white, dust cloud and later heard the trample of horse hoofs. Excitedly, they awaited the arrival. Hildaro untied his golden shield from Nada and used it as a mirror. Golden rays flashed towards the riders. Then, trill trumpet horns blared in far off answer. All eyes gazed westward as the riders drew steadily closer. Shortly, the riders were visible, rapidly nearing the arch.

Mindi watched the lead horseman. Suddenly she realized it was a woman! She could clearly see her now—a clear, stern, proud face, riding erect, her long blond hair flowing in streams behind her head. She was clad in heavy leather pants—yet her top was more akin to a dress. Her grey steed with black spots thundered forward as noble as its rider. The horsewoman flowed over the grass in a wide arc; both acted as if they were one. Swiftly the riders came upon the arch and halted in a great arc around the staring company.

"Felipe!" cried Hildaro rushing forward.

The young girl rapidly dismounted and rushed towards her brother. Their outstretched arms met in the sea of grass, and hugging each other tightly, Hildaro lifted her off her feet and swung her around him. They were talking rapidly and excitedly. Then, Hildaro led her arm in arm to the others; he nearly burst with joy and pride. Mindi had instinctively stepped forward and was the first to be introduced. If Mindi was surprised to see Felipe, so was Felipe to see a woman in the company. More and more wonder came into her eyes, as she met for the first time the other peoples, especially elf and dwarf. Implicitly, camp was made here by the arch, though no one actually asked permission. His sister explained that the riders had returned victorious, full of tales. All was well, and she had ridden forth to see herself the closed path and had hoped to find him. Everyone spent a most pleasant evening.

Mindi and Felipe talked far into the night. The two sat with their backs against the white wall. Before them stretched the grassland sea swaying, golden red, yet dark before the bloody, setting sun. Mindi observed her friend was rather robust, full of life. At twenty-three, she was in her prime of womanhood, standing bold with a well formed body, neither plump nor excessively muscular. Her clear complexion was accented sharply by her waving long hair, a dirty-blonde color. Her face still had the exuberance of youth. Everywhere she walked, she commanded the attention of men; this she plainly enjoyed immensely. Felipe spoke with a low alto voice, intriguing to the ears but not harsh or raspy.

Felipe talked of her homeland and of the beauty of Wancos—a white city amid unending grasslands. Most of all, she talked about her horse, Bonita. Mindi saw the equestrian pride with which the young girl took in her grey mare—a bond of love and respect shared between horse and master. Mindi also discovered that unlike her, Felipe was neither good with a sword nor was inclined to the more physical activities. With wide, excited eyes, the young woman confided her two loves: roaming alone among the grasslands on Bonita and men. Felipe knew the effect she had on men and loved every minute of it, using it as she desired.

With curiosity aroused, Mindi inquired about the role of women in Illanos and was rather surprised by the answer.

"Well, overall, stability is provided by us, with the men doing most of the wide roaming and hunting. Wives sometimes do join the hunt rides though. You see, we have strong family units. The duties of life are separated; yet there is much overlap, though the men invariably choose the heavier work. We just aren't as strong physically as the guys. Where we do the general cleaning, they will come and do—you know—the heavier stuff, moving things around. Actually, Illanos men rather hold us on a plateau; wives are honored, loved, and proudly displayed. We love it. In many little ways, menfolk await on us. Especially when we're bearing children— children are important for us. When a couple is ready, they will usually have four; and the fathers will spend much time with them, especially sons. In all our household needs, we are consulted; and usually our opinions are heeded, but in matters of state, the men rule almost totally. Only once do our legends tell of a woman ruling Illanos; Queen Victoria governed some twenty years after Madero died while his sons were still young children."

"And now I'm likely to go into the stories as well—serving as ruler, while my brother, Hildaro, is away. I dig that! Men, ooh!" she squealed with delight.

"Have you got one man in mind?" queried Mindi.

She giggled and answered, "Nope, not really. I like at least ten. I guess I could have the pick of my choice, but I really don't have any special one just yet. Time enough for that later."

She grinned broadly. Mindi returned an understanding smile. A myriad of bright stars shone in the dark sky; nearby a small campfire was crackling, casting yellow rushes of light. They suddenly realized it was late, and the others had already retired having posted two sentinels. Likewise, they retired sleepily.

The first rays of the chilly dawn shone upon the grass, covered with wet dew. The grass sagged heavily, glistening, bearing the weight of the large drops. One by one, the camp came alive with morning activity, and the girls rose late. Breakfast was already fixed, compliments of Hildaro and George. They joined the others already eating.

Hildaro was discussing the possibility of using horses. "I say why not? If we ride on the road north, they will cut our travel time immensely, leaving us fresh to do our work."

"Yes, but what happens to them if we need to travel on foot," put in the Drifter, "I just couldn't turn such beasts loose in the wild."

Before Hildaro could answer that one, Elwine replied, "Do not underestimate the intelligence of the horses. A horse, if given his head, always makes for home."

"You speak as a horsemen, elf." Hildaro noted.

Malazar ended the discussion, "All right, horses will speed our journey for a while, though I think we will be forced to return them before long. The real question is whether Hildaro can acquire nine horses more."

"Sure he can," broke in Felipe. "We can double up on our return trip."

It was agreed, and after their meal, the men began to prepare the horses. Mindi and Nache supervised the transference of most of the dwarf ponies' burden to the larger steeds. Hildaro and Felipe went aside and spoke together, presumably of matters of state. In an hour, all was ready, and the yellow sun now had climbed to the tree tops and shone directly on the golden fields. Then, the shrill trumpets sounded, and the two groups parted ways—Felipe and her men rode westward down the Wan Real while, Malazar and the others continued their northern trek along the Old Caravan Road.

Hildaro watched his sister ride off into the distance. He sighed and said mostly to himself, "What a sister!"

Mindi heard it and rode beside him. "I agree totally."

"Huh—oh sorry about that. It's just we horsemen appreciate beautiful women!"

"So I've found out," hinted Mindi subtly.

Suddenly he blurted, "Ever heard Twelve White Horses?"

"No," she answered and wondered what to say next.

Hildaro was moved by Felipe's departure and felt in great spirits. "Come; you shall hear one of the ancient horsemen's songs! It's called Twelve White Horses." Then, he rather softly but forcefully began to sing in a high, tenor voice that steadily quickened its pace.

Twelve White Horses
Twas a Friday night in our town,
And we sat there just a drinken'
We were playing cards and smoken'
On the porch, the sun about down.
It was just too hot there inside
And we sat there just a drinken'
At the back of Fannies playen'.
In the west, we spied them and sighed.

264

Twelve white horses a runnen' wild
High upon the great flat plain.
Twelve white horses against the sun,
Such a sight we never saw.
"Whose are they?" we all asked.
No one knew, no one knew,
Such a sight you'll never see, as
Twelve white horses 'gainst the sun.
Then we saw her on the bay mare
Four hands above the twelve
Riden' before with just no tack.
We saw her, fair Jenny Ann.
The biggest neck and finest legs,
The Bay, she just a went
Any place the gal did gest and
Twelve white horses came behind.
On they came to the canyon rim—
Did a pause at the fall—
The Bay mare seemed to know—
Down they went—all the twelve.
Twas the last we should ever see of them
The Bay, the twelve and the gal,
So we drank and played cards—
Haven' fun there on the porch.

Then we heard the beat
of hoofs upon the ground
There came the gal and all
a riden' down the valley floor.
Into town came the twelve.
Jenny Ann and the Bay,
up to us they did come.
There they stopped by the door.
They all got water and
Without a word up she jumped
on the Bay mare with no tack

and on they moved ever East.
Me, I just jumped up—
Started a runnen' fast and free
Leaped on the tail horse
who galloped to the lead.
While next to Bay, did we both go
Said she when I caught her
"I've been expecting you.
Come, let's just go."
So I took hold her hand
As the horses rode on
Now just eleven behind us came
And I found my true Love
that day in the town.

Hoofs pounded the road. The sun rose high and waned. They rode on with only a brief midday stop. Astride the swift Illanos steeds, they made good time. By early evening, they were reining in the horses. Before them loomed the dark, orange, jagged mountains of Quara Sud. Kyder Pass lay blocked with rubble in a multitude of sizes and shapes. Burly guards came forward to greet the newcomers.

"Hail Olaf, tis Vorag and company," bellowed the hunter.

The huge bulk laughed loudly, and swiftly Vorag dismounted and heartily welcomed his friend. Oran collapsed on the ground panting heavily, fatigued from the ordeal of keeping pace with the horses all day.

The company rested here for an hour, and Marc and crew had a guided tour led by Vorag and Hildaro. Scars of battle remained ominously visible. It was a bit sobering. Shortly before sunset, they continued their northern journey, and by dusk, the rumbling of the Cuero River was at hand. Horse and man alike refreshed themselves in the babbling, clean, shallow waters. Ahead to the right lay the tips of Quara Wund, fiery in the last rays of day. Dark lay the forest before them. Just beyond the river with the rushing water in the back ground, they made camp for the night. Supper was fixed and served, and the utensils cleaned. Around the cheerful fire, most rested complacently, staring into the flames, musing on private thoughts. Except Elwine.

He stood by the edge of the forest, a shadow in the failing fire light. His head was a glow and shone brightly. He stood aesthetic and somewhat ethereal, alone, singing softly, his voice blending into the night and the water cascades. Mindi watched him for some time. Marc had retired, but she was not yet sleepy. Quietly she joined him.

"You are absolutely beautiful standing here. What were you singing when I came up?"

"Of my love of the forest and all living things."

She quickly recalled how he had refused halter, bridle, and saddle earlier that morning. She remembered the dismayed look of the riders when he sprang lightly upon Asselore's back and how the horse had responded to his gentle touch.

"You are indeed a marvel," she said half to herself.

"None less than you, my dear," came the reply.

She blushed, and there was a pause filled by his melodic hum and the distant roar of water.

He stopped and looked into her eyes, "I wish that you could see Silvere and the Dionti trees—hear the music of a hundred wood loving voices. I truly wish to share such beauty with you."

"I do too."

"Actually," he began. "I have already written a song for you, if chance permits us to come to Silvere."

"Can I hear it now anyway?" she pleaded, suddenly becoming incredibly curious.

"Nope, it must be sung at just the right moment—the right setting."

"Then I shall have to make the opportunity," she pronounced defiantly.

"That would honor us both!" he replied. Then, the sweet sounds of elfin music softly floated to their ears.

"Hush now," offered Elwine. "Elves come." The chorus was not so distant now and straining her eyes, she saw glows, like fireflies in the forest night, slowly moving. Elwine looked long, and then a big smile formed on his face. "Aubrey comes. My brother."

Mindi looked again and saw still the tiny points of yellow light. They were closer. They waited patiently.

The music seemed to crescendo, and the golden glow grew. Soon dark shapes stepped out of the forest and surrounded the pair and the camp—music softly filled the air. A tall elf walked up and stood before Elwine, grinning broadly. "Welcome brother," he said almost in a chant. Lovingly their hands met and flowed the pattern of greeting. Then, Elwine introduced Mindi, and her hands met his likewise, but she stood nearly spellbound amid the glowing elves and the entrancing sounds. The rest of the evening passed by an enchanted Mindi.

At daybreak, everyone woke quite refreshed—minds washed clean by aesthetic charm of the elfin music. Even Malazar was moved by their songs of joy and happiness, for such was the power of their music. The other members were introduced, and a meal prepared. George was enjoying this immensely.

Malazar and Elwine spoke briefly, and Malazar announced, "Here on the edge of Eldamar, we shall part company. Elwine needs to speak to his father, Lord Mandell. With him shall go those who have not yet seen the splendors of Silvere, if you choose. The rest, Aubrey will lead on north to Elgladore, which borders on the Wild Marshes. There we shall meet together in two days' time."

There was no disagreement on this; and quickly Marc, Mindi, Nache, George, Vorag, and Hildaro followed Elwine's lead. Aubrey awaited the others; and shortly Malazar, Drifter, Tse Tse, Shannon, and the ponies continued their journey northward on Valmar Bypass toward Elgladore.

Soon a burned, blackened path veered off the road; sighing, Elwine turned his group down its charred way. He gave only a brief explanation of the destruction of the goblin hoard. A mound appeared. They turned in the saddle and, with somber faces, watched it pass—a grim reminder of the past. Presently, they were deep in Eldamar. The Viniere Woods opened wide about them, a living, breathing, spacious forest.

Vorag's comment spoke for the others, "Verily, this forest breatheth. It liveth."

Just after dark, by the silver-yellow light of the quarter moon, they come upon Silvere.

Speechless, they stopped and stared at the shimmering light. Yellowed moonbeams fell upon the wavering forms in a myriad of multicolored, glistening rays. Silvere glittered and sparkled in the soft light surrounded by the silver hued Dionti trees. Nache kept rubbing his eyes in disbelief. Uncountable, yet discernible, fragrances filled the air, tingling the nose, warming the body from lungs to fingertips in a rushing feeling of sensation. Light, high elfin voices filled the space with soft, gentle, relaxing music. Truly, Silvere was made for the pleasure of senses.

Elwine gently led Mindi forward into his world of exquisite, unparalleled, aesthetic beauty. The others stumbled along behind the two—eyes transfixed upon the mirage. As they neared the elfin city, all woes, worries, and troubles flowed away while a serene peacefulness gently took its place.

The elf saw the reflection of Silvere upon her exuberant face and softly spoke, "Now is the time for my song, dearest Mindi."

Her eyes met his excitedly, and softly his voice, barely separate from the others, sang to her: To You, My Love's Airy Note.

>Strangers meet on a passing
>Yet both on the same path.
>A gentle touch, a hi, a smile.
>Slowly comes the recognition.
>Timeless admiration and respect
>Flow and gently ebb
>The darkness of memory gone by.
>It's you!
>Bodies, now again
>On life's separate paths
>Yet the same trail still
>The chance to renew the friendship past.
>Yet, my flows arrived

And yours too.
Thank you.
I need not create a goddess
There's you.
With flows so clean
with a radiance so seldom seen
— a hornpipe in spring —
How I long to share your space
Once more.
And in your space
Just be.
No symbols reflect the joy
Of comm unspoken
Yet received
Of Beingness
With no distance.
Oh the joy of seeing you again.
Our Paths will cross
Me—less bent —
And recognition swift.
Til then and always
I **am**.
And you **are**.
Still as I recall.
Yet even more.

She felt a strange, tingling sensation flowing through her body as if huge energy flows were constantly discharging. When Elwine was finished, she spoke no words, but put her arms around him and kissed him, understanding. As Marc watched just behind the pair, he thought he saw a golden radiance swell and surround her head similar to Elwine's silvery glow, though not as large as his. He felt a strange sense of calmness that seemed to stretch across eternal time. Then, in an electrifying flash, a jolt, he suddenly comprehended the pair and understood.

The small company came to the Lord and Lady's

residence. There on the shining porch stood Mandell and Celina, awaiting their expected arrival. Radiant, they stood arm in arm against the backdrop of the incredible elfin creation, ready to welcome their guests. (These were now the first words spoken by many of the group since first beholding the splendor of Eldamar.) One by one, they were introduced. Vorag, with Oran close beside him, alone was speechless; he remained very awestruck. Nache, when presented, bowed as low as he could, and began talking excitedly, almost continuously, until they left the city. He was totally overcome with joy and had become wildly enthusiastic. Nache was such a sight that Celina herself took the half-man with her and personally guided the dwarf through the sights. He, ever afterwards, held her in the highest regards and forever praised her to any who would listen. Mandell had begun the greetings, when his son introduced Marc and Mindi.

"Welcome fair rose of the south, long unseen in my lands," and he gently kissed her hand. She wondered exactly what he meant.

"And welcome Lord of Metro, the bearer of Andrill. Tales of the fire sword are sung in our songs of old. Noble is the bearer."

He and Marc presented hands, fingertips touching in the traditional elfin welcome. Marc felt his fingers tingle with an energy of joy that rapidly flowed through his body; his toes tingled. Then the horseman was presented.

"Welcome steeded neighbor. Though borders we share, this is the first sharing we have had in many ages."

Hildaro could only reply, "In my shield lies only a snatch of the lights of these northern woods." They understood each other.

"Welcome Farmer of the Grey Fields. Long have we eaten your grains here. It is fitting that the producer should be seen." George blushed and mumbled inaudibly.

"And welcome to the Master Builders, the stone carvers, the rock sculptors."

Nache bowed low and began his nearly unending flow of words. "Oh fair and noble are the works of dwarf arms and hands upon the Stone of Armagh. But here lies a splendor above all Tulan. The glory. The beauty. The lights transfiguring—shimmering."

He continued as Vorag was presented. "Welcome Great Hunter of the harsh, southern Woods. The elves do understand the bonds you have with animals."

Both man and dog merely stared in speechless wonder. It was at this point that Celina stood and took Nache's hand and led him off to see the nighttime beauties. She felt the mother in her rekindled; Nache loved every minute of it. Elwine and Mindi took their leave and together strolled through the elfin city. Hildaro and Marc accompanied Mandell and counciled, as well as viewed the sights. Lana, Elwine's younger sister, swept George away. She knew he loved children, and George had a royal tour so orientated. In later years, he had many tales to tell his own. And the overwhelmed hunter and mastiff went with Ellena. She soon soothed his emotions and together relaxed and saw such sights as befitted the Mighty Hunter.

As Mandell led Marc and Hildaro around the area, he inquired about many details of the war and battles in the south, for now his long isolation led to an unquenchable thirst for knowledge beyond his lands. The two enjoyed bringing him up to date on the situations. Whether by fate or some such, the three arrived near the aged Elohir's home among the Dionti at nearly the same time as Elwine and Mindi drew near.

The old elf was leaning back against one of his silver trees, softly chanting ancient songs. As they approached him, his eyes opened. To Mindi as well as Marc, it seemed as if great visions of distant lands and times appeared in front of the old one as he sung. Elwine introduced his friends to Elohir. Long he gazed at each in turn as if fathoming every aspect of their beingness in one long probe. Finally, he spoke—first to Mandell.

"These are long unseen in Eldamar; you should pay honor to these before you. The Great Ones have been long from Eldamar."

Then, he moved his head to the others, and softly spoke, "I, Elohir, the bringer of Dionti, do humbly bid you welcome again to our land. It has been thousands and thousands of your seasons of years. I have kept the songs of the Great Age alive in the hearts and minds of the young."

Mindi bent over the glowing old one and gently kissed him and spoke ever so softly, "Thank you, Elohir."

Marc was moved by his words. *What had he meant exactly by all this? What did he mean about the 'Great Ones?' How could he recognize someone who had been gone nearly ten thousand years? These confounded pictures. I wish they'd just go away. I can hardly see the old one.* Marc saw a flood of pictures of bye-gone Eldamar. He saw or imagined Elohir as a young man. He continued to thrust them aside.

Hildaro merely mused upon his words.

After a pause, the old one spoke directly to Marc. "Would you, my Liege, grant an old man a favor, a treat for honor and old time's sake?"

Marc hurriedly agreed, hoping no one could tell he had this deluge of mental pictures.

"Long, long, long, has it been since I have seen the fiery blade. Too many years to count, but in time of need, Andrill comes again. Pray, here beneath the Dionti, and for an old one, draw and fire the ancient blade. Let me rekindle memories of old once more before I rest."

"Of course," Marc replied, and he stepped back away from the old one. Suddenly, he recognized the silence! He glanced around. Many elfin eyes sparkled in the soft moonlight about him. He felt a bit embarrassed for a moment, but it left him as he drew Tiny from its small, jeweled sheath. A confidence and power of command filled him as he held the blade with both hands in front of him. He murmured in a language foreign to all ears. All eyes beheld the lighting of Andrill. Quickly the blade grew to its full size of three feet and then burst into flame—leaping, red frames rose skyward. He held it aloft for several minutes. Then the flame went out; Tiny shrank, and he slid it into its sheath, breaking the awkward silence.

The old one began to sing (in the elfin tongue) a song of the olden days. Now and again, Marc caught the word "Andrill," and he guessed it was a song about his sword. After a minute, Elwine motioned the group to leave the old one, who was now lost in one of his trances. Instead, Marc stepped forward and laid his hand on the old one's shoulder.

To his surprise, the elf reached up, placed his hands upon Marc's, and softly said, "Thank you, Blessed One." Marc left and joined the others.

Now much could be said of the group's activities that night and their reactions to Silvere by day, but it only needs to be said that they were filled with a timeless joy and happiness. It was heartbreaking to find that the day had passed, and now they had to continue their journey to Elgladore.

After many partings, the company finally found themselves riding slowly among the shimmering trees of Viniere upon the twisting path of Vindal, which led to the northern elf city. None of the group spoke much, save Nache. It might be said that he talked enough for all—a constant stream of praise for his new elf friends and the Lady of Elves. On the following day, they arrived in Elgladore and rejoined Malazar and the others.

Chapter XIX—The Taming of Schlemloch

Elgladore was called the City of Brown, for here in the northern tip, the ground became brown just before it fell slowly into the marshes beyond. Here, the forest was only a few leagues wide. The city was founded primarily to guard their northern border from the foulness of the dismal swamp region that bordered Eldamar. Though horribly plain in contrast to Silvere, Elgladore was still elfin and displayed their typical craftsmanship and style of life. Elwine and the others rejoined Malazar in a large house on the eastern side of the city. There was both a large, grassy place for the horses and room enough for all to sleep.

After greetings and an exchange of comments, Marc took Malazar and Drifter aside with Elwine and said, "Okay, now what. Is there any news?"

"Ho! Ho! Ho!" exclaimed Malazar, who also was affected by the elf lands and was in exceedingly good humor. "Wizards cannot be rushed. Patience my boy, patience. Yes, we have some news gained from the elves of this area. However, most are rumors; in fact, there are very little direct observations here." The old wizard stooped and with a stick began scratching lines in the dry, brown dirt.

"Here lies the end of the woods; here, the Quara Wund mountains tower. Here lies Chooe Pass. Here is the junction of the roads: Wachoota going to the north, Banto going to the northeast, Ocalla Byway going southeast into Kahill's desert, and Valmar Bypass going south." Drawing a great oval circle in the dirt, he said, "Here lies the marsh, Witchachooie—the Dead Marshes." His voice grew silent.

Aubrey took up the tale. "We elves have long watched these wastelands. It is a great basin of stagnant water; there is little or no drainage from the mountains to the sea. Water collects and stagnates, becoming reek and foul. It is a great, swampy, marsh land. It is treacherous to pass into Witchachooie. Bogs lie for the unwary foot. It is said that a slip into the black mire spells certain doom, for foul creatures lie in waiting. Gators, like bumpy logs, float in the slime, as well as slithering snake serpents. The paths of sound ground, the hummocks, appear mobile, ever changing in position. Great groves of Mangrove trees, their arched feet curving into the tepid waters, twist their limbs upwards. It is a bewildering maize of filth and oblivion. Through the northern edge, the road, built ages ago, still twists its way. Though long unused, except by the nomads of Ocalla, it yet survives, but we have found it is now blocked by countless wargs and a few goblins None enter Witchachooie unless invited, and none are. The wargs need no invite and are widely scattered in the filthy mire."

"We have bad news from the north," the Drifter broke into the conversation. "Wargs have spread like a black plague over the hills of Ocalla. My people are scattered, and Yacs would be ill pressed to find anyone to battle. Yet wargs do us far, far more ill. Grouping in small bands, they come upon our flocks of sheep and devour our lifeblood. They are swift to attack, and before we can defend, they have run off leaving ripped bodies behind."

Bristling with excitement, Nache stood and loudly proclaimed, "Then, let us charge forth and slice their furry throats!"

Malazar raised his hand, saying, "Stay your jubilance yet a little longer, my dwarf friend. There is still more you should hear before you charge headlong into the foul marshes. There is another rumor of Witchachooie. From time to time, the elves have seen it. In this filthy place, a creature, a monster, dwells alone. As the elves describe it, the serpent is huge with many arms and probably blackish in color. Elwine says it acts as if the decayed marsh is its homeland, removing all trespassers from existence. Though it has only been seen twice from great distance, its presence can be felt by those who enter the dismal swamp. Now my hearty dwarf, are you yet as eager to charge into the black spoilt waters of decay?"

Though more sober, Nache said that he was, and the others agreed. Preparations were made. Loath was Hildaro to dismiss his horse, but there was no possible path except certain doom for the brave steed. So the horses were taken to the road and there given their heads. The elves had constructed special elfin boots for the company; the sides of which rose above the knees and were watertight. Their ponies, it was decided, would accompany them. Simply put, they could not hope to carry supplies for their journey on their backs, and though the risk was great, Nache put great faith in their hardiness. To their gear, Elwine added five lengths of elfin rope, shiny grey in color, light beyond guess, but strong. Everyone now had a lightweight, elfin cloak. Aubrey explained that they would help keep the flying vermin off them.

Late that afternoon with a western sun, the sobered company left the brown city of the elves behind, as they slowly trekked down Valmar Bypass heading for the dark world ahead. On their right the towering rocky peaks of Quara Wund slowly descended, each one shorter than the last. All were sheer, reflecting the orange brown hues of the sinking sun. The oak trees thinned, and more open space gradually appeared, filled only with stubble grass. The lands were mostly barren as brown soil turned slowly into grey. Lumbering steadily uphill for the last ten minutes, they reached the crest of the high hill.

Halting, the company viewed the bleak scene before them. Ahead the land fell downward sharply into the blackish foul of the Witchachooie Marsh. The hilly slopes were barren except for a scattered, twisted, stunted oak. The now reddened ball cast long ominous shadows. Far ahead, Elwine could see the convergence of the roads and many moving blackish shapes. Drifter knew well this sight; this hilltop represented hope or dismay, depending upon which way you were going.

He swiftly commanded, "This way—we should get off the ridge before we're seen." He led the company downhill and, veering left, quickly came to a small, grey basin or pit. No living thing grew in it; the acidic ground sapped all life from any plant that tried. Here they were sheltered from prying eyes. Peering carefully over the top, they could still see the dark swamp several miles below them. The rancid stink filtered up, and everyone had their first sniff of the bogs.

The wizard, Elwine, and Drifter held a brief council, for these three had passed through Witchachooie before, though mostly upon the road. A route had to be found. Here in the open would be a dangerous place to camp, and dark would soon be upon them.

"Many, many years ago, there used to be a path of sorts, rather through the middle—down that way," the elf said. "Whether it exists now, who can say? Perhaps we could go to the seaside, but there quick sands are plentiful. It would take a long time to skirt the march."

The wizard pondered thoughtfully for a minute, then spoke, "We cannot go by road. If we wander aimlessly trying to find a passageway, we may spend years getting through. Let us try the old path you spoke of Elwine, if it still exists, but if it does not, we shall discuss the matter further before we rush into the dark swamp."

"Agreed," spoke the elf, "I know of a reedy place near the start of the old path. There we can be comfortable. It is a shame that you all are not elves, for we can tread so lightly that most any path would do. Yet I will do the best I can for you."

"I agree," Drifter commented. "It seems best; lead on elf friend—into the bowls of the swamp!"

Slowly and remaining as concealed as possible, the company traversed the descending, ashen hills in the growing twilight and stench. After full dark, they paused briefly eating a hurried meal. Later after moonrise, they continued on their way across the bleak, dark hills. The black swamp appeared jet-black in the pale light, ominous and foul smelling. By midnight, the land became fairly flat with small stagnant puddles scattered underfoot; others had dried, cracked, mud bottoms. Ahead, creaking in the gentle breeze lay a tall mass of dark reeds. Here they made a hurried camp, lurking in the slithering reeds like hunted animals, cowering in their grayish cloaks. A guard was posted, and Elwine left them to explore ahead.

Though the reeds were soft, they also were very noisy. Few got any real sleep, but all desired the rest. As the first rays of dawn appeared, the company was up and about. Shortly Elwine returned to see his companions looking as dreary as the sober, grey wasteland about them. His news that the path still existed provided the sole good news. Hurriedly, they ate a breakfast, and as the sun began its climb in the clear blue sky, the group prepared to enter Witchachooie. Following Elwine in single file, they swiftly marched across the ashen mud flats toward the dismal swamp.

The path Elwine found began as a broad patch of grassy mud, several inches above the stagnant water pools. On either side, tiny slender trees grew tall and leafless, until they opened skyward far above—each fighting for precious sunlight. Below it was a toothpick world full of sticks, slime pools, and the narrow green way before them. Once inside, darkness fell; everything became gloomy. The stench of rotting things stifled their breath. The heat and humidity sapped their strength. Strange noises abounded from what wildlife lived here in harsh survival. A multitude of birds came and went as they pleased—Nache pointed this out, but other creatures lived in the shallow, rancid mires. Occasional sounds of a great thing exhaling in a mighty breath were heard, sending shivers down many spines. These were the gators, Elwine explained. The elf led, and Drifter followed, making great footprints for the rest to use as guides in the treacherous bogs. The occasional slip and resultant plop and gurgling sound accompanied by various curses reminded all to try to duplicate the other's exact steps.

By noon, they were deep into the rotten quagmires. Groves of Mangroves appeared here and there—roots reaching in great curved arches into the water, as if the tree was loathed to touch such rotten, foul slime. Everyone had slime up to their knees. Their path had steadily dwindled in size. Now the air had become infested with flying insects, mostly mosquitoes and biting fleas. They seemed to descend in swarms upon the guests. Drifter called a halt seeing the plight of the cloakless ponies. He covered their bodies with grey ooze from the slime pools. When dried it persuaded many insects to leave them alone. Yet they fared poorly.

It was early afternoon, they guessed, in the twilight of this ghostly world, when their path abruptly ended. For some time it had been only a foot wide, but now it failed altogether.

"There isn't even room to turn around," complained Nache.

"Here we get our feet wet," joked Drifter.

He and Elwine carefully explored the land ahead. Treacherous, greenish bogs lay scattered like crackers in a black soup. These could not be tread upon as Drifter discovered, crashing headlong into the marsh. He cursed, spat grey mud, and washed himself off with the polluted water. He continued to poke here and there and at last, found a narrow path through the slimy waters. Slowly, creeping one by one, they trailed into the soup. Mindi assisted Nache by tying his beard up into a bow because the slime came up to his chest. Carefully, they made their way through the black water, single file.

Suddenly, Marc noticed a curious, brown, knotted log was floating towards the ponies. Then, he saw eyes. Realizing the danger, he yelled to George and Shannon. "Gator! Gator!" Swords flashed, as the wide mouth of the gator fished in for his meal. Wild chopping accompanied with terror neighs, violent lurching, and splashing black waters marked the demise of the gator. Cursing, they continued their journey, but all were much more on their guard.

The elf, who had darted speedily ahead, now returned with news of a hummock ahead; they made their way painstakingly toward it. At last, they welcomed the dry land of the little hill above the blackened fens and pools around them. All were fatigued, soaking wet, and stinking badly. Camp was made here for the night.

Nache happily gathered firewood. He felt more secure with the roaring, smoking blaze. Elwine, Malazar, and Drifter spoke quietly together, so as not to upset the others, who were a bit merrier now, going about the duties of setting up camp and fixing dinner.

"Here the path seems to have disintegrated, but pieces here and there remain. Our progress will be very slow at best. I'd guess three days to cross the fens," explained the elf.

"More like four or five," grumbled the Drifter. "If we're not sucked of all our blood by the skeeters or eaten by the gators."

There was a silence filled by the noisy sounds of the others; then Malazar suggested, "Elwine, why don't you scout ahead tonight; see what you can do to pick the best path."

"My very intention. By your leave, I'm off now while light yet remains."

"Be wary, my friend," added the Drifter.

The warm meal was delicious and spirit-raising. With full bellies, the forsaken bogs seemed less evil. Hildaro even got them singing a round, but as the heavy darkness fell and the myriad swamp noises grew around them, their spirits sank into gloom. Quiet, they huddled, tiny grey bundles around the fire, trying to sleep. Three guards were posted at a time, and Malazar, Marc, and Mindi took the first shift, but little happened in that horribly uncomfortable night, save Nache turned one gator away with a blazing log.

Dawn found them in worse shape, being more bug ridden. Besides the flying hosts and those that they had picked up from the mud, scores had crawled over them while they had lain on the ground. Everyone was now vermin ridden with biting critters. Mindi fared the worst—save only the ponies. She tried vainly removing the beasts one by one from her long hair, but she gave up and was miserable. They had a gloomy breakfast, and Elwine returned in time for some as well. If they could cross some ten miles more of this soupy fen, they would arrive in a hillier area.

They set out once again. Only this time Drifter had cut a pole for prodding. He and Malazar forged the path through the foul, boggy waters. In similar fashion to the preceding day, they plodded and plopped along in the murky, mucky mire, fighting with the dense cloud of skeeters for air, itching and sweating, painstakingly duplicating the tiny path in the muck, forged by continuous trial and error by the two. Occasionally a deer would splash off in the distance, and once they disturbed a bear that growled and plopped off on a nameless trail of sorts. All around them were decaying, floating masses of vegetation in a vast morass of soft, ill drained, spongy ground. By evening, the totally exhausted crew had arrived at the hummock Elwine had found. They made a camp, set a fire, fixed a meal, and then collapsed in grey bundles on the ground.

It was dark. It stank. Shiny, mucky slime lay all about the filth covered, grey clad bodies. Malazar on his knees propped himself up by his staff, but his head had sunk almost to his knees. Elwine, though mostly just tired, stood behind the old man and gently massaged his shoulders and back. The wizard responded shortly with a long sigh. Raising his head, he spoke softly, and a red glow appeared atop his staff. Elwine could now see the other members of the company. Scattered in muddy, grey clumps about the hummock, the others lay sprawled in disarray in the positions in which they had collapsed. Carefully, he attended each one, moving arms and legs into better positions, even dragging Vorag's huge hulk the rest of the way out of the water. He had been too exhausted to consider his feet. Oran helped with the tugging, and then he lay beside his master. In the red light, the dismal swamp appeared eerie and gloomy.

Quickly, the elf unloaded the ponies and watched them roll their backs repeatedly in the dirt. Even Butterball managed to roll over twice. After feeding them, he at last helped himself. Then, he brought some to Malazar. While the old wizard ate, Elwine leaned against a small Cypress tree and began to sing softly. Whether there is magic in an elfin voice or not, Malazar relaxed considerably and noticed that the sleeping bodies of the others groaned, twisted, and seemed to relax as well.

Refreshed after the food, the wizard rose slowly, testing his weary legs. Then, he pointed his staff towards a large old oak standing centrally on the hummock. He spoke and flames issued from his staff; the tree burst into yellow flames, illuminating the dreary mire around them. They were on a small island in a sea of dark scum, the slime of rotting things.

"Much better. I'm too tired to chop wood for a campfire." He chuckled; the elf smiled. "Things don't look so hopeless when well lit!"

"Well put, Malazar. Now that things are going better, I will sleep a while." With that, the elf's eyes rolled and shut, mostly to fend off the insects. Normally, when he slept, his eyes were open, and a careful observer would see a distant gaze, sort of a not there feeling.

Meanwhile Malazar, though stiff and sore from the heavy work of picking a trail in the boggy land, paced about the hummock, stretching his sore legs. He resolved to stand guard, letting the others sleep as they may.

Some while after midnight, the moon, waning from full, filtered through scattered holes in the canopy far above. Like clockwork, Elwine stirred and rose stretching long. "That will do," he said, mostly to himself.

Whether he would have said more is unknown, for at that moment the familiar baying howl of wargs eerily floated across the dismal marsh. Both rose instantly alert. Elwine peered into the distant gloom for some time.

"What do you see," implored the wizard, when he could wait no longer.

"They're on another grassy hummock about a mile off—six or so wargs," came the reply. "I don't think they'll be a problem for us; there is much water between us. By your leave, I will do some exploring."

"By all means, we need to know where we are. I'll keep things guarded. Take care, Master Elf." Silently and almost as if walking on the water, the elf disappeared quickly into the gloom. For an instant, his cloak flickered in the firelight and then was gone. The wizard resumed his vigil. The wargs continued sporadic howling.

Sometime later, the wizard noticed that more voices had joined in the baying. The evil noise came from more directions, louder and louder. One by one, the others stirred and awoke grumbling, but aware of the danger. Soon all were awake, and while itching, scratching, and complaining, set about getting something to eat. This seemed to help considerably, and, within an hour, the group began discussing what to do about the wargs. Nache even inquired if it were possible for Malazar to burn down the entire swamp; he was disgusted with the whole place. In such idle talk, they amused themselves until dawn grew upon them.

Elwine returned as he had left. One minute he was not there; the next, he was stepping lightly upon the dry ground beside Mindi. He was immediately besieged with questions.

Laughing at their renewed vigor, he relayed what he'd discovered. "First the good news. We are just over halfway across the Witchachooie Marsh. There are some ten miles to go to the next large hummock. The path remains here and there. Beyond that, there are more frequent, firmer paths, though the old one is gone altogether. Strange. The rest is all bad news. The place is infested with prowling bands of wargs, devouring all living things in their path. I watched six tackle a gator and win! There is something else there too." Here his voice sobered and grew hushed.

After a long pause, he began quickly, "There is something alive in this swamp! I felt its presence. As I went exploring, I felt its eyes upon me. I used bursts of elfin speed and dodging, but I couldn't seem to shake those eyes. It is eerie at best, but friend or foe, I do not know."

"Hum, this is not good," mused the wizard.

Mindi looked long at Elwine, and she spoke very softly, "I have felt it too. I have had the feeling that something was watching us all night. I keep glancing around, but I see nothing."

"Maybe it's the swamp monster legends speak of," offered Drifter. "In any case, I don't like it one bit, but we have no choice but go forward, swamp beast or no."

Excitedly the dwarf stood and unfastened his axe. Setting his feet apart, he began to slash the air crying, "No swamp monster will get us as long as Kazab swings!"

The others laughed at his ferocious outburst. "Come brave one; let's ready the ponies," suggested Mindi. Nache instantly agreed, for his fair lady was the only one he trusted to properly pack the dwarf ponies. Eagerly, he set to work.

As the company once more set foot into the black, slimy waters, the sun streamed yellow rays here and there through the dark foliage high above. Misty trails of vapor rose about them from the temperature difference. The plodding and slopping began again. Mindi discovered how sore her armpits and crotch had become from the infestation of vermin that had been gathering there. In fact, she discovered she was actually bleeding in her tender spots. She became annoyed and irritable, but the others fared no better. Vorag, especially hairy, had suffered likewise; red patches slowly oozed down his sides. It was miserable going forward—one careful step at a time, but even worse to stand still. Great efforts were required to pull one foot up from the sticky mud and water. Progress was slow. Elwine occasionally glanced at Mindi. He noticed she kept glancing sideways. He wondered.

Three hours passed. They could see far ahead the low hummock Elwine spoke of, but Elwine did not yet reveal to the others that a dozen wargs now inhabited their refuge to be. Here and there, dry patches nearly a foot in size appeared and would support the weight of a person. These welcome pods as Drifter called them became more frequent, offering a brief rest to the weary feet.

Finally, Mindi could contain her feelings no longer and whispered to Marc, "Do you feel it? Something's been following us."

Marc grumbled; whether he felt it or not, she didn't learn, as his full attention was on the next step, and then the next step, but Elwine heard her. He felt the presence as well. He guessed it was not far off and was remaining at that distance.

They continued on in the filthy quagmire—a band of nearly lost souls. Suddenly Drifter called a surprised halt. He bent over and stared at the green pod before him, carefully observing it. Malazar sloshed up beside him, Marc just behind him. The elf barely skimming the foul water came beside the wanderer. "What's up?" inquired Marc.

"Look at this," came Drifter's probing comment. "See this bent grass and this squished spot. It's like a dozen feet passed over it! Here beside it, just under the water's surface, are hoof prints—ponies I'd say."

Confused, Marc antagonistically blurted, "Are you saying we've been here before on this pod? That's crazy; we're getting closer to yonder hummock. We haven't been walking in circles!"

"I know, Marc, I know; but I'd say these are our own tracks unless you can see anyone in front of us. These prints are only an hour old at most!"

The elf looked and admitted he saw no one save the wargs, of which he did not speak.

"All right you guys, let's be logical about this. Look ahead; now how many green pods do you see on our path?"

They all looked and counted. Consensus was ten.

"Now let us go to the distant one. I make it a quarter of a mile; count the pods as we go." It was agreed, but poor Shannon, who brought up the rear, only got the tail of the conversation trickled down to him. He heard something about the pods were the same ones he'd just used. He figured they were going in circles, and he grumbled—wishing for the sea to appear.

They had an exciting time covering the distance. Curiosity rose. Their pace quickened. When they arrived at the second extra pod, Drifter halted.

Mark yelled "Twelve! That's not possible! And there's two more ahead!" Drifter looked puzzled. Elwine and Mindi felt uneasy; an uncanny feeling was growing on them. Malazar alone appeared amused.

"I say it appears that we have unexpected help in our journey toward yonder hummock." His loud voice was answered by a low howl from the nearing hummock.

They all froze; Elwine embarrassingly blurted, "Oh, I neglected to tell you it's now got twelve, nasty, new inhabitants. I didn't want to get your spirits lower."

"Forgiven," spoke Malazar.

Finally having a target for his antagonism, Marc fairly yelled, "Let's get going, pods or no pods! The sooner I'm out of this filthy place the better. Just wait until I get my hands on one of those wargs! I may even do it Vorag style."

All shared his view and went forward now with renewed energy; the pods became more frequent and progress swifter, until Drifter called another unexpected halt. So sudden it was, the travelers nearly fell over one another.

"What's the matter now Drifter," yelled Marc. "Are your pods moving?" he jested.

"Damned right!" came the fierce reply.

They stared. Right before their eyes, a green pod floated into the line, straight for the low hill of solid ground. That sobered all, and they very carefully went forward testing thoroughly the well-used pods.

Finally, Malazar suggested, "Let's no longer doubt these pods. Let us take that hummock before dark." Now swiftly, though with many sideways glances, they swiftly moved across the swamp, pod by pod, while around them, other pods floated by and fell into line before them.

When they were some hundred yards from the dry land, they halted and drew their swords. Leaving George and Shannon to handle the ponies, they then charged forward into the slobbering, howling wargs. True to form, as they charged sloppily forward in the slimy soup, Vorag's horn blew loudly echoing in the close space. The violence of its blast dismayed the pack long enough for the party to lurch their way ashore unmolested. Against this group, even fatigued as they were, the wargs were swiftly exterminated. Against scimitar, broadsword, fire sword, axe, and staff, they had little chance. If they retreated, they met the fangs of Oran. The fight lasted barely three minutes. Then the ponies were brought ashore, and the wargs were pitched into the waiting black waters.

Nache watched the black furry bulks float slowly off, and then he screamed! The others were extremely startled and came at once. He was jumping up and down pointing to a distant warg carcass. As they watched, a slimy, shining tentacle-like arm rose up out of the dark waters, slowly dropping itself over the lifeless form; then the warg and arm disappeared in a similar fashion.

Finally, Nache yelled "Swamp Monster! Swamp Monster! Guard the ponies!" He ran to their side, as if expecting the black tentacles to slowly surround his ponies and drag them off.

Malazar spoke more thoughtfully, "I detect no evil towards us yet, but let us be on guard. Would you agree?" he inquired of Elwine and Mindi.

They nodded approval. Then, the company fixed a quick, anxious meal, and gathered wood for a fire, though it was still only early afternoon. None spoke of leaving the island—just yet.

Uneasy, they ate hurriedly, glancing constantly at the dark waters around the small hummock they were on. It was only a thousand feet across, a fairly small one with five large trees near its center. Malazar, Elwine, Marc, and Drifter went to the north edge and looked at the way before them. It seemed more hospitable. There were more patches of dry solid ground, though there were many treacherous, spongy bogs in their path. It seemed more friendly, if only because of more solid ground. They then started to return to the others, who were grouped around an oak tree on the southern end.

Halfway back, Marc cried unintelligibly, and they began to run headlong toward the group. Around the others, twelve large, shining, black, slimy, tentacle-like arms were rising out of the waters. It seemed to Marc that they could smother the whole group, ponies, and all. He drew Tiny as he ran; it flared into service. He headed straight toward Mindi, who stood directly before the menacing arms, somewhat further south than the others.

As the four came running up, Mindi yelled at them, "Don't hurt it yet. It means us no harm." They did as she commanded for she spoke with considerable intention. They halted beside her staring at the groping arms, six on either side of the island's end, wondering what would happen next.

"Elwine," Mindi called, not taking her attention off the waving arms before her, "I sense no malice, but rather a curiosity. What say you?" He stepped more forward and by her side.

After a long pause, he said, "I would agree. I feel no hatred flow against us." They stood watching it.

Vorag offered curiously, "Maybe it wanteth to be petteth as doth Oran. Cans that be?"

"Possibly," mused Malazar thoughtfully.

Mindi shrugged her shoulders saying, "Well, then here goes." She stepped carefully forward toward a slowly wavering tentacle. Slowly, slowly, she brought her hand close to the dripping, slimy, black arm. It made no move. Ever so gently, she touched it. The arm wiggled slightly, but did not otherwise react. Mindi felt the warmth of the slick arm. It felt solid and smooth. The underside had hundreds of suction cups similar to that of an octopus. Gently she stroked the offered slimy tentacle. Then a gurgling sound came from the waters and slowly a black form broke through the surface, growing steadily in size and bulk.

The monster's main body was a giant, bulky affair,

slimy, shiny, and black. Two great eyes were atop, near the center. Four more arms protruded below the massive body. It looked like a gargantuan octopus, with a giant fin attached to its rear. It was gurgling in front of them; the main bulbous body was over twenty feet across and nearly that deep. The tail fin extended ten more feet to its rear. Near its front, a cavernous hole appeared—its mouth. Water continuously gurgled in it.

Then, sounds came out; it sounded like "Glurg-glurg-schlem urg-urg-loc-urg. Schlem-urg glurb-loch-glurg."

It repeated this several times. Suddenly, Mindi realized what it was saying. She nearly yelled in the excitement of recognition.

"Its name, that's its name, Schlemloch. It's trying to talk with us. It can speak."

Then she said to the creature, "Hi Schlemloch, Hi Schlemloch. I understand. I am Mindi, Mindi."

To her surprise, it gurgled and repeated carefully, "glup Min-urg-urg-di glup min-ulp-di."

"Have you been watching us and moving those grassy pods around?" she asked.

"Glurb-yes-ulrp-test-urp-you-kill-glrp-wargs?" came the watery reply.

Mindi replied, "Yes, we have been all over the lands south of here. We have killed many wargs and other evil things. We heard there were wargs were up here and came."

This seemed to go well with Schlemloch, if from her looks one could properly guess. After many glurps, the following story was pieced together. Wargs had invaded her swampland. Where they went, they killed many creatures. They traveled in small packs. Schlemloch had a hard time being everywhere at once. Her animals were being slowly slaughtered.

"Glurp-can-ulrp-help-gulrp-urp?"

"We will try to help you. We want these wargs killed or driven back into the Quad," She paused and curiously asked, "Can you control the swamp?"

And after many "ulrps", they guessed she had some power over swamp animals and some over plants and water.

In a flash of inspiration, Mindi asked, "Can you get rid of these mosquitoes? They are really causing us trouble."

"Glrp-can-glrp-control-urp-that-glug-urp-Mindi."

"Also," Mindi added, "Is there any fresh water. We need some clean, clear water." She took the glurps that followed as affirmative.

"Glurp-north-urp-end."

Mindi then said, "Thank you, Schlemloch. We'll clean up now and council. When we have a plan, I'll call for you. Meanwhile keep a lookout for the wolves." She rubbed the black tentacle arm and let it go. Rushing gurgling waters rushed over the sinking blob and arms, which withdrew into the black, slimy waters, leaving no trace of Schlemloch. Everyone began talking at once and excitedly.

"Well done!" complimented Malazar above the others, shaking her hand. Soon they noticed the skeeters had disappeared entirely from their vicinity. The island they were on gave a small lurch, and very, very slowly began to move. Great swirls appeared at the south end of the hummock.

Drifter commented to Elwine, "Your island is not anchored too well."

"Marvelous," was the singular reply.

Shortly, the island halted in a small watery clearing. The late afternoon sun came through the breaks in the dense foliage, both heartening and warming. They discovered the north end of the island was now in fresh water. Elwine supposed it was a stream that fed the swamp. Cheerfully, everyone jumped into the water and washed off the slimy mud and vermin. Drifter had some medicine herbs in his pouch from which he created a salve. As they came out, each liberally applied it to their sore spots. Next, George and Nache got supper, while the others cleaned off clothes and picked the remaining creatures out of one another's hair. Spirits soared, and by sunset, they sat in a circle discussing how to handle the wargs.

Drifter knew the most about their ways, and he explained, "The biggest problem is that they tend to roam in small packs scattered over a large area. Schlemloch seems to understand this as well. How do you defeat an enemy that is so dispersed?"

"As we say in the south," interjected George, "Corral the critters."

"How does one corral wild wolf packs?" asked Shannon curiously.

Vorag laughed and jokingly said, "Hereth Wolfie, Wolfie, cometh wolfie!" Everyone roared along with the hunter.

Finally, Malazar with a sparkle in his eyes said, "Vorag, that's exactly correct. We call them." He paused long enough for them to grasp this twist and demand further data. This took all of thirty seconds.

"Well, you call the wargs by appealing to their instincts. Drifter, if you had a dead sheep lying around, how long would it take the wargs to come and get it? Well not long. But supposing it was tied to a tree dangling just above their reach. Wouldn't a whole bunch of wargs eventually show up to try to get it?"

"Yes," Drifter broke in seeing the wizard's idea. "Then when all are there in mass, wham, you spring the trap."

Malazar continued, "Suppose Schlemloch was the trap and we, the bait, say on a small island just beyond their reach, maybe treed. We let them howl and congregate in a great mass, and then cleverly turn them over to Schlemloch and crew."

The idea was well received, and Elwine took off to find an ideal place, while the rest merely waited and relaxed. The moon was already high when the elf returned. He had found an ideal spot ten miles further on. It was just off the northern edge of the marsh. There the land was grey and flat as it seeped into the swamp, which at that place was very watery with little grass bogs, fairly open. At this point, Mindi called Schlemloch. She went to the southern edge of their hummock and softly called her name several times. Finally, a long, black tentacle, shining in the pale moonlight, rose above the dark waters. Soon the familiar sight of Schlemloch appeared, gurgling. Mindi quickly explained the plan. The swamp creature was obviously delighted with the plan and emitted all sorts of gurgling sounds; one could sense her excitement. Then

Mindi asked her if she could move their island to the shore some ten miles.

"Glurg-yes-glurg-night-urp-move."

With that Schlemloch again disappeared. Again ever so slowly, the island bog moved almost unperceptively across the marsh. The others retired for the night, grateful for the ride across the swamp.

Daybreak found the hummock adjacent to the northern edge of the swamp. Here, as in the south, grey ashen ground ran down into the basin that made Witchachooie. All minerals and life sustaining particles had been long ago leached from the soil. Barren as it was, the solid ground underfoot felt delightful and was welcomed by everyone, after nearly a week in the obscure quagmires. Swiftly they set to work. Elwine and Malazar scouted round for suitable "islands," and Mindi had Schlemloch put them in place. There was one, small, boggy tuft held together by the gripping, finger roots of seven, tall, Mangrove trees. It was not much above water. On it, the others built a large fire pit and stored a great deal of dry wood, cut neatly into logs by Nache. The other trap island was a low, grassy bog, about five hundred feet across. This Schlemloch floated off shore some distance. Occasional moving bands of wargs spied them, but in daylight, they did little more than spread the word.

By evening, all was ready. After a hurried meal, they climbed aboard their Mangrove island. Nache lit the fire, while Elwine and Tse Tse scramble up the trees with readied bow and blowgun. Malazar joined them for a view fitting a commander. The ponies were secured to the center tree, and the others drew their swords and carefully surrounded them. Schlemloch moved them slightly off shore and they waited.

An hour passed. Patience grew short. Then a lone dark form sped across the less black, barren grounds. "There," called the elf.

Several cheers arose. Slowly others joined the dark warg. Carefully, they sniffed the grey ashen land where the company had spent the day. Satisfied, they stood staring at their victims a short distance across the water. In the flickering light, the victims' forms were outlined for the hungry prowlers, who began a low growl. As soon as six were pacing back and forth on the shore, they commenced loud howling and baying. Within a few minutes, the surrounding hills answered in like sounds. The plan to draw wargs here was beginning to work.

Nache threw more wood on the fire, which now roared. Flames leaped ten feet skyward. Now both could see the other even more clearly. Foaming white fangs glistened in the yellowish light. The howls continued as more and more wolves gathered. The word of the company's presence had been spread; eager mouths were congregating. Malazar gave the order; enticing screams broke the silence of the marsh. Mindi went first, screaming as if in dire peril.

"Very convincing," yelled Marc above the howling.

"Yes, I thought so too," she yelled back.

One by one, the others took turns in similar manners. They hoped that such action would communicate to the wargs that their intended victims were both scared and helpless. It worked rather well; the black beasts went wild, running, jumping, lurching, and howling. Yet none dared swim across the black marsh water.

In such a fashion, another hour passed. Some fifty wargs had now gathered before their prey. More were constantly arriving. Rising numbers brought rising confidence, and several wargs braved the foul waters, swimming towards the small Mangrove island. Quietly and without ceremony, Elwine and Tse Tse set to work. Elfin bow bent, and a soft twang and whir sent a silent arrow deep into the leading warg. Slowly, he sank into the slimy waters. A "twah" sound emitting from the blowgun was all that was heard from Tse Tse. His target swam a few feet, slowed, and likewise sank. Tse Tse's jungle poison had its effect. The swimming wargs merely disappeared, leaving those on land in mystery, for they had seen no blows delivered by their prey by the fire.

By very early morning, the warg's numbers were huge, many hundreds lined the dark grey shores. The noise was awesome and loud. Malazar observed that the number of new arrivals were few. Also, they were crossing the water in increasing numbers, and both friends were out of darts and arrows. Swords were now repelling the onslaught of swimming wargs. Indeed, Schlemloch had moved the island further out form the shore—continuously and slowly, it had moved for an hour now. Then the special island, which had been hidden in the dark reaches of the marsh, slowly moved shoreward.

Above the howling horror, Malazar yelled, "The trap is set. Spring it time!"

The company watched the grassy island slowly move between them and shore. When it was near the shore, the unsuspecting wargs in a blind frenzy rushed headlong onto the green bog, smashing, fighting each other for the best positions. Very rapidly, the floating quagmire filled. Then, ever so slowly, it moved farther out into the slimy waters of Witchachooie. Schlemloch was obviously having fun. For over an hour, she moved the two islands slowly around; and, finally, the positions were reversed. Malazar and crew were adjacent to the shore, while the howling warg island was far out into the black depths. Once safely on shore, the company attacked those few who had not been able to get to the island. Mindi signaled Schlemloch above the wild fracas. As the company watched, Schlemloch achieved her revenge on the scourge.

The howling suddenly died down; a great silence fell briefly upon Witchachooie. The island slowly sank, forcing all into the dark, slimy ooze of the marsh. A great host of logs came floating from all directions. Slowly and straight as an arrow, they made for the foundering, black, furry masses.

Suddenly Nache realized and yelled excitedly, "Gators, gators!" Hundreds of gators meandered into the mass. Cries of utter terror now arose. Amid violent thrashing and foaming waters, the wargs frantically tried to escape. Those that did found black tentacles encircling them, pulling them forever underneath the foul waters. A few actually made it to shore to meet swords and axe.

Within thirty minutes, a great silence fell on Witchachooie. Its surface carried a reddish scum as the slow currents moved deeper into the dark depths of the marsh. Gradually the logs disappeared into the dark depths. Presently, a gurpling noise came near the shore. Slowly the familiar black tentacles appeared and followed by the black shining hulk.

"Glub-done-urp-thanks-urp." "No-glub-more-ulp-wargs-ulrp."

"Well done, well done Schlemloch," congratulated Mindi.

Then everyone found a place to rest. Day came not long after, bright and sunny, though the air was definitely cooler. While the others established a camp, Elwine, Drifter, and Malazar scouted ahead to the pass.

They returned by noon. The wizard briefly explained that the marsh went nearly to the edge of the pass. The few wargs that were there at the pass had fled as they arrived. They now feared the swamp monster. Drifter was confident that the reign of warg terror here had ended; yet Malazar wanted to be sure. Carefully, he explained to Schlemloch via Mindi his plan. Then the dark creature left. The company ate and also broke camp heading for the pass as well. When they arrived, they found Schlemloch hard at work. She had taken small trees and was pitching them into the pass. Though it by no means sealed the pass, the terror of her did. From that day forward, at least once per day, another small tree would fly atop the mound. Evil eyes never missed it, and few ever had the courage to leave.

Malazar led the group a little way further north to the many crossroads. Here they decided to spend the night and council their next move. Everyone felt very relieved, hopeful, and happy. They were now on solid rock as Nache put it.

Chapter XX—Of Visitors and Minds

Hanging low, the yellow moon, now past full, cast her pale illumination upon the sleeping company at the northern crossroads. Tiredness and fatigue had caught up with them. That, combined with the relief of complete victory over the wargs, caused the group to retire just after at dusk. Drifter alone stood guard, sitting quietly on a large boulder just beyond the sleeping forms of his companions. They seemed to him in the faint light exceedingly beautiful; strong emotions waved upon him. He smiled. Familiar night sounds were all around this nomad, long accustomed to his role. The hours passed slowly.

It was nearing ten p.m.; a chill wind had begun to blow out of the west, carrying inland the faint odor of salt air. He knew fall was beginning. Farther north, he knew the familiar fall harmattan had come again. Every autumn, the easterly trades began, blowing hard and steady across the Zephyr Hills. Unceasingly, the winds would blow for fifty days and invariably become heavily laden with dust. But it did bring relief from the summer's heat. Drifter figured they would find this weather more to their liking. As Stephen Steadford sat musing perched high on the granite boulder, the southern sky arose in a dull yellow light, glowing brightest near the horizon and fading rapidly into the moon's, as it rose. Oran pricked his ears as if hearing some inaudible pitch. He cocked his head, and Drifter turned and quickly got up, staring at the light. It seemed nearby. Quickly he sounded the alarm, and the weary travelers, jogged from sleep, arose rubbing their eyes, muttering and staring.

"What is it?" George asked mostly to himself.

Malazar, stretching, replied, "I don't know." There was much discussion. Most felt it was very near at hand. It lighted the rising faces of the Quara mountains behind them. Elwine guessed that it lay near Chooe Pass. As suddenly as it came, it went.

"It can't be a fire; it didn't waver; it went out too fast,"

Nache offered.

Since there was no noise associated and nothing disturbed the night sounds, the questers quickly relaxed their guard; most sat down, chatting lightly about the nature of the queer light. Another hour passed uneventful, and many resumed sleeping. Elwine had not; he joined Drifter, Malazar, Marc, and Mindi near the great boulder at the southern edge of the crossroads. They spoke little, but were awake. Presently, the elf eyes caught a blur of motion some distance behind them just off the road. Simultaneously, Drifter saw it. Quietly many eyes stared at the intruder.

An elusive figure dressed in yellow slowly darted among the pine trees south and west of the crossroads, as if skirting them. He presented the image of an old man bent nearly double leaning on a staff; yet he made surprisingly good progress. Silent eyes followed his northeasterly, shaky path around the sleeping company. After some minutes, the yellow form had circled the company and was standing on Banto Road, looking back down at the travelers. For several minutes, they felt his eyes upon them, and they returned it equally.

No one moved or spoke. Mindi later described it as a chillingly, cold stare. Then, he disappeared on up the sharply climbing Banto Road and was beyond their sight.

"Who was that?" Marc questioned, breaking the long silence.

"Again, I don't know," came the wizard's dry response.

"It seems cold, disheartening, yet strangely familiar," spoke Mindi wonderingly.

"Agreed," tensely commented Drifter. "We should be more careful. We have been too lax this night."

"I'll take the watch with you," Elwine proposed. The others nodded.

Glancing northward, Elwine smiled and said, "This is like a grand station tonight,"

"Yes," said Marc also seeing the forms coming down the north road, the Wachoota Bypass from Ocalla. "It's like the Gate Docks of Metro! Here come some more night visitors."

"Ah, they're for me," grinned Drifter. "They're fellow rangers of the north. The smaller one is familiar even at this distance and light. Let's welcome them." Swiftly he slid to the ground from his granite perch and strode tall towards the approaching three. The others followed at a little distance behind him.

When the three neared the camp, barely a thousand yards from Drifter, the smaller one spoke questioningly, "Dad? Dad, is that you?" Drifter ran jubilantly forward, and the pair met in a great hug, father sweeping son off his feet. Drifter swiftly shook the other's hands, and Mindi heard their greetings.

"Arnold!"

"Stephen, it's good to see you!"

"And Errol! How be you?"

"Fine Stephen, you look good as well!" There were brisk, welcoming, handshakes.

Then Arthur, the young lad, began, "Dad, we've been looking for you for some time. See I'm a man now. Arnold is my guide, but only until you return, of course. The wargs got our sheep. We've been on guard in case you should come alone against these foul beasts. Somehow, yesterday most have disappeared." Only now noticing the other companions nearby, his rapid speech ended abruptly.

Drifter smiling broadly merely said, "Whoa. Whoa. You are abroad. I see you're no longer a child in Umatila. Much has changed, but before you fill me in, let me welcome you to our camp and the other members of the company."

As the Drifter led them into the camp circle, the others rose again. Nache threw more logs on the fire, which greedily increased its orangish brilliance. Then the proud father—that side of the lone, White Ranger yet unrevealed—one by one, he introduced Arthur to the others. The lad had just turned sixteen and had all the enthusiasm of youth—easily excited and no fear of withholding anything. Wonder and excitement shone on his face, as he met each in turn, for here was a sampling of people spoken of by the Nomads, yet never seen by the youthful eyes. Glowing elf, stocky dwarf, lean horseman, burly hunter, farmer, merchant—all were viewed by eager eyes.

The power the group did not escape his notice, as he

gaped and commented, "Dad, you have here an army mightier than those with hundreds of men!"

He nodded respectfully. "And finally, last but not least our beloved lady, Mindi Francos."

Here the boy faltered, uncomprehending, staring in utter disbelief, "You have a woman in the company?"

Mindi smiling stepped forward, throwing back her hood, "Yes a woman, though pleased to meet you Arthur."

She held out her hand, but he failed to meet hers and mumbled a bewildered "How do you do." He was obviously displeased and shaken to find a female in such a company.

The Drifter did not take kindly to his son's disrespect and rebuffed him at once. "I don't know what evil has befallen your tongue, my son, but never does one of the Steadford house do such discourtesy to a guest in welcome. Now stuff your tongue and greet Mindi properly or else!" He was obviously quite annoyed and irked by his son's distasteful showing.

Arthur, with his head bowed, as a wounded stallion, softly without emotion said, "Forgive me, madam, I'm pleased to meet you," and he hesitantly took her hand and quickly withdrew his. Yet Mindi felt in an instant his cold, clammy palm, and knew there was some kind of torment behind that clasp.

She quickly and skillfully ended the strained silence by saying, "Now how about these two rangers?"

"Arnold, at your service ma'am," spoke the taller without waiting for Drifter, bowing and then kissing her hand gently.

Unlike Arthur who still had the shyness of youth, Arnold was tall and well formed with a solid frame. She quickly saw that he had a keen eye that missed little, quite similar to Drifter.

"Arthur does have a well-chosen guide," she replied.

Arnold chuckled at the well-deserved compliment but added, "Nay, Stephen here would be far better." The welcoming continued to the others.

George offered their guests a brief supper. "That would be well received," said Arnold. "We haven't eaten yet."

"Hey, how about the rest of us?" implored Nache suddenly. "I'm already hungry again!"

Laughing, George said, "All right, all right. A midnight feast it shall be." Quickly George, Nache, and Mindi set about fixing the proposed meal. Meanwhile, the nomads, accompanied by some of the others, sat around the fire and exchanged news and events.

Even on such short notice, George concocted a reasonable feast. Starting with a soup base, at Mindi's suggestion, the salty dried meat was added, removing the familiar dryness. Mindi added some select herbs. Presently, the company and guests sat down to a hearty soup with fresh fruit to compliment. George apologized for having neither wine nor ale, but Mindi's flavorful concoction, vaguely reminiscent of elfin drink, more than sufficed. The mini-feast was well received by all, and after finishing, most retired. Shannon and George took the next watch over "grand station," as they jokingly came to refer to the crossroads. Mindi retired as well, troubled by Arthur, for she had seen his cold, covert stares directed at her throughout the meal. She wondered and then slept as well.

The chilly dawn came cold and grey without further events. Soon the fire was roaring again, and people were bustling about making ready for the day's challenges. Breakfast was swift and simple. Even in the cloudy light, the area of the crossroads was well defined. Towering jagged and tall to the southeast lay the Quara mountains Nord and Wund. To the southwest, the ground became low hills, greying towards the stark wastelands before the marsh. To the north and west the green hills, covered with intermittent clumps of pines, rose and fell; beyond, though out of sight, lay the Zephyr Hills, green sheep lands with virtually continuous breezes. However, to the northeast into the Ruenzorti Mountains went Banto Road. The road at once climbed upwards. Black, shiny rocks, smooth and round, lay upon either side of the dark, twisting road. Beyond the darkish rise of the mountains of Ruenzorti lay the lands long abandoned, the Serengreti Plains, ancient home of the Mizzinti. Truly, the crossroads was a land of sharp contrasts.

The group now sat around the large granite boulder sipping tea or puffing upon various pipes, endeavoring to plan their next move. In these matters, Arnold provided unexpected knowledge, though gruesome. Mindi sat between Marc and Elwine, but she felt Arthur's cold stare upon her back. Malazar was talking.

"We now must continue our search and go, therefore, to Obelos Magum, high upon the mystic plains of Serengreti. Long have I waited to set foot once again in the strange land of the high Ruenzorti mountains. From this high range, the legends state that the Mizzinti issued forth in times of war. For me, it is almost like coming home. I will state, openly for your sake, that I'm besieged with mental pictures; I feel here I belong. As you travel within Serengreti and the Mountains of the Moon, don't be daunted by the unfamiliar, for it is a strange place, even to me. And now it has been made stranger still by the knowledge Elwine gave us—some time ago. He spoke of a strange beast that would not let him pass. Now the time has come for us to confront this creature, friend or foe. On these matters, the nomads have gained more data. Let us welcome Arnold into our council."

All eyes at once shifted to the tall ranger. Somewhat unnerved by such an audience, he began hesitantly, glancing often at Stephen. "Many months ago, Stephen suspected some ill was brewing upon the high plains." He paused, choosing his words carefully. "At that time, he had to journey to the south at Malazar's command. Before he departed, he asked me to see to it that whatever was there was watched, but it was several weeks before I could get to the matter, having much to do near Chooe Pass. Long has it been the chosen duty of Ocalla to guard and spy upon the evil ones, especially the passes. Well, a curious event occurred several weeks ago now, before the onslaught of the wargs that drove us from the pass. Just after dusk, a small band of the Scourge came through the pass. It was more like a prison team, led by four blue goblins. They had chained together seven scrawny, half-dead, Yac men. They staggered instead of walked. Full of curiosity, we followed from a distance, careful not to be discovered. Well, they came to these very crossroads and then took yonder Banto Road.

They made very slow progress as the prisoners were in such bad shape. They could barely crawl up the steep road. We couldn't follow them further, but later on, guards reported that the four blue goblins returned down Banto Road two days later empty handed."

"Well, this intrigued me, and recalling Stephen's charge, four of us set out at once from Umatila: Benjamin, Errol, Arthur, and me. Ah, Arthur, ah, had become a man and, by our custom, becomes a trainee, a squire, under a suitable ranger, a mentor. You see, women and children are housed in our city. As each man-child becomes old enough, he is thoroughly trained. We are a nomadic people and . . ."

He was fumbling for the right words to explain his society. Obviously unused to such explanations and apparently unable to find the right way to say it, he eventually continued.

"Well, anyway, Stephen here was gone, and Arthur chose me in his place. I couldn't refuse such a request. Anyway, the four of us, under the darkness of night, entered the Ruenzorti by the northern Banta Road. It is indeed a strange land. Very strange plants. Not long after the day broke, we came upon a horrible sight. Ahead on the high plains stood a towering creature. It had the body of some gigantic lion, grayish yellow fur, but it had the head of a woman! It had long orangish hair—thick down its long neck. It had gigantic claws nearly six inches long. Also, attached to its sides was a pair of enormous wings. Despite its massive bulk, it could spring and pounce with startling rapidity and could fly very swiftly."

"Before long, it sensed somehow we were there. In a cracking voice, giggling, it said, 'Come out my pretties. Let's have a game.' Well, I ordered a retreat, but Ben insisted that one of us should cover our retreat and endeavor to find more about this thing. Try as we could, we could not dissuade him; he seemed intrigued beyond measure with it. He ran off toward it. While it was distracted, we rushed headlong back the way we had come. We heard scattered talk. She had some kind of guessing game. If you lost, she ate you. If she lost, you could eat her. As we began our final descent I looked back, I saw it flying up and down, the ground shook with her pounce. I assumed it was over for Ben. Then swiftly she flew towards us. Incredible speed! However, we were down the steep slope before she got to us. At the edge, she talked, pleading for us to come back to her lands."

"Once safe in Umatila, we scoured all our books and legends for any trace of such a monster, but we were only able to discover a rumor. A line in a long epic, 'Like the Sphinx of the Agean Desert,' that was all."

"Well," said Malazar, after a pause, "You have done well—bravely even. At least, we know we face a sphinx. I can add little, for such only existed in ancient legends. This is a living sphinx. Somewhere far from Isel in a vast desert dwells her race. It is a hallmark of them to eat only those that fail to answer the riddles. Can it be that such is in the service of the Evil One? These are indeed hard times. Our fears grow anew. For to control one such as this, even I should need the Orb! Yet Orbless, we must not stop! We must discover whether it lies in some secret crevice at Obelos Magum or not. We must. We must! Yet how?"

Nache bravely rose planting his feet apart and solidly on the ground cried, "Let us charge this beast. My axe will cleave a foot, if nothing else! She cannot stand such a charge!"

"Nay dwarf, I would not send all of us to certain doom," replied Malazar.

Drifter suddenly brightened up, "Say, we could learn from Arnold. Suppose half went in from Banto and half from Banta. Now let the southern one make noise—whatever—get her attention and stall her. That will give time for the others to reach Magum in safety. If the Orb is there, the sphinx can be controlled. If not, send some signal; let the others flee. All would not be lost."

"Yes", said Malazar, "It might work. Yet, who shall choose those who would be doomed to certain death? I cannot pick such."

"I will," Nache cried excitedly. "Never has Kazab failed on an enemy, man nor beast! It shall not fail on this one. I shall get a foot at least!"

"Me too," Marc hesitantly said, "I shall, for I bear the Flaming Sword. Naught has stopped it yet." He shuddered a moment, recalling the great cave trolls.

"Where Marc goes, so go I by choice," spoke Mindi softly.

"And I too, for such a tale for my children I may yet have," exclaimed George.

"Me not be good at towers—better blow darts at beast," decided Tse Tse.

"Well, if it's riddles, I have the most travel experience; I may be useful in the stall as well. Count me in," put in Shannon.

"Whoa, Whoa," broke in Malazar, "We all cannot go. I will take Vorag, Hildaro, Drifter, and Elwine with me. You shall keep the ponies and gear with you."

"Give us four days to get in place. Then go forward slowly and contact this sphinx. Do whatever you can to stall her. It will take about twenty-four hard hours to cover all the distance to the obelos in the center of the Serengreti Plains. After twenty-four hours, do what you will to save your skins. Above all, do not get yourselves killed! You are all too dear to me. If there were any other way, I would so choose. For our needs, we will take Whitefoot—Nache pack him light. The rangers will keep him at the entrance of Banta Road should any of us return."

Malazar then took his group aside and taught them a series of words in an unknown language. For hours, they repeated the phrases over and over, committing them to memory. At least, one had to gain the obelos. The wizard expected to leave in the late afternoon.

The others scurried about, making ready the one pony and gear sufficient for the five of them, and then set to fixing lunch. Shortly after eating, Drifter took Arthur aside by the big granite boulder to talk to him alone. Mindi saw the pair and became very curious. Slowly she drifted near enough to hear their words, yet not attract their attention. She heard Drifter scolding his son for his disgraceful conduct the night before.

"What has come over you? I can't say because I no longer know your mind. I can see that your body has become a man, yet I feel not your heart."

"But I said I was sorry. Can't I come with you? Must I stay?" he pleaded.

"I stand firm son. You are to stay and do as you may—to atone for your reckless conduct. When we meet again, I will expect a change in your behavior. Not just because you are my son, mind you. I would so order it for anyone. Consider it settled."

Drifter then noticed Mindi nearby and motioned to her. She came over unhurriedly, yet full of curiosity.

"I have a favor to ask of you," he began rather awkwardly.

Her long, black hair blowing in the wind accented her round face; and Drifter for a moment felt more like kissing her than talking.

She said, "Sure, anything. But I suspect it's about Arthur here."

"Ah—right. I've ordered him to stay with you for the next four days and to atone for his rudeness to you."

Arthur paled and nervously stared at the ground, embarrassed. Mindi felt it and saw the wall that had come between them. She instinctively went over to Arthur and put her hands gently on his youthful shoulders.

She spoke to Drifter, "A man who has to order another to atone for his deeds cannot expect much at all to result. However, a man who detects his own 'should not have done' and, then, by his own choice, rectifies the damage done will grow immeasurably. Drifter, give your son his own choice in this matter."

She put her arm around Arthur and moved him closer to Drifter, and put her other arm around him.

Slowly he spoke, "Long have I been without such a one to discuss family matters. You speak truly. I haven't thought clearly on the matter. Arthur, you have your choice—you can accompany me, no ill feelings—or you can stay and do as you will. The time to depart grows near. Make your choice."

The young boy looked at his father and at Mindi.

He said, "I choose to stay, Dad." He put his arms around both of them and buried his head in Mindi's bosom.

Drifter put his arm around his son; a tear was in his eye.

"Thank you, you have made me very proud, son."

Arthur blurted out, "It's her doing."

After a tender minute, Mindi broke loose and said quickly, "You two better spend some time together because Malazar will want to be off shortly."

She left them; they were talking rapidly and excitedly. Mindi was correct, for shortly the wizard grew impatient, "Come on everyone; let's get going."

He continued trying to act unconcerned. Swiftly his party separated from camp and stood beside him at camp's edge. There was a moment's silence. Spoken or not, everyone leaving felt they were taking their last look at their close friends. Marc's group was surely doomed. Suddenly, Arthur realized it as well, watching the two groups looking at each other.

He cried, "Well come on at least say good-bye, even if it's forever!"

That was spot on and broke the awkwardness of the scene. At once, everyone began to say what he felt, even Malazar, who actually had tears in his eyes. Ten minutes later more calm and relaxed, they set out northward along Wachoota Bypass.

The remaining ones stood still, watching them trail off into the distance.

Finally, Marc broke the silence. "Well, here we are again as a team. First, we must move our camp. It is too open here for us to defend, and we can be spied upon easily. I guess we should scout around for a more suitable place." Everyone nodded.

Arthur quietly said, "Marc I know a more secure place. It's where Arnold and I camped a while back. It's got water and is sheltered."

"Well, then young Drifter, lead on," Marc said cheerfully.

Quickly camp was broken; and they followed Arthur across the green grass blowing in the wind, heading northwest from the crossroads. Quickly they climbed and passed through scattered, sweet-smelling pines. The grey sky steadily darkened. Just above the hill, stood a small dense stand of pine. Nearby a small creek, barely a foot wide, trickled and bubbled through the grass and rocks. In the shallow, small basin of the trees, they could remain hidden and still see the crossroads some distance below them. The wind howling through the pines gave an eerie flavor to the hiding spot. Quickly a new camp was made. Nache gathered wood, and Mindi unpacked several canvas tarps. Barely twenty minutes later, lightning flashed around them, striking the tall Quara mountains in front of them; thunder rolled deafeningly in the small valley. Everyone huddled under a tarp as the rain lashed out in sheets. The pines blunted the force of the pelting rains, but they were glad to be under the tarps.

Marc had at first come towards Mindi, to snuggle with her, but she waved her finger negatively; her eyes twinkled. He knew that playful sign; she was up to something. So he had snuggled in with George and Nache. As the rains finally halted Arthur's eager drive to be helpful, she quickly got him under her tarp, before he realized what was happening. Then it was too late.

Very rapidly, Arthur's momentary enthusiasm for setting up the camp faded, as he realized he was alone under the tarp with a female. Disgust filled his heart; and it was felt by Mindi, who was expecting it. Arthur began to squirm nervously.

Her soft gentle voice finally broke the pattering of raindrops upon the tarp, "Want to tell me what you did?" she asked exploringly.

"Nothing—I didn't do nothing—damn women anyway. You're all alike," he burst out; but Mindi interrupted his critical flow of words.

"What did you do to women anyway?" Silence—broken only by the pelting rains.

"Did you murder a girl? Kill one?"

Her words dug deep, and at once, he protested, "No—No, nothing like that?"

"Well then, like what?" she quickly returned.

"Well, er, I, ah—I made Genny in bed, you know," he blurted out rapidly.

In the flash of lightning, Mindi saw his crimson face and sensed the relief he felt. Sighing, he relaxed considerably and cheered up rapidly. "How did you know I'd done that?" he sheepishly asked, followed by "You won't go telling everyone will you?"

"Easy and No," she replied smiling.

"What you have told me need not go beyond us. If it does, it will be your doing, not mine. It takes a brave heart and a wise mind to face and to say what those things are that one should not have done. But if they are not spoken of, gotten off so to speak, they fester a mind into a general bitchiness, an undeserved criticalness. That's how I knew."

"Oh," came the interested reply. Arthur was silent for a while, reflecting her words; here, he felt, was a great wisdom, yet coming from a woman. He was perplexed. They talked further and after a time, she and he both detected that he felt grief stirring in him. They were both lying on their sides upon soft pine needles.

She gently placed her arm comfortingly on his side and said, "Tell me about it."

"It's my mother," and for several minutes, he cried openly. Then she learned that Yacs had killed his mother late one night; then, he had gone to stay with his aunt, who also had been killed in a Yac raid. Arthur cried long and hard. From Drifter she had a guess that this loss was there, but now it was confirmed. She had him go over it again, telling her everything he could once more. And then again, as the tears gave way to sympathy and to anger. Gently, over his cursing and raving about the Scourge, she put him through the incidents again, and he moved more into antagonism. On the next pass, he became more cheerful about the whole affair.

Then he started laughing, "You know, I had been blaming mom and all girls for deserting me by going and getting themselves killed, but that's ridiculous. Oh, now I see why rangers must be so well trained. There's so many of them and too few of us!"

He laughed a bit; and Mindi smiled saying, "Thanks, Arthur, for telling me all that."

"No. It's thank you for whatever you did!" He looked at her, almost as if he had never really seen her and quickly asked, "Would you—could you sort of be my mom for a while?"

She responded by putting her arms around his head,

pulling him against her body, saying softly, "I'd be honored to." An hour or so passed.

The storm clouds broke up west of them, and the setting sun broke red and swift into the valley and the crossroads, creating a large rainbow over the rising wall of the Ruenzorti range. One by one, the small band crawled out from under the tarps. Tiny drops trickled down the reddish green pine needles, formed sparkling balls, and dropped. The air felt fresh, filled with the fragrance of the wet trees. Everyone spent a few minutes absorbed in the beauty.

A happy supper followed; no one said a word about what lay ahead of them. All were content to enjoy the cheerful present, and Arthur most of all. Marc noticed the change and commented upon it to Mindi. "Loss can be a heavy thing; I'm now his acting mother," was all he got out of her. He guessed the rest for himself.

When darkness fell on their corner of the world, Marc established guards, though security seemed lax. Arthur, Tse Tse, and Nache took the first watch of three hours, which was rapidly filled by tales. Arthur proved an enthusiastic listener, and the two loved an audience with which to share their narratives. In fact, it was well past midnight when Nache realized they were supposed to have awakened George and Shannon an hour ago. Promising more the next day, he awakened the next pair; and the three retired, and similarly, the night passed swiftly into a sunny cool day.

The day passed lazily for all. There was nothing that had to be done, save wait. At first, this was easily done; but by the second day, the band became restless, tired of sitting, tired of inactivity. The edge of doom slowly crept into their thoughts, though seldom into actual words.

It was just after sunset on the third night when a singular event occurred. "Central station" had no traffic since the night of its christening. However, this evening proved different. Tse Tse had gone to stretch his legs and view the sunset. Now he came running silently back to their camp in the tiny pine valley above the crossroads. Breathless he sounded the alarm.

"He comes! He—yellow—one—comes! Again—comes!"

Swiftly muscles tensed. Nache instinctively loosened his axe in his belt. Quickly everyone crawled to the crest of the small dale and peered into the growing darkness below. The outline of the roadbeds could be faintly discerned. There, slinking through the shadows down Banto Road, was the yellow man, pausing now and then, leaning on his staff, and listening for sounds.

For five minutes, they watched him curiously. He seemed to be trying to locate the party that was there days before. As if satisfied they had moved on, he paused at the crossroads bent over studying the ground intently.

Quickly Marc reasoned to himself, "If this is the same one, if he is a spy, then if he finds we've split up, if he relays to the sphinx—we must do something before that."

He issued a few orders. George and Tse Tse were to stay with the ponies. Marc and Shannon would stroll down first, followed by Arthur and Mindi; Nache would follow. Thus it would look like a slow wandering procession. As quietly as possible, Shannon and Marc slipped eastward a distance and hit the road. Pretending a leisurely stroll, they ambled toward the crossroads.

Soon the yellow clad man detected their coming. For a moment, he cowered and bent as if in recoil from some vicious blast. Marc distinctly heard the hissing sound of air rushing inward. The figure spat on the ground. Marc's plan was cleverly executed; the yellow man was taken off guard in the wide-open area. He could do only two things: run or stay. If he ran, well, that would solve everything. If he stayed, well, perhaps something could be learned. It seemed to Marc that the bent man was thinking the same thing; he saw him glancing around, evidently looking for the nearest cover. When they were within a thousand yards, Marc called out, "Hello there." That sealed the choice. The yellow man leaned heavily on his staff, awaiting Marc's arrival. Mindi and Arthur now had gained the road, and they too strolled towards the stranger.

"Well, as luck would have it, we meet again at the crossroads. Care to spend the night here with us. Marcos Blancas, at your service." He tried to be as casual as possible, alluding to the event several nights before.

Slowly with a cold piercing gaze, the dimly lit man stared first at Marc. He felt a growing uneasiness about this person. The glance struck him hard. A cold fear gradually crescendoed; Marc felt very nervous, bordering upon a chilly terror. As the old one glanced at Shannon, Marc felt the depth of the frigidness subside. The Mariner lurched slightly; evidently, he too felt the ominous presence. Finally, the seeming old one chose to speak.

In a high, mellow, singy voice, he said rather cracking, "I am Frederic, hermit of these parts. Who be yea, and what do yea want of old Fred anyway?" he added.

Marc felt the icy blast of covertness in his intention, though seemingly pleasant. Marc repeated his introduction, and Shannon did likewise.

Mindi and Arthur arrived and greeted the stranger as well. No word did Marc speak of their purpose, regretting that he had originally offered to share his proposed camp with him.

"Fredric, if that was who he really was", Marc thought to himself, "is a sly one." They exchanged a bit of courteous pleasantries, and Nache joined them. Five was a bit much for Frederic, who noticeably grew uneasy but continued in his sickeningly, pleasant manner.

"You are mightily armed warriors if my eyes don't deceive me. Brave noble men and fair lady." Mindi cringed at the compliment.

"These are not safe parts for such gallant ones to roam especially after dark. Have you not heard of the Swamp Monster or the Evil Ones. The nameless Scavengers, as I recall you speak of them?"

Nache blurted "Yes," but quickly restrained himself, adding, "yes, we are aware of the dangers, but we are confident, evils or no."

Marc decided it was time to switch to the attack. "You correctly call us mighty warriors. Yet you say nothing of yourself, save hermit. Why should we not consider you a monster and slay you here and now?" Mindi thought Marc was a bit blunt and covertly poked him in the ribs.

"I mean," he added quickly catching the icy stare full

on, "where do you live and that sort of thing. We, of course, never kill wantonly." He received no further pokes, so assumed he'd smoothed it out a bit.

For an instant, Marc felt the freezing stare waver in strength; he caught Frederic's rapid glances at the others. "Five to one," thought Marc.

Smoothly, even coyly, the reply came. "In a cave, over yonder, ten miles. This is my walkway. I have been walking here since before you were born, my lad. Tis a pleasant place. You wouldn't hurt an old man?" he added coyly questioningly.

"Of course not," Shannon began. "You see we have seen much destruction by the foul Yacs and goblins. Many have we here slain. We are the foes of evil, wherever we find it."

Marc caught Shannon's covert drive and watched closely for reaction. If there were any doubts in Frederic's mind, they were dispelled. Marc saw his smiling face falter slightly, but if there was any bigger reaction, he certainly contained it well. His reply was unexpected. "So I have gathered. That's why I steered clear the other night."

"Yes, but how could you tell we weren't a band of Yacs?" queried Marc, following Shannon's covert lead.

The reply was long in coming but reasonable. "Oh, I saw your spears and swords. The enemy does not possess things of such, such beauty."

Mindi caught his fumble. It was as if he were loathed to say the word. She pressed him. "Aren't they just beautiful," she said, feigning a primpy coyness and shoving Marc's sword hilt squarely into the old man's face.

He momentarily cringed and wavered, and then quickly regained his composure, saying, carefully yet smartly, "Yes my dear, they are visions indeed, very good. Yes, I have not seen one so well made; no, not since the time of the great wizards." He paused cleverly and added, "This wouldn't be one of the Old Wizard's, would it now?" Marc was taken aback with the sudden reversal of the covert thrust.

He stammered, but Mindi, acting like a pompous socialite, gaily proclaimed, "Oh yes, your eyes do not deceive you. This one is. This is the old Fire Sword itself! Is it not just the prettiest thing you have ever seen?" This last she threw his way with terrific intention. Marc saw him catch his breath momentarily.

Then he recovered and sweetly replied, "Oh my, I'm breathless. Old as I am, I never dreamed of ever personally laying eyes upon such a sword!"

Mindi now took a long gamble. She, acting daintily, drew it in a careful manner and offering it to Frederic, saying, "Wouldn't you, our new friend, love to touch such a majestic weapon of the gods?"

Marc, rigid, was loathed to have such a creature lay hands to his Tiny. He was pricked that Mindi should offer his sword., but he contained himself and waited. The man stepped back rapidly, the sweetness faded wholly for a second. His face grimaced as one in terror brought before the brilliance of day.

Amazingly, he recovered almost at once, "Nay lady, we shouldn't mock such mystery—such was the grandeur of the great ones. I would defile their very name if I were to touch so wonderful a thing, but I must soon be off. Can't you tell the old hermit whither you are going? Perhaps I can direct you safely upon your way. For me thinks you have been here for days. At these roads, there is nothing, not even an inn. Can it be you are lost?"

Once again, the attack was reversed. Marc stalled by carefully sheathing his sword. He was disturbed; this question above all was just too revealing, either way.

Shannon, having seen much diplomatic service as a Mariner, fielded this query adroitly. "Well you see, we really don't know. That's why we haven't gone anywhere yet. Actually, we are just more or less exploring, sort of an adventure. You know what I mean? City life gets boring, and, from time to time, we feel the need to be in the wilds, you know."

The old man nodded.

Shannon continued, "Do you have any suggestions of some exciting places to see or something exotic that travelers may enjoy?"

"Brilliant", thought Marc, "no wonder Shannon, of all the Mariners, could open up so many new markets in strange places."

Slowly, coyly, as if pondering Shannon's words, and as if trying to be genuinely interested, he replied, "Well, if you've never seen the ruins of Ruenzorti—the Grand Wizards' home in Isel, then I'd suggest taking Banto Road here. It's a steep climb, but the scenery is quite unusual, yes quite. I'm sure you would be surprised."

Shannon thanked him a lot and appeared sincerely grateful. The others joined in the game. Then, as dark was nearly complete—yet a full hour before moonrise and four more again before it would peak over the tall mountain—the old man took his leave, stating he had to hurry and get home. The band was very content to let him go. When he was far out of sight, they slipped back quietly to their camp and to George and Tse Tse. They spoke little. A quickly made fire kindled its cheerful, yellow flame and comforted both the chill, night air as well as their hearts. Instinctively, Mindi had a quart of tea brewing at once. With cloak drawn tight and hoods up, the group sat in a circle around the crackling fire, sipping the warm brew.

Shannon broke the long silence, "That was some encounter!" His words pierced the night stillness, ending the awkward silence.

Like a bursting dam, Arthur began, "Wow! That was the weirdest person I've ever met! So cold! So sneaky! I don't trust a word he said! I was spellbound. How did you all know what to say to him? That was marvelous!" He was obviously much impressed with the way they had handled him.

"Well for heaven's sake, will someone tell Tse Tse and me what the heck happened out there?" protested George. Tse Tse nodded in agreement. Quickly Shannon and Marc related roughly what had transpired.

"A number of points just plain don't jive," continued Marc half-debating with himself. "How can anyone live just south of here? It's a dead, grayish world and swamp. Schlemloch never spoke of anyone else living in her swamp. And not ever a single word or even a question about the wargs! One man and hundreds of wargs. They suddenly disappear and not so much as a word! It doesn't add up."

"Yes," put in Shannon, "and furthermore he went for a

walk in the Wizard's Vale, where a known monster lies, and he comes out four days later, alive and well—no word of the monster, and he recommends Banto Road for us!"

"And don't forget that yellow light too," Nache exclaimed. "First we see it, and then he comes walking from that direction just as big as you please, and he didn't even mention it!"

"Yes, something is very rotten here. That was the trickiest person I've ever talked to," added the Mariner.

Mindi, who had been silent now for some time, finally spoke. "The strangest part of all is the frigidity that emanated from his very presence. We all felt cold, cold to our very bones. Most unusual, most. I have no explanation."

"I know. We felt it way back up here, didn't we," inserted George with Tse Tse nodding.

Mindi eyed them, "You too, hum, and this far away even beyond hearing distance. Interesting."

"I don't know about the rest of you, but I felt like I was a chicken being plucked slowly. Yet, I don't think any useful data got revealed," Marc commented.

"Yes, very well done you two," complimented Mindi.

"Yes that goes for me too, fine show," added the boy enthusiastically.

"Strangely familiar," murmured Mindi half to herself.

"What's that dear?" queried Marc in sudden interest.

"Oh," she blushed, realizing she had been talking aloud. "I said strangely familiar. He was, I mean. I feel like somehow I know him from somewhere, but I can't place him or where. Did any of you also feel like you sort of knew him?" she asked exploringly.

There was a moment of silence. As horrible as the encounter was, this idea was even more startling.

"Hum, honey, maybe you've got something there. It does sort of feel like that. I don't know how or where but somehow it does, and I feel terrible just thinking about it." The others agreed and changed the subject.

"Shouldn't we change our camp?" asked George. "I mean if he isn't who he says, he at least suspects where our camp is located. Should we change it?"

"Good idea, George. You are right! He knows we came from the north so it wouldn't be hard to find us, if he sent a scouting party. Anybody got any suggestions?" Everyone had, naturally, but Mindi's proved the best.

"He has already suggested Banto. Why not head up the steep part a ways? At least it can be easily defended. It rises so steeply; we'd have a great advantage. Besides we need to go that way."

It was agreed, and within the hour, the small group, like small ants among the dark shapes of trees and boulders, made their way carefully and steadily down the road. The night was very dark. To the south, the horizon was obstructed by the towering, jagged, rocky peaks of the Quara mountains. To their left rising in a steep wall lay the basalt cliffs of the Ruenzorti, shiny, black, as dark as night. The lowlands crept away grey and dark to their right. Though everyone strained their senses, no one detected a presence beyond themselves.

Within minutes, the crossroads lay underfoot. Banto Road lay sheer, dark, and ominous to their left. On either side, the sheer, black, weather worn, basalt cliff rose steeply beyond sight. Here and there, a twisted gnarled form of a pine, tenaciously forcing its roots into small cracks, hung precariously to life. The road way was broad enough for them to walk three abreast, carved in ancient days from the solid stone. Now polished by the years, it glimmered faintly, as it rose sharply upwards in a series of steps cut into the uplifted basalt. A thousand yards up, the road began to snake its way up the sheer mountain face.

Without a word, Marc led the way, and by the time they reached the first switch back, heavy panting broke the night stillness. The steep climb was difficult for man, and Marc was very concerned for the two ponies. Nache had taken charge almost as soon as they faced the black road. To Marc's surprise, he found the ponies were surefooted and seemed very content, even pleased with the climb.

Nache explained it when they rested at the switchback, "They are in home-like country, and they like it."

After a brief rest, they continued the climb. After ten snaking loops, Marc discovered the ground now more gently rolled upwards—evidently, the steep part was behind them. Quickly, the group halted and scattered looking for a suitable place to camp. Shortly a spot was found, a large crack between two massive, dark rocks provided considerable shelter. The floor was nearly four feet wide with sheer walls for twelve feet. Huge splinters of fallen boulders blocked the western end. Here the new camp was swiftly established. Marc set up a lookout sight atop the western rock fall. From here, they could see the road snaking some distance down the sheer face. They retired sleepily.

Daybreak brought the exotic beauty of the Ruenzorti mountains to life. Gigantic blocks of black rose sharply all around them. There was little or no vegetation in this harsh environment. However, in the cracks and more sheltered areas, rainbowed lichens thrived. As far as the eye could see, the massive black mountain of basalt rose. In the space of four horizontal miles, the mountain of basaltic blocks rose some fourteen thousand feet. Marc's guess was that the slope where they were at was nearly one to one, forty-five degrees up! Nache estimated the sheer face to be nearly sixty degrees, quite steep! Nothing grew in the sea of blackness, save lichens. To the south, the black gave way sharply to the familiar orange granite.

Seeing this, Nache predicted that there was a sheer fault line where the two ranges met, and he was eager to go see it. So enthusiastic and excited was the dwarf that nearly everyone finally agreed that, when the chance came, Nache could show all this natural wonder. The day passed very slowly for everyone. Nothing marred the nearly absolute silence of this remote land. Occasional breezes broke the stillness. Shannon swore he could see and smell the sea, but nothing of significance occurred. The company amused themselves as they could.

Finally, the fourth night arrived, wholly uneventful. Excitement peaked as the moment of challenge and doom arrived at last. It was decided that Arthur should stay with the party. Marc felt he couldn't risk sending the boy back alone with the yellow hermit about. Arthur was quite cheerful about staying with the party. Indeed, he had already made plans to fake leaving if so ordered; he would follow them from a distance. So he was relieved to be asked to join their doom. The danger lay masked by the exuberance of youth.

Chapter XXI—Pixcies

As the red ball descended below the distant horizon, the company began their climb up the face of the Ruenzorti. The dark night fell swiftly and progress was very slow. Marc led, carefully picking the way over the well-worn roadbed. Occasional stumbles followed by a murmured grumble broke the rhythmic deep breathing, as they steadily climbed laboriously upwards foot by foot. The continual switchbacks of Banto greatly reduced the overall effort, by adding horizontal distance to the vertical climb. Nevertheless, it was a very toilsome climb, hindered by the blackness of the night. Their bodies began sweating heavily, and when they halted for a rest, the cool night air chilled them. In this matter, Nache was of great assistance, instructing the others on the principles of mountain hiking. Particularly useful was his advice on clothes. He told them to peel off their garments, one by one, as needed; when resting, one by one, put more on. Soon the others discovered the wisdom of this and continued more easily.

They climbed and climbed. After a few hours, Marc's mind became numb. He found himself thinking only about each painful step. "Step. Step." His mind mechanically plodded onwards. By midnight, their legs ached from the ascent, though Nache fared the best. They rested for a while, though the dwarf would only let them drink sparingly, eating mostly sweets and salt. Too fatigued to discuss the point with the dwarf, they pressed onward, ever upwards. Step after step. The moon, near the third quarter, finally rose above the forbidding blackness, but it was welcomed. They could now see the road, and the groping ended. They grimly continued the ascent toward the unknown.

Finally, the slope became gentler, though the ground became rougher and rocky. Now the endless snaking road bore straight ahead. More eagerly, they went forward, upper legs and knees, an aching mass of pain. Their lungs were now sore, and save Nache, all were deeply breathing—gasping for the low oxygen content air. They were nearly three miles high.

Within a few minutes, the ground became level. On either side of the road, massive black blocks rose randomly in a monstrous field of scattered boulders. The road snaked its way around this huge obstacle. Finally, passing between a narrow slit between two especially large ones, Marc came upon the Serengreti Plains, the high desert savannah of the Wizard's Valley. Instinctively, he stopped abruptly. Everyone, gasping for air, crowded around him, peering into the yellowish distance. "Camp here," gasped Marc. Quickly everyone scattered off the road, put on more clothes, and collapsed randomly. The respite cleared their spinning heads and exhausted bodies.

Even though the dawn came in just three hours, the

time revived the bodies. The prior four days of rest and relaxation also assisted. They rose and stretched sore muscles, and with mild interest, noted their environment. The air was quite thin and chilly, and at this height, the sun seemed to pierce the air, generating immediate heat on bare skin. They found the glowing ball incredibly brilliant in its splendor—to the point of hurting their eyes. Surrounded by massive, rugged, black blocks jutting westwards as if stacked by some giant's hand, the group ate a hurried breakfast and began their trek across the Serengreti Plains.

Banto Road left the basaltic blocks and made straight northeast. The high plains were a savannah: hot, dusty, and dry. Still, brownish grasses grew in sparse clumps upon the dry, solid ground—a yellow-brown soil, heavily leached, and exceedingly arid. The great plain was flat, so flat that George though he could see for ten miles or more. Above the surface, which shimmered in heat waves from the scorching sun, only an occasional tree grew. A solitary, twisted stunted oak was separated by a vast, brownish, hot, dry space. Trees were so scarce that you could count them easily. Underneath their shaggy bows, the only shade in miles, the grass grew more abundant and was a darker color.

Quickly, they began to shed clothing to avoid baking; but, at Nache's insistence, they kept on their loose fitting cloaks, though with hardly anything else under it. He explained that at this altitude the sun would fry their skin at a very rapid rate. The low sun was brilliant on their right, and most were squinting constantly, unused to so high a light level. They began walking by twos. Banto Road was here was just a brown, dirt road, but its smooth, dry surface felt soft to their feet, after the stone path.

Before long, they arrived at the first tree near the road. Marc halted; something sparkled and caught his eye. He gasped and turned away. The others did likewise, for scattered under the tree were the white, slim, bleached bones of men. Skulls lay scattered about, neatly stove in, as if something had taken care to devour every dainty. Nache pointed out that their ribs were uniformly crushed, but no one really cared to hear his anatomical discussion. They quickly resumed their march; Marc muttered something about the men the goblins had taken up the road a week ago.

After a half hour, Marc suddenly remembered. "Hey," he startled the group. "We're supposed to make a big, obvious noise."

The others recalled Malazar's words and nodded. Nache complied; quickly he retrieved a pot and spoon from Butterball's packs. Pounding loudly, he began to sing a dwarf working song. He looked so comical that the others roared with laughter.

Suddenly, something eclipsed the hot sun; a huge, dark form passed overhead. There was an abrupt silence filled only with gasps. The sun blazed once more, and the company stared at the flying form, as it swooped beyond them and came down to the ground by the basalt blocks where they had camped. Its wingspan was nearly fifty feet. A pair of huge, furry and feathered wings gracefully flapped, creating mini dust storms below. The wings were brownish in color and were affixed to the sides of a massive body. Mammalian, they guessed, rather like an enormous cat, or lion, a soured, yellow color, quite fury. As the outstretched feet neared the ground, the claws in its large footpads sprang out, sharp and white—like razors or curved scimitars. They gripped into the ground. The body was muscular and some twenty feet long—nearly ten wide. By contrast, it had a short stubby tail only two feet long. The real shock was the head, which rose boldly in front. It was the head of a giant woman. She had long yellow hair—all snagged and twisted, held coarsely behind her head, which was nearly two feet across. Its face was browned by the sun, yet definitely that of a woman. The sphinx had arrived.

"How the heck did she get here so fast," mumbled Shannon.

Treachery was the common thought—the yellow robed, old man, but now was not the time for reflecting.

Marc steadied himself and commanded, "Okay. Okay. Our job begins. So far so good. Remember stall, stall, stall."

The others, still staring, nodded. Slowly, like a cat playing with her mice, she pawed a small step forward. Instinctively, the group withdrew on down the road towards the center and obelos.

Marc gathered that she wanted to play, so he gladly obliged. Quickly the group began a fast walk, heading deeper into the Serengreti Plains. Slowly the sphinx pawed and crept forward, mostly on her belly, obviously amused. Marc's mind raced, it was some thirty miles or so to the center and the obelos. The others, if they achieved their target, would be a long way from being able to help them. If they could just get closer, say to within a few miles of the obelos and the central crossing of the four roads. If. It was a big if, but the sphinx was content to let her prey travel deeper into her territory—less chance of escape she felt, and so the dry, hot, mad race went. For nearly four hours as the arid heat grew, they retreated before the stalking beast. Perhaps she wanted to tire her prey, or let hopelessness sink in, but for whatever reason, she slowly followed behind them, cat-like.

In the early afternoon, Marc thought, "Well, whenever we stop, we'd best be under a tree."

The obelos grew and appeared as a white tower rising in the distance, some five miles off when the retreat ended abruptly.

Suddenly the sphinx, in a mighty cat leap, pounced unexpectedly right over their path, landing in front of them and blocking the road.

"Game's up; head for that tree," yelled Marc. Within seconds, the company crowded under the shade of the scraggy, stunted oak—the sphinx before them. "Here comes the game," Marc added softly. Quickly, Mindi broke out the water bag, and they continued, as unnervously as possible, to calm down, cool off, and relax. The dust settled down upon the parched ground, and the sphinx eyed them closely, as if counting them, ensuring none had escaped. Satisfied with her count, she crouched upon the ground; the sun was over her left shoulder now and waning. She spoke in the common tongue of Isel. Her singsong voice was feminine, yet very high-pitched and whiny, in stark contrast to her bulk.

"Ah my prettys—my prettys—these will do—do just nicely. Yes, it will. Won't it? Food must be cool. Not many trees in my land. Yes, rest yourselves my pretty ones. I'm Pixcies, queen of all these lands. And you, my delicious ones, have entered unbidden. Yes, yes, you shall face the challenge, my precious prettys."

Marc, having become used to her dreary whining voice, took a step forward, planted his feet dwarf-fashion, and with his hands on his hips and standing tall before her, spoke carefully. "Greetings great Pixcies. A wonder you are for weary travelers to behold. I'm Marcos, Master merchant of Metro, and these are my traveling companions," he said, gesturing with his right hand toward the others, who each stepped forward a bit uneasily. "As for this land being yours, we don't know for sure, since there are no signposts or people to so state. And as for trespassing unbidden, we saw no markers of warning or any such signs." He was attempting to stall, but she cut him off quickly.

"No matter, my delicious ones! I need no sign to tell me. Why should you? That is irrelevant for food. Does the cat place signs before the mouse? Nay, I say you've walked into my house, my prettys." She seemed to Marc occasionally to drift off in thought. Then, she would "pop" back, eyes gleaming. He wondered what she was thinking about. Some evil ideas he guessed.

"Hello Pixcies", Mindi said, stepping forward at Marc's side. "I'm Mindi of Metro. One such as you, I have never seen. Could you not tell our curious ears, who are you, what are you—tell us about yourself?"

"Ah I see, my dears, you are ignorant meals. I can't eat dumb ones, oh no. I'm Pixcies, a sphinx in your tongue. I'm powerful, yes the most powerful. None can slay me. I go where I choose and do as I choose. I'm free as the wind, yes free, my prettys. But you must forgive my speech; I've only recently learned the basics of your common language." She drifted off in thought once again.

Mindi waited until the sphinx's gaze returned to the

present once more, stalling. "Yes, I see that you are," Mindi agreed, "but where do you come from? How old are you? How long have you resided here?"

"Ah yes, it's history my dainties want. Ah ha. I'm old as hills, old as trees, young as the sky and the moon. My father Gentrix had me in the great storm of Sahara, which made the desert. So I am old as sand itself. There, food got scarce, and I flew over seas wide and blue. Nice fishes are there, but oh so small! Not good Pixcies' food. No—need man food. Soft juicy food, my prettys." She licked her chops, droolingly.

Nervously Marc changed the subject, "Say what about this challenge. Don't forget that."

"Oh, I make haste. Pixcies can't do that to delicious food, oh no. Pixcies loves games, yes, loves the game. Must have challenge. You know riddles, eh? Well Pixcies loves 'em, my dears. Yes, we must have riddles match—yes—oh yes, we must." She fell again silent, her whining, sing-songy voice trailing away into the wind that had come. They waited quietly, stalling. They were not eager to answer the challenge. Presently, she aroused herself and spoke again.

"Yes, the game. My dainties, I ask a riddle. You answer it. If my food gets it correct, then you shall ask Pixcies a riddle. We go back and forth from Pixcies to food to Pixcies. If you fail to answer the riddle correctly, then Pixcies shall eat the dainties that are offered here."

"Yes, but what if Pixcies fails to answer our riddle," pleaded Marc, looking for some small advantage.

"Ah, ieee," she shrieked so loudly that they all recoiled instinctively. "Pixcies never fails on riddles. Never. Never have I failed to guess a riddle. Oh no, my prettys, never."

"Yes, but," pleaded Marc, "a game must offer something to the winners. Now you eat us if you win. What do we do if we win? Eat you?" he said imitating her style. She had apparently never thought much about this, nor probably had so bold and challenging morsels before her. She thought for some time before speaking.

Questioningly, she queried, "You want to eat Pixcies if you win?"

"No," laughed Marc at the absurdity of it.

"Let's have high stakes here Pixcies. I'll tell you what," his merchant technique returning. "If we win, then you must promise to do whatever we command you to do. That will give some sport to your game. Your food will be very excited about the game this way. Agreed?"

There was a pause, and a slow smile spread across her face, "Yes it does, my danties; it does. Pixcies feels excited with the game now. I shall do as you order if you win. Otherwise, I eat food, my delicious ones. Yes, I will, yes." She paused once more and then said, "Oh yes, rules. The rules of riddles. The answer must be a known thing, in common tongue, like the sun or moon. You can't ask what the pony's name is. You can ask what has four legs, neighs, and is small. You get it, my dears? I shall show food how to do it first. Each time you get three tries to get the answer. Oh goody, game begins now. Pixcies goes first."

Marc took a deep breath, as she began whiningly and obviously excited.

"Its roots delve deep below,
 Its face touches the sky,
 Its teeth are sharp for the unwary,
 Its bare head is old and white,
 What is it?"

The group crowded around each other whispering together. "Answer please," she said grinning.

"Just a moment," pleaded Marc.

"Oh I get it," whispered Mindi, "a mountain. She's describing poetically a mountain."

"A mountain," yelled Marc; they turned and looked up at her crouching form.

"Argh," came the loud reply. "Yes, that is it, a mountain. My dainties are smart foods, yes they are, very delicious. Now your turn. Ask me riddle."

They floundered for a moment; then Shannon said, "Hey I got the idea." He stepped forward and said slowly,

"Some men love her,
 Others hate her;
 She surrounds us, even now

327

Threatening to swallow us,
Slowly crushes giant rocks,
Yet oh so gentle to the touch.
What is she?"

"Ah that is good one, my food. Let Pixcies see." She thought for a moment and quickly replied excitedly, "The sea, the sea. It is the sea."

"Yes," a sour faced Shannon said quickly.

"Now my turn. Oh good; this is exciting!" She mused a minute, itching her head with one paw; then, with a widening smile, she asked,

"She grows from bare mud
And, thru much time, just to be
a fleeting instant of beauty;
Then she's gone forevermore,
But later her kin will follow after her.
What is she?"

Again, they huddled, and discussed her clue. "How about a tree," suggested Nache, so Marc tried it.

"Oh no, no, no, my dainty morsels. Try again and see."

Disgruntled, they huddled and suddenly Mindi said, "Oh I know. I'll bet it is a flower."

"A flower," Marc suggested.

"Ahiee, that is it; that is it. Oh this is fun, such fun to play with food." She had risen and was stepping about excitedly. "Now you give Pixcies one," and she crouched down on her belly once more, listening expectantly.

This time Mindi had one for her.

"Sometimes friend; sometimes foe,
You cannot live without her;
You cannot touch her;
Always beyond your reach,
There's no escaping her; she's everywhere.
Who is she?"

"Hey that's a good one," Marc whispered. Evidently, Pixcies thought so too, and she growled and squirmed and tried, "Air."

Mindi said softly, "Nope," and the sphinx growled and

scratched her belly. Then, she brightened up, and glancing up, said, "The sun," but Mindi's soft "Nope" brought a frenzied growl and more scratching and pawing and more thought.

After a few minutes, she laughed and said "Pixcies got it now. It's the sky, that's what she is."

"Yes" Mindi said, crestfallen.

Once again, it was the sphinx's turn, and she was quickly ready.

"Sometimes warm, sometimes cold
When she comes the ground rejoices
But men hide in shelters
She swiftly comes and quite fast at that.
Can you guess her name?"

Once more, they discussed it and tried "The sun," but that brought a delighted, "Oh no, no she's not."

Then they guessed, "The snow" with equally poor results. Now they squirmed.

"Come on," said Marc. "Only one more guess left."

They talked. Pixcies began to hassle them, "Hurry up my dainties; you can't take all day. Pixcies is hungry."

"Wait, I've got it," cried Nache. "It's the rain—cold in the fall and warm in the summer."

"Argh, you tiny one, you guessed it, uch. Now it's your turn again." She sat expectantly like a playful puppy waiting for its master to toss its stick once more.

This time Marc tried one, trying to find a hard one, as well as to stall as long as possible. So far, the sphinx had not discovered the others. Marc didn't know how much longer they could hold out; the last one nearly had them. He took a gamble and spoke.

"She's narrow and slender,
but made of living stone.
Mortals dare not touch her.
She nearly catches the falling moon.
There are twelve in all.
What is it?"

That ought to keep her busy, he hoped. Mindi eyed him curiously. Marc seemed to be rising to the challenge. Pixcies was having a hard time with this one. Marc tried to further stall and confuse her. "Well, hurry up now Pixcies; you can't have all day now."

"Wait, my prettys; this is a hard one. Tell me it again."

Marc obliged, speaking slowly. She guessed a mountain and a tree, and Marc insultingly replied, "No my dear; now guess again." Now he played her game. "You only have one chance left Pixcies dear. Just one more—then we will win. Do you give up my dear? Come on; hurry up. Poor Pixcies, she cannot see this one. Ha. Ha."

She became angry and frustrated. She rose and her giant claws dug into the dried dirt. She pawed and scraped at the ground, dry dust flying in brownish clouds. Her eyes darted here and there, as if searching all her land for an idea. Suddenly, her eyes fell on the wizard's obelos.

"Obelos," she cried in surprise. "It's an Obelos you ask for. Whee. Now it's my turn." Their spirits sank. It had looked so hopeful.

Marc tried to encourage them, "Just one more, and I'll have her."

Pixcies began her fourth, getting more esoteric now, as the sun was nearing the horizon.

"You cannot stop her if you try;
 Yet everything has her.
 For mountains, she's large in size;
 For men, she's short.
 And for you, she's shortest of all.
 Who is she?"

Pixcies was obviously proud of this one, very carefully thought out. She crouched confidently down, certain that she'd dine at sunset, but her line was so familiar to elves that Mindi got it at once.

"Time," she said, "our turn again." Pixcies was upset and disgruntled by the ease with which her food got that one. She paced slowly around the tree, ponies, and group.

"Ok Pixcies, settle down; it's our turn again. Now we'll get you with a good riddle," Marc enticed her further. "This one will test your knowledge of old."

"Pale and blue and soft and old

330

Made in the depths of ages gone by
Yet still survives;
The good, cheers her; evil shrinks, crawls away.
What is that we search for?"

"Search? I can't answer what you search for. That's not fair. You cheat Pixcies, yes you do."

"No we don't," Marc yelled loudly. "All the clues are there; if you are as old as you say, you should know what it is. Now come on, think old girl or give up to us! Do you give up already without a guess?" He played right into her game, fending off the protest and forcing her to try an answer.

Half in a rage and storming in circles about them, she tried obelos, pyramids, and finally wizard's staff, maps, and swords.

"Ah," Marc yelled at her above the rising wind and her growling. "We have given you five guesses and still you know not. Come we have won the riddling—fair and square. It was a good game." He guessed from the first that she was most likely a bad sport. He was not disappointed. She raged; mighty chunks of turf went flying; soon they were enclosed in a large dirt cloud, coughing heavily.

Marc took action, drawing Tiny. At once, the Flaming Sword appeared with great red flames leaping skyward from the blade. The giant catlike creature ceased her rage and backed away—startled by this blinding turn of events.

Against the darkening sky, Andrill blazed; she backed off still crying, "Cheats—vile food cheats, trying to rob Pixcies of food that Yellow Man promised her. Cheats with fire stick. Pixcies not afraid of tiny sword." Still, she kept her distance. The others quickly seized the opportunity, as the wind swiftly cleared away the dust. They drew their weapons and stood beside Marc, tall and erect.

Marc cried in as commanding voice as he could muster, "Hear me now Pixcies. I, Marcos, will speak only once! Your food stands before you the victor at your own game, but food we are not. Have you ever heard of the Fire Sword of Old, the Mizzinti, the Great Wizards?"

He paused purposely; catching a glimmer of recognition in her orange eyes, he continued, "We're not food, we're the

331

Mizzinti; the wizards have returned. This is the lands of the greatest of wizards, the Ruenzorti. The Mizzinti issue forth from here. We have returned! Before you stand wizards and our magical blades. Andrill here has slain great cave trolls whose hides are like stone. The blade burns what it touches. Do not think you can withstand its touch, Pixcies. Size is no obstacle to wizards. Behold also Kazab, the Dwarf wizard axe, and the other wizard's weapons. Truly, Pixcies, you have never had a chance for this food. Never. I think you also realize this, for we acted like no ordinary squirming, terrified men!"

She glared, but said nothing, just one pounce away from her obnoxious food. Yet somehow, a force held her at bay in the growing twilight. Marc continued, "The answer you did not get was the great wizard's Orb. You have lost because . . ."

Marc was interrupted by a horn blast coming from the direction of Obelos Magum. All immediately recognized Vorag's horn. As they turned towards the Obelos, the tower walls ignited into a pole of light. Great red and blue swirls ebbed and creeped in random patterns against the white, piercing light of the tall tower. Its radiance brilliantly lit the northern sky in swirling colors. From the top, great bolts of lightning streaked jaggedly upwards towards the sky, followed momentarily by deafening claps and peals of roaring thunder. Everyone, including Pixcies, was held spellbound by the display. The effect was broken shortly by the nearby sound of a great horn blast.

As all eyes roamed instinctively towards the sound; Pixcies saw a glowing form running down the road as swiftly as light, singing aesthetically in the growing night. Not far behind, she saw three others rushing. In the eerie glow of the tower, she could see the sparkle and reflection of great weapons bearing down on her.

Marc broke the silence again, "You see Pixcies, the other wizards join us, and the obelos is active, ready to send a bolt of lightning your way. Shall I call the bolt to our defense? Shall I fry you as you stand?" He paused looking at the effect being created. He watched this mightiest of creatures. Anger turned to rage and then to fear. Like a frightened, wounded child, she lay on the ground and wailed pitifully and almost uncontrollably.

Marc stood domineeringly beside her, "Arise Pixcies, hold to thy own pledge. Promise, and you shall not be hurt."

She lifted her head slightly, great tears rolled down her yellow face, all twisted in despair. Between sobs that shook her massive frame, she replied, "I promise. I promise. Do not hurt Pixcies. You win; you won. I promise."

"Fair enough," Marc replied between cracks of thunder from the obelos. Elwine and the others arrived to hear Marc's final words. "Then I say to you Pixcies—my command is this; go now at once; return to your native land and never return to Isel. If you go now, no one shall hurt you."

Fumbling, she rose to her feet, regained some measure of poise, and said, "Pixcies go. Pixcies go. Food orders. I go, but was a good game. Never been beaten before. Must do it again, sometime." Then, she stretched her wings, extending nearly fifty feet on either side. As she flapped them in her takeoff, great whirlwinds sprayed dry dirt in two, great, dark tunnels. The company fell to the ground and covered their heads as dirt, grass, and sand blew everywhere. Soon she was well into the air. They watched her swoop around Serengreti in one big arch.

Then, they heard her whiny voice, though now distant, "Pixcies say was nice game, delicious ones. Come visit Pixcies. Must do it again." Off she sped, heading southeast. They stared after her until she was out of sight.

Marc relaxed and spoke for the others, "Yahhooiiee!"

"I've never been so glad to see a wizard's blast!" exclaimed George.

Everyone began talking excitedly together; the fear of doom was lifted from friends. The next ten minutes were filled with wild expressions and exclamations. Nache tried his best to tell all as fast as he could. It was a jubilant reunion. Drifter had spied Arthur, and the two stepped aside.

"Dad, they're wonderful! Tremendous job! Wow!"

"So I see, and how are you doing," he said a bit sternly.

Arthur picked his meaning instinctively, and with a carefree toss of his head, he stated, "Oh, just great dad. She's now my mom—in absentia," he added quickly and rejoined the others, leaving Drifter to ponder that one.

The dark night on the high plains quickly cooled the heat of day. Presently, the group realized how chilly it had become. Overhead the sky loomed black and clear. Myriads of twinkling stars filled the heavens. It was magnificent. One by one, the company stared at the incredible sky and shivered.

"Come you folks; let's rejoin Malazar and get out of this chilly wind." Elwine led the way for the star starers. The splendor of the heavens was magnificent, because of the much-reduced atmosphere. The group made their way slowly to the still luminescent, white, tall tower. Red and blue shapes still twisted and turned rising upwards to meet the heavens. In less than a half hour, they stood at the translucent glowing base of Obelos Magum.

Chapter XXII—The Mountains of the Moon

The bejeweled, high altitude sky seemed magnificent and close. All felt a sense of heaven's nearness. The companions stood before the massive doors of Obelos Magum, which rose upward for two hundred fifty feet, seemingly to the stars. It was made of a white, opalescent marble that shone with a translucent, white light. The stone, itself, seemed to contain the luminescence. Undulating bands of reds and blues slowly revolved upwards, not unlike barber poles.

Just behind the tower was the central mountain range. Here, in the middle of the Serengreti Plains (elevation: fourteen thousand feet), rose the Mountains of the Moon. They were neither tall nor did they encompassed a large area, being no more than "hillocks." The tallest was a mere two hundred feet above Serengreti. The range was confined to a length of ten miles by five. However, they were rocky, rugged, and volcanic. Most importantly, they contained the only water in the entire area, a small lake.

They paused for several minutes before the great doors, marveling at the incredible aesthetics of Obelos Magum. From far atop the obelos, the faint voice of Malazar broke the awed silence, "Come on up."

Mindi, startled from her musing, half expected to hear, "and don't touch anything" to follow next, but it didn't. Elwine led the way, as they climbed, single file, up the spiraling stairway. The walls were glowing mosaics of forms and shapes.

"Another time," thought Mindi, "I'd be content to take hours getting up. This is really beautiful!"

The long climb took its toll, reminding them of weary legs. Lungs, as well, felt the strain in the thin air, but all minds were clear and hearts, content. Though each felt strangely comfortable and quite at home here, no one had uncontrolled mental pictures flashing. Indeed, Mindi noted a distinct absence of mental mass. She filed the observation, intending to take the matter up with Malazar later.

One by one, they came stomping and clopping off the top step into the main viewing room. Each obelos was similarly laid out. The crystalline white walls glowed providing an internal, soft, subdued lighting effect. The room was nearly twenty feet square; a large Vishi table was centrally located. Each cardinal direction had a large walk-through window that led to a small balcony.

"Of all the towers in Isel," said a breathless Elwine, "yours is the singularly most aesthetic!"

"Thank you master elf, but each has its own special beauty as well," replied a very calm and tranquil wizard. The others crowded in and sat around in a circle, leaning against the marble walls.

"Thanks, Malazar," Marc began. "You had excellent timing. Not a moment too late! How did you know when to set off the fireworks?"

A large grin broadened into a chuckle, as the white bearded wizard said, "Well, I just waited for a sign from you. I began when your sword flamed. I figured that you would draw it only when it was time for action, but please, tell me about the sphinx. I saw that she flew off. At least, tell your wizard a few details."

Briefly, Marc described the events with Pixcies. Here and there, Nache added exclamatories that he felt were fitting.

"Verily. Verily. Thou has doneth exceedingly well against certain doom! Very well doneth, Master Merchant," Vorag heartily congratulated him, when Marc seemed to be more or less done with the tale.

However, Elwine, as well as Malazar, had detected the reference to the hermit, and he queried, "Marc, what about Pixcies' reference to the yellow hermit man—was that the same figure we saw circling our camp before we split up?"

Marc quietly related the goblin prison party and the second visit of the hermit. Arthur excitedly added a good description of the cold, chilling, fearful effect his mere presence had had on the group. Even Drifter marveled at the courageousness of his young boy; his pride and respect in the lad grew considerably, but the news of the hermit was souring to both the elf and wizard in particular.

"Interesting," mused Elwine half aloud.

"You know of him?" inquired Marc.

"Yes, well sort of. When I journeyed from Eldamar, nearly two years ago, I came across his path twice. We never met nor shared any signs, but I felt a cold chill at each encounter, almost a cold malice. I understood it not! What say you Cidithir?" Elwine noticed Malazar seemed to be lost in thoughts.

"Huh? Oh yes, the yellow one. I was wondering about him, could it be . . ." His voice trailed off into silence. With a jerk, he realized all eyes were upon him expectantly, but he shrugged them off. "No. I will not openly speculate. There's no need at this time. You all did well in this matter. It's intriguing isn't it. Now how about some food?"

"Yes!" exclaimed George, feeling how hungry he was. Malazar showed them the dumbwaiter system, and George and Mindi went down to fetch the necessary things. Nache joined them, intending to handle the ponies as well.

The time was filled by Drifter and Vorag, who briefly discussed their adventures—dry and perfectly routine— compared to the others. They had been very worried about them, had pressed ahead rapidly, and had come onto Banta Road nearly a half day early. They had snuck down the road slowly and carefully. Their plan was to get as close as possible before the headlong rush to the Obelos. Malazar and Elwine split off and went to the rear of the Mountains of the Moon, intending to come to the tower from the north through them. The other three headed for the Obelos on down Banta road.

A light signal from Malazar sent all running headlong towards the tower, but the elf and wizard had gotten there before Hildaro and crew. So they were startled as well to see the tower light up. Elwine came from the doors and yelled blow your horn.

"Verily didst I blast" Vorag added with a chuckle. Then the four of them charged.

"Positively dull compared to your adventure," added Hildaro.

Mindi and George returned, and shortly the food came

up the narrow elevator system. They ate voraciously with Drifter going down to fetch the seconds. Then one by one they retired, scattered about the floor, though Malazar continued to study and examine various features of the obelos.

Around 3:00 a.m., the waning quarter moon rose brilliantly white. Elwine roused Mindi, and together they stood, arm in arm, gazing from the southern balcony. They spoke no words, but only viewed the majestic heavens. They were on a narrow ledge; the ground, far below them. The blazing multitude of stars shone close and bright with the silver, beaming moon radiant—yet not obscuring the stars because of the thin atmosphere.

For nearly an hour, they stood transfixed by the beauty. Finally, something caught the elf's eyes. Far distant, to the southeast and near the not yet visited pass, many dull red glows could be seen, but Mindi did not see these. Then, the two retired as well, leaving the old wizard still lost in his inquiring search.

The company rose long after daybreak and found Malazar asleep, lying slumped across his Vishi table. Quietly, they climbed down the spiral steps to greet the sunny morning. The chilly night air was rapidly warming. They mulled around and had a leisurely breakfast, each fending for himself. Elwine offered a guided tour of the Mountains of the Moon, though only Mindi appreciated their name. As they were organizing the tour, Malazar sleepily appeared at the doors, "I trust you slept well and off so soon?"

"Yes sleepyhead," Mindi poked, "we're off to see the mountains."

"Well don't wait on me; have a good time," and he rummaged for his breakfast, while the others left, talking gaily and in good spirits.

One thousand yards north rose the ragged walls of the volcanic domes. They found the rocks gassy and dark—much lighter and more crumbly than the Ruenzorti basalt walls. There were many pathways into the mountains. The area looked like a giant bubble pot—George's description. The edges were barren, volcanic pumice, but, once well within, the elevation steadily rose. Grasses grew in the lower spots and crevasses. It had an unusual appearance that commanded one's attention.

They had not gone far when they crossed the highest ridge between two great domes. They stopped. Below them lay a large wide valley. In its center was a pale blue lake, absolutely still. Surrounding the lake, going clear up the hills, was vegetation—lush and queer beyond description. The plants or "treelets" were nearly neck high. None of the varied foliage was known to any of the group. Each was very unusual looking.

Principle among the treelets was the "moon trees" as Nache called them. They were large, extremely broad leafed— larger than Vorag's head. The "moon tree" twisted in at least ten directions; at each joint, a great leaf grew fairly parallel to the sky—like mini, deep blue—green tables.

Then, there were the "spindlers", twisty, vine-like plants. The "spindlers" grew or hung to rocks and treelets, with the same sickly, blue-green color, but were jagged-edged with narrow leaves and grew nearly six inches long.

The "orbs" were bulbous, white flowers that grew on short, large diameter stalks—reminiscent of bear grass. In the center of the open bulbs was a dark blob rather like a small, black orb.

The group wandered slowly down to the lake with unbelieving eyes. Purples, blues, and greens formed a queer, weird pattern of garden color.

Marc summed up their feelings, "I feel like I'm on a different planet—a different world!" Spellbound, they said little, but looked at everything slowly for nearly an hour.

The sun was now bright, hot, and high above them. Malazar joined them. "This is an unusual land, is it not?" He talked for a while naming each plant; they all had foreign names, which were quite unpronounceable Nache felt. He preferred his names. It was nearly noon before they arrived back at the obelos to have a brief lunch. Then, Malazar called for a search and conference.

"I haven't been able to locate that for which we search— the Orb. I call upon you for assistance. Let us all search—look into every crack, crevasse, and hiding place. Perhaps another viewpoint will show where I have not seen. Before we go onwards, we must be absolutely certain it is not here."

The game of hide and seek began; everyone rummaged throughout the obelos, making their haphazard way upwards from the entrance. However, one by one, they arrived sour faced at the top platform empty handed. Many things were located, but no trace of the Orb. They found Malazar at the Vishi studying volumes of scrolls—all written in a strange script. As each reached the last step, the wizard's eyes glanced at them. Pairs of doleful eyes met, and the wizard would resume his studies. By late afternoon, all were accounted for, save Nache.

"All right," sighed Malazar, heavy cares were upon his face, "Let's council. We have found no trace of the Orb, correct?" No one commented. "Legends here speak of its existence and use, but none tell of its history. Not one blessed clue!"

Suddenly, Mindi started said, "Hey wait a minute. Where's Nache?" Everyone looked around, but no dwarf. Then, they all yelled for him.

From just below the platform came a dulled voice, "Help! I'm stuck in here!" There was a scramble of searching bodies and exclamations of surprise.

"Where are you?" yelled a frustrated Marc.

"Down here—in a little room. I can't get out."

Suddenly as if remembering, Malazar cried, "Ah ha!" He ran to the middle of the room beside the Vishi. He crouched on his hands and knees. After a brief search, he pulled on a small knob, and, presto, a hidden door opened. Light fell in onto a worried dwarf.

It was a small storage room. Nache had found a side door into it. Unfortunately, once closed, the door gave no sign of being a door—even the cracks blended into a continuous, marble form. He had lost track of direction and had been unable to get out, but he was not too worried. He had a small torch of Mindi's. He was sitting with his beard tucked under his lap. Spread all across him were maps. About him lay piles of maps. He was excited.

"Thank you," he yelled. "Maps! Lots of maps. Neat ones.

Armagh and Khorizaba. Old maps!" Drifter lifted him out, maps and all. Quickly he crawled upon the Vishi and spread a yellowed scroll wide. "See, here's my country; just look at the detail. Here's Tulan; here's my Obelos."

He went on and on showing the course of the Yaca and Baca rivers. Finally, Malazar got him calmed down, so that they could continue their discussion. Chief topic: what to do next.

The main conclusion was that the urgently needed Orb was not here. That left only the evil tower in Kalhari. It must be there, but whether it was in the possession of Kahill or not, no one knew. Some said yes; some felt negative. It was dubious.

"If the Orb lies there, then our task is most urgent. We must remove Kahill before he learns how to use its power or finds it—however it may go."

Drifter proposed, "Well, we could charge into the Quad via Chooe Pass. Schlemloch's guarding it; it is passable."

"Yes, but," Marc countered, "we should then be facing, most certainly, a great host from within. Surely, the four passes are where his evil armies lie stationed, since the passes are the only way in or out. So how long can eleven withstand thousands? Besides, our fight is with Kahill alone—at least as I perceive it."

"I agree with Marc," added Elwine. "Even if we enter the last pass, Nyder, we would be besieged. Last night, I saw many fires that way. A large army inhabits the outer regions of the pass. Something will have to be done about them."

"Yes, or my people have bad time," added Tse Tse, now very concerned.

"Yes," commented Malazar. "We shall have to do something there. We certainly can't stay here and wait—to be trapped like pigeons in a roost." He paused.

Hildaro offered, "Can't we get an army and just rush them and get to the Obelos?"

"Yes, but then we'd lose a good many men."

"I keep forgetting."

"No offense, Hildaro" consoled Marc, "Choices are difficult. How the heck do we get into the Quad anyway?" In frustration, he joked, "Maybe we shouldn't have sent Pixcies away and had her fly us in—air drop fashion—right onto Kahill's palace." There was a long silence.

Vorag then asked, "Malazar, where doth all the great cave trolls cometh from?"

"That is a good question—a very good one. As near as I can discover, they reside in the very bowels of the earth, far, far underground. Legends state that they come from Boreal originally—rumored to be a city deep underground. Tales have been told of their occasional surfacing, here and there. At one time, ages ago, a legend tells of two appearing within the Quad. At once, the Orb drove them back from whence they came, but the whence is not detailed, named only Zahartos Kryptos. Where or what—there is no record that I so far have seen."

"Well, Kahill has obviously discovered this Kryptos," Hildaro noted, "and has brought many to the surface. If they come from a hole, perhaps we can plug it. Those trolls are something else!" They discussed the matter of the trolls for some time.

"True, true," Malazar replied, "but should we delay here while I search as I may? I fear time is pressing. Winter will soon be here. I'd suspect that this area will be snow covered, and we are ill prepared for heavy snows."

Nache had listened—well, sort of—throughout, but mainly he was carefully studying the map of his country. Suddenly, he got so terribly excited that his small frame was literally shaking.

"Nache, whatever is going on?" asked Mindi, who suddenly saw him about to fall off the table.

"Look! Look! Look at this," he cried in glee.

Everyone got quite curious and crowded around the table to see what had gotten this dwarf so fired up. He was pointing to some faint hash lines midway down the western wall of Khorizaba, where the Armagh mountains met those of Quara Ost, in the area known as Mazatlan. There were strange letters faintly written beside the two tiny lines.

"What's it say Malazar?" the dwarf begged.

Malazar leaned over and stared at the unusual writing.

342

"It's in the same script as my other scrolls—Mizzinti in nature. Let's see."

Carefully the old wizard stared at the tiny writing, "Two words I'd guess—one is Meina and the other is Krypte. Yes, Meina Krypte. Translated literally, it says: mine hidden. Hum, a hidden mine. It must be Khartos Kryptos, the lost dwarven mine."

"Yeowiee," Nache cried, and he began jumping wildly about the table top. For several minutes, all they could get out of him was "yahooie" and similar exclamations. Finally, he calmed down a bit and tried to explain.

"Hidden mine—Kryptos! Found at last! Yahooie!" He explained, "I have studied all of Belwain's records—our ancient wizard—he speaks often of Khartos Kryptos, the fabled mine. We know it only in legends as the mine of grandeur and of immense beauty. After the Great Battle, all trace of its location was lost to the dwarfs. It was rumored that its caverns produce many rare metals and ores, and that it was a natural beauty unsurpassed in Isel. Before the Battle, dwarves worked the mine relentlessly, bringing much wealth from the earth. Kazab, here, is said to be made from metals from Kryptos. As the tales tell, some fell catastrophe occurred, and the dwarves abandoned the mine; its location became lost. Now in recent times, dwarves have searched long and hard for the mine. Its discovery would add immeasurable wealth, materials, and beauty to all of Khorizaba and Isel, but alas, all searches ended without even a clue. Yet here is a map! Oh boy! I must memorize this map and find the mine for all dwarves."

Suddenly with a cold stern eye, Malazar asked the dwarf stiffly, "Are there no legends, tales, rumors that describe or tell about this catastrophe? Think before you answer!"

Somewhat surprised by his seriousness, Nache tried to think as hard as he could. "Only Daelos' Stone. Daelos was said to have found some evil stone in a newly opened shaft. But whatever that is, none say. I never could figure how rock could be evil. It makes no sense."

"Sense and nonsense," the wizard said slowly, "sometimes get confused—or perhaps, literal. I recall other legends, my good dwarf. This mine was made by the dwarves.

Night and day, they toiled far underground. The tunnels are said to pierce through the Quara Ost mountains. A passageway to the desert they needed in order to dump the tailings. The dwarves were loathed to dump such in their own mountain valleys, but dug through and used the desert as their waste pile. So this would be a way into the Quad and unguarded for sure."

"Hey!" said Marc catching his drift, "If we went through there, we probably could get to the tower, most likely without meeting armies."

"Right you are! Nache, I bid you keep the mine secret a bit longer until we have used it. We shall pass in secret into Kahill's nest. Many hours would we have before his host could answer any call from the tower. It's in the center. Loathed am I to leave my Obelos now. It does feel rather like home, but we must get that Orb before Kahill finds it or learns its use! We simply have no other choice. Our fate is sealed. We shall be the first to pass through the lost dwarf mine since the ancient days. All that remains now is to choose our path to it."

"Yes," Nache cried. "My fair lady shall see the wonders of the dwarf builders at long last! Everyone is invited to visit Tulan, set in the snow-clad, Armagh mountains." He was filled with joy. His long wish was coming true.

The sober voice of Malazar brought him back to their current situation. "We now must choose our path. The Vishi of Magum shall assist elfin eyes," and he spoke a solitary word in a strange language.

The others clustered around the table, as its solid form became translucent and then vanished. Images came like three-dimensional pictures on a screen. Slowly, Malazar brought the Vishi to bear on the northeast pass into the Quad. Elwine's red lights were verified. The late afternoon sun cast long shadows from trees and Scavengers alike. They were clustered in small camps of some dozen per site—Yacs and goblins mostly. The pass was crawling with the Scourge. The wizard backed off and scanned the Old Caravan Road for some distance. They beheld campsite after campsite, but the area north of Ruenzorti, near Banti Road, seemed deserted. He scanned a bit more and then ended the session.

"We shall go northwards. It seems we will have to devise some help for Tse Tse's people as we pass through. Now then, leave Nache and me here; we shall study the maps. The rest of you prepare the ponies. Arnold will be here momentarily, and we shall depart ere the sun sets."

Quickly, they stumped their way to the tower's base and set about getting everything in order. True to his prediction, Arnold did arrive shortly, bringing the third pony heavily laden with fresh supplies. Here Arthur said farewell to his father and newfound mother. He knew he could go no further with them, and his parting was sad. For a while, he had felt part of a powerful group, but as his father had said, he knew that he had responsibilities in Ocalla. The war was not yet over. Shortly, Arnold and Arthur left; Drifter wanted them both safe in Ocalla by full dark. It was nearly sunset when the wizard and dwarf strode out of the large doors. He closed the heavy doors. Now the obelos stood like a lonely, white finger pointing to the heavens. Mindi heard him mutter to himself, "I shall return."

Swiftly they set off on Banti Road heading northeast; and the sun, rather rosy, sank. Twilight was very short at this altitude, and the dark sky burst forth once more, emblazened with myriad points of light. The brown, dusty road was discernible even in starlight, and they made good time. They talked little, pausing near midnight for a late supper and rest.

At daybreak, clouds filled the sky—streaky, high cirrus. They marched on again with only a passing tree and growing cloudbanks to mark the time.

By late afternoon, it began to drizzle. Ruenzorti got very little rain. What it did get, came mostly in slow drizzle. They halted, surrounded by gigantic, black, basalt blocks. Here they waited for the drizzle to end. Malazar said that the steep descent over polished rock would be treacherous when wet. So they had no choice but to spend several hours under tarps again. The dreary rain continued until the following dawn, when at last the sun broke through. By mid-morning, the rocky path was dry enough to descend.

Now as fatiguing and difficult as the ascent was, they found the descent even worse. Some tried it standing up, slipping and sliding, but most followed Mindi's example and slid down on their butts. At least, it felt much safer and less steep. Tse Tse took considerable coaching for he was unfamiliar with mountains and was a bit afraid of the steepness. Nache alone remained upright, scampering here and there assisting the poor burdened ponies. To everyone's surprise, the dwarf ponies did far better than they did. As it worked out, the descent took until late that afternoon to complete with nearly everyone relieved and exhausted.

Quickly they moved off the road into the thick jungle growth and made camp. No one objected. Tse Tse was much relieved to be in the jungle once more, and his spirits rose. They had dinner and surveyed their location.

To the north and east lay a dark massy jungle known only as the Anuir, as Elwine named it. Somewhere, some sixty miles northeast, lay the Old Caravan Road, striking obliquely for the Quad. Southward lay a green jungle area—the Winianie and Tse Tse's homeland. Far to the south lay the Scavengers. Save Banti, going in the wrong direction, there were no other roads.

Chapter XXIII—The Jungle of Winianie

It was night; it was humid; it was hot. Having left the high Serengreti plains with its thin air and chilly October nights behind them, the questers were camped at the base of the sheer rise of Banti Road on the northeastern edge of the Ruenzorti mountains. For many miles in all easterly directions, a dense jungle fought the low-slung foothills. The living vegetation smothered all things—all the way up to the sheer, black wall that formed the Ruenzorti mountains. It was a clear line of demarcation: black, straight, and long. Cradled at the fringes of the tepid jungle, the company slept uneasily, now unused to the higher temperatures and humidity. Tossing, turning, and writhing marked their ill sleep.

Somewhat past midnight, Mindi cursed softly and got up. She observed that the others fared no better than she, save only Tse Tse. She strolled around the small camp, rubbing her face and neck in the darkness. Red coals were all that remained of their small fire. Idly, she added a couple of small branches and gazed absentmindedly at the renewed flickers. Presently, the small clearing was illuminated again. Hearing a low mumble, she suddenly noticed the solitary figure of Malazar sitting nearby on top of a large basalt block. She joined him.

"Can't sleep. This heat. Ugh. How about you?" she inquired.

The reply was slow in coming, "Yes, the heat, but also there is the future. An army I must find amid this." Frustrated, he motioned toward the black jungle, hopelessly. Silence grew, broken by cracklings from the small blaze.

"Malazar," she sighed deeply, "there is something I've been meaning to ask you about." He grunted curiously, so she continued, "It's about mental pictures. These images. Does altitude affect them?"

"Um, I'm not certain what you ask my dear. Tell me more."

"Well, when we were up there, on the high plains, I felt

347

more powerful somehow. Pictures were very few. I felt cheerful most always; even when we encountered Pixcies, I felt no mental mass. By contrast, down here things seem—well, heavy somehow. I'm massy; I feel heavy, and I have masses of unseen pictures—more like blobs." She yawned a bit.

"So you have observed it too. Well, well, I thought I was the only one aware of that. Yes or so it would seem. You have accurately described the phenomena except for one thing. After a while you'll get use to the denseness, accepting it as life and giving no further heed to it."

"Oh," came her blank reply.

"I have been looking for the cause of the effect myself, having observed it in me several times. Care to hear my theory?"

"Sure."

"Okay. First assume we are all eternal spiritual beings that operate; we go from body to body as they wear out. The difference between us is how much does one operate the body compared to the other. Well, suppose that there is an exchange of energy necessary to operate the body's controls, and let the mind act as a relay point. Resistance affects the flow and potential flow of this energy. Now what is different between the high altitude and low? I thought for hours before the utter simplicity struck me. Air. It's air. Up on Serengreti, the air is thin—less resistance, the greater the power. Down here, the air is dense. As our dwarf said, 'It's so thick that I can cut it with my axe.' Well that means more resistance, less force, less power, and more difficulties. Perhaps the mind gets clogged so to speak." He paused to see if she followed the hypothesis.

She thought briefly and suggested, "Then, old Missar, the Great, was very smart in building the greatest obelos high atop Serengreti. A very smart move."

"Yes, yes, I think it was so." Both were silent a while staring into the flickering fire light. Then, he spoke once more, "The night ebbs, my dear; we should try to get as much sleep as possible." She agreed, and the two retired. Mindi slept a bit better.

The incessant cackling of a number of gaily colored parrots overhead marked daybreak. The members of the company arose in an ill humor, cursing the noisy, feathered creatures. Breakfast did little to cheer them. They now could clearly see the jungle before them. It grew very dense almost at once. Banti Road, though ten feet broad, trailed off under a perpetual canopy. Vines hung from great heights above the road. It looked more like a tunnel. North of them, the jungle deepened into a dark mass, the Anuir section, uninhabited, Elwine had found. Southwards, the jungle was dense but not so foreboding. Banti Road ran northeast for some one hundred twenty miles before it intersected the Old Caravan Road, which then wound its way south-southwesterly to the corner of the Quad.

None liked the idea of going over two hundred miles out of their way.

"Can we not strike south by southeast, Tse Tse, and hit the Caravan Road, shortening the distance considerably?" posed Malazar.

The brown-skinned man replied, "Can go that way. Difficult. No path. Slow going—much dense—much animals. Can do perhaps, yes. Much hard."

In the end, the "much hard" gave way to shortening their journey by several hundred miles. Thus, the group, single file, struck out south through the uninhabited regions of the Winianie jungle.

The native, at first, went in front, picking his way through the dense vegetation. Large trees, just off the road, towered, forming a dark, shady, canopy—some fifty feet above their heads. Twisty, tangled vines dangled everywhere, clear down to the ground. Great broad-leafed plants grew from the ground upwards. Rapidly, forward visibility shrank to nearly zero. Painstakingly slowly, they picked their way, twisting and turning through the steaming, jungle maze. The sun raised the temperature considerably by noon. All were sweating profusely. Insects buzzed constantly, as they blindly stumbled over rotting logs and decaying mats.

Soon Tse Tse was replaced by Drifter and his blade. Chopping began with vigor. Now slashing right and then to the left, he endeavored to create a pathway. Others followed with widening actions. However, Tse Tse kept his blowgun raised, dart inserted. His sharp eyes ranged ever forward. After an agonizingly slow hour, they rested, perspiring heavily. Drifter's arms ached.

Tse Tse now cautioned them, "In jungle now. Harsh here. Many dangers. Big tigers. See easily. Smaller dangers worse. Many snakes. Very poison. Vipers. Watch steps careful. Also hanging snakes. Constrictors in trees. Crush you. Also stingers under feet. Scorpions, see."

He lifted a log carefully. At once, many creatures, exposed to the daylight, went scurrying for cover. Among them, two large scorpions, as big as a hand, paused with stingers raised high, and then darted off under some leaves.

Now the noise of the jungle filled the air. Far off, cries of a host of monkeys, screaming and chattering, could be heard mingled with the voices of a thousand birds. Here indeed was a harsh survival zone, where only the hardiest dwelled for long. Spirits lowered further. They began once more, Marc spelling Drifter for a while. Passage slowed as they entered jungle grass nearly ten feet tall. The ponies became nervous, as well as the company. Progress was step by step, preceded by much chopping and slashing. Shannon replaced Marc. Suddenly, the Mariner froze stiff. Tse Tse behind him aimed and blew. "Toooh" softly came from his tube. Ahead of Shannon something thrashed noisily among the grasses and became silent, as Tse Tse reloaded from his bag of darts.

"Viper," he said.

One by one, the group passed the lifeless form, some six feet long, as big around as a fist. It was colored in many bright patterns, but its head looked as dangerous as it was.

Wearily, they continued on and on. The darkness of the day finally darkened. They guessed evening had come and searched in vain for a reasonable camping spot. They ended up clearing a small circle among the tall grass as best they could and collapsed. Only an hour later did they endeavor to fill their very empty stomachs, but the heat reduced their appetites.

They spent a sleepless night fighting off a multitude of eager bugs, both crawlers and flyers. Day came gloomily, and the cacophony began once more. They said little and ate less. Soon they began again. Drifter did the slashing, while the native poised his tube right behind him. On and on, they drearily chopped. Near noon, they passed under a branch of a tree with a speckled, green, parallel branch. They marched on like zombies. As George passed under, the greenish branch dropped swiftly and skillfully around him. Startled, he yelled. As they halted and looked, a large python had encircled his body three times and was beginning to constrict its lunch.

Elwine tried to shoot an arrow but the vegetation hindered him greatly. Nache swung Kazab wildly, while Shannon tried to chop its head with his cutlass. A "thoong" quickly issued from Tse Tse's golden gun; and a small, black dart stuck in the snake's head. It swayed momentarily, before slowly loosening its hold on George, slipping to the ground, twitching.

Tse Tse called out, "Poison works fast. Ok now. Careful. Must not be mindless—no not here."

Determinedly, Drifter turned around, and the trek continued. For a while everyone was alert, especially aware of hanging things, but the heat, humidity, sweat, and fatigue took their toll. They ended before sundown; camp was little different from before. Supper consisted of salt, dried meat, salt, and water. They were miserable, and the night passed poorly.

They continued drearily the next day. More animals were roused by their passage. Tapirs and even an occasional tiger growled, as it gently crept away from the company. The point-job was wearing them down. Drifter, at first, worked four-hour spells. Now the point was replaced every hour. They spoke little. It was as if the living jungle refused their passage and was now fighting them openly.

By the fourth day, their water supply was nearly gone, a cause of great concern. Luckily, at noon they came upon a small stream and gladly refreshed themselves, but carefully. Tse Tse told them about flesh eating fish that lived in jungle rivers. They had carefully examined the small stream, but had not discovered any. The warm water, though muddy, had revived them a bit, and they were up to conversation. Likewise, two squirrels in a branch a hundred yards away chattered loudly. Then, they began to argue. Their racket finally caught

the company's attention, and they paused and watched.
Presently a brown one was de-treed and fell down, landing
safely in the water. He bobbed to the surface and swam for
shore.

Suddenly, Tse Tse pointed at a number of small waves.
The flesh eaters arrived. Suddenly a horrible squeal resounded
and echoed in the jungle. The small squirrel yelled twice and
sank slowly. The water bloodied. A great flurry of thrashing
water surrounded his location. Then complete silence and
order returned. They all watched stunned.

Tse Tse said only, "Man lasts bit longer."

Now they dared not cross the stream, and so Nache
directed a footbridge construction project. An hour later, they
were safe on the other side—ponies and all, but the jungle
enclosed them once again. They plodded onwards. With each
new day, they grew more fatigued and lower in spirits. Five
days passed. Distance wise, only a pitiful thirty miles. All the
sixth day, they plodded along. The jungle was relentless;
tangled growths were everywhere. Minds went blank; all
emotion, all thoughts were numb. Their bodies apathetically
chopped a forward path. After a week, eleven zombies hacked
their way through the foliage. It was as if each had entered a
dull, endless nightmare, filled with relentless noises and
unyielding vegetation. The living jungle was ruthlessly
bending their wills towards its. Soon a great weariness set in.

Tse Tse called it jungle fever. One by one, he watched
his friends enter that familiar trance-like, carefree, whee-state
of joyousness before death. Only too well did he know the
signs. The company began singing and wildly jeering, yelling
at the earless jungle. He alone knew the horrors that would
befall his friends in a few hours, when the utter glee and
elation blew off. They had halted all forward progress now and
were cavorting wildly about a small thicket. He felt very alone
and very separate from his friends, who now all had the
"fever." What could he do? He had to try something and fast. If
they should scatter in their madness, all would be lost.

Quietly and unnoticed, he snuck off into the depths of
the jungle. Their wild yelling and laughing filled the jungle.
Presently, he returned with a handful of greenish leaves oozing

a sticky, grey juice. Carefully, he mixed the juices in a small flask of water. He measured a cup full, and, with a big sigh, approached a laughing Drifter.

"Here drink," he offered.

"Oh boy. Here, my friends we have the juice of the gods," and he drank it in a gulp. It was bitter. "Ugh, we best teach the jungle how to brew better water." He laughed uncontrollably.

Tse Tse thought, "One down, nine to go."

In a likewise fashion, sometimes goading, sometimes teasing, but always somehow, he got each of his friends to drink the bitter mouthful. Vorag was the hardest to handle. The mighty hunter was three times the native's bulk, but by teasing him about being too big of a baby, Vorag also drank the juice.

A half hour had passed after the last had downed the potion. Drifter had now quieted down and sat drooped. Tse Tse had drugged them with just a pinch of a wild, manioc juice. It produced a drugged stupor and blind obedience, given in small quantities. In larger doses, it swiftly killed.

He got the company of drugged zombies into order in a single-file line up. Then he commanded, "Follow the one in front of you."

He repeated this many times. Slowly, he led the way, back down the path they had cut through the jungle. Painstakingly, Tse Tse led his string of cattle northwards. The brew, he guessed, would last for several hours, but he found that they made good time now, not fighting the jungle—merely returning on their own path. They stared glassily ahead and stumbled along after those ahead, some pulling along the poor ponies. Tse Tse was everywhere at once. He had to guarantee the safety ahead and keep a sharp eye for stragglers. He knew that their instincts would soon cause them to desire nothing but sleep. He could not afford this.

An hour passed and then another. Tse Tse was weary beyond belief. Yet he kept the pace going. Vorag was now rousing; he noticed the telltale moans.

Stumbling beside Oran, he groaned. "Ohh. What hitteth me? Ooh!"

Tse Tse called, "Come up front here."

Stumbling out of the trance, every muscle seeming to throb, he passed by the others and got to the front beside Tse Tse.

"Nearly all perished. You ok now. Keep us going down path."

Vorag holding his head between moans, mumbled, "Ok, wilst do," followed by low groans.

Relieved, the dark-skinned native rested as the others, dreamlike, plodded by him. He counted all present and took the rear for a time, pausing now and then for a brief rest. Already they had passed by the sixth camp. He recalled that on the fifth day they had passed by a small brook of fairly clean water. There was a small, relatively clear, glen there. Here he resolved to stop. Already it was growing dark. Monotonously, he staggered back up to the line and followed along.

Just at full dark, Vorag yelled, "Stream ahead."

He sighed and hollered back, "Vorag. Camp here."

The hunter needed no second notice. As they halted, others were coming out of it, and soon there was a chorus of moans and groans, but all were together, and all were very much alive. Vorag's head had cleared, and now he took charge of the grumblings and made camp. The utterly exhausted native washed in the small creek and collapsed on the ground. The jungle had defeated them.

He awoke to the noise of dinner being prepared. Familiar yellow, flickering light created an eerie glow to both vegetation and faces. Around him, the others were busily fixing a comfortable camp. Savory odors of hot food hung in the humid air. Getting to his feet, he noticed that George was busily roasting a tapir pig. The others seemed not nearly so gloomy.

"Hey, he's up," Shannon's voice cried.

Suddenly at the focus of attention, he felt a bit embarrassed. A dismaying array of thank you's and handshakes came his way.

"It is obvious we are returning the way we came and have covered quite a distance already. But, brown one, what happened back there?" Malazar inquired, speaking what was on everyone's mind.

Tse Tse looked apologetically at the ground and began. "You got fever. Jungle fever—all go mad—soon run off—die in jungle. Me drug you—lead you back path. Now all safe. Now all ok. No more fever. Jungle wins. We go back. Try Banti."

"Very well done, Tse Tse," Malazar replied. "We all owe you our lives. Our haste nearly made waste of us all, but how come you didn't get the fever?"

"Me lives here," came the obvious answer.

George's "come and get it" ended their discussion. Famished bellies were well filled that night. Most got a reasonable amount of sleep. In two days, they were back where they started from having been defeated by the jungle and having lost nine days.

Their provisions were running dangerously low. So now, Elwine and Tse Tse hunted daily for fresh meat. It slowed their progress, but there was no choice. Grim and determined the company began the long walk down Banti Road. The way was easily passable, though care was needed. It was still a jungle. They made good time, nearly twenty miles a day. None complained on that account. After their defeat, their spirits rose once more. The roadbed was a breeze compared to their overland attempt, but the heat, humidity, and bugs were ever-present.

On the third day on the road, they passed the darkest part of the jungle they had yet crossed. Here the road ran adjacent to what the elf had called Anuir, the strange forest. It was a very dense, hilly jungle. Deep bellowing sounds could occasionally be heard not too far off. At other times, the thud of heavy feet could be felt. Elwine said only, "The big ones." That night the company camped next to the strange jungle, dark and foreboding on their left.

Hot and steaming, the jungle seemed to close in on the travelers; they made camp right on the roadbed itself—clearings were rare along Banti. The path was made of a soft, crushed, alkaline rock, rather grayish in color. So strong was the basic nature of the rock that no living plants could get a root-hold in it; the road remained void of jungle plants—a pale grey strip. Overhead and beside the road, the jungle did grow, attempting to devour the road from other angles. Here the air was heavy; the sounds of cooking pots rang with a dull, damp thud. Voices seemed oppressed as well.

This evening a brace of furry squirrel-like creatures was the main entree. Their other supplies were over half-gone, which concerned George considerably.

Actually, their major problem now was dysentery. In varying degrees, everyone had contracted the loose bowels disease—quite a messy affair, as well as providing hurting guts.

While George tried to boil the brace and keep from steaming himself, Tse Tse, accompanied by Elwine and Drifter, scouted the underbrush nearby looking for some herbs that the brown little man knew would help the dysentery problem.

They rummaged to the south in the less dense area, struggling between the twisted mass of tangled plants, but were unsuccessful. Unfortunately, Drifter was at a loss. Though a ranger, he had absolutely no understanding of jungle plants, and after thrashing around to no avail, he gave up the search. Feeling utterly bored, Mindi replaced him, trying to recall all the plants she had studied about so many months ago in Metro. The elf was glad to have her along; Tse Tse led the forage, this time north into the dark gloom of Anuir.

Ten feet of pure, struggling effort found them inside the dark, dank, forest jungle. "Weird," Elwine muttered to himself, straining to see in the dim light. The trio remained motionless for some time, permitting their eyes to become used to the dark. The October sun had just set, and dusk came swiftly to this place. Yet dimly they perceived that they stood in an open area. So great was the foliage above them that few plants could grow on the heavily leached floor below. Instead of the lush vegetation south of the road, here was a soft bed of decaying rotting mulch. Giant trees with bases nearly three feet across opened umbrella-like fifty feet overhead, each one interwoven with its neighbor's, fighting for the suns' rays.

Mindi turned her Black Bone torch on—its sudden yellow rays flashing brightly and unexpected in the gloomy darkness. Instinctively, the two men recoiled from the startling illumination.

"Oh, sorry, but I brought a torch. We can see better."

"Excellent, but warn us next time," protested the elf.

"Yes!" added Tse Tse.

They carefully scrounged the area for the herbs. Just as George yelled for supper, they found one plant. Tse Tse eagerly confiscated it, but Mindi's and Elwine's attention had now gone to two glittering eyes. They were being watched! Just beyond the fading light of the torch, something was studying them. Both felt it and grew uneasy. The native did not seem bothered by it, and happily, they crashed through the tangled barrier and were on the road once more, quickly at camp.

George as usual had whipped up a tasteful meal, in spite of the climate. Tse Tse only modified the soup slightly, adding chopped pieces of the herb plant he'd dug. The meal passed with relatively nothing said. Elwine and Mindi found themselves aside from the others after dinner, but neither said anything for some time.

Finally, she said what she felt. "You know, it seems as if we were being spied upon. That's how I'd say it."

"Yes, it was most curious about us, but I sensed no malice in its stare," the elf replied.

She looked at his face with his glowing radiance about his forehead and pointed facial features. He seemed particularly beautiful to her. She nestled up to him and put her arm around his light body and said, "Let's go for a walk."

He likewise grasped her gently, and together they strolled down the road, heedless of heat and steam. Night jungle sounds surrounded them in an endless cacophony. They spoke little until the camp was behind them, sweltering in the night heat.

Around a small bend, the pair halted and began discussing the eyes. The elf told her about the strange animals that he had seen nearly a year before, when he journeyed from Eldamar. He had an attentive audience, eager for the tale. She found his description of the large animals particularly interesting. Nearby a twig cracked. At once, both were silent straining their ears for further sounds.

She whispered, "We're being watched."

"Yes, it's just inside Anuir—right there." He pointed to

the dark, black edge, four feet from them. For several minutes, no sounds came from either side.

She whispered, "Sing an elfin song." Questioningly, he looked at her dim face, shrugged his shoulders, and began a slow, soft, elfin chant—a gentle soothing music. Mindi felt she heard a sigh from just beyond in the black void.

"Come on," she pulled his arm and together, they trashed and struggled into Anuir once more. All sounds from within were mashed by their noise of entrance. Once inside, the forest opened up into a vast space.

"Go ahead—sing again," she implored, while her eyes darted inquisitively all around. He began once more. Presently, Mindi felt she could see eyes glowing ever so faintly. They were now just ten feet in front of them.

"Continue," she said and crept slowly towards the eyes, her hands upraised before her in a blind man's walk. She stood just feet before the eyes. She could hear it breathing. From the heavy sound, she guessed it was large. By some strange sense of knowingness, she reached out her right hand. It touched something warm; both recoiled slightly and met again.

Slowly, Mindi began to understand and to communicate through using little words. Presently, Elwine joined her, as fascinated as she was.

For five feeling minutes, they touched, and then suddenly, the large creature backed off and moved away. The encounter was ended. Taking each other's hand, they crept back out through the dense wall of underbrush and returned to camp, full of an insatiable curiosity. What was it?

So excited, the young woman could scarcely sleep. Finally, dawn broke in the unseen, eastern sky, spreading a pale illumination that filtered down through the green canopy. While the sleepy others rummaged slowly for breakfast, she and Elwine quietly stole off and returned to the place they had entered the night before. Without a pause, they reentered the dark jungle thickets. Once inside, the dawn had come, but colors were paler. Dimly they could see the forest jungle opening wide before them. Then they saw the eyes and the form standing not ten feet from them.

Before them stood a large, grey elephant—two great

white husks protruding almost two feet in front of his head. He stood at least fifteen feet tall. Instinctively, Mindi stepped forward very slowly, raised her hand, and placed it gently on his long, dangling trunk. He wiggled; the nose curled up, and she faced his nose squarely in front of her face. He seemed to be sniffing her. She felt his urge to communicate and strained her senses to their fullest. Likewise Elwine.

"Hey, his name is Bobo," the elf said, startled.

"Yes," she grinned, "and he doesn't think we're the dirty ones, but he doesn't know who we are."

Quickly, they spoke softly to Bobo. They kept to the simplest ideas; but had to repeat some several times. At last, he understood them, and they, he. It seemed Kahill's evil Scourge had passed by his realm. Wantonly, they had killed many of the herding animals in Anuir—or Tepo as Bobo called his lands. He hated the Scourge, but as yet, he had not been able to do more than trample a few. When at last the pair had to return, Bobo seemed disappointed at their leaving. Mindi told him to wait; she'd be back.

Quickly and very excitedly, the two left and ran back to the company. Elwine answered the party's curiosity by explaining about the elephant. They were amazed. Soon everyone crawled through the now well-made path into Anuir. Bobo was a bit overwhelmed by their numbers, but Mindi was a calming influence. When the initial excitement had fallen off and when they were returning to the road to continue their hot journey, Mindi said farewell to her new friend. She was the last to return to the road.

They then began their long, hot walk once more, talking excitedly about the sight of such a huge, friendly animal, but as they walked that day, from the dark woods on their left, the sound of heavy feet came trampling, paralleling their progress. When they finally camped for the day, Mindi, Elwine, and Marc pushed through the underbrush. Sure enough, there was Bobo waiting for them.

They talked, reading each other's minds for nearly an hour. George's supper call ended the rendezvous. Elwine had to pull her away for supper, for she was so engrossed with her new friend. They rejoined their companions for a meal of stewed salted pork. The others ate it grumbling, but Mindi only picked at her food, lost in thought. Sundown came, announced by a host of parrot calls from high in the canopy above. Mindi set her plate aside, left camp, and slowly rejoined Bobo, lost in thought.

An hour later, she felt the gentle touch of an elfin hand on her shoulder. He had quietly, elf fashion, joined her. Elwine found that she and Bobo had just finished resolving something.

"Oh, hi Elwine. It's done. Bobo and I have arranged it! Come on; he's got to be off." Together, they returned to camp. As the ground thunderously shook, Bobo departed rapidly as well.

"What was that all about," Marc inquired when she returned.

"Let's council," was all she said; there was a bright twinkle in her eyes. Nache made a small fire and Shannon passed tea all around. Even Malazar seemed curious.

"Well, now my dear, we're all here and all ears. Tell us what is up," the wizard asked with keen interest.

This was the first reasonably cheerful word they had received from him in the last two days. For he had been ill of temper, grumbling incessantly about the Orb. Now he seemed a bit more outgoing, interested in Mindi's turn of events.

"Well, I've got our army for us and transportation as well!" She fairly beamed with pride.

"Well?" Marc implored.

"Yes, you are looking at your newest general," she joked. "Commander Mindi!" She saw that she would be trounced if she stalled further and so told them. "Yes, Bobo and I have arranged for an army, a grey army, composed of Bobo and friends." She paused for effect and continued, "He has gone to round up the 'big grazas' as he calls them, oliphants, rhinos with big horns, and a thing called a murmonsk—sort of a wooly looking cow I think. He says he will have them mustered at the tee ahead, where Banti Road ends at the Old Caravan Road. Also, he'll send several elephants for us to ride. Not bad, eh?" she added.

"An army of beasts," mused the elf.

"Not bad, not bad. It just might work," the wizard replied, slowly realizing the effect that such an army might have, "an unlooked for grey army!"

Chapter XXIV—The Grey Army

The news acted like a pressure release valve; everyone seemed greatly relieved, and spirits rose in spite of the sweltering heat and swarms of bugs. They talked far into the night. The morning parrot calls were crowned by the trumpeting calls of several great elephants just beyond the walls of Anuir. Mindi and Elwine woke and at once went to them. Presently, amid a great thrashing and crackling, ten of the huge beasts crashed through the wall of vegetation and stood inquisitively on the road, looking timidly at the camp. The party returned the timid stares. It was one thing to contemplate riding an elephant, and quite another when facing one. If the company was timid about the elephants, the beasts were even more so of their newly acquired allies. They spent an hour getting acquainted.

The leader was called Lobo, and Mindi learned from him that Bobo had gone off to gather the grey forces. They loaded all the ponies' gear atop one of the beasts, and one by one, they struggled aboard. The technique most workable was for the beasts to lower their front legs to their knees and, by use of their powerful trunks, lift the passengers aboard. Many doubled up. Only Tse Tse, the lightest of the companions, would remain on foot. He tied the three ponies together and then riding first one then another. Freed of their burdens, the ponies would be able to keep up. Mindi rode alone on Lobo, who led the way. Soon the grey riders were off.

The huge beasts were swift and sure. It seemed to Mindi that their walking had been as a snail compared to this.

Even Hildaro remarked, "Though not like a horse, exactly, they're sure welcomed!"

In two incredible days, they arrived at the fork in the road. Camp was established, and their steeds returned to the forest jungle to feast. They now awaited Bobo's return.

Moods were mixed and had changed during the ride. Vorag, who had been a bit reluctant if not just nervous about elephant riding, was now cheerfully discussing their merits with Hildaro. Shannon definitely preferred walking, while Tse Tse who felt dwarfed by the beasts, seemed greatly relieved to be on foot or pony back.

Tse Tse's general reservedness melted as he announced to Nache, "Near home country—good feeling."

"Yes, the smallest in size may not be the smallest in grandeur," his stable friend replied, anxious to get on with the travel.

The camp was very lax; a sense of security prevailed for a time, as dinner came and went. Then, above the harsh distant cries of survival in the jungle came drum beats. Fairly low pitched with a breaking rhythm, it throbbed not too far away. Quickly, the lax nature dissolved, as instinctively the company prepared for some unknown action. Noticing that the brown man alone had not gone into action, Marc came over to where Tse Tse was standing by the south fork of the Old Caravan Road. He noticed the native seemed to be listening intently to the drums.

"Friend or foe?" Marc queried.

Tse Tse's smile was answer enough, but he motioned for Marc to remain silent. So he returned to the others and whispered, "Friends, quiet."

They all gathered around their guide for this foreboding country. As sharply as the drumming began, it ceased. Far off another took up the stroking, as if in answer.

"They relay messages," Tse Tse began, noticing everyone had surrounded him. Sheepishly, he explained, "My people pound drums. Warning messages get sent. Faster than runners. First one at Falls of Mala, maybe five miles that way— east. Other comes from Paomoho Camp many miles south— big drum there—Grundi—big man—beats loud."

"Yes, but what do they say," Nache impatiently tried to hurry him up.

His eyes fell; a look of sadness cringed his smooth features. Falteringly, he answered, "Say Wauli camp destroyed—guanies—sorry—goblins stopped."

Mindi stepped to his side and comforted him.

He appreciated her caring and, taking a deep breath and forcing a smile, said, "Say also strangers on road at tee.

363

Investigate. My people come soon. Must meet."

So a guard line was established with Elwine on the northeastern road and Tse Tse on the southern side. To be helpful, Nache threw more logs on the fire, which now crackled and blazed brightly.

"Can't be missed now," he mumbled to himself.

A slow hour passed; large black reflections darted here and there among the heavy jungle beside the road. The fire died and was renewed twice by an attendant dwarf. Several members had retired already when Elwine noticed that the nearby cries of the jungle had slowly ceased; it was surprisingly quiet. He hurriedly left his post and came to his friend.

"The jungle is strangely quiet."

"Yes," his brown friend replied, "people sneak by—no see yet."

The two strained their eyes peering into the abysmal blackness of steaming heat. Aroused, Marc, Mindi, and Malazar joined the pair, but said nothing.

"There, a shadow," pointed Elwine. Try as she might, Mindi couldn't see what he pointed at.

"Be better, I go alone," and the brown man slipped quickly away from the others. He went south on the road some distance and halted. Mindi could see his outline dimly if she tried hard. Soon she observed there were two outlines. Excitement grew as the two forms moved closer to camp, stopping around a hundred yards from where the others stood.

If Tse Tse was a shy fellow, then the newcomer could only be said to be super shy. Yet shyness was one of the characteristics of these jungle people. Isolated in such a hostile environment for so long, self-preservation demanded a minimization of risks. The companions could hear the two voices speaking in a high singsong fashion—a somewhat musical, clucking sound. Though the elf had spent some time with them not so long ago, he still understood little of so strange a language. They could only wait.

After fifteen minutes, the pair shook hands, and the newcomer swiftly disappeared into the jungle darkness. Tse Tse returned to camp, a smile on his face. The shadow of sadness lifted somewhat.

He saw their faces full of curiosity, and for once, he almost laughed. "Was Malo there. Good scout. Much news. Say goblins thrash forest—evacuate Paomoho camp—they come—many dead—but burned village—no house stands—many filthy bodies dead—few of us hurt. Big battle. They go back to Nyder now."

"Excellent. Excellent," said Malazar. "I had hoped that the scourge would avoid the tepid jungle lands. It seems that has been the case for the most part."

"I tell Malo about us. He goes to relay drum. Let rest know it is safe. Can sleep now."

After a few more questions, they did just that, listening to the music of jungle drums, which had once again began their rhythmic throbbing.

Daybreak came grey and bleak. Dense rain clouds seemed to reach down to the very canopy above them. The day promised to be bleak and dismal. Tse Tse's comments added to the dreariness, "Monsoon season comes."

He and Elwine explained that the October rains were about to start. For weeks now, torrential rains would be the order of the day. Though it would bring relief from the heat, the vast amounts of water would turn the jungle floor into a vast sea of grey mud, knee deep in places. The day seemed even drearier than before. No one liked the idea of wading through mud. Visions of everything being soaking wet passed through many heads. Gloomily, they prepared for the rains.

They had not long to wait, for soon without warning the sky opened up; sheets of rain poured down upon them. As the day passed, torrential rains did not abate but continued to dump vast quantities of water upon the jungle. Quickly the ground saturated. Now great puddles formed in the low spots. One by one, the puddles connected and joined with others. By late afternoon, the road was a small, sloshy sea, nearly everywhere under water. The long day crept by as the company remained dry for a time huddling under their tarps, but soon there was little choice but to get their feet wet. Grumbling became the most frequent utterance. Still no word had come from Bobo.

"I don't like sleeping in a water puddle," cried Nache in utter disgust!

"Verily, dwarf, thou speaketh truth. I liketh it not as well. Canst we not do something?" the drenched hunter imploringly asked the others.

Tse Tse explained that they built their homes on stilts to remain dry. They took little comfort from his words. However, with a sudden gleam in his eye, Nache loosened his axe, and the others watched him curiously, as he felled a small tree and stripped its bark. An hour later, he had constructed a small platform on six-inch legs. Proudly, he wrapped himself up in a tarp and proceeded to lie on his dry bed. The others laughed loudly at his action, and then the others followed suit. Soon nearly a dozen of the floating beds were built and occupied.

As supper time came, marked mostly by hungry stomachs, they discovered the next problem; wet wood did not burn. They ate a cold dinner. Grumbling, they retired on their raised beds. Unrelentingly, the heavy rain continued throughout the night. By the grey dawn, the monsoon had ebbed a bit, and the rain fell more gently, but the road was covered by a sea uniformly two inches deep.

It was not the dull sky that roused the company, however. Distantly, at first, came a rumbling noise, accompanied by far off trumpeting. They sat up on their beds, gazed at the water surrounding them and listened to the growing noise.

Soon the ground began to vibrate, and the noise of heavy trampling feet grew louder. The animals were coming. Louder and louder came the din. So heavy was the footfalls of so many that the water began to shimmer and shake. Nache's bed began to rattle, and his teeth chattered as the ground trembled in a quake. Suddenly, Marc had an awful thought, "What if they were not seen in time—to be trampled beneath the feet of the great host!" Others had similar fears. Suddenly, they started yelling wildly.

However, their fears were groundless. Though the noise became deafening, Bobo halted the company near the edge of Anuir, while he slowly plowed through and came searchingly down the road, plodding as he came.

As he neared the company, he halted timidly. Mindi waved her hands. Reluctantly, she stepped down into the muddy, grey waters. "Oh, it's cold and yucky," she exclaimed, and waded toward her large, grey friend.

The others watched, very content to let her get her feet wet. Marc mused; there she stood grey-green, shimmering in her elfin cloak, which was drawn tightly about her body, rain water falling about her in the fading light. Alone she stood before this huge, grey shape, many, many times her size. An animal. Yet he knew that somehow she and Bobo were communicating. "She's incredible!" he thought to himself.

A half an hour later, she splashed her way back and crawled on her floating bed. "Well," she began, noticing everyone was staring at her, "the grey army has arrived. Bobo said they were easily aroused, and now that there's the opportunity, they are uncontrollable. The want to charge the Scourge. We shall leave at once. Bobo insists we all ride the elephants once more, but the ponies must go up front beside Bobo and me; great is the danger to them if they lag behind. Many of the beasts are wild, and he has little control over their actions. These he has put in the rear, but we must go quickly."

Somewhat reluctantly, they climbed off their raised platforms and got the gear ready. Meanwhile the great steeds quietly appeared again ready for their job once more. Shortly everyone was aboard his elephant. Only Nache was refusing, worrying about the ponies. Hence, Mindi had him tie the ponies in a string, and he mounted behind her upon Bobo. He held the lead rope. Nache's job was to keep the ponies coming along beside the tall, massive elephant.

Then Bobo snorted a loud blast, and the two felt his whole body shake and vibrate from his effort. Deafening was the resounding trumpeting and bellowing that came in reply. Slowly the grey army went forward on the Old Caravan Road with heavy, sloshing steps.

The sounds of cracking timbers could be heard on either side. Even in the poor light, the length of the herd could still be discerned: a wall of grey forms went to the rear for nearly a quarter of a mile. Nache guessed that they extended for a thousand yards on either side of the road, and everything in their path was trampled, save large trees.

Bobo slowly led the way down the water-covered road as the rains continued. All that day they continued slowly making their way southwards. By evening or what should have been sunset, masked by the overcast, grey, rain clouds, the herd halted.

"Feeding time," Mindi announced, and carefully, everyone was set on the water-covered, roadbed.

While the hosts ate as they might, the company fixed a meal such as they could. Several hours after dark, they were aboard the grey steeds. Now they went very, very slowly, for in the rain-drenched darkness, the road was nearly impossible to see. Mindi figured they were going on by feel alone, but it felt reassuring to be making some progress. It meant the end of the jungle was just that much nearer.

With no significant change of scenery or rain clouds, the grey army passed noisily onwards for three days and nights. Occasionally, small brown shapes appeared in front of them, curiously searching for the makers of the thunderous noise. Nache would watch their startled faces and then watch the brown natives flee for their lives, as the host, ignoring them, plodded relentlessly forward. It was the passing of the grey army.

The fourth day dawned. They noted that the jungle was less dense here, and Tse Tse explained that they were nearly opposite his villages. Indeed, it seemed to be the case, for they could see many brown forms timidly peering out among the trees ahead. They would stare in disbelief for a while and then swiftly run through the drenched forest to get out of the path of the great host.

Perhaps some of Tse Tse's people had occasionally seen an elephant up north, but now passing down the road beside their villages were thousands of the beasts. They were accompanied by rhinos with large horns and the horned cow-like creatures. All headed for the Scourge. Even more incredible: strange people plus one of their own were riding atop these mammoth beasts. Tse Tse knew that his people would talk of this singular event for years to come. He felt both proud and happy that he had a hand in it. He even took to waving to his people. It became catching. Soon they were all waving to the startled natives. Nache exclaimed that it was like a great parade.

Still the rains fell, and the elephants slowly plodded onwards; darkness once again grew on the jungle world.

The fifth day saw action. It was just before noon as the rains abated. Here the jungle was definitely thinning, and the ground became hillier and a bit more rocky. Suddenly, Mindi saw the smoking fire of a Yac or goblin camp ahead. Bobo saw it too. For the first time since they started, he raised his trunk and bellowed loudly. Cries came from the camp ahead.

Now she could see clearly. They were smaller, blue goblins. They had two, white, carved horns across their forehead and great ugly teeth. There were nearly a dozen running wildly about the campsite. Bobo did not vary his pace. The smoking fire lay in the middle of the road. The others in the herd took up Bobo's cry. Hue and cry of the grey army sounded from all sides, deafening to all ears. Mindi and the others held their hands over their ears, so great was the trumpeting tumult. Freaked, the goblins screamed wildly and, splashing and sloshing, ran down the road ahead of the grey wall. As Bobo neared the campfire, he purposely scattered it. Small clouds of vapor rose when the hot embers hit the water. Likewise, those that followed continued the trample. She knew their arrival was now announced.

By noon, the ground was rising gently; the rains had stopped. The area now looked like a hilly forest. They were only some twenty miles from the pass. Ahead loomed the craggy, towering, Quara Nord mountains, orange against the grey clouds, which seemed to be breaking up. They had come upon campsites more frequently, but the warning of their coming seemed always to reach there before they did. Some ten had been deserted, fires still blazing. Here the ground was not covered with water, though still muddy. Before one of the fires, Bobo halted and the company dismounted.

Mindi quickly explained, "Here we must depart. The grey ones grow restless for the charge. We would be a dangerous burden in such a run; for if we fall off, the wild ones in the rear may trample us as a goblin. We should swing way to

369

the left and let them pass, and then we can follow safely behind."

Not one complaint did she get; everyone was only too glad to exercise cramped leg muscles; the feeling of dry, firm ground underneath was heartening, along with both the change in weather and terrain.

As quickly as they could, they headed due east; and, in some ten minutes, they were beyond the last grey bulk. When the last elephant saw they were beyond him, he gave a loud, trumpeting bellow. Bobo answered it, they assumed. Then, once again, the trumpeting was taken up by all, and during the deafening roar, they began to charge forward. The earth shook violently beneath them; such a thunderous trample had never occurred.

The company crouched in hiding and covered their ears, while their bodies shook along with the ground and trees. A huge, grey, moving, bellowing mass thundered by them. In ten minutes, the rear stragglers roared past, and the ground shaking subsided. In the distance, the roar could be heard clearly. No one moved or spoke for some time.

Finally, Drifter stretched and said, "Man I sure wouldn't want to be in front of that herd!"

The others wholeheartedly agreed. They ate a quick snack, for none were too eager to follow too closely. Then, they once again made the road.

Presently the crushed forms of goblins and others began appearing in the debris before them. Most were squashed beyond recognition, save the telltale blue skin. No one spoke. By nightfall, they were within five miles of the pass. Here, Malazar urged the group to camp for the night and wait for daybreak, before actually going to the front line. No one disagreed with that for the distant trumpeting could still be heard. Quickly, they left the road and trampled forest, making camp among some large boulders, which they felt offered considerable cover. All throughout the night, the trumpeting continued, and they slept uneasily.

Dawn came rosy red, the first in many weeks. All noise had subsided. A great silence spread before them, broken only by an occasional crackling in the distant brush. While the others ate breakfast in the most cheery mood they had displayed in a long time, Elwine scouted the area towards the pass. As the others were finishing up, the elf reappeared. He discussed the scene, while he ate.

"All is done. They are returning slowly down the road. They look tired and exhausted, but few injuries do any carry! It is probably safe for us to parallel the road. Strangest thing though, I didn't see a single fallen enemy! Very peculiar."

Soon, the group was walking southward, some distance from the road among the shattered remains of the forest, while the great beasts were going north down the road. They looked tired, yet proud of their deeds. So strong did they emanate their feelings of victory that Marc noted to Mindi, "It's as if I can almost sense or feel their pride. It is so strong!"

"Yes," she replied, a twinkle in her eyes. "That's the way you can communicate to them. They have done a great deed and are justly proud of it." Marc pondered this for quite some time.

When they were within two miles of the pass, Bobo came slowly down the road, bringing up the rear. The company went towards him at once. Red patches covered his grey frame, mostly on his front side. There was an ugly gash across his nose between his two great eyes. He walked very slowly, but seemed uplifted to see Mindi again. Quietly and quickly, she issued orders and began tending his wounds. While she cleansed them, Drifter scrambled around the rocks and found several herbs for her. These she mixed into a mud salve and closed the wounds. He was feeling much better when she finished, and the pair stood silently facing each other for several minutes. At last, she stepped aside and waved goodbye, as the large elephant hurried down the road to catch his friends.

Of what they said, she only related that all was completed and that they had their revenge. The company continued towards the pass.

Now the land rose sharply upwards, and pine trees flourished among increasingly large boulders. The road twisted and turned as it snaked its way up towards the pass, and now far to the east, white capped in the noon sun, the

Armagh mountains rose mightily. Nache, of course, became exceedingly excited and insisted on telling everyone rapidly the names of all the distant peaks. Finally, they rounded the final bend; before them lay Nyder Pass, surrounded by the massive destruction of the grey army.

Scattered remains could be seen of hundreds of guardhouses, the homes of the northeastern Scourge. Towering orange and tall stood the Quara Nord mountains, sharp and craggy. Between two sheer cliffs of orange stood Nyder Pass—painted checkerboard yellow and black at the base. They all gasped, for within the pass sealing it shut was a gigantic mound of dead Scavengers.

"Very clean, these elephants are," Malazar commented.

It was a ghastly, sickening sight. Hundreds upon hundreds of trampled and squashed goblin and Yac bodies lay piled within the pass. The plug of dead rose over twelve feet and was beginning to stink.

Quickly, they retraced their steps, and once out of sight of the pass, they halted in the damaged zone, pondering their next step. There was little for them to do here. The grey army had done its job very thoroughly.

Once seated, Shannon began with the obvious, "Well, Malazar, what next? We are dangerously low on supplies and in the middle of nowhere."

"Right," added George. "We are indeed almost out of provisions. We can ration them I guess, but how far can we hope to go?"

"Well Khorizaba lies yonder," exclaimed the dwarf, but he added with a sinking heart, "but our cities lie far to the south, and Armagh now is heavily covered by snows. We have no gear for the cold stuff."

Tse Tse added, "My camps be north—also big distance back into jungle."

No one liked that idea very much. Whether Malazar had a plan for their situation or not, he never had an opportunity to speak. Just then, from the hills behind them came the clearly audible clanking of armor and shields—far off, but nevertheless there.

"Sure sounds like armor," said Shannon.

Hildaro replied, "Yes, you know, it sort of reminds me of the dwarves." Malazar gave the order, and they set out at once in the direction of the scattered noise.

"It sounds more like the clanking of marching men," Nache commented. They entered the area of the pass once more and veered eastward toward the foothills of the Armagh mountains from where the sounds seemed to be originating.

Presently, moving shields beamed random rays towards them. They scrambled over the rocky hills, as quick as they could. Finally, reaching the top of a larger hill, the majestic, snow-capped Armagh mountains rose before them. As far as their eyes could see, whitened peaks rose in an endless array. On the next hill, halting as suddenly as they, stood a band of thirty dwarves, clad in bright shining mail, silver helms, and shields sparkling in the noon sun. Gleams radiated from spear tips, swords, and battle axes. Beneath the silver mail, the familiar gaily-colored, zig-zag patches shone through. Nache yelled wildly and raced down the shallow valley towards the company. The others followed more reservedly, and the dwarf band did likewise. The two groups met in the browning valley beneath the towering Armagh mountains.

For several enthusiastic minutes, Nache and the leader of the band, named Dorti, conversed in their highly accented, coarse tongue. Quickly, four dwarves were dispatched and returned back towards the mountains, while Nache introduced Dorti and company to the questers. They quickly learned that the dwarves, under the command of Aaron, had taken up the war here on their northern borders and had been slowly pushing the Scavengers back into the foothills. Last night, there came a noise of thunder and a sound like trumpets blaring; the dwarves were afraid that Kahill had loosened something terrible upon them. At dawn, the noise subsided, and since they weren't attacked, Aaron ordered small bands to scout the area, for the scourge had disappeared altogether.

Nache quickly told them about the grey army. They stared at the company, eyes getting wider and wider, their mouths opening wide in astonishment and disbelief. "Come and see," the dwarf excitedly added. Slowly in single file, the awed dwarves passed by the others, staring constantly at them.

When they were out of hearing range, Vorag roared with laughter; it was catching, and soon even Malazar was chuckling. Sometime later, the dwarves returned and sat down some distance from them. Their eyes were wide in awe.

Dorti managed between swallows to exclaim, "All hails to the wizards!"

Just then, the now familiar clanking of armored dwarves was heard, and over the hill came a tramping double line of dwarves, nearly a hundred, led by Aaron himself. Seeing Nache and company, Aaron smiled and seemed greatly relieved. He strode right up before the company and halted. He bowed very low and said, "Aaron Thrombdale, Supreme Commander of Dwarven Armies, at your service."

Nache stared at him and cried, "You've been promoted!" Aaron blushed and acknowledged it.

They spent the afternoon bringing each other up to date. With wide eyes, Aaron received the news of the grey army. After a quick visit to the pass, they were even wider, and he complimented and thanked them for nearly five minutes. The company also learned that all was still well, far to the south. The Scourge remained contained, and though much of the pass had been cleared, none dared venture out.

As afternoon wore on, Aaron invited them to join him that night for a celebration feast. Now the word "feast" did it. Though no one wanted a celebration, everyone's mouth watered at the word. Swiftly they set off across the barren foothills towards the Armagh mountains. Already the air was cool and refreshing, and in the sinking sun, the picturesque mountains radiated, beckoning before them.

"A feast would definitely be in order," thought Nache, rubbing his stomach gingerly.

Chapter XXV—Out of the Oven and into the Icebox

Orange hues, cast by the late October sun sinking beyond the western ridge of the Quara Ost mountains, made the Brown Feet, the northern foothills of the Armagh mountains, seem even more rich and enticing. The company eagerly followed Aaron's marching lines of dwarves. Before them, in a sharp silver contrast to the rich, rolling, brown, tree-scarce lands, the armored little men, marching in pairs, formed a flowing, gleaming, endless line that crawled like a silver streak over the hills.

Radiating a cold beauty in a multitude of colors, the taller peaks, snow-clad and purple hued, stretched endlessly across the entire southern horizon. The mural-sight was breathtaking and inspiring to everyone in the group. Nache felt home.

As dusk grew, they arrived at the dwarf army base cradled in a deep, though not steep-sided, rounded valley. Scattered pine trees dotted the gentle slopes of the mile high, glacier carved vale. As they descended, tiny, silver, moving dots covered the valley floor like swarming ants. Scattered bonfires illuminated darker areas. At least a thousand dwarves were encamped below. The long, thin line trailed down into their midst. The sight brought smiles and chuckles to the faces of everyone in the company. It was a pleasant surprise. As they descended, the chilly mountain air, coming down from the snowy heights, was both refreshing and invigorating. They halted near the middle of the large camp.

Here stood a large pavilion done in purple and orange striped canvas that contrasted sharply. Aaron stood beside his door welcoming them. Nearby, several teams were hastily erecting several large yellow and red striped tents for their guests. Although those for dwarven use are small, Aaron had brought along several larger, guest versions, just for any eventuality. Already the odor of fresh, cooking meat floated in the gentle breeze. The company was more than a little surprised to see the dwarf version of a campfire. They were more like large bonfires! The company quickly established themselves in the three tents, and when a large gong resounded echoing in the valley, the feast began.

Aaron apologized for lack of civilities, no table or chairs. Large rocks served admirably, and soon all were lost in endless conversation, in feasting, and in song. The dwarves loved to eat and sing. Mindi had already observed that; the little she had seen of Nache at the Dew Drop Inn had obviously been much subdued! Far into the night, the dwarves ate, sang, and danced around the huge bonfires blazing ten times their height. Eventually, the party retired with a feeling of tranquility they had not known in a long while. Only slowly did the revelry subside and give way to the coming cold dawn.

"Where's the damn fire," Marc chattered, when he scrambled out of the tent. The yellow sun felt warm on his cheeks, but he was cold.

Mindi was right beside him, "Yes, where are those bonfires when you need them?" she asked.

They rushed to the nearest fire. Already the dwarves had rebuilt them. The two, rubbing their hands for warmth, snuggled by the fire.

"Boy, it sure is getting cold around here. You sure we got on all the clothes we brought, dear?" Marc asked for the tenth time.

"You bet," she joked. "Come be a good boy, give me your woolens."

"No way!" he laughed.

The others joined them, likewise chilled, but the climbing, yellow ball soon took the cold chill off, and after a hot breakfast, they felt acceptable again.

Now they surrounded Malazar and stood looking at him silently. "Well?" he asked realizing that he had become the center of attention.

"Now what will we do, for starters?" Marc laughed.

"Oh, we must seek the Orb of course," he replied.

"It lies over yonder," Nache pointed towards the snow-clad but not too distant peaks, "the—the—well, you know—it

376

does," he added trying to avoid open words.

"Let us hasteneth, then," pronounced Vorag.

"Whoa, wait a minute," cried Hildaro, thinking things were getting off all wrong. "It's too darn cold. We're not prepared for snow, and besides, our food stock is nearly gone, right George?"

"Yes," came the short response.

"Malazar," Marc interceded, "Hildaro is right. We're not prepared for such a journey. Right Nache?" He hoped the dwarf would concur.

He needn't have worried, for the mountain dweller piped up, "Yes, for sure. We have no clothes, ropes, boots, snow shoes, packs, food, fire wood, dry kindling . . ."

Malazar chuckled. "Whoa, patience my little fellow; great deeds can go ill, if one is not prepared. Your points are well taken. So eager am I to end this thing, I would have begun that which could not end but ill. So come now, what do you propose to do? We shall need considerable preparations, as Nache says, and food. How shall we acquire these?"

Here Aaron took charge. "If I might add a word of council, everything that you would need to travel Khorizaba in the glorious winter can be had or made in Tulan. Now that the end has come, at least temporarily here, I shall take most of the army and return to our capital. I'll leave a garrison here, just as a precautionary measure. You're most welcome to accompany us across the mountains," he pointed southwards to the snowy heights. He continued, "But Nache is correct; you do not seem prepared for such a bitter cold journey. I would not recommend it. Perhaps you can wait here. We can send back appropriate supplies."

"But that'll take weeks," muttered Malazar. "We thank you for your gracious offer. But is there no other way?"

Shannon broke the silence, "Well, if we can get to the sea, the Mariners can be signaled. Then, we can sail to Cuicatlan and come overland along the great road to Tulan. With good luck, we may even beat Aaron here to Tulan."

"Splendid, splendid!" Malazar became excited and seemed greatly relieved. "Nache, how far is the sea from here? And the terrain, is it passable by us?"

"Thirty-five leagues and yes," came his quick reply.

"Good, then it shall be done. So let us prepare ourselves for the journey to the sea. Aaron, if you arrive before us, we would greatly appreciate your getting preparations under way, for our next journey shall be to cross Armagh's middle."

Aaron bowed low, and whether he was curious about the hint, he did not indicate. Soon the camp was bustling with activity. For the dwarves, there was much to be done.

Before long, tents came down, and everywhere the sounds of chopping were heard. Nache explained that great loads of firewood were carried on their ponies. "Safety first," he explained.

Though they couldn't acquire clothing that fit from the dwarves, they did replenish their provisions with bags of dried and salted deer meat, a form of dried sweet potato, and bags of dried fruit. Water bags were filled, and George carefully replenished his salt and spice bags. At noon, a gong sounded heralding Aaron's departure.

"Come," cried Nache, and he led his friends swiftly to the southern hilltop. Here the mountains seemed close and particularly breathtaking. They watched below. In long lines, ten abreast, the dwarves marched up and out of the valley. Their silver mail and armor flashing in the sun made a magnificent sight. Soon the endless silvery line stretched up hill and down, heading off over the hills southeastward. As far as they could see, the silver hued line stretched.

After taking leave of Dorti, who was now in charge of the hundred garrison troops, they were off themselves. Leading their heavily laden ponies, they went in pairs up and out of the large valley heading due east among the brown foothills. Great herds of wintering deer and elk startled before them.

The trip took nearly a week, for progress was not exceedingly rapid in the rocky country, but ever their eyes were drawn to the beauty of the snow-clad Armagh to their right. As the cold drew more intense, they would veer more to the north, for in Tse Tse's land, it was still hot. Thus, they sought a comfortable compromise. At night, they acquired the dwarf custom of large bonfires for warmth. Overall, it was a peaceful relaxing travel—the best any had yet had on their long journeys. From time to time, Nache and Elwine would walk together composing or reciting appropriate songs. It was indeed a happy journey to the sea.

By the sixth day, Shannon was constantly sniffing the air. "Can you smell it? It's her, the sea," he enthusiastically proclaimed to any who'd listen.

By late afternoon, they climbed atop a hill with the distant rumble of waves crashing upon a shore. Below them lay the shore and endless miles of green water. Nache cried in his own tongue, "Shebab," while superlatives merely rolled from Shannon.

On the dark, sandy beach, they pitched their borrowed red and yellow tents and established camp, while Shannon and Vorag assisted the dwarf in collecting wood. At dusk a large signal fire was blazing, and the company sat upon rocks enjoying a hot dinner, listening to tales of the sea as told by Shannon. Then, in the quarter moon light, everyone gathered firewood, for the Mariner insisted that the fire must not burn low.

"They will steer by it," he explained.

The next day having little to do, they scouted the land. Here there were no inhabitants, save animals. The Brown Feet hills rolled lazily into narrow, sandy beaches—mostly dark colored. Further south, the beaches would diminish. Nache explained that there the mountains rose from the ocean depths. Some spent the day scampering about on land. Mindi, Marc, and Shannon went swimming in the cool waters. Getting out was the worst but the bonfire helped. By the end of day, nearly everyone except Vorag had a bath.

He protested, "I needeth not a bath. Tis not yet six months since my last one." Laughing and yelling, the others peeled his clothes off and threw him into the water, and playfully Oran joined him. Then they supped and collected more wood for the fires. The sky was clouding heavily by then, and in the chilly evening breeze, they retired hopefully. Elwine had seen a light far out at sea. It was too dark to see what it was exactly, but they were hopeful.

At daybreak, they awoke to a white ground. It had

snowed lightly during the night covering everything with a soft, moist, half inch of white flakes. Marc, Mindi, George, Hildaro, and Tse Tse had never seen snow firsthand. The fun began just after breakfast and after Elwine's sighting of a boat coming their way some twenty miles off.

At first they had walked in the white stuff, fingered, and tasted it. Then, Nache demonstrated snowball making. Vorag started the snowball fight by tossing one Marc's way. For ten minutes with cries and roars of laughter, white balls flew thick and fast. They even ganged up and rolled the wizard in the white stuff. Then, they ended, warmed up by the fire, and had several rounds of hot brew.

Shannon and Elwine concurred about the arrival time of the ship, and accordingly, camp was broken. The gear was stowed into packs once more. At last, they crowded the beach, watching intently as the boat took form on the horizon.

Elwine's keen elfin eyes read the name of the side: "The Lucky Lady."

"Yes," exclaimed Shannon, "that'll be Erving Seafund's ship, all right! That's a good one!"

Soon the three masted schooner drew closer and closer. Now the others could see the crew waving, and they waved excitedly back. Presently, she hove to just off shore. Broadside, she looked quite impressive and very seaworthy. Rapidly, the crew dropped sail, and an anchor rumbled noisily into the shallows. Simultaneously, a small dingy was lowered. Erving and another rowed swiftly to shore and received a jubilant welcome. Later, the Mariner signaled his first mate; a large long boat was lowered, and four crew members rowed to shore.

It took four trips to get all the gear, themselves, and the three ponies aboard. The latter required a good deal of effort, though. Eventually, a small raft was constructed. The three nervous ponies, standing dead still and huddled in the center, accompanied by Nache, Mindi, and Elwine, made their way out to the waiting ship. They were pulled by the long boat with ten oarsmen and were lifted aboard by winch.

At sunset, the ship weighed anchor and set sail for deeper waters. They found the Lucky Lady more like a home than a boat and were extremely comfortable in the stern cabins. They slept in beds and ate well. Erving was an excellent host, and between the two Mariners, the tall tales seemed unending. There was a moderate breeze, and the ship creaked, groaned, and rolled gently. It took only three days to make Cuicatlan, the dwarf port.

They learned much news from Erving. Best of all, he had guessed from the rumors of their movements that they would eventually be near the dwarf mountains. Knowing that they were ill equipped for a winter's journey in the mountains, he had acquired a great store of the necessities and had them sent to Tulan in readiness. Further, he himself had been sailing these eastern runs for the last month now, just in case of a signal fire. They were unanimous in their thanks.

Both Marc and Mindi were pleased at the news from Metro. The Mayor had formed a large army of sorts and had systematically removed all remnants of the Scourge. George was pleased to hear that East Flats had done similarly, having acquired an arsenal of Burly scimitars and dwarven blades. The others had similar messages from home. Perhaps none was better received than that from Pali Camp. Tse Tse's people had now partially rebuilt Wauli Camp, and the endless filtering of Evil Ones from the north had ceased.

Malazar's only comment, as he sat feet propped on the railing, thumbing his beard was, "We must strike now; we can't let him launch a spring offensive. The Orb—if only he doesn't get the Orb."

By late the third afternoon, the dwarf port was sighted from the crow's nest, much to the glee of both Vorag and Tse Tse, who both had become a bit seasick. As they neared Cuicatlan, Shannon called everyone on deck. "There is only one port in all of Isel that is such a wonder. You must see it from the seaward point of view."

No more would he say. Nache crawled as far forward as he could, staring ahead. To their right, the jagged mountains thrust steeply upwards from their water depths. Shear, steep walls reached from the sea, forming the exposed sides of tall mountains of black. Heavy metamorphosis had created a hard stone whose basic color was black, but great swirls of schist and other multicolored rock created giant flow patterns in the exposed rock, forming great loops and twists of oranges, reds, and yellows. Here and there, great swatches of green olivine merged with darker hornblende and black dikes of long cooled volcanic flows. The overall characteristics were sheer walls interlaced with colorful swirls and loops. The area had once been heavily glaciated, and the typical "U" shaped valleys appeared all around. Always the exposed rock faces were layered with blended colors. Mindi now realized how fitting the colored zig-zag patterns were to their land.

"But where was the port?" she wondered, realizing suddenly the obvious problem. She had not long to wonder, for around a large out thrust black arm lay their port city. Many gasps filled the air when they entered the flow path into Cuicatlan.

The dwarves were the Master Builders. Cuicatlan was a stunning example of their handiwork. The city was cradled between steep walls of two mountains. Here a semi U-shaped valley met the sea sharply. This being the nearest thing to flat land, the dwarves had long ago turned such ruggedness into a serviceable port. Seaward, standing like lone sentinels guarding the sea lanes, stood two rows of massive black towers, each filled with many patterns of colored swirls. They rose some twenty feet above the water's surface and were at least six feet in diameter, spaced uniformly six feet apart, and ran in a straight line seaward. These served as a storm breaker.

The Lucky Lady turned to starboard and followed the long lines of marching towers inward. Before them, the sheer cliffs rose abruptly to great jagged heights, displaying colorful reddish swirls and loops. The valley rose steeply before them. Carved out of the living stone were houses and buildings. Great doors and windows with balconies of stone were everywhere in the narrow valley and climbed a considerable distance up either side. The central area was a maze of stone stairways and paths. All lines of the buildings were precise, with squares of black blocks spaced evenly, like the top of a giant's castle. Stone arches and bridges in midair crossed over the valley, striking off at unusual angles and directions. Everywhere small clouds of smoke curled their way upwards, but no snow had yet fallen here.

Thrusting out to sea were six large stone platforms each ten feet wide, the docks. Cuicatlan could berth and load some two dozen Lucky Lady's at the same time. As they slowly glided inwards, the docks seemed alive with dwarves. All were gaily clad and running about like busy ants. Three large schooners were moored to the southern docks and were being swiftly unloaded by the industrious dwarves. Everywhere dwarves were in action. Slow carts lumbered along filled with grains, crossing dizzily above on the great bridges and crossways.

Now as the Lucky Lady slowly crept alongside of a stone platform, from what appeared to be a guardhouse carved precariously high upon the northern cliff side, a giant deep gong sounded. All the little men paused and a cheer arose. A small welcoming party quickly formed, while the others resumed their tasks. Nache was wild with excitement. He jumped ship and ran to the welcoming gathering.

Presently, ropes as big as a man's fist were cast aboard by stout dwarves on the dock, and the ship was moored. The others quickly joined Nache, but their heads were looking up and around, trying to grasp the magnitude of the city. A fairly plump dwarf, dressed a bit finer than the others, stood by Nache's side as they came up to him.

"Allow me to present Mayo, Mayor of Cuicatlan."

The stout dwarf with a well-combed, grey beard bowed so low, Mindi feared he might topple over. His beard wrapped around his shiny black boots. "Humbly at your service," Mayo said in a deep, throaty voice. "Welcome to Cuicatlan, most honored guests, revered wizards. Saviors of Khorizaba and all Isel. We are deeply honored by your presence. The entire city is completely at your service. You merely have to speak, and it shall be done."

Somewhat taken aback by his sudden overwhelming generosity, everyone fumbled a bit clumsily, but Nache quickly began introducing them. Mindi watched the poor dwarf become completely awestruck, as one by one, Nache presented the company. So when at last she was introduced as his fair Lady, she kissed Mayo's hand and said, "No mayor, it is we who are pleased to be here. We all thank you for your hospitality. We merely need a place to stay briefly and a royal tour." The last brought gleams to the dwarf's eyes.

Then quickly, Mayo sent a number of dwarves to tote their gear to the way house, where he had rooms prepared. Several others assisted the Mariners' in unloading the ponies and took them to the stables. While royally, Mayo led the small procession on the paved, cobblestone roadway up from the docks. As they walked, Mayo apologized if anything seemed rushed; he had only received the light signal this morning. Nache quickly explained that in the mountains, signal messages were sent by reflecting sunlight off a polished silver mirror. Very fast communication.

The streets were made of highly metamorphic stone cut into paving blocks; once above the wide hemispherical docks, the road narrowed and ducked under an oblique course way perched high upon tall towers; it stretched across the whole valley on trestles. As they began the climb up toward the end of the valley, more and more bridges zigged and zagged across the space above them in a myriad of trestles—each one, each block, cut to an engineer's precision.

Steadily upwards, they climbed; each stone step was as precise as the last and at an easy height to handle on foot. Nearby were smooth ramps for carts; the smooth floors of the bridges were scoured every foot, presumably so the ponies' feet could have traction. At last, the valley came to an abrupt end. Now it rose very steeply for a thousand sheer feet. Twisting and turning, a stone step-way led upwards. At frequent intervals, some twenty-five feet apart, were large platforms carved out of the rock face. Nache explained that each had a large crane on it. Thus, cargo could be raised or lowered a step at a time, serving as an elevator should.

On either side, black walls of stone rose to great heights, but carved into the stone walls were houses! Windows opened uniformly in the shiny, black walls, flared here by twists of green and orange granite globules.

"Our way," pointed Nache; some gasped. He indicated a steep winding stairs off to the right; the end was not in sight.

"Must we," implored Hildaro, a bit reluctantly.

"The view is worth it," came the reply, though not unexpected.

Mayo led the way, followed by Nache. Those two scampered up the steps like mountain goats, but the others, considerably more reserved, lagged behind. Finally, the two slowed their pace to match the others.

"Don't look down," Marc suggested to Hildaro. A grunt came in reply.

Twenty effort-filled minutes later, they stood on a platform nearly a thousand feet up the wall of stone. Still, for some four thousand feet above them, the cliff continued. The stone base was actually the veranda of the guesthouse. It overlooked the whole city below, giving a breathtakingly spectacular view. A stone gateway and arch led into a chamber, carved from the living stone itself. After marveling on the view, Mayo led them inside to inspect their quarters.

It was like a jeweled cavern, deep, roomy, and pretty. Small, metal-worked lanterns burned high above and beside the various columns that separated the arches. The ceiling was ten feet overhead. Walls, floor, and ceiling were polished rock, interlaced with marvelous patterns of schist and other swirls. They had turned a cavern into a treasure room. While they were inspecting their quarters, ten puffing dwarves came in with their gear and quickly departed. Mayo, satisfied that he had welcomed them sufficiently, bade them clean up, and when ready for the royal tour, to let him know. He left the company alone in the splendor of the royal guest house.

They found a small stream had been diverted into the end of the room; flowing down through a small hole, it formed a shower. A stone table and intricately carved wooden chairs surrounded the central area by the door. The other end had numerous beds, bunk fashion, with neat ladders going upwards.

Hildaro took Nache aside and asked, "This is really neat, but I fear I'm leery of such heights. Can we not have an easy tour—no steep climbs?"

Nache laughed, and Mindi, who had overheared, said, "Right. I'm pooped, and it is a bit scary out there looking down."

"Sure thing," he replied. "I myself will pick the route, Fair Lady."

Then, they cleaned up after their own fashions. Refusing a shower, Vorag complained bitterly that it had only been days since his last bath. However, he at least washed his face and hands.

While they were so engaged, a large crate was lowered onto their platform. Erving recognized it and announced, "Here we have a change of clothes for all!"

The crate was brought inside and opened. It contained, as the Mariner promised, heavy, warm clothing for all. Ten minutes passed while they sorted it out, matching sizes as best they could. He had acquired heavy, woolen clothes from Ocalla, Burly, and the dwarves. Though not particularly dressy, the clothes were exceedingly warm. In addition, fur lined boots, some parkas, and gloves completed the stock. Erving got a round of applause and thanks well deserved.

Late afternoon here was dark, for the sun sank beyond the mountains early. Undaunted, the company took their grand tour. Most displayed the keenest interest in crossing the many terraced crossways that were like bridges across vast spaces. Mindi said they were thrilling; Hildaro, scary, but neat. Nache explained that these bigger feats had been created in the ancient days of Belwain, the great wizard. Most of their handiwork these days was in maintenance and carving new lodgings for the growing population.

Upon their return, they found that their table had been filled with food. Ale was in readiness for dinner. The mayor joined them, and everyone had his fill and was questioned at length by Mayo, who loved tales as much as Nache. His ears were eager and seemed insatiable. George, Nache, Vorag, and Hildaro delighted in filling his ears.

After dinner, Marc, Mindi, and Elwine stood side by side at the edge of the balcony peering into the abyss. Lights flickered from the multitude of windows on the cliff wall below. Far below, a number of torches dimly illuminated the dock. Small street lamps lit the various paths and stairs. Dreamily, the three stared for some time. Marc recalled how, so many months ago, he had gazed from his balcony at

Bellview, and he felt startled—all this, was it worth it? He mused.

Finally, the elf spoke what was most on their minds. "Here is a beauty like no other. The old songs from ages gone by do not do this place justice. I will have to create some new ones that do. Here is a place of immense beauty—hard toil's reward."

"Yes," they both replied. Later they retired and slept well, except for Hildaro who tossed and turned. He woke in a cold sweat, a fear of falling ever gnawing on his mind. All at once, he realized that the fear came from a picture of a Yellow Obelos. Smiling, he relaxed and slept soundly.

Here in Cuicatlan, days and nights were both early to arrive, and by 7:00 a.m., the city was bustling with activity. The company awoke to the clamor of dutiful toil. Refreshed and eager to continue their journey, they had Nache get things ready for their trek to Tulan. Meanwhile Erving told Shannon that their supplies were in the keeping of one master Boba in Tulan. By afternoon, toting only their parkas, they took the elevator cranes up to the "station" as it was known. The swinging ride up the sheer black face of Borgdad, as the dwarfs referred to it, was breath taking, physically as well as mentally.

Five thousand feet up, they found the "station" was a large cavernous building, constructed of stone with a similar handiwork. Huge arches and columns supported a domed ceiling carved with images of history. From here looking westward, one got a splendid view of the sprawling mountain range. The station was actually on a small mountaintop surrounded by small stone dwellings. Evidently, the cavernous room was a central meeting site; roads ran from it in all directions.

Here they found their ponies were already waiting for them, loaded, and ready to go. A fourth pony had been added, laden with wood logs. "Insurance," Nache notified their curious looks.

The mayor was there to see them off and invited them to return anytime with tales for ears. Around noon, they departed on Baca Road, heading westward, traveling a cobblestone road with large blocks spaced evenly at the edges of the road, like a castle's barbican. The dwarf explained that when the snows came, the road can be found by the blocks, and the snow cleared easily by shovels.

As they walked along the winding road, mountains loomed tall and huge all around them. Far below, creeks in steep gorges thundered and roared. Baca Road was slowly meandering its way around the side of one mountain, joining onto the next one at connecting ridges, while climbing slowly upwards. The odor of pine filled the air; lazy cumulus clouds hung about the higher tops. The dwarves' maintenance of the roadway was immaculate—nary even a stray rock could be found, but they were not alone.

Frequently, they met small companies of dwarves. Heavily clothed, they were coming from the west. Sometimes pony carts accompanied them. They snaked their way around one mountainside; they could see the road going first behind them and then snaking in a great curve around the side of the mountain that they had just passed. Behind them four carts heavily laden with lumber crawled along.

Occasional lookout towers stood high above the road, overseeing everything. There were occasional guardhouses where unwanted travelers could be stopped. Also at particular scenic spots, large balconies had been built. Nache explained that this was the dwarfs' finest roadway. Several places, a deep gorge sliced ravenously down the mountainside. Here the Master Builders had constructed elaborate stone bridges, called Gorzbads, which, made from precision cut blocks from the very mountain gorge it spanned, blended beautifully.

At various places, steep escarpments revealed the nature of the dwarven range. Eons past, silt and gravel had been deposited in layers, and later compressed under terrific pressures and heat. The soft layers underwent a metamorphosis and were converted into a very, hard stone. Later on when the mountains formed, the layered beds were folded in great loops creating the bulbous appearing swirls. Next, glaciers had carved the area exposing nature's beauty. Each escarpment laid bare the ever-changing pattern of colorful folds.

Baca Road was called Khadzbongh, God's Path. It was

justly named, for at irregular intervals the black stone bed crossed folds. The anticlines were especially colorful, for here the road sliced through the exposed layers, and the road's surface appeared banded in a multitude of colors and hues. Nache was constantly pointing out the synclines and anticlines and the great fold bulbs and bends, especially at the escarpments. Indeed, it was Khadzbongh—for at the scenic overlooks, one could gaze for hours at the rainbow mountains, filled with pine at the lower elevations.

They climbed steadily upwards in a shallow but continuous gradient. Every five miles, there was a gordaz or shelter house.

The dwarf explained that at night, these would provide shelter from weather, enemies, or whatever. These stone buildings were bare of fancy trappings, but in a snowstorm or lightning storm, a lifesaver. As they reached the higher elevations, the topography of Khorizaba became clear. Glaciated valleys with trees climbing half way up the steep sides presented a green floor, while far above, jagged cirques thrust their stony teeth skyward. There were multitudes of isolated promontories and hog back ridges. While even higher, cirques contented with saddles in a vast jagged array. Sometimes two gorges nearly met leaving a rugged, stony arete to mark the junction. Yes, it was Khadzbongh.

Finally, the entire range took an eerie, ruddy hue that intrigued one's senses, as the day ended. Nache halted at the next gordaz, which was already beginning to fill up with other travelers. Though toilsome beyond measure by day; by night, the dwarves were light of heart and prone to revel far into the night. Nearly everyone had heard of the coming of the wizards, and being honored by their presence, rightly insisted on parties in their honor. Fire, ale, and tale were the dwarf bywords to happiness on an otherwise cold, winter night, and the company quickly became accustomed to the habit, though they did tire of repeating the same tale.

On the second day on Baca Road, they crossed the timberline. The heavy snows had not yet fallen this far east, but were due any time. Here light snow had fallen and stood two inches deep already. Green and brown gnarled trees, floored in a white powder with colorful boulders protruding, lined the road side, while just above, the trees disappeared. Tough, scraggy bushes, only inches high, although many feet wide, took their place, occasionally protruding a dark, greenish hue above the snow. When pressed, Nache advised that by January, the mountains here would have a blanket of snow some twelve feet thick, while nearer Tulan, twenty. How much in the Mazatlan ahead, no one got a word from him.

All was going extremely well on the God's Path; they made good time.

"Very efficient, these dwarves," was Malazar's statement.

By the fifth day out from the port, the dawn came cold and grey. Dark clouds hung engulfing the higher more distant peaks. The road now was meandering across saddles between peaks, going down small troughs, and circumscribing deep, rugged cirques. Occasionally, far below these steep walled cliffs, small, blue iced tarns could be seen. These lakes would be surrounded by thriving patches of greenery in summer time. Now it stared deep blue with cold.

Nache only said, "Today snows come, overdue actually." Each was left with his own interpretation of his meaning.

Chapter XXVI—Khorizaba, Land of Snow and Ice

The winds picked up, hurling icy blasts that, no matter how tightly one clasped his parka shut, always seemed to find a way to seep in, chilling to the bone. Bent nearly double, the dwarf urged them onwards, for they still had two miles to go to the next gordaz. Without warning, the snow came—a blinding sheet of white flakes. At once, visibility shrank to nearly zero. Nache halted the party. While they stood with their backs to the blizzard, he quickly got ropes out of the pack, and awkwardly in his huge mittens, tied each person to the next. Yelling as loud as he could, though barely audible above the howling, raging winds, urged everyone forward.

The going was turtle fashion. Slipping, now falling, bent always nearly double, they pushed onward into the teeth of the storm. Snow drifted and began to form large mounds. It rapidly became exceedingly fatiguing to go forward. Those unused to such cold and wind began to desire to lie down and sleep through the storm. Nache yelled repeatedly, urging them to their feet.

Then, Drifter and Marc realized what was happening and even louder urged them forward. After an effort-filled hour, they finally reached the gordaz. Everyone stumbled inside. It was dark and cold but a tremendous relief to the raging blizzard outside. Quickly Malazar held his staff aloft and created a blue blaze. The windowless room was empty save themselves. Quickly Marc and Mindi issued the torches from Metro, and a dull, yellow light filled the room. Nache quickly retrieved some wood from the store bin, and adding some kindling they'd brought, soon had a welcome, though smoky, blaze going.

"Now we wait," explained Nache. "Eventually, the snow will end."

"Do we go on then," inquired Hildaro, unused to snow.

Nache hemmed and hawed and rested his weight first

on one foot and then the other, before he finally replied, "Well, we shall see."

He didn't want to startle them needlessly. Dwarves were always prepared, but, well, sometimes when the road was totally buried under snow, it would be a while before one could just "go" again. This he kept to himself. However, Drifter understood or had guessed, and he alone kept insisting that some measures of food conversation be implemented. With full bellies and nothing to do, they lay down and slept or dozed, while all around them the outside wilderness raged in the snowy blizzard. Time passed slowly amid the constant roar of wind. Occasionally, Drifter would pace to the door, open it a crack, and peer outside. In such a manner, he discovered night had come along with a flurry of in-rushing cold and snow.

Many hours later, the dull roar subsided, replaced now by periods of stillness followed by great, sweeping rushes of wind. When Drifter peered out this time, a blinding, white light flooded in along with the cold. "Storms over; it's day," he announced, through it was obvious to everyone.

They struggled to their feet, tightened all their clothes, donned their furry mittens, and together attempted to file outside for a look. The door naturally opened inwards. However, they did not go far. A three-foot wall of snow was now in front of the door. Blinding whiteness was everywhere. Many grumbles followed.

Elwine said, "Okay, you guys, it's elf time again. Let me go take a look see."

To their amazement, he stepped lightly on top of the drift and quickly strode off, barely leaving a footprint. The others commented on this for some time, wondering how he managed this.

Presently, Elwine returned smiling and singing. "Oh it's pretty outside. Yes indeed."

"Well, tell us what's up," grim faced Drifter demanded.

"Oh well, there's certainly a lot of snow! The road's gone—buried I'd say. A couple of places a mile off you can see it cropping out of drifts. This whole area here is probably buried by four feet."

The news was disheartening to all, and they shut the

door and sat down beside the fire.

Nache began cheerfully, "Never fear. Dwarf is here! This is expected. It is why we have frequent shelter houses. Each one has a storeroom, see," and he showed them a clever, stone door that opened. "We have enough food in here for at least two weeks and firewood as well, though it's best to keep some in reserve. Seldom does anyone get stranded that long. Usually it's just a matter of days. Dwarves are always at work. Even now, the road crews will be busy shoveling off the road. It is only four feet. Now when the January snows hit, it can be ten feet at one time! So take heart. Who wants to shovel first?"

From the storeroom carved deep into the mountainside, he produced four shovels, each just the right size to be pushed through the gaps between the edge blocks along the road. Drifter, Vorag, George, and Nache went outside to begin. Elwine went as well to watch. Presently, he told Nache that, at the house across the valley, ten dwarves were busily shoveling. The others took heart at this and began shoveling in earnest. Soon they were panting and were sweating heavily. Over their protests, the dwarf took them indoors at once. After they caught their breath, he explained.

"At this altitude and in this cold, one does not work so strenuously. Heavy sweating can be dangerous, and the intense cold will harm lungs that are unused to such labor. You must go slow and easy."

They then tramped out once more. Later, they switched off, and others took their place.

By nightfall, the large, open area around the shelter house had been cleared as well as part of the roadway toward Tulan, about one eighth of a mile. After a sound sleep, snow removal began anew. The sky was clear, and the sun shone brightly illuminating an intensely still, soundless, white world. Only the scraping sounds of shovels broke the stillness.

On the third day, Drifter and crew ran into four dwarves coming from the next gordaz. They hailed, cheered, and shook hands, and each group returned to get his companions. After restocking their pony's supply of firewood, they continued their journey. They made the next house before nightfall and shared it with a dozen dwarves. The little folk proved full of energy and were eager for partying and tales. Mindi was glad that they had been snowbound by themselves!

On the sixth day, a new sound greeted their ears. The alpine stillness was now broken by a distant, low rumble—a roaring sound.

"The mighty Baca," Nache cried! "You can hear her song from afar."

Two hours later, the road traversed a steep escarpment and rounded a ridge. Below them, a steep, rugged gorge fell sharply for four thousand feet. Rushing foaming white in a loud endless roar flowed the Baca. The opposite side was just as steep and rugged. The sight was breathtaking.

"Aesthetic beyond measure," pronounced Elwine.

The road snaked its way precariously around the side of the ridge. The road was carved out of the ridge side, but the ridge proceeded another thousand feet on up. Cradled against the sheer side, the road picked its way for a quarter mile to a large, shelter house. Then came the bridge, Bacazdan! On either side, two towering, black, stone archways held the huge, long bridge in suspension across the deep chasm below. The suspension wires were as thick as a man's head, and at either end, disappeared far underground, held tightly. Smaller wires hung vertically, like harp strings, supporting a planked, roadbed.

Hildaro was relieved, when he spotted the large, thick, guard rail. The great bridge, like its sister across the Yaca river, was nearly a half mile long. Dwarves, like tiny crawling dots, were going across in either direction. The company spent an entire hour crossing very slowly, trying to capture all the splendid scene in their memories. They spent the night at the next gordaz beyond the bridge with the roar of the Baca in their ears, for Nache said from here they'd easily make Tulan the following day, only fifteen more miles.

Day broke bright and clear with only a few, scattered, high cirrus clouds in the deep blue sky. They left the gordaz and continued along road, which began its slow descent, curving in a great arc about the middle of the small, domed cliff. As they rounded the northern edge, Nache cried, "Behold, Cidthorn, the northern mountain of Tulan."

Tall and barren, the snow-capped, fourteen thousand foot peak loomed ahead across a wide valley. They descended through the timberline once more and passed the next way house, continuing to curve around the dome. Distant Tulan appeared below them, with Althorn towering over fourteen thousand feet just beyond.

The dwarf capital, Tulan, city of the Three Peaks, was cradled in a twelve thousand foot, alpine valley, surrounded by the towering peaks that forced the Yaca and Baca rivers to merge between Althorn and Blithorn, forming the Kanandrul river that flowed southward to the distant sea. As they descended, the folds became more pronounced. Now the roadbed cut across anticlines and synclines regularly. The black roadbed became continuously banded in gay colors, mostly reds, yellows, and greens. It sloped down from the heights into the snow-covered pine valley. Bordering each river were the remains of once large domes now eroded by the rivers. They formed a continuous chain of saddles some thirteen thousand feet tall and created a V-shape where the rivers joined. Nestled snugly within the V was Tulan.

As the company descended into the valley, Tulan spread before their feet, a sprawling alpine city. Every building was made of stone from the surrounding mountainsides; the stratigraphy of the blocks formed great zig-zags of contrasting colors. Most stone buildings were capped with arched domes, adding to the unusual visual display. Additionally, the dwarves never seemed to build a straight road! Typical dwarven-style, stone lined, paved roads ran bewildering curved courses in an endless array of directions, seemingly without any form. And the arches—oh the great archways and trestles. Dwarves delighted in their construction, and every imaginable place, every conceivable spot and direction was filled with archways and great trellises supporting oblique causeways, striking at various angles horizontally and vertically. It was a three dimensional city of domes, arches, elevated roadways, and winding streets.

Everywhere, dwarves in gay-colored, zig-zag parkas busily scampered—some pulling carts straining upon the elevated causeways. Tulan was bustling with typical dwarven activity. Down into the city of myriad colors, hues, arches, domes, roadbeds and elevated byways, the company slowly passed, trying to comprehend the creation of the Master Builders.

And gaily colored in similar fashion, towering far above the city, stood Obelos Khander.

Presently, a gong resounded somewhere near the center of the city. Instantly, the multitude of dwarves stopped and began cheering. Nache saw the welcoming party coming forward to meet them. For the dwarf, it was a triumphant homecoming—such seldom, if ever, occurred in Khorizaba. They halted.

Mayor Dorin was a stocky, plump dwarf with very grey hair and beard, rather old looking. He stepped forward. In as formal a manner as he could muster for the occasion, he solemnly began. "I am Mayor Dorin of Tulan. On behalf of all dwarves in our land, it is my honor and duty to welcome you to our capitol. Welcome and great honor to the saviors of Isel."

With a keen glance and twinkle in his eye, he added, "And perhaps the return of the Mizzinti. For greatest of deeds in recorded history have you undertaken and completed. For us, it is, therefore, with the greatest of honor and pride that we welcome you to Tulan. And it is altogether fitting and proper that we give thee the honor due. There shall be a great celebration on the Diorn, the winter festival, in two days. Aaron is scheduled to arrive by then as well. Until then, may I present to you the key to the city?"

He turned to one of his aids, who nervously produced a golden key. Dorin looked at the troop and quickly handed the key to Nache, who graciously accepted it.

Nache asked the mayor where they were to stay and where the crates Erving had sent were located. Dwarven efficiency prevailed once more, for the cargo was already awaiting them at the large-people guesthouse, and two runners were dispatched to get the last minute touches complete. Dorin proudly led the company down the zig-zagging streets. In the center of Tulan not far from the obelos, he halted before what might have been called either a small castle or a hotel. It was a huge, stone building whose construction was carefully done so as to produce zig-zag striped bands of colors up its sides. Every window opening had protruding arches, and the doors were heavy, ironwork and appeared strong enough to withstand a siege. Parts of its roof made a viewing balcony. The company could each have ten rooms apiece, if desired!

Once inside, they found that a huge hallway led into a cavernous, square, meeting room. Private rooms surrounded the square—three stories worth. In the center stood a huge oak table capable of serving twenty at once. Food was already prepared, and no one complained, as it was past lunchtime. There was nothing to be done, except enjoy the hospitality, which they did.

Now, the awe and mystique that the dwarves associated with this remarkable group of wizards was made complete by Oran. The grey mastiff stood as tall as the dwarves. As the party entered and passed by their smiling, big eyed hosts, Oran began sniffing them. In fact, Oran was immensely curious, for here he had found a whole city of the little folk. He wondered if they played well; they were a good size to playfully pounce. One poor befuddled dwarf had been backed into a corner and was shaking in his pants as Oran sniffed him and offered his paw.

Nache saw the little man's plight and called, "Oran, over here boy. Lunch is served; come here."

To the growing wonder of the little man and Vorag as well, Oran in four great leaps bounded to Nache, who deftly diverted his arrival to the bench. With forepaws propped on the oak table, face hungrily looking down at his empty plate, Oran looked so comical that everyone roared.

Secretly, everyone welcomed the delay; one adventure in the snow was sufficient. The journey ahead was not particularly appealing, save perhaps to the dwarf. After the lunch, the company chose rooms and settled down to examine the gear Erving had acquired for them. The afternoon was spent opening crate after crate, sorting and identifying the items. Included was gear sufficient for an expedition: heavy, fur lined boots with an inner shoe, cramp irons for ice, ice axes and picks, coils and shanks of various ropes, hammers, pitons, carabineers, slings, and mittens. The list went on and on. Shannon marveled; his friend had been painstakingly thorough. Beyond provisions, little had been left for chance. Nache calculated at least two more ponies would be needed, and the others concurred.

The following day was spent in a grand tour of Tulan and in acquiring the necessary provisions.

Just after dark that night, the group gathered on the observation roof of their gigantic, guesthouse. Ominous and close loomed the dark masses of Tulan's three mountains. The air, filled with the distant rumble of cascading white water of the Yaca and Baca rivers, felt cold, clean, and scented with pine. Here the stars seemed to fall from the heavens and touch gently the bulky peaks. Towering like a huge, fingered rock, the dwarf obelos rose among multitudes of stone dwellings and elevated crossways; the obelos protruded skyward, in challenge to the more distant peaks.

The next day Aaron was scheduled to arrive, along with the celebration of Diorn, the winter festival. Preparations for the largest holiday of the dwarves had been under way since November. Each year, just after the first heavy snows halted much of the construction industry, the little people would prepare for their grand festivities. Included were feasting, merrymaking, sharing of small presents, and honoring deeds accomplished both great and small. In general, it was a time to share a year of successes that they had had.

Shortly after dawn on Diorn Day, a deep metallic gong sounded; echoes reverberated. Soon smaller gongs heralded the arrival of Aaron and army. Mindi watched for a while from the great balcony; lines upon lines of the silver clad warriors marched gaily and proudly into the city. Though tired and weary, they were cheerful at having made it back on time. Bongs, cheers, and general merrymaking filled the air, as dwarves everywhere took to streets and inns in a day of fun.

Around noon, Dorin and a large group entered the guest hall and quickly converted it into a meeting place. Dorin ushered the surprised guests to the oaken table. They found themselves seated upon the table. In front, dwarves packed the hall—elbow-to-elbow—all straining to see the company. At last, the mayor began the meeting.

Aaron was introduced and gave a general report of the army's deeds; catcalls of oohs and ahs were interspersed with cheers and hurrahs, but an awkward silence fell when he told the tale about the mysterious, trumpet blaring in the night that ended with the destruction of their northern foes. Seeing the opportunity, Nache stood upon the table, and with wild delight and a few, little exaggerations, related the passing of the grey army—to everyone's obvious delight. There were roars, cheers, and tumultuous applause when he finished. It ended only when the company took a bow.

More ceremonies followed, but Malazar had the final chilling word, "Dwarves. Dwarves. Though you believe that the great deeds have ended your foes, do not yet count the war ended. It was just a battle. Kahill still lives, though for a while he remains confined within the Quad. Still, spring may not be rosy, if we sit all winter! There is more to be done, if we are to be free peoples, much more; perhaps the worst yet."

His words, though true, greatly sobered the festivities. A hush resulted, broken only by faint whisperings.

But to everyone's surprise, he added, "However, you are right—great deeds have been done and deserve to be acknowledged. Tonight when the quarter moon zeniths, I myself, with your wizard's aid, shall create fiery works to light your sky!"

Thunderous applause and wild yelling spontaneously broke out; for the dwarves knew Malazar, and many could recall fireworks of his design set off years ago. Jubilantly the meeting disbanded, and the company split into groups for tours and fun. Drifter, known as the White Ranger in these parts, took Elwine, Marc, Mindi, and Hildaro to visit some of his dwarf friends. The others went with the mayor for a royal tour and drinking, but it was an excited Nache, who led the old wizard through the curving streets to his obelos.

For an hour that night, the dwarf obelos was activated. Glowing swirling colors caught the eye below, while from above, Malazar caused giant, fiery blasts that briefly vied with the starry heavens in glory.

Then, the company retired. They were to leave the next

morning for Malatzan, a smaller village just across the Yaca river where the God's highway ended. Here westward trails began.

Dawn came cold and grey. Another storm was brewing, as the company gathered their gear and packed the ponies, now six in all. Few were up early; most slept in from the night's gaiety. Unceremoniously, the company left Tulan heading westward on the last of the well-built dwarven roads. The road followed the curves of the great cliffs that channeled the Yaca river. Before noon, they rounded the last great escarpment and crossed the sister bridge, Yacazdan. She was an almost perfect duplicate of Bacazdan. Five miles beyond, cradled in a small valley north of Althorn mountains, lay the small village of Malatzan—most of whose residents were still in Tulan.

Now the sky grew ominous; snow threatened. The cold blasts of wind increased in force and blew continuously from the west-northwest. At the edge of the quaint village, Nache pointed out their path.

A faint trace of a path could be seen snaking its way narrowly along the distant mountainside. The peaks were rugged and snow-clad with patches of barren rock still protruding. Below, but right at the tree line, the small line of their path could be discerned. As they gazed gloomily into the chilling winds, the first snowflakes fell. The next village lay ten miles ahead, but Drifter convinced them to ride the storm out in town before trying the path. They took shelter in the village hall.

Though not much larger than the small shelter houses on the main highway, it was cozy enough and comfortable. Outside the December blizzard raged all that day and on into the next. At last, with flakes still sprinkling down and under a grey sky, the company bundled up and began the trudge. No need waiting to clear the snow. It didn't occur here until spring. In fact, these outlying villages usually became snowbound by January; only the hardiest and most pressing needs would drive anyone to travel during the heavy snow months of January and February—during which time, only the main highway from the port was open.

Elwine alone had no great difficulties in the deep snow, for elves are light of foot. The others gathered behind Nache and Vorag who blazed the trail with considerable effort, plowing through the four-foot drifts. Hildaro never ceased marveling how able his dwarf friend was at picking out the trail buried under the thick white blanket. By noon, the cloud cover broke, and the white became nearly blinding. Snow goggles were issued. They strained onwards; by nightfall, they had covered a painful ten miles. They found the shelter house very inviting.

For the next ten days, they fought the growing cold, snow, and fatigue. The mileage covered varied greatly, because Nache endeavored to always end the day at the next village. Painfully slowly, they meandered their way across the land of towering, jagged cirques, sharp aretes and hogbacks. Always the trail was deftly chosen to avoid the steep escarpments with only a gradually increase in altitude. Sometimes, the path even crossed a glacier. It was a world of cold stone, snow, and ice. The winds blew relatively uniformly into their faces from the west. Try as they might, it continued to chill them. Conversation ebbed, and few words were spoken. Everyone was lost in the continuous plodding effort to make forward progress.

The tenth day brought snow once again. For two days, the sky dumped a deluge of the white powder upon the already snow-covered lands. When they resumed their journey, they found the going even more difficult. At times, the snow drifts were so tall that snowshoes were needed, being the only way to traverse the growing obstacles. After fifteen days out, they reached Bizzdan, a tiny village, which was the westernmost, dwarven village. Only fifty dwarves lived here. It was a barren desolate area, seldom traveled even in good weather. For the dwarves, it was far from homes.

Yet in ages gone by, it had been a prosperous region, but the harshness of the environment gradually forced all but the hardiest to seek an easier life eastward. For here, the snow could reach depths of fifty feet. Some of the taller peaks were snow-capped year round. While the blizzard raged outside, the others snuggled together inside, keeping warm and discussing the next phase of the journey. It had all the promise to be even worse. Even Nache did not deny it. Yet, Malazar drove them on, forever remarking about the Orb and time being precious.

The dwarf and wizard discussed the way ahead for hours. Nache calculated it would only be fifty miles as the crow flies, but maybe a hundred on foot. There were no known trails; one goof could spell long delays, if not disaster, should their supplies run out. Hence, there was much discussion and careful planning during the next two blizzard days.

In late December, they left the last shelter house for the unknown wilds. Poor Nache had only been in this area once. He carefully guided the company—now snow-shoed, roped together, and using ice picks constantly. They established a camp early, being their first in the open wilderness.

The tents were pitched, and such wood was gathered as could be found. It was bitterly cold and harsh, yet endurable if you could get enough clothes on and were careful.

That night, Nache came to Mindi and took her to a corner of the tent. He seemed awfully fidgety, quite disturbed. She instantly recognized something was wrong, and when they were as alone as possible, she put her arm around the little man and said softly and reassuringly, "Tell me about it, Nache."

Falteringly at first, not knowing or having just the right words, he described his plight. "Remember that spiny arete back a ways? Well I came here once long ago, but I went south back there, not west. I'm supposed to guide, but I haven't ever been here. And one slip, one tiny slip spells doom for us all. I don't even know the way."

He paused looking searchingly into her pale face. She knew that he had not really defined his trouble yet and coached him, "Yes, go on."

"Well, as we climbed beyond that spine—well, it's like I—oh, ah, well—the snowy land faded from my eyes—sort of. I kept dreaming or so I thought. I'd see pictures of these mountains in all sorts of seasons. There was even a path there too. All sorts of jumbled pictures. I saw them several times along the way—they were trying to get me to follow them. I resisted them, but somehow I kept ending up following them.

This could be terrible. Where do they come from? Am I going crazy? Is all lost already? I'm confused—and then that eerie, haunting melody came. I got snatches of some poem—an epic I think. But one part kept rolling over and over in my head."

She looked fascinated; so he continued, at first speaking the words. Then, he sang the haunting melody once through as well.

> In the lands of snow and ice,
> Snow-capped domes and pillowed vales,
> With frosty beard and frozen toes,
> Tramping, dragging, crawling goes,
> In the land of ice and snow.
> In the land of snow and ice,
> At heart's loss and hope's depart,
> Cast thine eyes upon Kazander's height,
> And keep him ever upon thy right,
> In the land of ice and snow.

"What does all this mean? Am I going nuts? Have I cracked under the pressure so soon? Or can it be—are they real? Is it real? Am I here or there or here and when or how?" His voice trailed into a bewildered silence.

She began slowly in reply, soothing his head and back, "Relax my little one. In truth, you are our only guide. We all implicitly trust your guidance. Mental pictures exist, of that I'm sure. Sometimes their meaning is not clear until one looks more closely. Only a fool, Nache, would attempt to tell you if they are true or not. I shall not. But close your eyes and take a closer look. Are they yours? Did you make the pictures? Remember one point: a thing is true for you only if you have observed that it is so. Always, trust yourself. If you have at another time been this way and can now in the hour of need recall the path and are certain of it, why doubt it? Use what you know—feel to be true. We cannot ask more of you."

For an hour, the pair sat silent, the little man cradled in her arms. Finally, his mind's webs were torn, and he smiled and said, "Thanks. However, it is or was, I do know the way. I shall not err."

For the next ten, pitifully, slow days they fought their

way, foot by foot, around canyons, gorges, and endless hogbacks and aretes. The brief and only relief from the deep snow was the crossing of the saddles between domed peaks. Here increasing winds cleared the rock of its white burden. The days seemed long and filled with an endless toil; day by day, they grew closer to their goal. Nache was forever darting back and forth for a better view; always he kept the highest far-off peak, the tallest in the Mazatlan range, Kazander, always on his right. As luck or fate would have it, there always was a possible pathway through the endless cirques and gorges. Progress was always forward; luckily they never did have to retrace their steps, having come into the basin of some towering cirque.

Nevertheless, the journey took its toll in weary limbs and provisions. By the tenth day, dry firewood was running very low and food likewise, but Kazander loomed tall and massive before them. It was late afternoon, and storm clouds were again gathering. They hastily made a camp, setting large stones on the edges of their tents, in case the wind became too strong. Several members assisted Nache in gathering pine branches. In fact, they spent three hours doing so, for Nache felt it was crucial to have a large supply for the storm. Darkness fell sharply when the last group returned with great loads of wood.

The camp was cradled against a sheer escarpment bounded on each end by large rocky boulders open only to the east. They were, in fact, on the east side of Kazander at nearly fourteen thousand feet; yet the craggy peak rose more than two thousand feet above them. Being above the tree line, wood had been scarce. A small fire kept the small hole considerably warmer than the surroundings, but food was scarce.

The elf finally protested the scanty food, "This is ridiculous! Come on Vorag; bring Oran; let's get something reasonable!"

The two heavily clad men lumbered off into the gloom. Above the wind, far off howls and jackal cries were audible. The others stared at the fire and watched the first snowflakes fall. Malazar was the first to notice the change, "Hey, the beasts are silent! Something is up out there. It was a dumb move letting those two wander off. If the blizzard comes before they get back, they'll be frozen stiff."

Hardly had he gotten a search party ready, when the hills echoed with a horn blast. "That'll be Vorag. Come on."

With his wizard's staff blazing yellow, the small rescue party could see well enough for Drifter to track the pair across the snows. After going barely one thousand yards, they abruptly halted. Before them puffing heavily came Vorag sinking in over his waist in the snowfield, while beside him tugging at him was Elwine and Oran. The great hunter had a small deer draped across his shoulders.

At their sight, he yelled, "Hail, musteth we doeth all the work? Giveth us a hand."

He puffed and unslung the deer off his huge frame. Food. They needed no other coaching. Within a few minutes in a makeshift spit, the deer was being slowly roasted before eager eyes. Hungrily and hurriedly they ate, for the blizzard had already begun. Then, stocking the fire, they divided the remainder of the deer and other goods, and crawled into the three tents. The wind howled and swirled around their hole, and snow fell, flew, and piled all that night and through the next day. The crackle of their fire could scarcely be heard above the winds roar and whine. Biting cold filtered through the canvas walls, and everyone huddled into a mass of bodies, each keeping the others warm. Some slept, some dreamed, and slowly the hours drifted by.

By the dawn of the second day, the last log had been cast on the fire, and anxious watchers gazed skyward. Finally, a tiny strip of blue marked a change in the weather. By noon, all were cheering; the sun had come at last, and they were alive, although their tents were nearly buried, and the poor ponies were nearly frozen. As a first action, the camp was cleared of the snow blanket, and ponies warmed. Then, a search for wood was organized. Darkfall brought twelve loads of wood and another deer. Rather cheerfully, the group ate heartily in the fire light, while the stars shone brightly overhead. Now their thoughts were ever bent on finding the mine and getting on with the job.

Chapter XXVII—Over Peaks and Under

The air, crisp and clear, was bitterly cold. The stillness was unearthly; no sound could be heard except the harsh exhaling and frosty breaths. The rugged stone mountains lay subdued in rounded, blinding white mounds that forced the use of dark goggles. Eleven figures stood motionless, viewing the eerie, silent, white world. In front, several miles distant, towered the massive dome mountain, Kazander, the highest peak in Khorizaba. Between them lay a wide, slowly rising sea of white snow. To either side of the peak were two gigantic cirques, deep vertical bowls sliced from the very rock itself. Bluish ice appeared at scattered intervals, nearly half way down the distant cirque—a reminder of the glaciers that remained, year after year, slowly cutting away at the mountain. A pair of saddles dropped gracefully downward to smaller peaks on either side of Kazander.

January was arriving, bringing with it the heavy snow. The field before them was twenty feet thick. Movement was difficult even with snowshoes. However, their provisions were holding out, even if firewood wasn't. Day by day, the temperature decreased, and now frostbite was becoming an increasing problem. At these higher elevations, both fresh meat and firewood were scarce, but they were in the area of the lost dwarf mine and were hopeful, though the terrific reality of finding a small entrance somewhere ahead, probably buried under snow, had not made its impression yet, except upon two.

Malazar and Nache were conferring on the next stage. As the little man, stamping his cold feet and rubbing his gloves, spoke, large white frost clouds surrounded his face.

"Well, Malazar, now what? Here we are. Ahead lies the general area on the old map. Now what? Which way?" He was eager to get on with some action, and the dwarf found Malazar rather perplexed—his polite way of saying that his friend seemed quite troubled by something.

"Patience, my dwarf. It is cold, and I'm trying to think,"

he grumbled. "It lies ahead, but I have a growing fear of what unknown lies ahead. A strange foreboding. I, Malazar, am scared—well, just a bit," he added hastily. "The map was in large relief; no small details were on it, right?"

"Yes, just the general area," Nache replied, recalling the ancient map he'd committed to memory.

"Well, we must get closer and search the area."

"Yes, but how? Where? If it's under twenty feet of snow, then what? Wait till spring?" the dwarf complained.

"Oh I don't know. We must, we must—darn it—the Orb—why did it—well we must. It has to be here; it has to be there. It just has to." The wizard seemed to be slipping away from the present time, drifting in thought to another time and place.

"Malazar," the dwarf was tugging on the wizards arm, "Malazar, please, please. How are we going to find it? Which way do we go? Malazar!"

"Huh, yes. Well we must get closer." After a pause, the wizard said, "It would be stupid to build a door in the cirque's area; glaciers, avalanches, what have you, would easily shut it forever. It must be ahead on the side of the mountain. Let's make for the right cirque side," the wizard pointed.

The dwarf became rigid. "But, that would mean having the peak on the left! I don't want to do that," he pleaded, remembering the "Snow and Ice" poem he had followed so far.

"Well, then why ask me?" Malazar snapped angrily and complainingly.

Nache held his ground and led the others towards the left cirque side, keeping Kazander always on the right. He told Mindi about how grouchy and ill-tempered the wizard had become. She was aware of it also, but offered no explanation.

The ascent of the snowfield began eagerly but ended two steps later. Gently blanketed in downy, white, soft, cold flakes, the snowfield was over twenty feet deep. Drifter, who took the two steps forward, ended his second step engulfed in snow up to his waist. Though the blanket was only three hundred feet across at this point, it took nearly five hours to pass. The bigger men in snowshoes tromped and stomped a trail, packing the powdery flakes into a denser form that would support some weight. Finally, they had a channel way made, and the company walked single file through this tiny channel, leading the ponies. It was two feet wide with sides over four feet—so much had it compacted. Still the ponies hooves were forever poking through, and it took a good deal of effort and prodding to cross the snowfield.

From here, it was only a short, easy climb up the long, stony saddle. When they reached the top, they were dismayed. Instead of being right upon Kazander's mountainside, there was yet another valley below and another climb beyond, but the valley was very curious. It was exceedingly deep and had a thick pine forest growing in the lower ranges. It was maybe two miles in diameter, fairly circular in shape.

Elwine's comments brought sighs of relief, "Hey, there are animals down there: sheep, deer, and elk. It's a natural shelter place. No lack of food and wood here!"

They were close to the huge peak and could clearly see the lay of the land. Like an immense tongue, the mountain sloped downward towards them. To either side of the great, twin cirques, gaping, steep-sided glaciers filled chasms, slicing the sides of the mountain. From the right cirque, the land fell sharply into a maze of aretes and steep sided, river valleys. But to the left, just beyond the talus slopes of the cirque, the ground basined deeply, supporting trees and larger wildlife. They were standing on the long sloping tongue, which if they stayed on it, led slowly upwards to the craggy domed peak.

Picking his way carefully along what seemed to be a convenient passageway that was cleared of snow by the heavy winds whipping up over the lip of the hill, Nache felt a growing eerie feeling. This was all somehow very familiar. He felt he had been here many times before. The path he found was more like a roadway for carts! It did not lose any altitude and circumscribed a wide arc around the forest basin below. As the others were marveling over how lucky they were on finding such as easy passageway, Nache suddenly cried aloud.

"There! There! Look there!" he pointed wildly.

Nestled just below them in the shelter of the trees was a town. A ghost town, long abandoned.

But the stone block structures were definitely of

dwarven origin, and Nache fairly ran down the cart side road to the town. There were some twenty ancient structures, each adjoining the others, cradled together in the wilderness. As the group explored the town, Marc could scarcely believe his senses. Here was a whole town in perfect order. Walls, doors, windows, streets—all were like the day they were made, virtually no decay, save occasional lichens that had begun growing on the walls. But no people—not any trace. Very dusty tables were inside, weak with age and dry rot.

Here they made their base camp. Marc pointed out that with a good, sheltered, base camp, they could daily explore far and wide, yet still have a nice shelter, warm and snug, to which to return. After freezing nights in the tents, no one disagreed. With a new relish, the group industriously made themselves at home. Some gathered firewood and others, fresh venison. Everyone enjoyed the warmth of their newfound shelter and were quite merry. All except Malazar, who only got grumpier as time passed.

Adding credence to the lost mine theory, the town became a welcome base for the company. The next day, the search for the lost mine was organized. Somewhere nearby, most likely buried under the snow and/or ice, lay a concealed set of doors or a hidden tunnel. But how to find it? In the spring, it would have been a difficult search in the rocky country. Some felt it was hopeless in the winter, but none was ready to give up.

"After all," Marc said, "we can stay here till spring, if need be!"

After daybreak and a hearty round of flatcakes and leftover meat, search parties were organized. Tse Tse, Vorag, and Hildaro took the forest area; it was more familiar ground to them. The other eight broke into four teams and began scouring the mountainous area, but it was dole, sober faces by day's end. Nothing had been seen.

The second day proved equally fruitless save two events. First around noon, Nache had discovered a melted snow area. Further investigation revealed a narrow, twelve inch, air-shaft coming from far underground. The warm air rising out of the top had melted the surrounding snow, but it was only an air-shaft. However, it meant they were close. The second involved Malazar. He had become down right upset. Constantly grumbling, alternating with angry outbursts about the Orb and mine, the others grew uneasy around him. An angry wizard was dangerous. His incessant gloom had lowered the others' emotional tone as well.

The third day of the search, Mindi and Nache went off together. "Nache, we must find the opening today, for the wizard is getting harder to handle."

"Yes, but I don't know where it is," he whined with a lost feeling.

Mindi saw his forlorn face and put her arm around his heavily cloaked shoulders. Together, they silently walked the cart road toward the mountain. Suddenly, she stopped. "Nache, I've got an idea."

"You know where the door is ?" he asked hopefully.

"No, but why not use the skill we already possess?" He looked baffled, and she continued. "Well, you are a Master Builder, right?" He nodded. "Well then, Master Builder, let's play a game. We're walking on a road that you've built. Somewhere before us lies the mine. Now let's say you were going to build a road. It comes from the mine entrance and goes here past the town. Here we are on the road. Where would you build the road to the entrance?"

"Oh, I get it." Catching her idea, he said, "Well for sure, heavy carts prefer level ground—less toil either way. So I'd build it as level as possible, probably veering over that way."

Together they walked around the basin's edge. They continued discussing, pointing, climbing, and scrambling over the snow-clad mountain side, ever drawing nearer to the peak and leftmost cirque. Here and there, they were rewarded to find another piece of the cart path, which the winds had blown free of snow. Confidence grew. Finally, a steep escarpment with swirls of yellow rock rose up towering before them. They veered around this barrier and gained a high spot on top of a large boulder just beyond the edge of the escarpment. Here they halted.

The wide ledge they had followed had petered out. The chasm opened wide in front of them. Falling away beneath their feet, they found themselves on the lower left side of the cirque. Below lay a blue, ice covered form, surrounded by huge and small rock piles—talus from the cirque, which rose like a sheer, jagged wall to the right. The top was nearly two thousand feet above them, blanketed for the most part with snow. So breathtaking was the view that for some minutes neither spoke but merely stared into the vast cirque.

Finally, Nache spoke, "Well, here I wouldn't build a road. See how the crumbling rock litters the floor below? Any road would never last. Landslides would bury or destroy a road here. So I guess it was a nice game but it led us nowhere. Oh well."

Both spirits sank. She'd been so hopeful, but the dwarf was right. No road could go any further. They rested here on the boulder, which was sheltered from the wind and was warmed by the near noon sun. She silently gazed at the majestic panorama, but Nache began to ramble on, speaking of this and that, drifting absentmindedly in and out of the common tongue.

"Oh, Mindi, no! Meina, Kazbad! Kazandaz Ach! Bachdan! Forest and trees, da do da do dah—oh Khartos Kryptos where are your mines of old; mine of old; fair Khartos Kryptos, open your doors to meet the. . ."

Here his voice stopped abruptly! Both heard a low, rumbling sound—a heavy, low-pitched, noise bordering upon a vibration or tremor. It came from behind them near the escarpment. Gradually, it grew louder and now sounded metallic. Startled, they looked blankly at each other. Suddenly, as if they both had the same idea at the same instant, their faces moved into a huge grin.

"Come on," yelled Mindi. The noise stopped. They began a headlong, stumbling run over the snow piles on the road. Rounding the bend, they stopped abruptly, mouths open.

Two gigantic, heavy, metal doors opened from the base of the escarpment; they had pushed both snow and boulders out of the way. A deep, dark hole lay gaping in the wall; warm air rushed out rapidly; and hundreds and hundreds of startled bats swarmed out of their dark home, soaring into the cold heights.

Before either could say a word, a dull thunder began shaking the ground. "Avalanche," screamed Nache, and he instinctively pushed Mindi inside the opening and covered her head. Now growing to a loud ominous roar, snow came cascading down the cirque. Rocks and boulders dislodged and added to the deafening thunder. Then as quickly as it had begun, the roar subsided. The silence of the heights returned.

"You ok?" he asked, as he shook the snow off his clothes.

She did likewise. "Yes, thanks. Let's go see. I hope no one was below!" Together they returned to the boulder and peered into the wake of the avalanche. Tons of snow, ice, and rock had fallen down into the depths of the cirque. Only a little had made it as far as the trees. Quickly, they hurried back down the cart path to the ghost town to find the others. They found the rest had returned before they did, and everyone breathed a sigh of relief when the pair came in. After a quick glance at the others, Nache, wild with excitement, began telling them of the mine.

"Yah hoo!" yelled Vorag, who quickly shut up, remembering the avalanche, though the hills continued to repeat his exclamation for another thirty seconds. They held their breath, but no avalanche came. Then, they jubilantly hurried to the doors and saw for themselves. Nache explained that the doors were voice activated. "You only need speak the name of the mine, and the doors will open. Clever isn't it?"

The others agreed. The rest of the day was spent in transporting their gear from the base camp in the abandoned town up and into the mouth of the mine. Here, they found the dwarves had torches stuck in notches on the sidewalls. Great vats of dirt covered oil still lay about, and for the first time in centuries, the torches of Kryptos blazed, illuminating the outer area of the mine near the door way.

By nightfall, they'd brought up all their gear, along with a goodly store of wood. Surrounded by blazing torches, the company shut the doors and soon found that the mine warmed up to a nice fifty-five degrees! The only problem was the bats. Having made the mine their domicile for hundreds of years, they were not about to be made homeless by the new arrivals. Even worse was the stench from the pile of bat guano!

"This mine needs to be cleaned out!" Hildaro said in jest to the dwarf.

Nache didn't disagree. So they moved their camp deeper into the mine and eventually camped just beyond the piles of guano. The air was fresher here, coming from some unseen shaft far above.

Black and cool was the lost dwarf mine; yet from the frigid outside, the uniform temperature felt warm and welcome. Kryptos had been painstakingly carved in the metamorphic, folded mountains during the time of the great wizards. Everywhere were the signs of the master craftsmen. The walls were square and smooth, highly polished. Apparently, the shafts and tunnels were designed to cut across the folds and swirls of multicolored rock, forming aesthetic patterns. Indeed, the walls were so polished that it was like walking within a jewel box—splendid and breathtaking. The ceiling was ten feet above the floor. As polished as the walls, the ceiling was a perfect arch. Only the floor remained dull, for here carts ruts were worn into the solid bedrock. Nooks were carved at regular intervals in the walls. The decaying torches still angled upwards; though no longer lit, they were silent sentinels of bygone days of splendor. Progress might have been swift indeed, save for two things.

First, everyone walked slowly, studying and admiring the great beauty surrounding them, illuminated by both flaming torches and the chemical torches of Metro. Constant streams of praise, wonder, and excitement issued from the dwarf; the others shared his exuberance. Secondly, the wizard seemed even more troubled. Since entering the mine, Malazar alone had been sober and silent. He and the dwarf along with Marc and Mindi were in the lead. While the trio cheerfully pointed out features and swirls, Malazar remained gloomy for the first quarter mile into the long, straight tunnel.

At the quarter mile point, the entrance tunnel suddenly flared into a large, crossroads room; Cavern Room Number 1 was carved on the wall in dwarf runes. A thousand feet across from them, the tunnel continued. In between, the ceiling rose to a hundred feet. Tall arches and columns grew upwards at regular intervals, and sounds echoed wildly and brilliantly off the polished walls. Striking upwards at oblique angles, vent shafts, nearly one foot in diameter, sliced to the outside world, bringing life-giving air below. On either side of the chamber, side shafts angled their way gradiently downward, and at the rear corners, others went upwards.

Decayed, wooden carts lay neatly piled in the far right corner, and many mining picks, axes, and metal chisels lay in an ordered stockpile. To the left in the flickering light, several piles of ore gleamed, separated by types: gold, silver, iron, copper, and several others. Though no one needed a break, the company instinctively took a break and went exploring in the strange, cavernous room, while Malazar slumped onto a stone bench gloomily.

At last, with delightfully satisfied desires, they were ready to continue. Now the problem of which shaft to follow arose; there were five choices. Nache had felt that straight ahead should be the choice, but asked for Malazar's view.

Angry words came, "Oh, I don't know. I don't care. You choose. The darn Orb. Oh why can't I find it? We must have it. I need it. Oh where, oh why—oh well—doesn't matter anymore. Just go on."

Silence weighted heavily in the cavern room; no one spoke. The unexpected reply tended to lower everyone's cheerful tone. The others really didn't know what to say to the wizard. It was awkward. Finally, Mindi arose and put her arms around the wizard comfortingly. She quickly spoke to Nache, "You and Marc get going; we'll follow. Let's go your way."

At once, they obeyed, and the dimly lit company resumed their single file, torch lit, march into the black depths far underground.

"What's the matter, Malazar? Can you tell me about it?" inquired Mindi, genuinely concerned.

After a long pause, he sighed; a tear was in his eye, "I feel lost, so helpless, so useless. My—the Orb is lost." He paused. "It must be found, but it's no use; all's lost. I've tried so hard." Mindi said nothing, but stayed at the old man's side.

The subterranean silence was broken only by tramping

feet; yet ears were attentive, alert for danger. None came. They continued their march. For the rest of what must have been that day, they marched onwards through six more great cavern rooms. A bewildering number of side tunnels offered many diversions, but always Marc and Nache held to the straight level tunnel.

Marc was pondering the wizard's condition as he walked along. "Malazar seems to have gone mad right when we need him the most. Whatever can be the matter? How can he act so badly anyway. I—I—Oh. I guess I did—at Obelos Sud. I wonder if—I'll talk to Mindi tonight."

True, the emotional tone of the company was dampened somewhat by their leader's growing madness. Hildaro wondered if it was due to the closeness of the mine. In Cavern Room Number 7, they halted for the night, though there was no way of telling the fact that evening had come. Camp was made, and the dinner fixed and eaten, but few words were spoken. Marc took Mindi aside afterwards.

"This is an ill blow; our leader lies half mad, and we are far underground. Not good," he began. She agreed, and he said inquisitively, "You know. I was wondering if Malazar is having trouble with mental pictures—like I was at Obelos Sud."

"Hum," Mindi replied pondering his idea, for she had been suspecting the same thing. "Let's see," and she went slowly over to the stone bench the old man was laying on, shrouded in darkness. "Malazar," she began barely auditable.

He rolled his eyes and met hers; she continued, "Do you see any mental pictures?" A barely discernible grunt was heard. "Tell me about them," she commanded firmly, yet softly.

There was a long silence; the wizard closed his eyes, and tears swelled in his eyes. She watched him closely. She could feel his immense sense of loss of the Orb. Suddenly pictures of Enchendar began flashing in her mind. Constantly, she kept seeing King Faegor's royal palace upon the hill and the columns and the moon ball. At once, she cried loudly, "Oh!"

Everyone jerked, startled into the present. Everyone looked or came to her. She felt a bit embarrassed. "What's the matter love," Marc asked much concerned.

"The Orb—the Orb—I think I know where it is!" Malazar opened his tear-filled eyes. She looked at him and said, "Describe it—Malazar describe it!"

Slowly wiping away the tears, he said with a slight note of hopefulness, "Well, legends say it's small, holdable in one hand. It is like a glowing, silver ball on a silver shaft. It radiates a soft, whitish hue."

She became very excited, "Then that's it! That's it! The Orb. Oh wow and right under our noses all the time. We missed it—went right by it! Whew!"

"Hold it. hold it," interrupted Marc, "Where is it?"

"Oh—it's in Fairy Land—Enchendar. Remember—it's the moon ball in front of Faegor's palace!" Yes's and ah's echoed as the others realized it as well. "That's what Queen Miranda's poem spoke of. Wow. Now I understand!"

She quickly retold the words Miranda had recited to her of Lenora and the great battle. Missar, the Great Wizard, had come in grief and gave them their charge, the moon ball, and its oath. Wild excitement prevailed. Nache danced with Tse Tse around in circles. Vorag laughed and petted Oran happily.

"Well doneth, Mindi! Verily, twas right before mine own eyes, and I didst not see it. Verily." He spoke as the others felt, and a great relief came to everyone.

Malazar too was moved, and the mental blocks gave way. Yawning heavily, he volunteered, "The pictures are becoming clearer."

"Tell me," Mindi quickly replied, setting down beside him again.

Slowly, with many interruptions for yawns, the old wizard spoke, "The great battle was over. I had lost. All my friends, my peers, all were gone in that evil, self-consuming blast. I hadn't been strong enough or quick enough to prevent it. I left Magum, and carrying the Orb, I came into the Quad, sad, dejected, no hope left. The evil in Kalhari I quickly handled and came to the dwarf mine here, abandoned since the start of the war. I passed through the mines in darkness. The heavy grief I bore alone. Several times, I neared an abyss wondering if a fall was the answer. But I could not. I walked in the darkness for nearly a week; only the Orb glowed softly still.

Finally, I saw a tiny ray of hope. The fairies, the land of no change, where time does not pass. I forsook the guardianship of Isel. As I journeyed to Eos woods, I resolved to keep my last ray of hope alive there. So without telling Faegor what the moon ball was, I placed it in the ground for all to see. I cast the spell upon it—that it should not answer to my or anyone's will until she came once more. Boy, do I feel better!" he exclaimed, a comment that everyone appreciated.

"But what would break the spell? That part is not very clear to me yet," questioned Mindi softly, half in thought.

"Well, the spell I placed could only be broken by the arrival of Lenora. By her hand alone could the force of the Orb be removed," he explained with another yawn.

She wondered to herself for some time. Meanwhile, Malazar seemed much more cheerful. The company broke into small groups, discussing the turn of events. Marc helped the wizard, who now seemed famished, find a late supper. Then sleep took them all, and it was a peaceful one.

Drifter ushered in the next day, if one could call it day. He was like an alarm clock, ever a nomad. He somehow sensed morning had come far above them.

When he was awakened, George grumbled half-asleep, "How come it's day; it's not even light yet." Then, he embarrassingly remembered his location and got up.

The journey this day went as the one before. Through cavern rooms and tunnels they marched in single file.

Nache asked Malazar, "How come the dwarves abandoned the mine, after the war I mean."

"Yes," put in Marc, "that's a good question. This place is incredible!"

Back to his usual self, the wizard spoke calmly, "Well my good dwarf, there is much that this wizard does not know. Again, you have stumbled upon my ignorance. I do not know. Perhaps we shall get a chance to find out; we just may," he mused. If he had an idea, he did not reveal it to the others.

What must have been late afternoon was interrupted quite suddenly by Cavern Room Number 20. As they entered, everyone noticed the sudden change. Half of the dimly lit room was black stone of Armagh, but exactly in the middle, the stone abruptly changed to an orangish hue. The Quara Ost mountains. They had finally come to Kalhari, though in secret.

The granite side was similarly polished, but it definitely lacked the immense aesthetic appeal of the black stone. It was mainly granite with large flakes. The fissure line between the two dichotomous ranges had been a mineralogist's dream come true. It was a great slice filled with settlings of various precious metals and superb gems. Here the dwarves had carved tunnels following the great crack. Five tunnels and shafts bored their way in each side. Nearby were piles of gold, silver, and gems of many types. They halted and fell upon the pile of wealth, not from lust, but by the sparkling beauty that the huge pile formed.

"A king's treasury of gems could not surpass this," was how Hildaro described it. An hour passed, filled with: "Look at this one!" On and on.

Then Nache proudly stood tall and announced, "On behalf of all the dwarves, let us each accept one gem as a token of the gratitude and friendship of the dwarves."

So insistent was he, that everyone accepted his offer. Each rummaged in the granite hall for a treasure to his liking. Marc found his choice and went over to Mindi, who was inspecting her choice. "I chose this cloudy agate," she explained, "because it reminds me of the dwarves. See how the colors ebb and flow in swirls?"

"Beautiful," he said and added, "I might have guessed."

"What did you pick out," she asked gaily.

He showed her his choice—a large, deep, ruddy, ruby. "Like Andrill," he said. They hugged each other and walked over to the granite tunnel they intended to continue following. By the entrance, Marc paused suddenly recalling an image long forgotten. Mindi watched, as his face grew serious yet calm. She could perceive his thoughts were not on the passage or her or on the present.

She finally asked curiously, "Marc. Marc, what's the matter?"

"Oh—oh nothing's wrong. It is as it should be, as it was foretold. Hey all of you come here a minute. I have something to say. I've been meaning to bring it up, but never did." The others, happy with their newfound stones, noticing his serious, sudden prominence of command, responded quickly.

"What's up," queried the wizard.

"Oh nothing dangerous or serious yet. I just have something I want to say to us all," Marc replied in a commanding tone. When the others gathered around him, Marc began, "We are about to enter the orange tunnel. Our destination is just ahead. I have something I've only now recalled. Let me begin." Others nodded.

"Karzam has done things that he should not have done—things that harmed much more than they helped. He has done overt actions—actions that harm more broadly than they help. Some are of commission—some are omission; all are evil for the most part. Each of us has followed Karzam's lead—either by omission or by failing to handle or by direct or indirect aid, we have committed overt actions ourselves—that is, things we regret, that we should not have done. Full of shame, blame, and regret, we became blind. The mistake was to think that responsibility lies in this shame, blame, and regret trio."

"Ah poor, poor wizards, consumed in their own fiery blasts of self-pity, but such does not amend the evil that was done; it does not handle what was begun. It merely removed ourselves from our actions for a time—done, perhaps so that we could not do any further damage! Each of us has since had his own hell in which to live, surrounded by guilt, problems, remorse, and many half-hidden, pain-giving pictures of our ill-fated deeds. We know now for certain that these actions were irresponsible, and we are now gathered to rectify our past deeds, our past overt actions."

"Now Karzam has gone further in his deeds. So much evil did he do that he desperately needed a 'reason' to justify his actions. So he got someone to attack him. Now being attacked, Karzam is safe in saying, 'Oh look what he's doing to me, so I am now justified in crushing him.' But he commits more evil and needs to have even larger 'reasons.' And on and on and on and on it goes! Overt action and harmful reaction on doer—which prompts further overt actions, and so on, unending."

"But relief can only come by thoroughly viewing one's own acts and then doing what is necessary to correct, to remedy, and to rectify the damage done. For my money, I'd guess that Kahill may be Karzam. It fits the pattern very well, but I have no data, just a strong hunch."

"And of this brings me to the real questions. What needs to be rectified and how? Once done, each of us will be freed of the haunting past. If we do not handle it, there will yet come another time and another."

"At the pool of Ian in the land of the fairies, I saw a vision full of fear. I haven't spoken of it until now. Now I'm sure. We shall come at last to the orange opening ahead and shall cast our eyes in fear and terror upon the yellow and black checkered obelos. However, the fear and terror comes from atop the obelos, not from us. It comes from Kahill, Karzam, whoever lies before us. Our time shall come. We must be ready for the what and how."

"Malazar has counseled that the evil Yacs, though terribly debased, still have some goodness deeply buried within themselves. Perhaps they can be saved, but what of the wargs, the goblins, and the Evil One himself. Of the first two, I don't know, but of the Evil One, I feel he must be made to confront his evil actions and their cause, and then fully repair his doings, if that be possible."

The others found this a heavy talk. All had or felt some form of shame, blame or regret. It was real to them, though hard to bear, especially when given so bluntly, but none disagreed; inwardly they knew he spoke truly. Sobering silence fell as he ended.

After a long, unbearable silence, Malazar spoke slowly. "Marc is, of course, correct in his analysis on all counts. You have learned well, my friend, perhaps faster than I intended, and perhaps more than I myself know, but are we not all wizards?" He shrugged his shoulders and hands in a questioningly manner. There was a wry smile on his face.

"The source of the Scourge, its driving power, comes from the man in the tower. Unseat him and the Yacs will easily handle. Not so for wargs and goblins or trolls. These come from another place and time; where, I cannot say. Borrowed evils they be. I believe we yet don't have enough knowledge to handle the loaned trio of Evil Ones. Let us pass on this question at this time. But of the evil leader, Marc is right; we must make him see his track of overt actions. Somehow. How, I don't yet know. Let us ponder this one."

This was agreeable to all, and without much further conversation, Nache and the wizard led the company onwards.

Down into the dark, orange, arched passageway, dimly lit by their torches, the company marched, once more heading toward the confrontation they all knew to be just ahead of them. Onwards marched the determined company through narrow, orange-hued tunnels, which periodically opened into spacious caverns with precisely constructed pillars and arches supporting vast domes far above. Always like orange tentacles, shafts and tunnels bore to the cavern sides. Always their path went straight, beyond huge rooms filled with pilings and debris, as well as miner's tools and ore.

Occasionally, signs of ancient volcanic activity could be seen. Black dikes and pillars of basalt rose upwards; its seam melted the orange rock; and thin layers of green olivine marked the blending of the two stones. Through an endless array of tunnels and giant chasms, they strode all that day and the next, moving swiftly in the uniformly cool temperatures. Here and there, drafts of fresh air filtered down the deep oblique shafts that rose to the world above. The company rested little and strove to make their greatest speed forward.

Chapter XXVIII—Of Death and Life

The third day since entering the orange-hued tunnels proved eventful. Around noon, the tunnel they were using came to an abrupt end. "Iee!" cried the dwarf, as everyone worriedly gathered around him looking ahead, torches pushed forward. The passage way was blocked by fallen rock; a great fissure had opened in the ceiling.

"An earthquake?" queried Drifter.

"Perhaps so," mused the wizard.

"Well, let's get the debris cleared," commanded Marc.

And painstakingly slowly, the mass of crumpled granite was shifted, shoved, and pulled apart. In this endeavor, Vorag proved quite useful. Nache seemed to be everywhere at once, directing the clearing of the passageway.

They were nearly done clearing a passage through the rubble when Elwine gasped and spoke hurriedly and quickly, "Quiet, I hear someone; quiet."

At once, everyone froze in their motions, ears strained. Soon everyone heard the of telltale tromp of echoing feet resounding in the tunnels. It came from somewhere up ahead, beyond the cave in. The tromping grew ever closer. Now unmistakably, voices could be heard grunting and cursing. Two great goblins were moving towards them, talking in the common tongue. Thus, they were evidently not from the same ghoulish tribe.

"Umargh! Where is the cursed hole anyway? Damn this tunnel." They carried only a feeble light.

The second answered, "Shut up. We're nearly there. You should not let the Lord hear you talking like that. He'll throw you to the trolls or worse yet, the sphinx."

"Well, curse him anyway," the first grumbled. "I hate mines—smells of dwarves. Hardly a mouth full."

"Well if you quit grumbling and help me find the hole to the trolls, you may soon get to sink your teeth into better meat! You should praise our Lord. For it is he who has found this hole to the great trolls. It was he who got them for us in the first place."

"Well curse those Burly fat men. How dare they kill all the trolls? We nearly had our feast," the first responded.

"Yes, well, the yellow Lord is not defeated yet—haven't you heard, with more trolls, the passes will be cleared, and then he'll loosen a hundred of the stone monsters on Burly. Sweet shall be our revenge. This time, all we have to do is eat our fill." They both laughed hideously, with snorting and grunting.

They were getting dangerously close to the huddled company by the cave in. Just then, the second cried, "Ah—there it lies—see the Lord's hole to the trolls! Ha. Ha. Ha."

"Well let's get it over with. You go first. You've been below before."

"Grr, all right."

Swiftly Elwine motioned to the others, and quietly with elfin stealth, he climbed over the nearly cleared, rubble pile and disappeared into the ominous blackness of the tunnel. Fainter and fainter came the sounds of the goblins' passage.

Finally, Malazar gave the all clear sign; they relit their torches, and as quietly as possible, finished clearing the passageway. As they finished, Elwine returned to them, taking them by surprise.

"Boy, you sure are quiet!" whispered George.

"Yes, I followed the two. Ahead is a ragged hole smashed into the wall to your left. It goes steeply downward, very rough, very jagged. Our two had to go down it bent over. They're now far below. A foul stench comes from the passage way as well."

"Okay, well done," replied Malazar. "Let's go check it out. I fear we have discovered where the cave trolls have come from!"

As quickly as possible, the company stumbled across the cleared rubble and walked on down the orange tunnel. Around a thousand yards ahead, they halted. Here a roundish hole had been smashed into the polished wall. Jagged, rough, and poorly made, the hole stunk badly; a foul breeze rose up from the very bowls of the earth. Lit by their dim torches, it appeared dark and ominous, and very, very crude next to the craftsmanship of the dwarves.

They stared. It stank. Silence grew heavy. Heartbeats thumped in drum-rolls, as the company peered into the blackened, gaping, deep rent. No one spoke. Ill memories flashed through many minds, especially Marc and Vorag— memories of the stone-skinned trolls. Finally, George questioned himself in a whisper that seemed to echo loudly, "Now what?"

Shaken, the others mumbled inaudibly; whether in agreement or answer, the former couldn't tell and didn't want to know anyway.

The old wizard recovered first, and glancing toward his elf friend said, "Well at long last, we know from whence the aged creatures of darkness and doom have come. I'd bet the quaking tunnel gave way back there under the force of their footsteps! So a passageway exists to another time and space. Interesting. I wonder what it's like below in the dark depths? Ghastly, I'd guess." His musing added to the ominous silence.

Nache finally stirred from his awed trance. "Oh. Oh. Oh, for only a hundred dwarves. Now I wish Aaron and company. For in a day's passage, we could block and seal the gap forevermore. Block by block, stone by stone, each one sealing tight against its mate—not the merest crack through which the foul air could seep or fingers creep. Oh, for a thousand dwarves. Mightily could we build a plug for the orange hole, stronger than the very granite stone of the mountain. It would be a cork stronger than the flask! Oh, for ten thousand dwarves! For then we could . . ."

"Whoa, whoa, my busy dwarf," Marc cried laughingly, and the others, sensing the humor of the serious dwarf, joined in with amused chuckles. "With that many dwarves, you wouldn't even need to plug the hole—you could charge below and conquer the trolls' kingdom!"

For a second, he caught a fleeting gleam in the little man's eye, as if—but just then, the dwarf saw the humor of his exaggeration and laughed, leaving Marc wondering.

Now Malazar's voice rose above the others, "Sometimes the smallest have the biggest ideas. Yet here I deem he has spoken the best. Obviously, we must close the hole. Clean and simple. No hole, no trolls!"

"Yes, but how dost we doest this thing," pleaded Vorag, already exhausted from the heavy labor of clearing the rubble pile behind them.

"Well sometimes even a wizard does not have all the answers at once. You have me there, great hunter. That is a good question. How do we close the hole? Any takers?"

He threw it open to the floor. Quickly, the little man described the toilsome task of carving solid, basalt blocks. When he explained that by working day and night, a week would see one small cube cut and polished, Vorag moaned, loudly joined by the others. A realization of just how much effort and toil had been involved in all the perfectionist, stone block works they had seen hit them heavily.

"Dwarves are incredible," Marc quickly compromised, "but—but if we carve from this softer granite and neglect the polishing, it'll only take two days and nights per block." He smiled at this hopeful time reduction. However, the others continued to grumble.

Rubbing his hands across his face and through his hair, Hildaro exclaimed, "And if we spend days piling rubble in the hole, the beasts can probably dig it out faster than we can stuff it in. Is it hopeless?" As if in answer to the horseman's words, there came once more the familiar far off, faint sounds of doom.

Boom. Boom. Boom.

"Ieee", cried the dwarf.

Nerves tingled, stomachs clenched, fear stuck. The floor and walls shivered from the distant quake of stamping feet— the telltale pattern of eminent doom.

Boom. Boom. Boom.

The sound drew ever so slowly closer, nearer the shaken company.

"Oh lord not again," Marc cried, fumbling for Tiny in the dim light.

Boom. Boom. Boom.

Thundering footfalls grew steadily nearer. In the narrow and dark tunnel far under the mountains, with the tramp of doom echoing, and with the quaking stone underfoot, the company felt as if they were imprisoned alive in a tiny crypt already buried under ground! Intense fear and even a controlled terror gave way quickly to a hopeless waiting for the certain doom that crept ever closer.

Boom. Boom. Boom.

Echoing loudly now, the voice of death resounded loudly off the walls. Small stones began dropping randomly from the arched ceiling above them, like a rain of stone, a harbinger of death, preparing their burial mound far underground.

Boom. Boom. Boom.

They stood transfixed to the spot, vainly trying to resolve eminent death and cave in with ways to survive. In terror, the ponies began to wildly neigh and rear uncontrollably, dragging their masters about the narrow stone coffin to be.

Boom. Boom. Boom.

Everyone began to scream and cry out wild ideas at once, in a hectic din above the thunder of approaching doom. Sand and gravel began falling uniformly from the ceiling, forcing all to bend and cover their heads with flailing arms. Confusion grew as the voice from earth's bowls grew steadily.

Suddenly out of the chaotic confusion of rearing ponies, falling debris, and yelling people, Malazar rose to his full size, undaunted by his doom. His staff blazed brilliantly white. The wild melee hushed at the sight. In a commanding tone, the wizard yelled, "Flee! Flee! Run down the tunnel towards the desert. Flee! Flee! Get out! Get out! Run as fast as you can! Run! Flee! Go now! Go!"

So forceful was his command that without knowing how or even ordering their bodies, the group found themselves scrambling and running on down the tunnel towards the desert end. In a wild headlong rush, with hands holding torches, heads, and ponies, the company determinedly fled. Amid the clamor and confusion of doom, they had an action to perform. All intentions strove towards fleeing down the downwards sloping tunnel.

Boom. Boom. Boom.

The voice of doom grew fainter and at last seemed far

off. The company slowed down gasping wildly for air. The headlong run had calmed their nerves, channeling their energies to a faithful, survival path. Now, the horror was dispelled, and they bent over taking great gasps of the cool air.

The elf recovered quickly and began a head count. Suddenly he cried, "Malazar! Malazar! He's not here! He didn't come! He's back there!" Like a bolt of lightning, his exclamation electrified their minds.

At once Marc cried, "Some of you follow me," and he began running back up the rising tunnel, now heedless of the voice of doom. Elwine, Vorag, and Oran followed after him.

However, Mindi restrained the others saying, "Let some of us stay; no good will come of all of us perishing just now." They agreed with her logic, yet their emotions swelled to a crescendo. Their friend was back there, alone, facing, certain doom, and here they stood in safety and couldn't assist the wizard. But logic prevailed.

Amid the peals of doom, the wizard had watched as his friends' precarious position worsened with every new step of the unseen beasts. Quickly, he resolved that he himself must handle these monsters of another age. So he'd taken command, and with a sigh of tensed relief, he watched their pell-mell rush on down the orangish tunnel. A lonely blackness crept around the old one. Alone and surrounded by darkness lit only by his staff, he slowly scrambled over the stony rocks into the gaping, jagged hole. Deafening came the trolls tramp.

Boom. Boom. Boom.

He felt an increasing calmness. As he slowly crawled down the steeply striking shaft, waves of tranquility, a sereneness, flowed over him, replacing the dull reactive terror. He knew what he must do. His fate he accepted. Isel would at last be free of the ultimate weapons of the Evil One. He felt certain that Marc could handle the Evil One himself.

Now three thousand yards into the steeply descending, rough shaft, he waited leaning upon his staff, which glowed a pale white. He waited as the thunderous, magnified sounds gradually approached him.

Boom. Boom. Boom.

Then a great grey form, bent over in the narrow

427

passageway, loomed before him; the voices of doom ceased. Silence fell in the shaft to hell. Staring in wonder, the troll tried to fathom the meaning of the old one bent over on the staff, dully glowing. He repeatedly blinked even in this much light. He took one more slow step towards this intruder, now about a half thousand yards away from his huge bulk, which nearly blocked the shaft. Malazar stood erect and rose to his full height, head touching the orange rock above. His staff blazed and burst forth in a blinding, searing, white light.

Above the cries of pain from the troll covering his eyes, his voice cried aloud, "Halt evil one. No trolls shall pass here. This way is now closed. Go back! Go back to your foul den in the foul bowels below! Go before my wrath bursts upon you."

The troll, recovering from the sudden onslaught of the brilliant light, bellowed slowly, "Nay—get thee gone old man. No creature stoppeth Cirnook. I'm Cirnook, guardian of the caves below. You shall die."

He took another step forward, his last. Malazar muttered in a strange tongue and from his staff great fiery bolts of lightning streaked forward, striking walls and troll alike. Tremendous peals of thunder, magnified by the tunnel into a deafening roar, echoed and rolled along the sound channels, the walls. The earth began to shake violently. The ground quaked, and the tunnel began to collapse with a furious rapidity. In a great crashing, crushing collapse, the entire mountain fell in upon the troll and shaft. A huge, billowing puff of dust and rock blew out either end of the shaft, taking Malazar with it.

So strong was the force of the blast of the earth that Malazar was swept off his feet and blown back a thousand yards towards the dwarven section. He flew down the tunnel like a paper airplane, along with many boulders, gravel, and yellow-orange dust. More ceiling sections gave way, and he lay piled under orange debris and dust. The cloud, now less in force, carried a dust puff actually out into the dwarven tunnels and into the running trio. The wizard breathed no more.

Straining every muscle in his body, Marc raced back up the slowly inclining tunnel, holding a torch in his waving left hand. He no longer heard the sounds of doom, did not hear his feet on the rock floor, nor the crackling of his torch; he had his sole attention upon his headlong race with time. He had to get to Malazar before—before. Rounding a bend, he ran headlong into the orange cloud of billowing dust as it puffed outward from the hole of hell.

Visibility was zero. Choking on the air, he stumbled to a halt and covered his face with his cloak. Behind him he heard the other two doing likewise. Then, he became aware once more of the thundering noise of the cave in ahead. Fear and concern hit him in jolting waves; he struggled to his feet and pressed onwards slowly feeling his way. Shortly the concussion noise subsided to a distant rumble; then silence came, broken only by an occasional kerplop sound of a rock giving way.

Through the slowly settling, orange dust, he fumbled his way along the hole to the trolls, stumbling over the fallen pieces of what had been the ceiling. Progress was slow and precarious. Jagged boulders and stones were strewn upon the passage floor with smaller bits and pieces still crumbling and falling, as if in parody of the larger ones before. He felt the bump of the others as they collided into him from the rear. It felt encouraging.

The trio crept along for about a thousand feet, before Marc cried loudly, as he saw the lifeless form of Malazar, half buried under the orange debris.

Quickly the three set to work, heedless of the danger of further cave in and polluted air. The wizard was unearthed, but with sinking hearts—they saw no signs of breath or life. Marc felt sick! No one spoke; no one moved for a minute. Crumbling sounds from the fragments still dislodging and settling broke the silence. Then, Marc unknowingly yelled releasing some of his grief. More calmly, he said, "Let's get him out of here."

Startled by his unexpectedly loud outburst, they jerked, and together responded. Slowly they carefully lifted their friend, companion, and leader, and they began stumbling their way back out of the hole. By the time they reached the dwarf mine tunnel, the air had cleared considerably, but everyone's lungs were filled with orange dust. They were coughing and spitting.

Once in the well-built, dwarven tunnel, they made excellent time and had gone several thousand yards, when the telltale crumble and roar reached them, momentarily halting them. They had been just in time, for the remainder of the crudely dug tunnel had given way under the stress. The very mountain seemed to settle downward, closing the crude hole to the depths forever. Quickly they grabbed the lifeless form and rushed with all possible speed down the sloping tunnel. They coughed, spat, raced, and stumbled.

How long it seemed, none of the trio could afterwards say. Their very intent was solely on the next step and the next. After an eternity of effort, Marc saw a dim yellowish light ahead: the company. Soon other arms relieved the trio's and helping hands reached out to ease their coughing. George had instinctively retrieved water flasks, and the three drank and spat orange mud, while everyone moved forward as fast as they could on downward in the sloping tunnel.

An hour passed and then two and then three. No one spoke. Everyone knew and could see, yet said nothing, feeling sick; a tempest of tears was restrained. At last, they rushed into another large, open spaced cavern. Floods of cool air blew in from many air-shafts. Long yellow sunbeams shone from high holes above down to the floor, creating brightly lit spots. Had Nache been alert, he could have welcomed them to the Cavern of Light, as it was called.

Another time, this hall would have been entered in highest spirits; the form and beauty were incomparable. Sparkling, the well-lit and well-vented chamber was the last one before the tunnel entrance into the desert. Here the company halted instinctively. They placed their fallen leader upon a bench warmed by the soft, yellow, broad beam of sun, which fell from a shaft thirty feet above. No one spoke, and each slowly found a corner of the cavern where he could be alone for a while. Mindi could hear and perceive the overwhelming sense of grief and loss. Some were crying openly, some sniffling, others sighing and withholding tears. Others were solemn and grave, but Mindi felt confused.

As soon as Marc had dashed from her side, she felt strange. She wanted to reach out and keep him from going, yet she could not. Then left standing with nothing to do but wait, she had never felt so helpless before in her life. Using all her long unused and long unknown senses, she felt the mountain's lurching. It was if she could somehow sense actions, through the solid rock itself. The stone seemed more like water to her feeling, reaching, probing senses. In a flash of knowingness she realized the cave in. She had probed relentlessly for Malazar, but could find no life form in the collapsed shaft, either from the dwarven side or beyond the collapsed section. Her senses retraced the path gropingly and found his body. She "just knew" was her only way of describing it, as she later explained to Marc. Thus, when the trio had actually arrived, she already knew the situation and had no further reaction, except a bit of marvel that her expanded perceptions had been correct. Bitterly so.

The others had left the lifeless body lying in the yellow beam upon a stone bench. Here she knelt and laid her head upon the crushed chest, her arms rested upon his shoulders. For a moment, she felt a twinge of grief, but it subsided rapidly. No one saw her there. Perhaps, had they done so, they would have been freaked, startled beyond measure.

Her draped form began to glow. Actually, it was as if a whitish glow grew around her body, rather similar to the elves, except it engulfed her entire body and slowly crescendoed. Brighter and brighter, the white energy grew, equaling and then surpassing the brilliance of the solar beam falling on the pair. And still brighter. Had anyone now seen her, the white brilliance would have forced their eyes away in pain.

Then the crumpled, crushed, splintered legs and chest began to move! The twisted right leg jerked perceptibly and began to straighten into proper form, rather like the inflation of a twisted, flat balloon. The sunken chest expanded ever so slowly; the bloody gash upon his forehead slowly sealed; the flesh joined, mended. Five minutes later, the glow subsided slowly. Malazar breathed and suddenly began coughing heavily.

Mindi helped him up, and he spit wads of congealed orange silt for several minutes afterwards. Elwine, who alone had seen the glow, saw the ending of the singular miracle. For though the elf's grief was heavy, the new, radiant glow had caught his attention, and he had quickly explored the source. Elwine had found them, as the glow was subsiding, and had quietly watched; his mouth hung open, eyes wide in wonder.

When the wizard's coughing broke the silence of the cavern of light, one by one, the startled members of the company came over to the bench and stared in awe and total disbelief and surprise. Such a shock none had ever had! Some cried his name aloud; others, unable to speak, cried tears of uncontrollable joy. It was as if a great, black mass was rapidly blown from their minds. Relief gushed in its stead, followed by wild exuberance.

Finally, Hildaro wildly cried, "He lives!" This was nearly everyone's singular thought, and they all began cheering.

Unused to such a flow of love being directed his way, Malazar muttered, "Of course, it's Malazar. Who do you think I am? Am I not a wizard? What's with all of you? You act as if I was dead or something. What happened back there?"

His amused face suddenly cringed as he recalled, "Ooh, Oh!" Now his face looked perplexed and slowly his gaze met Mindi's. The others turned to her. The last trace of the white glow was still receding; her face was calm, filled with serene countenance of one who has immense power and certainty.

For an instant, no one spoke; all eyes were upon her. She smiled and said cleverly, "Am I not a wizard?"

Then the restrained joy of life burst, and everyone began cheering wildly, and dancing around the floor and shining pillars and columns. The wizard, slowly tested his legs, and Mindi helped him up.

"Oh man, are my legs sore!" he exclaimed.

"Yes, I believe it, but if you exercise them a bit and rest up, you'll be as good as new!" she replied.

With newfound hope and life, the others gaily established camp in the Cavern of Light. George and Shannon prepared a feast, and Nache lit every torch in the place. Elwine and Drifter went exploring the tunnel that lay ahead. By the time that dinner was prepared, the two returned with the welcome news that the entrance lay only a half mile ahead. It was unguarded and at the base of the mountains. Desert would soon be underfoot. They had the happiest, gayest meal they'd had since entering the lost dwarf mine.

Chapter XXIX—Kalhari

For three agonizing days, time seemed to move pathetically slowly. Malazar, who was quite weak after his ordeal in the foul shaft, needed rest. Healed and returned to the living by Mindi, his body now ached and felt drained. Daily he exercised, gradually doing more and more, and all the while, eating as though he were famished! George would make jokes concerning the wizard's appetite. As he served the old one, he would receive a cold stare and a grunt. Both enjoyed the game.

The company had little to do or to occupy their minds. They were in the last cavern before the western doors, the Cavern of Light. Well lit by numerous overhead air-shafts, which allowed warm refreshing beams to fall onto the floor, the large chamber was some five hundred feet square. Great columns and arches supported the thirty-foot ceiling, and scattered about the floor were typical dwarven stone benches. (Only the dwarves would build a bench of rock that would last centuries.) The orange colored walls were highly polished and made of porphyritic granite; great crystals sparkled in the sheen of the golden walls. Here the air was fresh, clean, and warm.

However, the others grew exceedingly bored, "Like rates in a cage," Hildaro suggested. So to ease the monotony, Marc had let each wander on down to the doorway gate of the lost dwarf mine, only a half mile from this, the last cavern room, but he watched them closely, recalling his vision from Enchendar and the Pool of Ian, which now seemed years ago. His vision was borne out in fact, for as a companion reached the door gate and gazed at the world beyond, into Kalhari, a great fear slowly grew upon him. Only Elwine seemed unaffected by it, and of course, both Mindi and Malazar, who had not yet come to the doorway.

The ancient gates that shut the mine off from the desert world had been hurled open by foul hands and lay askew and unhinged. The great doors were made of iron and silver nearly six inches thick, and they now hung ajar by one hinge.

Evidently, strong hands had forced them open. Kahill's hands—most assumed. The great gates lay at the base of a small cliff in the Quara Ost mountain range. The orange, rugged mountains rose sharply behind the gates, and like jagged, broken, razor blades, they rose for nearly a mile, snowless.

Lying westward was the vast Kalhari desert; its sands were a mixture of orange and red. The orange came from the Quara Ost mountains. The red came from the scattered, red sandstone buttes. Since most of the Quad was a desert, it was called Kalhari Desert, though Kalhari Buttes would also have served. Towering vertical, red walls rose up a sheer two hundred feet. The tops, fifty feet across, were small and flat— the nesting place for flocks of black birds and others. The buttes were like towering, red cylinders, defying nature, and were very widely scattered.

From their viewpoint at the tunnel's mouth, the land sloped gently downward to the arid plains. Scattered buttes dotted the horizon, and a faint trail crawled from the gate, snaking its way into the distance around the red fingers. Always, the trail bore towards the west, to the central regions, where some small hills, three or four hundred feet high, rose blackish in color. From this westerly direction, an unwary viewer sensed or felt the greatest fear. If he dared to peer to the west, fear would seem to flood upon his mind and body. For there, rising among the distant, black hills rose a solitary, narrow tower, yellow and black checkered, Obelos Cerban.

Just as he had seen in his vision from the Pool of Ian, Marc watched the others cringe as the great fear grew. He pointed out to each that the terror came from the tower. Instead of feeling a general fear of everything, this observation alone channeled the dispersal to its source—a welcome relief to each. Marc wondered what madness would have resulted if the company hadn't spotted the source of the fear flow. Ruin, he guessed.

Here in Kalhari, the winter season produced chilling nights; yet the days were warm, a cool seventy degrees. Many varieties of cactus thrived. There were those that spread in circlets on the desert floor; others grew like miniature towers.

These proved useful, for Drifter had some knowledge of them. He produced a delicious tasting cactus juice, with George's assistance of course.

The elf spent three days on his own private, reconnaissance mission, though not straying too far off. Marc had suggested it would be poor to be attacked and trapped within the abandoned mine. Hence, everyone was careful about attracting the eyes of the Evil One. Marc was both relieved and encouraged by Elwine's report.

They sat around a small fire in the cavern, after supper the third night, and listened to the elf's report, marveling at his ability to perceive. In the area of the four passes, four armies were quartered; each nearly fifteen hundred strong, he guessed. Yacs were mainly at the southern passes, while the goblins were, for the most part, stationed at the northern pass. Only a very few wargs could be seen and no jackals. Evidently, their numbers had been reduced completely. Elwine said they were camped in flimsy matchbox houses, shabby and barely erect. All were quite distant from them. "Those to the south," he explained, "seemed to be building a gigantic crane, perhaps to clear the passes." But it was very slow going, he guessed.

"Now near Cerban," he continued, "hope rises. There are very few men; they are clad in checkered tunics and carry black shields. Probably Kahill's personal guards. I'd guess only fifty remain at the obelos. There are few shanties there, so a large army can only pass through."

"That's terrific," Hildaro broke in, "really encouraging! If we can get in quickly and end this thing at once, we shall not have to face fifteen hundred!"

The others agreed and discussed the situation further. Then the elf spoke once more. "Also, I think that I have found an answer for your old man and yellow glow."

A hush of excited expectancy quickly fell, as half the company recalled the cold, frigid man and the mysterious, yellow glow they had seen near Witchachooie Marsh.

"I saw a yellow glow coming from atop the obelos, several times," the elf reported.

Minds raced to the inevitable conclusion; and Marc cried aloud to himself, "Kahill, that must have been the Evil

One himself!"

"Eieee," cried Nache. "One swift flash from Kazab could have ended it all back then. Oh, had I only known!"

The others felt similarly, but Malazar arose slowly and raising his hand spoke, "Nay, to have killed the Evil One would not fully have handled it. He must be made to clean up his own mess."

"He's right," Marc asserted, once more hoping they'd see what he'd been trying to get them to understand. "He has to clean up his own actions and deeds, if we are ever to have a full peace." They reflected upon this and retired for the night. Since the wizard said that he was now recovered enough, their excitement rose.

At last, the sun did too, throwing the familiar yellow glow down into the cavern far underground. Hurriedly, they ate and quickly covered the half mile of orange tunnel to the gate. Everyone crowded around the gateway, peering into the desert lands before them. Unfortunately, it was a false start. Malazar leaned on his staff and surveyed firsthand the land of arid sand and red buttes. As the others excitedly waited for him to give the word to get going, their impatience grew.

Finally, he did speak, "Well my friends. It is nearly two days journey to the obelos, and only slightly more to the passes. If we go now, we shall be seen at once and arrive only to be greeted by fifteen hundred men. No, our path now lies at night. We shall journey only by night. Days, we shall sleep tight against the buttes. If we aren't seen until our arrival, then we shall have two days' time or one full day, if they charge without stopping from the passes."

Though many complaints were voiced, no one disagreed with the wisdom of the wizard, but rather the thought of having to spend yet another day cooped up underground. The daytime slowly passed, as each tried to rest or sleep the daylight away. Only the wizard and Mindi seemed calm and relaxed. He slept many hours. Mindi gave Marc a back rub, and he too relaxed and drifted off into a shallow sleep.

She felt uncommonly at peace, indeed, serene. Since reviving Malazar, she seemed to have grown. No fear or doubts were in her mind; in truth, nothing came into her mind unless she herself called it there. She found her mind clear of unwanted pictures and emotions, and she felt very strong and powerful. She needed no bully's words to sound convincing; she was convincing. She just sat reflecting clearly upon whatever she chose. It felt delightful.

At the first sign of dark, Nache was up and about, hurriedly packing the ponies, anxious to get under way. Marc suggested that they take only the three ponies with them, and the others agreed. Quickly, the dwarf made the cavern into a stable for the remaining ponies. Finally, the company began the walk down the narrow tunnel to the gate. The last stage of their quest was upon them. All knew it. As they stepped out from the dwarf mine, the clear dark sky dotted with tiny jeweled lights flowed upon them. For a moment, they paused and gazed at the starry heavens. Hanging low in the southwest shone the early March crescent moon.

After a brief pause, Malazar and Drifter took the lead; the others fell into pairs and followed them. The path slowly descended into the arid basin that formed the Kalhari Desert. High by the gate, the air was fresh and clean, but only minutes later as the company descended onto Kalhari proper, the air bore a faint stench, which rapidly grew to a very foul odor when they reached the flat sands. It was the smell of Scavengers, for here was their home, and everything they touched stank. Soon in the faint light, the telltale signs of the Scourge were present. Burned, tall, cactuses stood—silent specters of the Scourge's passage. Blackened campfires with bone bits scattered about became frequent. Occasionally, foul, rotting flesh, perhaps an arm or leg, lay forgotten by the creatures of night. It was sickening and ugly. The closer they drew to the obelos, the more bone pieces they found. It was disgusting, and many stomachs reacted from the foul smells.

They stumbled on in the darkness; the starlight only outlined the trail, showing no details. Yet they made progress and entered the area of the buttes. Dark, tall specters, they seemed evil and ominous.

"Indeed, Kahill couldn't have picked more fitting land," mumbled Drifter aside to the wizard.

Step by step, they moved on through the night, stopping

only once for a rest. As the sky lightened with the first sign of twilight, they halted and made camp beneath the base of a sandstone butte. Here, they were out of eyesight from the passes and the obelos; it was a small security.

Marc and Mindi sat down together, leaning their backs against the red wall. He looked at her rubbing her nose and face, and suggested, "I'd guess the smell is so bad because there's little or no ventilation in here, you know, surrounded by mountains."

"Yes, but this is, is, well, it's just—something else." She refused to say what she had just thought. Then, as the sun rose high in the east over the Quara Ost range, the warm rays fell on them, and they dozed.

Each was lost in his own thoughts and lay basking in the dry morning sun. Dull warmth gently put tired bodies and minds to sleep. The day passed uneventful save only the muttered curse of Tse Tse, who discovered a cactus with his rear. Blue sky prevailed far into the afternoon, and as the shadow of the butte fell upon the sleeping company, the chill of the desert winter slowly supplanted the sun's warmth. Now sporadically, they arose, anxious to get on with it, although unable to do anything till dark. Restless on the eve of the climax, they felt constrained—horribly so—only to sit still and not be seen until dark. So far they had been lucky; not one Scavenger had been sighted in the area.

They guessed the two goblins were not due back from the trolls for some time, and evidently, no one detected the cave in of the tunnel. Their presence was still unknown and hopefully unsuspected; their biggest chance of success lay in surprise. By Marc's reckoning, Kahill had to be overthrown and his spell upon the Scourge removed within twenty-four hours after their presence was known. If not—well, he'd not think of that—fifteen hundred to eleven. Poor odds.

Finally, the sun sank blood red in the west, magnified by the dark, sandstone pillars of the region. The sands seemed to flow blood—well, at least the color. Presently, snacking done, they began once again, eager, excited, and yet a bit fearful. No one, except perhaps Marc, could pinpoint exactly the source of the gnawing, growing fear, but they felt it. Their steps toward the obelos became increasingly heavier and harder to take. By midnight, progress was slow, painfully slow, even though the trail was soft and straight. In each, there was now a yearning, a craving, to turn aside—to leave well enough alone—to go home—to forget their purpose.

Efforted footfall followed footfall, as each struggled against the unseen force of fear. A terror force that was somehow sensed or felt by all grew and gnawed, ever on their minds and via that, their bodies. They were breathing jerkily now, and their eyes darted, flittered, and glanced seemingly everywhere at once. Had someone yelled "get out," undoubtedly their bodies would have so reacted, while they wondered why they would be fleeing.

Even as they felt the force of cold fear, Kahill sensed them. This night, as most every night for years now, he spent alone, high atop his confiscated obelos, ever watching, ever planning. He was only thirty years old, but he always seemed to have had an evil or mean streak in him. Before he'd taken Kalhari, he'd stood just under six feet, a fine mesomorphic body, strong rippling muscles. Though he didn't need to use treachery to be the champion in sports events, he always did so. He'd spent most of his years way up north in the wilds beyond Isel, where the frontier town of Portabee lay, a small town nestled in the hills. Every contest he'd entered, which had become a yearly event, he'd contrived to rig. Coy and clandestine, there was no way he could lose.

A traveling merchant had entered the town when he was sixteen. His folks discovered that this newcomer was attempting to take over control from them—his father being the "elected" ruler. So for a handsome price, Kahill had murdered his parents, and when the crafty merchant had become the ruler, Kahill had cleverly blackmailed him into being Kahill's puppet leader. Well, Kahill had tired of that game early and left in search of a bigger conquest.

Alone in his tall tower, he reflected upon his good fortune of hearing about Isel from travelers to the north country. Yes, he remembered how he'd explored the country, and how strangely familiar it had seemed. In fact, he'd felt right at home as soon as he laid eyes on Obelos Cerban. Had it not opened at his command? He recalled how he'd discovered its powers over men and had built up an army the size of which Isel had never seen. For years, he'd taken great pride in his plans for the domination of all Isel; he'd be the master ruler.

He gloated over his luck in finding the tunnel to the evil goblins some three years ago. One night, while exploring his tower, he'd found a secret map that showed a hidden passageway. So he'd opened the secret rock door just outside the obelos and ventured down into the haven of the goblins. Exactly where the tunnel led or where the goblin main cities were, he still didn't know, but so strong was his bidding, his parleying, his offers of spoils, that they'd sent him armies of creatures and wargs.

But his greatest weapon, he himself had found—the great cave trolls. He coyly chuckled to himself every time he thought of that. He'd located the lost dwarf mine, and once inside had heard a noise far underground. By slow trickery, he'd gotten the goblins to burrow to the rumble. He had personally bargained for the ten trolls, the ultimate weapons. Even the goblins, as foul and evil as they were, were totally terrified of his great monsters from the depths of the earth. He cursed and swore vengeance upon the coming of the great slayers who dared defy his weapons of doom! He'd already sent a request for another bunch of trolls for his surprise spring offensive. This time he knew he'd win. Time was his weapon as well. He knew it. He could feel and taste the sweet victory.

"This time those meddling fools won't have a chance," he mused. A dull yellow light glowed atop the obelos, as Kahill paced back and forth. Across his Vishi were piles of maps. He'd cleverly worked out a new plan of sneaky treachery. Objective: to swarm en-mass to South Isel and the Flats. Let the Burly men come to him. He wondered when his dignitaries from Khorizaba would return. They were overdue. The idea was a stroke of genius. Remove the dwarf threat by getting all their outlying villages, the remote ones first, onto his side by threats and shows of force. With dwarves fighting dwarves, he'd only have to face the others. A three way attack would keep the elves boxed in, and his force could flow to the Flats by the thousands. He smiled at his good plans and laid them aside.

Soon he was gazing in his Vishi. Scenes of his guard posts flashed, and all seemed normal. No sign of anything wrong. Kahill felt ill at ease. For several days now, he felt a growing sense of the presence of the "good fools" as he referred to the company. To him, it felt awful; he sensed somehow their presence, a brightness, a whiteness. Kahill himself felt a growing uncertainty that led into a mild anxiety. He turned his Vishi from pass to pass. Still nothing came to his evil eyes. He paced some more and again surveyed his passes.

This night the presence felt stronger than other times, somehow. "Damn, something is wrong somewhere," he declared to himself. Then, he clanged a large cymbal and watched as several goblins and Yacs rushed outside their tiny huts far below. He glared at them and yelled, "Something is wrong somewhere. Some treachery perhaps. Send a pair of runners to the passes. Have them report at once. Find the treachery or it's your head! Oh yes, send someone to check out the mine as well."

He added the last on a mere whim and watched the scared men below rushing about getting his orders obeyed. Still he felt a growing uneasiness. In a few minutes, he watched the runners, rapidly moving like ants over the road ways. In twelve hours, he could watch the action on his Vishi. He went inside and paced the room, reflecting.

Marc had now taken the point with Elwine, relieving Malazar and Drifter for a spell. Suddenly, the elf halted and quickly spoke in a hushed voice, "Someone comes—a goblin I'd guess, nearly five miles off."

Quickly they looked around for a hiding place. The nearest butte lay ahead of them five miles. Flat desert ground lay all around. As the others discussed their plight, Drifter hit upon a plan. Carefully, everyone moved off the trail on either side leaving the ponies standing on the trail. Avoiding the cactus, they laid down in the cool sand, waiting, swords drawn. An hour passed slowly as the goblins neared.

Around a quarter mile off, they halted, seeing the three

ponies ahead alone. Cautiously, they slowly came forward, being careful not to shy them. Their bellies had plans for them. As they neared the ponies, the beasts reacted a bit, sensing the evil goblins. Just as the blue horned beasts were about to charge the ponies, the company sprang on them. The goblins cried out briefly, but died at once. Arrow, dart, and axe hit, followed by several swords. They were silenced. Quickly the party buried the bodies in the sand and resumed their journey. Dawn twilight was growing; they had to make the butte before daylight. Soon the company broke into a run. Swiftly and steadily, they made for the red finger; slowly the light grew, just another mile to go.

From far above in the checkered obelos, Kahill grew increasingly restless; the sense of a foreign presence had steadily grown. Nervously, he paced his fiftieth circle around the Vishi. At last, he stopped and gazed frantically into his viewer. He could see his runners bent towards the passes. All seemed well, but he knew it was not. Fidgeting his cloak nervously, he decided to do something. So around five in the morning, Kahill issued his call to arms.

As if by some magic spell, half of the men at each pass felt their Lord's command. The Evil One, using the Vishi as a transmitter, had sent his fearful summons for them to come to the obelos. Repeatedly, flows of intense fear commanded the Scourge to action. Whether they chose to or not, Yacs and goblins alike found themselves walking, and then running wildly, down the roadways towards the center of the Quad. For so great a power the dark Lord had that none of evil could choose their own actions when he summoned them.

As he watched nearly a thousand of his brood rushing headlong at his will, Kahill relaxed. Now he moved his viewer towards the runners who were heading for the lost dwarf mine. The company, scrambling for cover, felt the flows issuing from the obelos.

Nache cried, "We're discovered!"

Malazar quickly stemmed the growing waves of fear they felt, "Nay, the black flow passes high overhead—it is a command to the passes, not to us. Run! Run! We're not discovered yet."

Every muscle strained as their bodies increased speed to the fullest. Suddenly everyone knew. It felt like a cold shock wave. Some stumbled and fell headlong into the sands; others just tripped. The company now knew. They were spied. Their presence was now known to the Evil One. As Kahill strained his Vishi in search of the runner, the viewer presented to him the image of the company's flight towards the butte nearest the obelos. So great was his surprise that Kahill fell back upon the floor, breathless, heart pounding rapidly.

Precious seconds passed for all. In a wild scramble, the company made the protection of the red butte and huddled, gasping for air, sweating profusely. All senses were keenly alert. Then, the large gongs of Cerban sounded the intruder alarm. In wild disorder, the guards of Kahill rushed out of their flimsy shelters, grabbing weapons and crying loudly in many voices. They seemed to pour over the very hillsides of Cerban in a foul hoard.

From the temporary shelter of the towering butte, the company re-established a resemblance of order.

Malazar took command, "All right, our hour has come. The future of Isel lies before us in our hands. We have maybe twenty-four hours before the hosts of Kahill descend upon us at a hundred to one odds. Before us lay his guards, perhaps fifty to one hundred, only five or ten to one. Within the tower is the Evil One himself, one to eleven! Elwine, how far away is the obelos now?"

"Four or five miles," the elf replied hastily.

The wizard stood tall and flowed a radiance and power that he had seldom displayed—showing that reservoir of power Mindi had guessed was present when she had first met the wizard ages ago.

"We shall charge and stand before the obelos. Then, we shall get Kahill down, and then we will see. Let us conserve our energies for the battle before us. Precious is time now, but likewise our strength. We shall jog only."

He added somewhat more slowly, "My friends—my dear friends—whatever occurs, remember one thing. I love you all dearly. We will succeed."

The others, as if echoing the wizard, repeated his last

words, for in their last hour together here in the desert sands, those two single sentences seemed to say what all felt deep inside. At once, the final jog began with Malazar in the lead.

As they slowly moved forward, Nache sang loudly.

From far above in misty heights
Mighty Mizzinti issue forth
to conquer all our fears and foes
Isel freed once more.

The others smiled at his words. Whether they were really the old Mizzinti or not, it was irrelevant. Each felt at this instant that they were powerful and able beyond description. The words rang true, wizards or not.

Kahill's throng of Yacs and blue goblins scrambled around the grounds surrounding the obelos. Presently, they spied the attackers coming their way and began to jeer wildly and charge towards them. From atop the black and yellow tower, Kahill, by force of fear, restrained them—congealing his home guard into a solid mass of fighting force. He spread them around the base of his retreat of power. Mustering all the command power of dark terror he could, he urged his already running armies from the passes to greater speed. So great was the urge that many would lie dead of exhaustion beside the road before they ever gained the obelos. Such was the dark one's command power over those of evil.

Then, he watched and waited; a slow smile spread over his face, followed by the coy, cold laughter of one who sees victory finally within his grasp. He waited and watched. Timing was crucial. The company jogged determinedly straight for the obelos and Scourge. Ten anxious minutes passed; then another, but still the enemy showed no further reaction to their charge, evidently content to greet them on the doorstep of their evil leader. It now lay only a mile away; everyone could discern the Scourge lying in wait for them. Then a half mile. Then a quarter.

In an instant, the top of the obelos blazed into a brilliant yellow glow, which, like an explosion, swiftly grew. It was an explosion of energy—not that of fire or lightning, but that of pure terror. Wild screams of utter terror came from his driven men, and then the expanding blast hit the company.

A wave of bone chilling coldness swept over them; minds filled with pictures of horror; bodies jerked from the violence of the force unleashed. Any normal man would have been swamped by all the mental pictures of fear and dark terrors stimulated, re-stimulated, and unleashed to do their will. The Yacs and goblins fell to the ground in a wild torment of hell.

The force had no real physical effect, only mental.

Malazar was the first to recover from the shock wave of terror. He scrambled to his feet and cried loudly, "It's only mental! Rise! Rise to action! Let not your minds affect you. That's its only power! Rise Mizzinti, rise!"

Like a razor, his words sliced through the minds of the company. Truth shall set one free. It did. Instant realizations followed realizations, as each suddenly saw through the will of Kahill and rose ready for action. Thus, it became only spiritual being plus body. Minds were ignored. However, the ponies went wild. Leaping and lurching in a frenzied terror, they nearly broke free. Rapidly Elwine and Mindi went to work on them.

It took their combined efforts to calm the poor beasts, but soon with the assistance of Shannon, they were brought under control. They started forward once more. Now before them lay the outskirts of Cerban. Heaps of garbage surrounded crumbled shacks.

Chapter XXX—Kahill, the Twelfth

Safely atop his obelos, Kahill grimaced; his ultimate weapon proved ineffective. Fear crept into his mind.

"Can nothing stop these, these, these damned fools?" he wondered.

Seeing his own forces groveling uselessly in the desert sands, he cut back the yellow force of fear and commanded them to attack. He had nearly a hundred below. He knew he must push them, control them, and force them. They must not fail.

Only a thousand yards separated the forces, when instinctively the company halted before the swarm of Scavengers. Marc, wild with excitement cried loudly, "Shall we charge now?" He'd already drawn Tiny and was ready, but to charge into nearly one hundred seemed foolhardy, even to him.

Then of all people, George piped up, "Malazar, we need to take the obelos, right?"

"Yes," came the old wizard's instinctive reply.

"Okay," George was now yelling at the top of his voice. "Vorag come here!" The great hunter, muscles rippling and tensed ready for the onslaught, stepped forward; Oran, head held high, was at his side. The two men picked up two immense timbers from an abandoned, half-burned shelter. They held them balanced in the center and stood apart forming an immense V-shaped wedge.

"Get behind us," George yelled at the top of his voice.

"Verily," Vorag added loudly.

Since he couldn't blow his horn, the Burly hunter, yelled and bellowed a loud "Charge!"

"Yahooiee!" added Nache.

At the point behind the logs, the fire sword blazed, and the others fell in behind the wedge. Slowly quickening their pace, George and Vorag began a power charge, fairly running, straight towards the obelos and the Scourge.

Both men bent low, mustered all possible speed, for

each knew well the laws of jousting. He who delivered the greatest momentum—or force—won. Determinedly, the wedge rammed into the mass of yelling Scourge. Stationary as well as fleeing forms slammed into the rams, groaned, and collapsed underfoot only to be trampled or neatly stabbed by the others inside the wedge. Veering one way and then the other, the timbers creaked and groaned under the sudden impacts. Both men labored greatly, now and again stumbling over their fallen marks, but always they moved closer and closer to the obelos.

One clever Yac avoided the crush and dived under the oncoming timber. His knife flashed, and blood gushed from George's leg, pouring down his thick pants, but only a stumble acknowledged the gash, and Kazab ended the Yac's days. George, total intention upon making the tower, barely noticed the gash and gave it no thought. Afterwards when he remembered it, he tried vainly to find the gash that produced all the blood on his pants, but no gash could he find. A face of amazement glanced at Mindi, who gave him a smile.

On Vorag's side, Oran proved a good guard, and any that tried to sneak under, the dog eliminated swiftly. He tore out the evil one's throat with a powerful bite. Within minutes, the group gained the obelos and quickly formed a semi-circle in defense around it.

Vorag looked back at the way they'd come. "Verily, George well doneth! Well doneth!" For a thousand yards, there was a trail, a path of smashed trampled bodies.

"The odds decrease," George replied casting his timber into the faces of the oncoming tide of Scavengers, throwing them backwards.

Now the Yacs, seeing the display of force by company, backed off, holding their distance—victims of growing double fears. Terror from above drove them forward, while fear of the company held them back. However, the ugly goblins, having virtually no good remaining in them, relentlessly pressed forward, undaunted. Indeed, the success of the company spurned a greater rage to destroy within them. Thus, it was primarily the great blue goblins that charged the semi-circle defense of the company at the obelos.

Above, Kahill now smiled once more. His attackers

were as close to the source of his power as they could get—the obelos. Now he would win. His foulest army was charging. He'd just help them along a bit. Carefully, he energized his yellow energy beam of fear and terror.

Suddenly, the company became surrounded, encompassed in the hideous, yellow field of energy. Craven terror ran rampant in their minds, which sought to control their bodies. Under such pressure, the members cringed; some bent double; their fighting effectiveness lowered. Hildaro knew that none could handle both attacks simultaneously. Suddenly, he realized he could do something about it. As the others, half-willed, fought off the first onrush of goblins, Hildaro raised his golden shield above his head and spoke softly to it.

The others, cringing, bent, fighting both the foes before them and the specters energized in their minds, labored heavily under the onslaught, giving way before the screaming goblins. Then the great, golden shield of Illanos held high above Hildaro's head began to grow or seemed to do so. Shortly under the gigantic umbrella of golden shield, the yellow beams of energized terror ceased to fall upon the company. Without questioning the rapid removal of the terror from their minds, they escalated the battle with renewed effort. Elidine flashed in a high arc before swiftly falling to its mark. Flaming and burning all it touched, Andrill chopped and smote all who challenged. Kazab, under the control of the dwarf, now flew through the air and made a pair of sweeping slices, felling two per throw. Evidently, Nache's prowess grew. Even Malazar's two-handing of his elfin blade took a heavy toll of blue, hideous faces.

All the while, Hildaro, nearly squashed to the ground by the force, continued to press his shield to the sky. It had, apparently, grown immense, and acting as a mirror, it reflected all Kahill's flow of yellow fear back from whence it originated. A blood curdling, piercing cry of utter and complete terror sliced through the din of battle. All action below the obelos ceased in reaction. The yellow field died instantly, and the Yacs, howling, crying in fear and wonder, fled the area. They saw that the one who had for so long controlled them with terror lay beaten within his own tower. However, the remaining twenty or so blue beasts renewed their attack, for nothing short of death would end their unending hatred of goodness.

They rushed headlong in a mad frenzy into the waiting blades of the company. Amid wild, mad shrieking, they met their just end. Within seconds an incredible silence, broken only by labored breathing, fell on the field before the checkered obelos of the Evil One. While inside, Kahill squirmed like a fish out of water.

He had thrown every ounce of strength he had into the yellow field of hideousness, attempting to give his blue beasts the advantage. When Hildaro had unexpectedly raised his shield and it had somehow reflected his energy back at him, Kahill was caught off guard. Indeed, the master of evil was crushed, smashed by his own field of terror. The Evil Lord had his own mind run rampant, filled with terrors upon terrors. With his last tiny strength of will, he had managed to kill the spell. Now he lay shaking violently, curled up in a ball in the corner at the top of his tower. Great balls of nervous sweat poured down his face, tasting salty on his lips. His pants were now soaked and stained with brown; they stunk. Still, he shook and fought for self-control.

Below him, the company leaned on swords and wall, recovering from the attack. Around them, the mounded arc of hideous, blue carcasses lay; the odor was oppressive.

At last, Vorag grabbed his friend George and pulled him into the air, "Verily Farmer, tis time we bringeth some order here."

Together using the remaining wooden beams, they pushed, prodded, and rolled the slain goblins farther away from them, creating a breathing space. Catching their purpose, Drifter and Marc and some others joined in. Before long, the nearest was well over a hundred feet away, and each felt some order had returned. Heat waves were now shimmering across the distant view of endless desert sands; a reddish haze engulfed the nearing noon sun.

A keen eye could catch glimpses of the scattered Yacs, who no longer had any heart or will to fight. The bondage of the Evil One had been broken, and they were fearful. Hiding behind cactus and stone, they watched the checkered tower and group intently, dreading the wrath that should inevitably come their way.

However, the call of stomachs can be put off for a time, but not forever, and Nache was the first to yield, "George. Hey George! We haven't eaten since midnight. I'm now a starved dwarf! What have you got in the bag for me?" His directness broke the general quiet.

"How can you eat at a time like this?" implored Malazar! While few felt like eating, most took refreshing drinks.

After drinking a mug of ale, Marc inquired of the wizard, "Well, Malazar, here we are. Maybe twelve hours before the armies arrive. Now what?"

The wizard spoke ever so slowly, as if he were still studying the options. "Here we have need of both haste, extreme haste, and yet wisdom. Those two tend to be mutually exclusive. Wisdom cannot be hurried; yet hurry we must."

Ears quite curious, the dwarf had been listening to them, and interrupted the wizard, "Say, Kazab and I can probably remove the door in—oh, say, a day's time. With all of us chopping, the time can be considerably lessened!" He swayed from side to side patting his silver axe, a chunk of meat dangled from his other hand.

The wizard brightened up and laughed, "My friend, you and that axe of yours yearn to chop; there is no tiring a dwarf for long! No wonder you are the Master Builders! But if we need the door down, and if chopping is the only way, I shall surely call upon your services." Then in a louder voice, he said, "But come my friends. We've rested enough; it's time for the last, bitter confrontation."

With that he stepped close to the obelos, tilted his head back, and yelled towards the top. "Oh Kahill, your time is up. We are here. We have come for you. Come down to us now!"

He screamed the last word, which echoed softly through the nearby hills and off buttes. Kahill started out of his dreamlike state; the challenge had come. Rising slowly and stretching his body, a smile began to grow into a grin, as he realized he was not defeated. Not just yet.

A pale yellow light began to grow atop Obelos Cerban; at first just barely perceptible to those below, then it became fairly brilliant.

"The same glow as before on the road," Marc muttered, his voice trailing away into the desert silence.

All eyes strained upwards. Hildaro raised his shield just in case. They waited. At last, the glow reached its peak, and the icy, bone chilling, pleasant voice that some had heard before pierced the air to their ears, like a lightning bolt of fear.

It began coyly, "Yes, you call upon the Great Kahill? Yes, I see that it is a bad hour for you, maybe even a desperate one. For I do detect, as you already have, four armies marching. Your certain doom draws near. You have need of me. I am here. Yes, for a long time now, I have asked my servants to beg you to come to visit me. The desert is a lonely place, is it not? I longed for your noble company. Yet, as I remember, you Marcos, Merchant of fair Metro—did you not reject the humble offer extended by my emissaries at Feanor Bridge? You even killed the poor, honorable man, who was only delivering my loving invitation! For shame. Bad times have fallen upon Isel when mere messengers are slain for delivery of invitations. But you have come, my noble friends. Yes, Yes. Have you had a comfortable journey? Did you find Ruenzorti a beautiful place to visit, my dearest Mindi? I find that land positively enchanting. But no matter my lovely friends, you are here, safe and sound now. So again, I, Kahill the Greatest, ask of you, what is it that you desire? Assistance in your plight ahead? Be not bashful. I will understand. We are not enemies."

A fear, both cold and cruel, hit each right from the first piercing, impinging, sweet word from above. Shudders of recognition flowed through half of the company, as well as curses, and "I wish we had slain him before."

Marc mused dreamily, "It is no wonder men come under his spell! That voice is virtually enchanting, and what doesn't agree is filled with a terrible cold fear! Poor Yacs. They've been abused no end."

"Verily, it feeleth as if very agreement canst not be

withheld! But I canst not agree!" The Burly man fought the growing spell.

Malazar grew impatient with the flowering, crafty speech, and at last, interrupted that sweet, flowing, singsong voice, whose words pierced into minds and bodies. Harsh, no coarse, seemed his voice, as he halted the rich melody from above. "Stop, Kahill, your treachery is known to us. Pixcies knew us; she felt our power. Now I say for the last time, come down or we shall come up!"

With the arrival of the wizard's words, the yellow glow disappeared in a flash. Kahill cringed as the truth impinged upon him. He knew. Anger began to boil. Tensely, he stepped near the window and spoke softly to the walls. Then a ball of fire sprang up beside the wall—an angry, flaming sphere full of all the anger and hatred the creator could muster. For several seconds, it hung there in space—its maker flowing all his hatred into it. At last, he let go of it. The blazing, raging inferno of energy began its roaring, accelerating descent, bent upon engulfing all below in an all-consuming fire of ultimate scorn and mockery.

But even before Hildaro could react and raise his shield, Malazar raised his hands and cried aloud strange words never heard by other ears in Isel. From his hands, two bolts of a cold, blue energy streaked, raced upwards forming an enlarging cone. The group instinctively dove to the ground, covering their ears in great haste. The blue cones enlarged as they arced upwards. When they hit the seething, red, flaming ball, there came a terrible blast of destruction, disintegration. The flash of light would have blinded any who gazed, and the noise was deafening. The ground trembled and shook; the door to the obelos was shaken ajar. Nearby cactus were uprooted. Much later, when the sound shock wave hit the mountains, avalanches of loose stones thundered into desolate, nameless valleys.

For a minute after the great noise had subsided, there was an unearthly silence. The expanding shock wave bounced off all four distant mountain walls and returned to its point of origin. The echo blasts arrived to shake the obelos once more. The lesser shock waves lurched the great tower in four directions. For an instant, Drifter feared it would topple over. But strong was the ancient Mizzinti handiwork. Obelos Cerban, bent, groaned, and swayed, but did not yield to the reflected force. And for well over ten minutes, the echoes came and went, only to reappear—each time fainter than the last, with more separation in the four echoes as the distance factor multiplied.

Throughout all, a lone figure, whose clothes were now torn and tattered rags, stood tall and unmoved. Malazar seemed changed somehow, as if a tremendous power, long withheld, now came unleashed into its full potential. Again, Malazar spoke, only now his words were not loud. So powerful was his intention—the command value of his words—that even the company felt awed. "Come down now, Kahill. Your powers have been destroyed. No longer do you control Obelos Cerban. It has been wrenched from your hands. I now control the obelos. Come down now. I command thee!"

Into that last fireball, Kahill had sought to place all the force he could possibly muster. He watched its descent, confident of ultimate victory. He had seen the blue streaks and had a cursing doubt. The searing second of blast seemed to Kahill to be hours long, for during that brief interval the true battle was fought. Kahill faced the forces of Malazar, each side endeavoring to crush the other. In that second, Kahill felt all his years of control of the obelos force being wrenched from his hands. He fought that second with everything he had. For him, it was a terrible instant, for Malazar swiftly and easily wrenched his years of control and power from him. The Evil One was bodily thrown across the floor by the shock of Malazar's attack.

Powerless and naked again, he lay groveling on the platform floor, crying and shaking; the terror had recoiled upon him. Kahill was mad with terror. With his body now beyond his control, he writhed in a mass of irregular convulsions. He was crazy with fear. Then came those commanding piercing words. His body involuntarily began to stand and moved towards the stairs.

Kahill could not surrender, could not give up; he fought the terror still. In his ragged state cried aloud, "Thou shall never take me!"

He forced his quaking frame over to the window and plunged; his last word coming from his mouth as he fell. The others looked in horror, as Kahill accelerated in his fall earthward. Quickly, eyes, heads turned aside, but ears heard the sickening thud and squishing sounds with the forced exhalation of air. Slowly, they turned around and looked.

Twenty feet from them lay the crushed, squashed, mangled, lifeless body of their enemy. Kahill the Great lay at their feet. Victory was at hand. Yet bitter and sickening was the achievement.

Disgustedly, Marc muttered, "Curse you."

From the others came various comments as, "That's no fair." "Coward." "Such an escape." But mostly a staunch protest came from the company, who had for so long sought this confrontation. To such an end, none had foreseen or was desired.

Suddenly, Marc had an idea and said, "Mindi, do you think," but she had already stepped forward. She knelt before the crumpled body of their foe. Already various bodily juices were slowly oozing onto the desert sands from numerous lacerations and punctures. Everyone was silent, watching her every move, but she only placed her hands upon the lifeless back and closed her eyes. Slowly, a blue glow surrounded her body and then the Evil One's. It grew steadily and soon was a brilliant, blue blaze of energy.

Before their eyes, small changes in shape and form of Kahill transpired; slowly the chest swelled in size towards normal. As if by magic, the body jerked and coughed, breathing once more. Then the glow rapidly subsided, and she stretched and stood up.

Breaking the silence, she commanded, "Get up Kahill; you are weak; you are not dead yet!" She stepped instinctively back to Marc's side; he put his arms around her; she leaned her head on his shoulder, exhausted.

Malazar now stepped forward. "Arise Kahill! I have not given thee permission to take your leave just yet." A look of utter bewilderment was in his eyes, as he stood up staggeringly, exploring limbs by feel, wonderingly. "There are a number of loose ends that we have to attend to, Kahill."

Satisfied his that his leap had failed and he was here, even unbruised, Kahill's coy smile returned once more. "What is it you wish, oh noble wizard? Long have I waited your arrival here. Tis a pity you did not come sooner. I asked my men . . ."

"Oh cut out that crap, Kahill. Sweet words do not hide your true meaning. Your intentions have been laid bare."

A stern look was in Kahill's eyes now; they flashed from the wizard to Marc and to the others. Barely perceptibly, he backed up and bent over, eyes fixed on the company. He fiddled with his black boots. Springing tall, he cried, "You shall not have me!"

They jumped and gasped, startled by his sudden lurch. In his hand was a small, black dagger; evidently, he'd kept it in his boot. Before anyone could react, Kahill using both hands plunged the curved, S-shaped, black blade deep into his heart. Blood oozed and flowed upon his black and yellow tunic. He slowly collapsed onto the ground. The ultimate victory of death as his last effect was upon his face. His eyes shut as he fell on the dry, sandy, desert floor.

"Curse you," Mindi cried and sprang forward. "Messy!"

"I'll help," Marc came forward, tore a rag off Kahill's tattered clothes, and carefully pulled the dagger out. Gushing, blood poured out and subsided. Once again, the blue glow appeared around Mindi, spreading rapidly over the prone form. She was evidently losing patience and was hurrying. Or perhaps this was becoming easier to do. Marc couldn't tell. He was beside her, and he watched the wound close before his eyes and then saw the body breath once more. However, it was several minutes before Kahill stirred.

Just as soon as the glow subsided and she arose, Marc began searching Kahill, producing a matching dagger from the other shoe. Backing away he exclaimed, "Now, he's clean! Thanks Mindi!"

"He'll be a bit weak this time; blood loss was not totally restored, intentionally."

He stirred, and once again, the wizard called him.

"Kahill, arise once more. Did I not tell you that I was

not finished with you? You cannot depart until I so command! Now get up and stop being a snake in the desert!"

If Kahill was bewildered before, this time he was even more so, for he had himself stabbed his heart. He knew it, but this time as he arose, he began to yawn heavily. There were no more ways out.

"Well, Kahill, now we meet. Your actions have been despicable, to be polite. There are only five ways to handle them. You cannot flee from your actions; we shall not let you. You cannot pretend any longer that they don't exist, for they do, and we know. You cannot avoid or go around them, for they are well known to us, and we shall not let you take that course."

Kahill's yawns gave way to a crazed anger as Malazar spoke. Only too truly did the Evil One see the exactness of his words. At last, he slumped limp and lifeless.

"I know; I'm to blame; I did it. I guess I regret it, but there's nothing I can do now. Just kill me, and let's get it over with. I'm too bad to be allowed to live. I'll just do it again eventually. Kill me now. It's all over."

"No, Kahill, that's the fourth way, succumb. No, we shall not offer you that path. No, for you there shall be only one way out. You shall attack your own actions and handle them. In short, you shall face your own causes; you will confront what you have done."

The reaction was gruesome to watch. Kahill screamed wildly, cried, protested, refused, cursed, swore, and bawled; but all to no avail. The stern eyes of Malazar remained unmoved by it all. At last, Kahill sank upon the ground, groveling in the sand, crying and talking to nameless things. Malazar knelt beside the belittled form and put his hand on his back, gently. The others, full of curiosity, crowded around, eager to hear.

Malazar said softly, "Tell me about the recent things you've done that you should not have done."

The ensuing minutes were filled with alternating whimpering, crying, protests, yawns, brags, and anger, but always about his recent evil actions. His treachery was confirmed with Pixcies as well. Marc quickly lost count of the number of overt actions he'd committed in just the last few months. However, Elwine interrupted Marc's reckoning and pointed away to the south.

"Company," he whispered.

"How long?" Marc asked.

"Four hours or so," the elf replied.

Then, they both resumed listening to the hideous tales of Kahill. At times, Nache reacted, cursed, and spat, but Elwine put his hand on his little friend whispering, "Quiet, it's okay; he's coming clean." After a half hour, most of the company felt rather sick from listening to his continuous stream of butchery. Some were fingering the sand, others their swords. Still Kahill continued, getting off more and more of his actions. Here and there, Malazar would interrupt him with "and before that what did you do?" He always seemed to blaze a path straight for the action done. They heard the sobering tale of how he'd killed his own parents for money and more.

Crime after crime was revealed. Indeed, as Marc later put it to Mindi, "He should write a book. Every conceivable, imaginable treachery, he's already done it." On and on for hours, Kahill continued his tales of destruction and evil actions.

Then he ran out, but he did look somewhat more pleasant, less reactions but more yawning. Malazar kept probing for more, but Kahill kept saying that's all he'd done. Finally, the wizard said, "Picture, got any pictures there?"

"Yes."

"Well, what did you do there that you shouldn't have?"

"Oh," then more yawning. As he began to describe Isel of old, the others pricked their ears, quite curious. They now heard the ancient tale once more but from a different viewpoint and slant. Whenever Kahill got off the track of what he'd done, Malazar nudged him back onto it. Finally, Kahill paused evidently out of pictures; he was back at the beginning of Isel, in the olden days.

Suddenly, he began to laugh good-naturedly. He actually seemed pleasant! No one else laughed though, and at last, Kahill, seeing that the others weren't laughing, said, "Don't you see? I didn't know what a desert was." More laughing, followed by, "We divided up the land, and I chose the desert area, but I thought it would be sweet and delicious." This was just too much. The company roared with laughter along with Kahill, who somehow now looked civilized.

The fun was cut short by Andrill bursting into flames. Quickly, other swords were drawn, as they gazed upon the first army that had just arrived full steam from Begrundi Pass. The goblins had halted, mouths foaming, yearning for a battle. However, the Yacs seemed to lose heart when they came upon Obelos Cerban and the company, surrounded by heaps of fallen blue forms. They held back while other goblins pressed forward hoping to avenge their fallen ones. Most striking of all was the absence of the cold terror all had felt when near the obelos. All seemed natural; it was just a pretty tower in the afternoon sun. Malazar was the first to speak.

"Kahill, here is another of the little details that yet remain. What do you propose?"

Coolly, as one long used to such scenes, Kahill pondered the goblins, then the Yacs. "The Yacs, they'll obey me, er us, but the goblins are full of hatred; they come from the bowls of the earth. Compassion is not known to them."

"Then you shall still have the Yacs," commanded Malazar, "but the goblins will have to go!" The wizard drew himself up and began to speak domineeringly to the blue hoard, and Mindi aided him. To the goblins, Malazar suddenly seemed a hundred feet tall. As the others watched, they cringed and fell back in awe.

He said, "Goblins, the Evil One is destroyed; there is no more evil here. I am here, and I order you to return to your own lands at once. To attack will mean your deaths. As you can see, fifty of yours lie dead, and we have not a scratch. Flee before our wrath and take your brethren that have not yet arrived with you."

A hideous howling and wailing set in at once, as the blue forms, shaking in familiar fear, only now reversed, began to scramble over one another heading for the northeastern road. As they left in a free-for-all, he added, "Stray not from the road, for if you do, you shall meet the grey army and shall never again see the road!"

They routed and ran helter-skelter across the desert forming into a long blue line on the Old Caravan Road. Both Marc and Nache looked at Mindi. She smiled back at them, knowingly. They guessed what she had done to the goblins. Malazar had not and said to himself, "I must be really getting more powerful than I know. I expected more of an argument!"

Then he caught the trio's glances and instantly guessed what had actually happened. "So you had a hand in that one, eh? Well, good job, Mindi. Now for more loose ends. Kahill you have much to set right here."

"Please," Kahill pleaded, "Let me and the Yacs have this desert region. With time, we can fix it up pretty for all. I'm not certain how else I can help undo all the damage done, but let me try here. Hence forth, all travelers through Kalhari shall be honored guests, honored as if kings."

"And queens," Mindi added jokingly.

The wizard turned to the company and said, "You have heard his crimes and have heard his offered amends. Shall it be accepted? You are the representatives of the lands involved. What do you say?"

"Okay by me," Marc quickly said. The others agreed uniformly, wondering just how far Kahill could be trusted. Yet he seemed much improved. The evil intentions had vanished altogether. But would they remain so? Marc had his doubts, still he agreed, as he could offer no better solution.

"You may start," Shannon stepped forward addressing Kahill, "By bagging the salt. I saw many dried beds of the stuff on my way here. Salt is a much needed commodity in parts of Isel. Now the Master Merchant here may be able to market it for you. In Mari, we have grown tired of drying sea water for it and would relish a change."

"Verily," added Vorag, "And openeth the passes at once; perhaps we may lendeth a hand."

Thus, a future track of possible survival opened to the leader of the Scourge. He graciously accepted the offer, and genuine tears of happiness filled his face.

Finally, Malazar ordered him to go to his Yacs, for they needed handling. Kahill realized that would be so small task. For years, he had implanted fear and evil in their minds. Now with no weapon or power, he alone had to undo that work. Justice would be well paid for.

The company, all talking at once, relaxed and set up a camp. While Nache and Drifter got a fire going, the others set up the camp and began a long needed dinner. Golden rays of the sun setting over the craggy, distant orange Quara Wund mountains fell upon the camp. The end of the day came, welcomed by all. Wearily, they slept soundly, though they still posted guards.

In the ensuing days, they watched as Kahill gained some control over his area. Half of the Yacs fled back to their northern wild. Fairly five hundred chose to remain. Kahill had managed to convince them to assist. In fact, he suffered a broken wrist while "reasoning" with a brutish captain. Crews were dispatched to begin salt mining, for food was scarce in Kalhari. Their bellies were to know hunger well before the caravans of grain arrived two weeks later, ravenously welcomed by the new workers. Kahill seemed to be enjoying his new post as creator. He'd held elections, and the Yacs elected their own leader, responsible only to the Creator. All actions were watched for nearly a week by the relentless eyes of the company. No signs of reversion were seen, only a thrust for bare survival.

Finally, Malazar held a brief council. "It is time; our job is ended. Let us return to our homes. George, I know, has a great longing. So let me say thanks to one and all. I am honored by all your services. Pray, let us meet here in Kalhari, say two years hence, and view the changes, for I shall miss your company. I have grown fond of you all!"

His voice faltered briefly. Mindi felt she saw a tear in his eye. He said no more. Quickly the others agreed—two years then. Preparations were made for the return journeys, and they spent over an hour saying farewell.

Elwine and Drifter left together for Witchachooie Pass; Vorag and Nache headed for Begrundi Pass; Tse Tse and Malazar, for Nyder Pass in the northeast. And Marc, Mindi, George, Hildaro, and Shannon, headed for Kyder pass in the southwest. In spite of emotions, it was a tear-filled departure of friends. Nache had given each group a pack pony to use for the trek; Mindi had Butterball. They departed in early March for home.

As the five walked along the Old Caravan Road southward, they watched Vorag, Oran, and Nache going obliquely away from them. Mindi and Nache waved many times. Everyone had invited everyone else to come for a visit. Mindi laughed and had said that they'd spend the entire two years just in visiting everyone. All laughed, but repeated their offers.

In two days, they were scrambling over the bolder-filled pass into the arms of Garth, who followed them on down the road, sharing news. Soon horsemen rode up, for at Felipe's request they'd kept a small garrison in Burly. Hildaro welcomed the opportunity to ride once more. Shannon also said farewell, for he yearned for the sea, and Uvalde was the closest port.

Marc refused the offer of horses because the snows had melted and spring was coming. Besides, he felt like walking, un-urgently. At last, Marc, Mindi, and George found themselves walking together slowly down the Old Caravan Road as it paralleled Illanos.

George seemed exuberant; Sharon, the kids, and home were ever on his mind. His time came, as well, when they neared Klee. He gave his farewell and added, "Hey Marc, let's not make it another six years before we meet. Come on and drop by some time. You too, Mindi."

"We will," they replied waving.

Alone at long last, the pair, with Butterball ambling behind them, walked slowly homeward through the low hills of northern West Flats. For a while, neither spoke; she rested her head on his shoulder, arm in arm. It was springtime, and greens were sprouting from the ground. The air felt fresh; both felt alive.

As they walked along, Marc said softly to her, "Hey, want to hear a poem I've written?"

"You don't write poems," came her reply.

"I know, but I did. Want to hear it?"

"Sure."

So Marc began.

I cannot give the Sun to you,
I cannot give the Stars aglow.
The sky, it seems so far away
And the world, she's just not mine.
The trees, I cannot give to you
Nor grass and flowers all around
Nor dogs, they are my friends
All this, I cannot give to you.
I can only give to you
All the love I can create
All my life I'll share with you
Full of admiration and respect for you.
Come with me and feel the sun
Come with me and be the sky
Kiss a raindrop on the wind
Come with me and see a land.
Let's find our friends somewhere
Who only care for what we are.
There to find a life that's free
Where love is all that is.

She squeezed his arm playfully and kissed him. She said softly, "Marc, I'd like to have a family now."

"Would you?" he asked imploringly.

"Yes," was followed by a hug. "I'd really like a daughter."

"A daughter!" Marc cried, "I was thinking about a son."

"Well, what's wrong with a daughter?"

"Oh well, nothing I guess." After a pause, he added, "It's just not a son, that's all."

She stomped and said "Men!"

He halted, and they embraced lovingly.

Marc added, "Only if you promise that we can do lots of traveling. You see, I've become rather fond of this wandering. Actually, I'd like to do it all again; I missed so much of it before."

"Agreed," was her reply. "And you must let me go to Enchendar from time to time."

"Of course."

Nearly a year had passed since the pair had undertaken the challenge. Both felt confident and satisfied.

Spring had come.

The End.

A Favor to Other Readers

How about helping other readers? Many readers rely on reviews to make the decision whether to buy a book. You can help them make their decision by leaving your opinions and viewpoint in a short review of the positive things of this book. Writing the review and expressing your opinion only takes a few minutes, and other readers will appreciate your efforts.

Click this link: The Return of the Wizards, Volume 1 The Twelve Companions
scroll down to Customer Reviews; click on Write a Review, and enter your review. Thank you.

Author Information

Visit My Amazon.com Author Page
Vic Broquard Author Page

Follow My Blog
Vic Broquard's Blog

Follow Me on Social Media
Facebook
Google+
LinkedIn
YouTube

Other Books by Vic Broquard

Without Warning (fantasy)

The Trident Series: (fantasy)
Volume 1 The Trident and the Book
Volume 2 The Trident and the Scepter
Volume 3 The Trident and the Resurrection

The Adventures of Elizabeth Stanton Series: (science fiction)
Volume 1 The Evolution of the Path
Volume 2 The Great Messiah
Volume 3 Of Kings and Queens and Troubadours
Volume 4 Chaos in the Aftermath
Volume 5 Power Plays
Volume 6 Age of Exploration
Volume 7 Abducted
Volume 8 The Emperor and Empress
Volume 9 A Job Worth Doing
Volume 10 Degradation
Volume 11 The Second Crusade
Volume 12 When Worlds Collide
Volume 13 Dark Ages

The Lindsey Barron Series: (fantasy)
Volume 1 The Rod of the Apocalypse
Volume 2 The Board of Governors
Volume 3 The Crown of Moses
Volume 4 Dominus for President
Volume 5 The National Health Care Program
Volume 6 States Justice
Volume 7 Cross and Double-cross

Zoran Chronicles Series: (fantasy)
Volume 1 A Dragon in Our Town
Volume 2 Dragons, Power, Courts, and War

Planet of the Orange-red Sun Series: (science fiction)
Volume 1 When Kingdoms Fall